"D[...]

Her tone was c[...]

"Glad you left y[...]

"In case you've gotten the wrong idea," Serena said, "this trip is dead serious. I don't intend a replay of our marriage."

"Me, neither."

"Promise?"

"As far as I'm concerned this is a job," Michael said. "You're paying me a thousand a day, and I intend to collect my paycheck. Just because the working conditions are pleasant doesn't change that fact."

"What working conditions are you referring to?"

"The boss smells good and she doesn't make me ride in front with the rest of the help. What more could a man ask for?"

Serena gave him her hand. "I don't know about you, but I have a feeling Rio is going to be quite an adventure."

"For once you may be right, Serena. Maybe I sold my services too cheaply."

"A deal is a deal," she said.

"Yeah," he replied, "like 'till death do us part.'"

Bestselling husband and wife team of Ron and Janice Kaiser deliver a sizzling tale of love and bullets with *Last Night in Rio*, their second novel for MIRA® Books. Both the Kaisers are former lawyers and now write full time. Janice has already begun to make her mark in the world of women's fiction, with over 20 books to her name, while her husband Ron has published several non-fiction and mystery titles.

Already available in
MIRA® Books

PRIVATE SINS

LAST NIGHT
IN
RiO

JANICE
KAISER

MIRA® BOOKS

*First published in Great Britain 1997
MIRA Books, Eton House, 18-24 Paradise Road,
Richmond, Surrey, TW9 1SR*

© Belles-Lettres, Inc. 1996

ISBN 1 55166 174 8

58-9710

*Printed and bound in Great Britain
Caledonian International Book Manufacturing Ltd, Glasgow*

For our fathers:
Al Kaiser
and
Harold C. Bender
(1904–1988)

We wish to thank Robin Rue
for her wit and wisdom,
and Dianne Moggy and Amy Moore
for their vision and exceptional judgment.

T U E S D A Y
September 12th

Inyo County, California

They had been at the lake for two days. Mount Mallory—bleak, rocky, commanding—rose above them in all its granite majesty. They'd slept on the ground, fished, gathered firewood, built campfires. And they'd talked into the night, the stars twinkling down through the crystalline mountain air. The boy was having a ball.

Mike Hamlin, on the other hand, was making the best of a marginal situation. Somewhere between age twenty-five and thirty-eight he'd become a little less enchanted with nature. He still loved it, but he now had a greater appreciation for toilets, running water and firm mattresses. In other words, the bright lights of Las Vegas were starting to look good to him.

Mike put a couple of small pieces of wood on the fire and replaced the frying pan. He glanced up at Jason, who was squatting on a boulder just above the camp, peering across Meyson Lake through Mike's prize eight-hundred-dollar binoculars. Serena had given them to him for a trip to the Kentucky Derby before they were married. Christ, it had already been ten years. Nearly eleven. No wonder his joints rebelled at dining on the ground.

"There's somebody on the other side of the lake, Mike," the boy announced.

Mike stood, startling a chipmunk that had been watching him from a nearby rock. His knees were reluctant to unhinge after bending over the fire for so long. He tried to see where Jason was pointing, but there was too much underbrush. "Probably a fisherman up for the day," he said.

"Nope. He doesn't have a pole or gear."

"Maybe he's a hiker."

"No backpack, either," the kid said.

"Maybe he's a serial killer then, looking for a victim."

"Could be. He's packing heat."

"Packing heat?" Mike said it as much to himself as to the boy. Where did fourteen-year-olds pick up language like that? Television?

It wasn't the first time his eyes had been opened this trip. During their man-to-boy conversation around the campfire the night before, Jason had wanted to talk about hookers and call girls. "Do you arrest many at the hotel?" he'd asked. "Ever catch them in a room with somebody?"

Mike had answered candidly, telling him the streetwalkers knew to stay away and the call girls weren't allowed to solicit. If they came, it was because they were invited. The practice was not encouraged, but it couldn't always be controlled.

"But you comp the high rollers with a girl, if that's what they want, don't you?" Jason asked.

Mike could see candor wasn't getting the result he wanted. "Son, you're letting your imagination run wild. You'd be better off concentrating on girls in your English class and not worrying about matters you shouldn't even know about."

"The girls in school are all stupid and stuck-up," he'd groused. "And they're not even interesting."

"You'll find they can get very interesting if you give them a chance."

"Bullshit," Jason had said, tossing a stick into the darkness.

Mike had tried other approaches, but Jason hadn't wanted to talk about himself, though that had been the purpose of the trip. The kid had the usual adolescent problems—mostly, to do with hormones running amuck. His dog-eared copy of *Gallery* was clearly his prized possession—his window into the world of naked women.

Unfortunately, Jason's preoccupations had gone beyond magazines. He'd had run-ins with the cops—picked up twice for peeping in the window of the two showgirls who lived in the trailer next door to him and his mom. The fishing trip had been inspired by the second arrest.

"Mike, I don't know what to do," Connie had lamented. "He's not a bad kid, but I feel like I'm losing control. He's outgrowing me."

In a fit of compassion Mike had volunteered to take Jason under his wing, though it was more for Connie than her kid. He'd always been a sucker for a woman alone with a child.

She'd leapt at his offer, and the post–Labor Day fishing trip in the Sierras was arranged. What better place for a man to build a rapport with a kid than out in nature? Before they'd fallen asleep the night before, Mike had made a little speech about sex being a natural desire but, like anything, you had to learn to channel it into socially acceptable behavior. Jason had listened without comment. A few minutes later he'd been snoring away.

"This guy looks to me like he means business," Jason said. He still had the glasses to his eyes and was sitting crosslegged on the boulder, staring across the lake. "And he's definitely coming this way."

Mike took the skillet off the fire, set it on the ground, then climbed up on the boulder to have a look. Jason handed him the glasses and pointed.

Meyson Lake was less than a quarter of a mile across, too far away to see details of a figure moving through trees and undergrowth without a good pair of binoculars. Mike's glasses put the guy right across the street.

"That heat you see, son, is a service revolver. That guy's law enforcement. The matching shirt and pants he's wearing is a uniform."

"Shit," Jason said, "what did I do now?"

"Let's not jump to conclusions. The man could be Fish and Game, checking fishing licenses or something." Mike said it to be reassuring, but knew it was unlikely. The officer appeared to be a deputy sheriff, judging by the uniform, and what's more, he wasn't dressed for a hike. There could be an emergency, but Mike wasn't going to tell the boy that. "Let's wait till he arrives before we get excited."

Hamlin handed back the binoculars, climbed down from the boulder and returned the skillet to the fire, fanning the smoke from his eyes.

"Lunch is about ready," he told the kid. "Go wash your hands."

"Where? In the filthy lake? I peed in it last night."

Mike rolled his eyes, fully aware that a quarter of a century earlier the words might have come from his own mouth. "All right, forget washing and bring your filthy hands over here. Time to get your plate ready."

Jason climbed down from the pile of boulders, taking the last four feet in one huge jump and kicking up a cloud of dust in the process. He was at that awkward stage when his body was half boy and half man. The fuzz on his ruddy cheeks was getting coarser, as was the hair on his long, sturdy legs. But his shoulders and chest hadn't developed, giving him the appearance of someone who was growing from the ground up.

Mike fanned away the dust and smoke. "I hope you like your food gritty."

"Huh?"

"Get two cups of water from the pot so we'll have something to drink," he said, pointing to the log where he'd set things up.

"We should have brought Pepsi or something," Jason said. "I hate water, especially knowing it's out of the lake."

"Next time, think where you're peeing before you do."

"How can *you* drink it?" Jason asked, dipping two tin cups into the water pot.

"I've already had all the childhood diseases, including puberty." He stood again, painfully unfolding his knees. "Come on, kid, grab your plate. This fish'll be cold before you sink a fork into it."

They were halfway through lunch before the deputy arrived. First they heard a voice calling from the other side of the boulders. Then a hatless head in sunglasses appeared, followed by the rest of him. The badge on the deputy's chest glistened in the sun.

"Afternoon, gentlemen."

Mike gave the deputy a casual salute. "Howdy, Officer."

Jason watched in silence, his broad forehead and small-ish mouth pinched with concern. Mike was glad to see the kid was intimidated rather than defiant.

The cop, a tall, fair-haired man in his mid-thirties, was sweating profusely, the underarms of his shirt soaked, the rest of it spotted. He took a couple of deep breaths. "Whew!" he said, taking off his sunglasses and wiping his forehead with the back of his hand. "I'm looking for Mike Hamlin. This the right camp?"

Mike straightened his back. "I'm Hamlin."

The deputy stepped down from the rocks as Mike got to his feet. They were about the same size, the officer maybe an inch taller.

"I'm Deputy Anderson, Mr. Hamlin," the officer said. "Inyo County Sheriff's Department. There's been an emergency, sir. I was asked to track you down."

"What kind of emergency?"

"A family matter, as I understand it. Your wife is waiting for you at Whitney Portal."

Mike blinked. *"Wife?"* he said. "Deputy, I'm afraid there's been a mistake. I don't have a wife."

The cop's mouth sagged open. "You *are* Mike Hamlin out of Las Vegas, aren't you?"

"Yes, but I'm still not married...not unless I was drunker last New Year's Eve than I thought."

Deputy Anderson scratched his head. "What the hell's going on? The lady's with my partner down at the trailhead. She flew up to Lone Pine from Vegas this afternoon. We met her at the airstrip on orders from headquarters. She had your name and knew your location, Mr. Hamlin.''

"And she said she was Mrs. Hamlin?"

"She said she was your wife."

Mike glanced at Jason, who was hunched over like a little monkey, eating and listening at the same time. "Did the lady say her name was Connie Meyers, by any chance, Deputy?"

"No, sir. Serena Bouchard."

"Serena?" Now he understood. "Oh, Jesus."

The deputy appeared bewildered.

"Serena's my *ex*-wife, officer. We divorced five years ago."

"She didn't say anything about ex-wife. We just assumed..."

"Serena induces people to assume things. It's her style. But you say she actually came up in the mountains?"

"Yes, sir. She wanted to hike up herself, but we told her it'd be quicker for one of us to find you."

A sense of urgency was beginning to sink in. "What's the emergency?"

"Something about a death in the family."

Mike's expression turned cold sober. There wasn't anybody she'd come all the way here for, unless.... "It wasn't Christina, was it? Did she say it was her daughter?"

The man shook his head. "She didn't say who. I think she wants to tell you yourself. That's why she was ready to hoof it up here, dressed for church."

A sick feeling went through him, the sort that made a man feel helpless and small. Christina had been his child as much as any biologically unrelated offspring could be.

His gut twisted uneasily. It was either Christina or Jeffrey, Serena's brother. Those were the only two people he could think of who meant enough to her that she would swallow her pride and come all this way to ask him for help.

He hadn't seen Serena in over two years. They'd settled into an arms-length relationship, communicating, when they did, mostly about Christina. He and Serena had gone their separate ways, and their marriage was just another part of the past, like high school or the navy.

There had been only one lapse—when they'd run into each other at Tahoe a year after the divorce. Serena had claimed it was a meaningless aberration, but he wasn't so sure. One thing was certain, though: she was embarrassed about having slipped. That in itself had given him a degree of satisfaction. Victories over Serena Bouchard, however small, weren't easy to come by.

Mike glanced at Jason, who was swatting at a pesky fly, seemingly oblivious to what was going on. Kids were amazingly passive about some things. Life, it seemed, just came to them, randomly and with capricious inevitability, like the scenery in a video game.

"We've got us a problem, son," he said to the boy.

Jason licked his finger. "We have to go back?"

"Possibly." Mike ran his hand over the stubble on his jaw, knowing he looked like hell and smelled worse. "I suppose she's expecting me to jog right down," he said to the deputy.

Anderson nodded. "She said she had to be back in Los Angeles tonight at the latest. Something about catching a flight for South America in the morning."

"Oh, shit."

"Sir?"

"My stepdaughter's in Rio de Janeiro. Or she was as of a month or so ago. That means she *is* the one." A sick pain went through him again.

The image in his mind was of the little girl he'd led out of that hotel kitchen a decade earlier. Big, blue, trusting eyes. A helpless child in a sick adult world. Hamlin the hero, stepfather-to-be. Serena in tears. And poor little Christina. Of course, she wasn't little anymore. She was a grown woman—as much as a girl could be at nineteen.

"Serena definitely said 'death in the family'?"

"Yes, sir."

"Damn," he muttered. "It's just like her to send somebody up here with a message like that and not say who."

Deputy Anderson checked his watch. "Hadn't we better be hitting the trail, Mr. Hamlin?"

"Yeah, duty calls." He turned to Jason. "You ready to get back to MTV?"

"Are we leaving?"

"We don't have much choice. We better start packing up."

"If you'll excuse me, sir," the officer continued, "Mrs. Bouchard said if you'd allow me to bring the boy and the gear down, she'll send her Lear jet to pick him up at Bishop in the morning. The strip at Lone Pine won't handle a jet. That's why she flew in a single-engine charter from Vegas."

"That's Serena, having things all worked out." Mike went over and sat down next to Jason. "Well, my friend, it's up to you. You can come with me now, or let Deputy Anderson take you up to Bishop and ride home in my ex's jet in the morning. I suppose you'll be staying in a motel tonight under the watchful eye of the Inyo County Sheriff's Department, which means no women in your room. At least none over sixteen."

Jason smiled sheepishly. "Could the jet fly over the Grand Canyon on the way home?"

"It would be a little out of the way, but I'm sure it can be arranged."

Jason screwed up his face. "I guess I go back in the jet, then. But can we come fishing again?"

Mike tousled the boy's hair. "Sure. Next long weekend I get. But don't expect it to be this way every time. I've only got one ex-wife." Then he mumbled to himself, "God knows, that's more than enough."

Mike made it to the trailhead at Whitney Portal in just under an hour. He was hot and sweaty, and running down the steep, rocky trail had given him hellacious blisters. He was limping by the time he came to the sheriff's four-wheel-drive vehicle sitting at the entrance to the picnic grounds. A deputy was slumped behind the wheel, smoking a cigarette. There was no sign of Serena.

"Excuse me, Officer. I'm Mike Hamlin. Where's Mrs. Bouchard?"

The man sat upright, recovering from his daydream. "Oh, yes, Mr. Hamlin." He had a red face and was heavier than Deputy Anderson. "Mrs...uh, the lady is right over there." He pointed to a picnic table tucked in a cluster of pines thirty yards away.

"Thanks." Mike started toward her. There weren't many people around. An older couple with a camper were at a table on the other side of the road. Through the trees he could see a larger family group. Children's voices echoed faintly in the woods, overlaid with the caw of jays.

But his eyes were on Serena, sitting at the table, a beam of sunlight cutting through the woods, illuminating her as though she were under a spotlight. The closer he got, the more strikingly beautiful she looked. The pain of divorce and the passage of time couldn't change the fact that she was an attractive woman, with a presence and an aura that went beyond mere physical beauty.

She could be a hellion, too. Serena Bouchard seized life by the throat, doing things her way, though she was not without her subtleties. For all her grit, Serena was a lady, feminine right down to her painted toes. She could be hard or soft, depending on her whim or the exigencies of the situation. She had balls, but her big gray eyes could tear up, wringing a guy's guts. She was the only woman for whom he'd never lost his sense of awe, even after five years of marriage.

Screwing was the only area in which he was clearly her match. Toward the end, it had galled her. "Too damn bad great sex is not enough," she'd said during their last fight. He knew she'd meant it.

Maybe that was why Tahoe had been such sweet revenge. But the real victory he wanted was the only one he couldn't have—putting her from his mind once and for all. A part of him still loved her. That was his Achilles' heel, and maybe hers, as well.

As he got closer, he could see that her eyes were closed. She seemed to be meditating, her hands folded on the table. Was she praying?

He thought again of Christina, once more taking a hurtful jab in the gut. He slowed his gait, unsure whether he was seeing a grieving mother or the femme fatale who'd been a little too fatal for him.

He stopped across from her, running his dirty fingers through his hair. He knew he was disgusting—three-days' growth of beard on his jaw and smelling like a horse. But he wasn't the type who apologized for what he was, even to Serena Bouchard, though that insight had come to him only *after* their divorce.

Sitting in the calm of the forest, Serena looked cool and pristine, a mountain wildflower in a country meadow. She wore a delicate lavender silk dress that was more appropriate for a garden party in Bel Air than a wooded camp in the high Sierra. He allowed himself a moment to savor her, to remember, before plunging ahead.

Her hair was shorter than when he'd last seen her, her skin just as smooth, her figure still as trim and enticing. Time had been kind to her, kinder than it had been to him.

"Serena," he said softly.

Her lids slowly lifted. Her gray eyes focused, but a full three seconds passed before she seemed to recognize him. "Michael," she muttered as a tiny smile appeared. She got up and moved around the table, insinuating herself into his arms. He held her uncomfortably, knowing he was sweaty and dirty. He resisted the temptation to stroke her head. This was, after all, his ex-wife.

"What's happened?" he asked, his voice wary. "Is it Christina?"

"What?"

"The death in the family. The deputy said there was a death in the family."

"Oh, that." She went to the table and got her purse, removing a tissue. She carefully wiped her eyes so as not to smear her mascara. She didn't turn back to him until she'd finished. "No, Christina's fine." She dabbed her nose. "Well, she's not fine, but she's not dead."

"Well, who the hell *is* dead?"

She took note of his tone, but let it pass. "Haven't you read the papers?"

"I've been in the woods for three days," he said, forcing an unnatural calmness. "Where am I going to get a newspaper?"

"Oh, I hadn't thought of that. I just assumed you knew about Drake."

"Drake?"

"Drake Manville. He's dead, Michael. Murdered in Rio three days ago."

"You mean Drake Manville, the actor?"

"Yes, Drake Manville, the actor."

"What does that have to do with the family? He's not a relative, is he?"

"No."

"Then why the hell did you come up here to tell me about him? Surely I didn't run down the goddamned mountain to get the latest Hollywood gossip! Jesus Christ."

"Michael, please don't get testy right off the bat."

"I'd like an explanation."

"Well, if you wouldn't shout, you might get one."

"I'm not shouting," he said, tempering his voice. "I'm asking."

She sat on the bench and crossed her legs. "It's not Drake I'm concerned about. It's Jeffrey. They think he killed Drake. He's in jail in Rio de Janeiro, accused of murder."

"Your brother killed Drake Manville?"

"No, of course not! But the police think he did. That's the point. We've got to save him, Michael. We're all he's got."

Her voice was plaintive, but not quite pleading. She knew the line separating the two and was careful never to give an adversary the advantage in a negotiation if she could help it. And that's what this was—a negotiation. It suddenly became clear to him.

His feet were killing him. He sat down on the bench, as far away from her as he could; it was bad enough that he could smell himself. He looked at Serena and she looked at him.

"It's the word *we* I'm having trouble with," he said. "You and I are divorced, Serena. I was under the impression your brother and I got divorced at the same time."

"Very funny."

He sighed. "I'm sorry, I don't mean to be glib—"

"Cruel is more like it."

"All right, I don't mean to be cruel. I'm sure you're very upset about this, and I'm sorry about that. I truly am. But I fail to see why you've brought the problem to me. What can I do for Jeffrey?"

She gave him a hard look.

"Really, Serena, what can *I* do? I know you're not here to cry on my shoulder. You wouldn't give me the satisfaction."

She shook her head with disgust. "You're incapable of seeing this as a human problem, a family tragedy, aren't you? Everything has to be judged on the basis of who wins and who loses. Ego, that's all that matters to you."

"You convinced the judge I was an asshole five years ago," he said. "You don't have to convince *me* now."

She lowered her head. "I should have known this would happen. It was unfair of me to come to you asking for help. You don't owe me or my family a damned thing. I'm sorry I disturbed you."

He groaned inwardly, feeling the full impact of the guilt she was leveling on him. It was hard to say how genuine her emotion was and how much of it was intended for effect. With Serena he'd never been completely sure.

"Listen," he said, "let's start over. Erase the last two minutes. Just tell me what happened. How would Jeffrey even have known Drake Manville?"

She got to her feet and began to pace, like an executive who needed to walk,in order to dictate. Serena *was* an executive, of course, though she neither looked the role nor played it the way people expected. That was consistent with her freewheeling style.

Serena Bouchard headed one of the largest privately owned hotel empires in the world. She'd taken it over at the time of her father's death, shortly before Mike had met her. According to what he'd heard, the company was worth eighty or a hundred million dollars more now than when she'd taken the helm. Serena clearly had her talents, not the least of which was a canny sense of people, knowing who to hire and fire.

She stopped pacing. Her pretty face took on that mask of seriousness she adopted whenever her mind was on something important she wanted done.

"Jeffrey and Drake Manville were lovers," she said.

Mike was surprised. "Manville the pirate, the gunslinger, the macho...whatever, was gay?"

"Honestly, Michael, for an adult living in the last decade of the twentieth century, your naiveté astounds me. There have been gay pirates as well as gay actors, not to mention gay football players and gay cops."

"I wouldn't know," he said defensively. "Certainly not from personal experience."

She scoffed and resumed pacing. "I've never understood why men are so fragile when it comes to their sexuality."

"Self-confidence comes with age," he replied, unable to resist. "You associate with younger men, you got to expect fragile."

She did a slow burn. "Amusing. You could have gone all day without saying that."

"Don't despair, babe, you're the best looking forty-two I've ever seen. You haven't aged a bit since we got divorced. Body's dynamite. So's the face. If you want to know the truth, I still find you attractive."

"Up yours, Michael."

He smiled, feeling a vague sense of satisfaction. Things between them hadn't changed all that much. Tahoe had started out testy, too. Somehow, though, he doubted this encounter would end up the same way.

"So much for friendly banter," he said. "Go on with your story."

"That's it. I hardly know a thing, except that the police in Rio apparently have decided Jeffrey's guilty of murder and they're trying to hang him."

"The police?"

"Everybody down there. The police, the prosecutors, everybody who knew Drake. All of Brazilian society, from what I've been told. It's like the lynch mob is at the jail-house door."

"All without cause? They've picked on him because he's gay?"

"Michael, my brother is not a killer!"

"All right, fine. But why are you so sure there's a con-spiracy? Could this be a Serena Bouchard hyperbole, by any chance?"

She looked at him through narrowed eyes, then contin-ued. "I really don't know what's going on except that they've decided to make Jeffrey the scapegoat."

"Okay, so your brother's in trouble, serious trouble. Why are you coming to me?"

"I want you to go with me to Rio, Michael. I need some-one I trust completely." She checked her watch. "Our flight from L.A. is at nine-thirty tomorrow morning. I hope to hell your passport is current."

"Forgive me for pointing this out, but aren't we forget-ting something?"

She seemed genuinely surprised. "What?"

"I haven't agreed to go. As a matter of fact, I *can't* go. There's the little question of my job."

"Oh, Michael, don't be tedious. You know there are ways of dealing with that. Take a leave of absence without pay if you have to. I'll pay you triple your normal salary."

"Serena, I'm the head of security at the Desert Palms. It would be like the captain of the ship just taking off. I can't do that."

She bowed her head, obviously forcing herself to be patient. "Don't make me beg you, Michael. Please."

"Listen," he said, "let's be practical. What could I possibly do to be of help? Really. I don't speak a word of Spanish—"

"Portuguese."

"Right, Portuguese. I don't know shit about Brazil. And I'm not even a P.I. So what good would I be to you?"

Serena took a couple of steps in his direction. "It's not just for me, Michael. If you must know, it was Christina's idea. I didn't want to use your relationship with her. I'd hoped you'd do it for *me*. But the truth is *she's* the moving force in this. She insisted I bring you with me. Absolutely insisted."

"Bullshit."

"Michael, it's true!"

"Then I'll call her and explain."

Serena turned her face heavenward. "I hate this," she said. "You know I hate this."

It wasn't clear if she was addressing her remarks to him or God, but he assumed it was him. She wasn't used to people saying no to her. He was one of the few people who ever had.

She turned away, pondering her next move. His feet were throbbing, so he began to unlace his boots.

Serena ended her conference with herself, came to the table and slipped down beside him. "All right," she said, using the matter-of-fact tone she employed when she was ready to get to the bottom line—and with Serena every situation had a bottom line. "Can we solve our problem with money? Name your price."

"Goddamn it, Serena," he snapped. "This has nothing to do with money."

"What is it, then? You haven't given me a good reason. Not a legitimate one. Your job's a bullshit excuse. You want me to get on my knees, don't you? You want me to prostitute myself. You want...what? A dozen blow jobs? What's your price? Name it and it's yours."

He pulled off a boot and picked at his bloody sock. "You know, you really are your own worst enemy. I told you that when I married you, and I told you that when I divorced you."

"*I* divorced *you*, Mr. Hamlin."

"Correction. I told you that when *you* divorced *me*. And it's still true. You are your own worst enemy."

"So it's no?" she said. "No, period? Just goddamn no?"

"If I was the slightest bit inclined before, I'm definitely unwilling now. I just can't go to Rio with you, apart from not particularly wanting to. I'm sorry."

"Is it because of your girlfriend, Connie?"

Mike was surprised.

Serena nodded. "I talked to her. That's how I found you."

"How did you find *her*? How did you even *know* about her?"

"Money talks, Michael. Or have you forgotten?"

"No. Or maybe I should say, yes," he said, pulling off his other boot. The sock was bloody, but not as bad as the first.

Serena glanced down at his feet. She didn't say anything, though she did give him a sympathetic look.

"Well, you're resourceful," he said. "I'll give you that."

She stared off into the woods. "Connie seemed nice."

"She is."

"Is it serious?"

"No, not really. We're friends." Mike took two Band-Aids from his pocket and began applying them to his bloody blisters.

"You know what's surprised me most about you?" she asked after a while.

"What?"

"That you're flitzing around in marginal relationships. I was sure that within a year of our divorce you'd be married to some young thing yearning for babies. I pictured you with a couple of rug rats by now, and another on the way.''

''Well, it didn't happen.''

''Why not? You were so gaga over kids, so eager to have a family. Frankly, I thought that was what ultimately did us in.''

He said nothing. Their marriage and their divorce were the last things he wanted to discuss. She gazed into his eyes. He couldn't tell if she was thinking about the past, the present or the future. But it seemed she was starting to resign herself to the fact he wouldn't be going with her to Brazil.

''I'm sorry I interrupted your camping trip,'' she said. ''It was selfish of me.''

''Look, Serena, if it was really something I could help with—if it would make a difference, I'd do it. But you'll be fine. Believe me.''

She sighed. ''I'll just have to tell Christina that we couldn't put the past aside for the sake of the family.''

''Don't try to lay a guilt trip on me,'' he warned.

''Michael, I've already accepted that you aren't coming. I was simply sharing what I'll have to say to Christina. I know you value your relationship with her.''

Mike saw what she was doing. ''There's nothing you'll stop at, is there?''

''You're right, Michael. I was wrong to come. It was unfair of me to put you in this position. I'm sorry. Just forget it.''

''I have no right to condemn you. You're in a tough spot. I realize that.''

She appraised him the way she used to in the early days. ''You've mellowed,'' she said, her voice barely a whisper. ''I'm impressed.'' She stared at his mouth like she wanted to kiss it—for old time's sake.

He stared back. Damned if she wasn't getting to him. Despite everything.

''Well, I've got lots to do before I get on that plane,'' she said, breaking the mood. ''Not the least of which is getting back to L.A." She patted his hand and glanced up at the trees as a couple of jays cawed. "This was an interesting diversion, the closest I've been to nature in a long time. Peaceful. Ideal for meditation."

"Is that what you were doing when I came up?"

"Yes, I've been studying with a Zen master for four months now. It's wonderful for stress."

Serena never failed to surprise him. "I guess you've mellowed, too," he said.

She smiled, reflecting. "For all the problems in our marriage, it was never boring, was it, Michael? We had a few good years, some good times."

He nodded.

After a moment, she leaned over and kissed him lightly. "I love you, Michael. In spite of the fact that you've failed me." She squeezed his knee and got up, saying, "Tell Connie's kid I'm sorry I messed up the trip. I appreciate you talking to me."

Mike nodded, not knowing what else to do. It was so typical of Serena to end a conversation with a zinger, leaving him completely off-balance. The "I love you" didn't ring false, but he knew damned well it was said for effect.

"I'll give your regards to Christina," she said. Then she sauntered off, swinging her hips like she knew his eyes were glued to them. She never missed a trick. Sex, guilt, pity, intimidation, love—Serena had every weapon known to woman, and knew how to use them. The remark about blow jobs, the profession of love, the walk—nothing she said or did was innocent.

She continued to saunter away. The appropriate moment to call to her came, but he let it pass. He wasn't going to give in. He'd put on his boots and return to the lake.

Serena didn't break stride; she didn't falter. She moved across the dusty ground, her derriere swinging just so, rekindling memories, making the synapses in his brain crackle. It wasn't often that a man had leverage on Serena Bouchard, but he did now. Could he really afford to let the opportunity pass? *Really?*

"Hey!" he called.

She stopped, but took a moment or two to turn. She'd gone twenty-five yards and was closer to the sheriff's vehicle than she was to him. A pair of marauding boys ran between them, whooping gleefully.

"Were you calling me?" she asked.

"Yes. I was wondering what, exactly, Christina said. Did she really ask you to bring me with you?"

Serena began walking back toward him, her expression inscrutable. "She said, 'Bring Michael. It's our only chance to save Uncle Jeffrey.' Those were her exact words."

"Why would she say that?"

"Because she's been in Rio for four months and she knows what's going on down there. She told me what people who matter are saying."

"A nineteen-year-old girl?"

"Jeffrey and Drake were well connected. They introduced her around. She's made friends. Now everything has blown up in her face. She's alone down there and she's calling for help."

"Shit," he grumbled under his breath. "Serena, tell me straight. Are you bullshitting me? I want an honest answer."

About five yards from him she stopped, cocking her hip just so. "I wouldn't expect you to believe me, so I won't answer that. When you call Christina to offer condolences, you can ask her yourself. Why trust me?" She started to turn away, but he stopped her again. "Yes?"

"I'll give you three or four days of my time, long enough to check things out and give you a reading," he said. "But that's it."

"Three or four days, exclusive of travel time," she replied without so much as a smile. "In other words, a week."

He grinned, shaking his head. "You can't resist turning the screws, can you?"

"I know what I need and I know what I want. When the two coincide I do what I have to do. You know that, Michael."

"I hope you realize I feel like a dope, a gutless wonder who can't stand up to a desperate, determined woman."

"You've got your problems and I've got mine." She checked her watch. "Can you walk or shall I have a stretcher brought over? I'm already an hour behind schedule."

"We haven't discussed terms," he said.

"Oh, yes." She reflected. "I'll give you ten thousand up front for holding my hand. Plus a thousand a day, every day you're on the job."

"How about fringe benefits?" he asked.

She arched her brow. "I was kidding about the blow jobs." She smiled. "But then, you knew that." With that, she turned and headed for the sheriff's vehicle, her swing more exaggerated than ever.

W E D N E S D A Y
September 13th

Beverly Hills, California

The phone rang, harsh and real as a gin hangover. Serena did not want to leave her dream, but the ringing wouldn't go away.

"Michael," she murmured, "would you get that?"

She'd uttered the words mindlessly, so mindlessly that it took a couple of rings before she realized there was no one in her bed to hear them. Certainly not Michael.

The persistent ringing forced her to look at the luminous dial of the clock at her bedside. Five forty-five. Jesus. She crawled to the edge of the bed and lifted the receiver.

"Yes?"

"Hello," came a man's deep voice. "I would like to speak with Senhora Serena Bouchard, if I may."

"This is Serena Bouchard," she said numbly.

"Oh, *senhora*. I am Roberto Cabral, telephoning from Rio de Janeiro. A thousand pardons for calling at such an early hour, but I was told you are leaving Los Angeles on an early flight and I wanted to speak with you before your departure."

It was the smoothest, most resonant voice she'd ever heard, a veritable musical instrument. And the accent made her insides quiver. Serena cleared her throat.

"Yes . . . okay . . ."

"You will perhaps recall it is I that your lawyer, Mr. Soloman, contacted regarding the defense of your þrother."

"Yes, Mr. Cabral," she said, her brain finally clicking into gear. "Walter said you'd be calling."

She'd asked her attorney to find someone exceptional to defend Jeffrey, and Walter had come up with Cabral. He was reputed to be the biggest gun in the Brazilian legal profession and, according to Walter, was the best money could buy. Cabral was a former government minister of something or other and was extremely well connected.

"Have you talked to Jeffrey?" she asked. "How is he?"

"I spoke to him very briefly, Senhora Bouchard. As you can imagine, he is upset. But for the moment he is—what is it you say?—holding it together."

Serena smiled at the awkward use of the colloquialism, but she was not distracted for long. "They haven't hurt him, have they? I mean, is he in good health?"

"He made no important complaints, but he was most distressed. He asked when you would be arriving."

Serena pictured Jeffrey's dear, anxious face and had to struggle to control her emotions. "The poor thing. I've agonized over what he must be going through. I hope they haven't put him in a filthy dungeon with a bunch of perverts."

"Prisons are never pleasant, *senhora*."

Cabral's indirect response told Serena more than she cared to hear. But sexual abuse was not something she could deal with just now, particularly when it concerned someone she loved.

"Did he say anything about the murder?" she asked. She knew Jeffrey would refute the accusations against him. It was just a matter of him being able to get out his story.

"Our conversation was brief, *senhora*," Cabral replied. "He insisted that he did not shoot Senhor Manville, but that was all."

"Of course he didn't kill Drake," she rejoined. "Jeffrey is incapable of harming anyone."

"Certainly, Senhora Bouchard."

"The important thing is that we get him out of that prison as quickly as possible."

"This I understand, *senhora*. Everything possible will be done. But as you can imagine, the authorities have their view and their responsibilities."

What the hell did that mean? she wondered. Of course they had opinions—misconceptions. It was Cabral's job to change them. He had to understand that.

"If I may, there are certain arrangements I wish to inform you of *senhora*," he continued.

"Concerning what?"

"Your visit. I retained an excellent private investigator. Mr. Pericles Kotomata, the most celebrated detective in Rio, has agreed to undertake the investigation and provide security services during your stay."

"Good."

"I have taken the liberty, *senhora,* to instruct Mr. Kotomata to meet you at the airport and escort you to your hotel. He can also brief you on the case. He speaks perfect English, better even than I. He was educated in America."

"Sounds good."

"I wanted you to know this, and so this is why I have called at such an unfortunate hour. Again, my apologies."

"Don't worry, Mr. Cabral, I'm pleased that you phoned."

"Thank you, Senhora Bouchard. I look forward to the honor of meeting you. If I may, I will contact you at your hotel tomorrow afternoon."

"Yes, of course. Until then, Mr. Cabral." Serena hung up and looked at the clock. She could afford to spend another five minutes in bed, but it was basically time to get rolling. She lay for a moment, thinking about the call.

Roberto Cabral seemed impressive on the phone—God, that voice was a wonder. But she'd been around long enough to separate form from substance. Latin men, in her experience, were especially adept at atmospherics. This was not about a resonant voice that could make a woman's ovaries throb, it was about her brother's life.

Sex was the last thing on her mind, though seeing Michael had stirred some latent feelings. It wasn't unusual for her to think about him when she was horny, but this was not that kind of situation. Her neediness was more emotional than sexual. She was vulnerable. And Michael played into that so nicely. He was the one man who had never bought into her Superwoman persona, and that was probably why he'd had such a hold on her.

He did have a soft spot, though. He'd loved her. That had been his undoing. And hers. He'd gone down like a row of grain before the scythe. But at least he'd succumbed for the right reasons. That had impressed her, so much that she'd married him.

But that was then and this was now. Serena wasn't sure she knew Michael anymore.

It had been touch and go up at that picnic ground. For a while she'd thought he might actually let her walk away. The bastard had made her pull out all the stops, but at least he'd given her what she wanted in the end. Michael might still love her, but he was fully capable of screwing her, then taking a hike—the way he had at Tahoe. That might even be what he was planning now.

If so, she'd just have to deal with it. She had her resources, too. Her strength was that when it came to feelings, she was more clever than he. As with most things in life, winning and losing at love came down to willpower and guts. Michael knew that. She knew it better.

Serena was about to crawl out of bed when the phone rang again. She groaned, picking up the receiver.

"Serena, it's Blake, in London. I know it's terribly early, but I've got to talk to you."

Blake Peters was the head of her European operation. He was a charming man who'd made the mistake of trying to use his sexual prowess to climb the corporate ladder. If he hadn't been an outstanding hotelier, she'd have canned him the first time he came on to her.

"What's up?" she asked.

"Bumgardener agreed to our price on the Happy Host deal, but won't carry paper. Wants more cash. I told him we can't do it."

"And?"

"He'll take stock instead."

"Stock is practically the same as cash, Blake," she said. "Only worse from our standpoint."

"He'll take class B, nonvoting."

"How much?"

"A million."

"Do we have it to give?"

"Yes."

"Same price and terms otherwise?"

"Yes."

She thought for a moment. "What's the downside?"

"He's more in bed with us this way than if we gave him cash."

"Honey, I don't mind having a man in bed with me so long as I have all the votes."

Blake chuckled.

"That wasn't meant as a joke."

He cleared his throat. "Sorry, Serena."

"Listen, I'm getting on a plane for Rio this morning and I don't have time to deal with this now. Can you tell Bumgardener I'm incommunicado and you'll need a few hours to reach me? That'll give me a chance to talk to Walter."

"Okay," he said, not sounding pleased. "Whatever you wish."

"Get him drunk, Blake. Tell him I'm suspicious of sudden erections. And if he doesn't understand that, we shouldn't have been doing business to begin with."

Blake Peters chuckled again. "Check."

"I'll talk to you later," she said, and dropped the receiver back into the cradle. "Damn," she mumbled, rubbing her eyes. "What a way to start a day."

Getting out of bed, she padded off to the bathroom. Moments later she was standing under the shower, trying to focus her mind on the horrendous day that lay ahead. She

hated long flights, and this one would be particularly oner-
ous considering she was on a mission to save her brother's
life.

But the sensuous feel of the water lulled her, and her mind
went back to the dream she'd been having before Roberto
Cabral's call. She couldn't recall the details, but it involved
both sex and anxiety, the worst possible combination. Michael was in it, she remembered that.

Rubbing herself with the loofah brought erotic thoughts
of Michael to mind. Not a good sign. She certainly didn't
need that kind of distraction on top of all the rest. The reason for taking him to Rio was for his counsel and maybe for
his emotional support, not hanky-panky, as her mother
would have called it. Sex oughtn't be a problem when it
came to ex-husbands, of course, but Michael was no ordinary ex.

Sergei Rosenkrantz, her shrink, had once said former
husbands were useful as frames of reference—a way for a
woman to measure herself against the past. Every woman
had a before-during-and-after self when it came to the important men in her life.

God knew that's how it had been with Eric Lorimer, Serena's first husband. He'd been much older, more a teacher
than a spouse. The marriage had been a statement aimed at
her father and had lasted only fifteen minutes—barely long
enough for her to get pregnant. Had it not been for Christina, history would have remembered him as no more than
a blip in Serena's diary.

Michael was a different matter. He was like a tattoo on
her posterior—whenever she undressed he was there. Part
of it was that she was older than he. That hadn't been an issue when they met, but the sands of time had brought the
twin demons of immunity and aging to the fore—his immunity and her aging.

As she rinsed herself with the hand spray, Serena thought
how blessed life had seemed as recently as a week ago. Her
biggest problem then had been Christina's rebelliousness.

Compared to what she was facing now, that was a piece of cake.

Then there was that damned thirty-million-dollar deal in London. At this moment two men were sitting in some stuffy Mayfair club, drinking warm Scotch and wondering what in the hell that self-important bitch in California was going to do. She could picture Cy Bumgardener, pasty-faced and cursing the fact that he had to deal with a woman. That was more than enough reason to give the screw another turn. She wouldn't, though. Her father had warned her never to allow her ego to come to the negotiation table.

Getting out of the shower, Serena wrapped herself in an enormous bath sheet. She pressed her wet face into the soft, warm towel, luxuriating in the sensation. It was always the best moment of the morning—like the first thirty seconds after an orgasm or the last sip from a bottle of champagne. It was the destination.

Serena carefully examined her face in the mirror, just as she did every morning. "First you look for the tiny fissures," her mother had said. "When they become gaping cracks it's too late for anything but graciously growing old."

There were hints in the mirror of what was to come, and had been for a couple of years. But they were hardly noticeable to the naked eye. Doom was over the horizon, but creeping closer.

As she ran a comb through her hair, Serena peered into her eyes, seeing a glint of her brother. She recalled the time they'd hidden in the bathroom and put on makeup. Serena had been nine and Jeffrey six, a tart even then. Her poor brother, locked up in a filthy prison with a bunch of hairy brutes.

It was impossible for her not to worry about him. Jeffrey was her obsession. He was like her child, and always would be.

Not that they had a wonderful relationship. He resented her, especially in the surrogate-mother role. There was sibling rivalry at play, of course, but the real problem was that he didn't want her "running his life," as he put it. That wasn't quite right—except with regard to finances. The simple truth was Jeffrey was weak, she was strong and he couldn't deal with either fact very well.

Their father had arranged things so that Serena controlled the family fortune, including Jeffrey's trust. At forty he'd get five million and at fifty another five. The balance would remain in the trust, to be managed by Serena, and then go to his heirs upon his death. Underneath he realized that having her make the decisions was best for him, but it still wounded his pride.

Jeffrey complained that their father had treated him like a teenager with an allowance. When Serena offered to loan her brother whatever he needed to start his own business, the complaining stopped. For a while.

But Jeffrey's principal problems were not financial. He had a strong morbid streak. And that worried her. How could he possibly handle a rat-infested prison where he'd be preyed upon like a helpless child in a den of deviants? Serena felt her stomach knot.

Sex. That was what life was all about: people begetting people. Only last week she'd asked her shrink if women lost their sexual appetite in middle age for emotional or physical reasons, and if it was a sign of menopause.

"I wouldn't worry about it," he'd said. "With most of us sexual drive is cyclical. This is a downswing for you, that's all. The old drive will come back. Trust me."

"Maybe I'm getting old, withering," she'd told him, feeling uncharacteristically unsure of herself.

"Nonsense, Serena. You're in the prime of life. You're just more particular now. Are you dating anyone?"

"No, and I haven't really wanted to. That's what's got me worried."

"I doubt it's physical, but if you want to be sure, go see your doctor."

The next day she was in Bernie Silverstein's office. He sat at his desk in his white lab coat, listening to her go on and on about menopause, his pudgy face fatherly and wise.

"There's one sure way to find out," he said. "Let's check your hormone level."

And so she'd had them draw blood for an FSH test and then had gone home to brood, anguishing like an unmarried teenager afraid of killing the rabbit. She'd insisted on knowing the minute the results were in, so Bernie had called her at the Plaza in New York, where she'd gone for a board meeting. She'd just gotten out of the shower and was sitting on the bed naked as a jaybird to take the call—fitting given that she was speaking to her gynecologist.

"Your estrogen level is down a smidgeon, Serena," he said, "but that's not unusual. It could have dipped a trifle when you were twenty-five just as easily."

"So what's the bottom line, Bernie?"

"You're still a girl, my dear. But I wouldn't wait too much longer to have a second baby, if you want one."

"The way I've been feeling about men, you'll have to artificially inseminate me," she replied.

"If there's a problem in that regard, talk to your analyst. On my end, everything's copacetic."

She'd laughed. "Bernie, was that a bad pun?"

"You're one of the few patients I could say that to."

"I feel honored."

"Have dinner with an attractive man," he said.

"Then take in a porno flick?" she returned.

"I'll leave the details to you."

She'd planned on a book and bed that evening, but instead she got dressed up and went to a relatively classy pickup bar in Midtown to show off her hormone level. She'd let a few young studs paw her on the dance floor and got a tingle or two, which was reason for optimism. That night she'd slept better—if alone—knowing her femininity was intact. Two days after she'd returned home, Christina had called about Drake's murder and Jeffrey's arrest. So now her sexual rehabilitation program was on hold—or it had been until she'd seen Michael.

Serena hated to admit it, but seeing him had done wonders for her libido. She'd had that sexy dream, which was a hell of a note! Sergei would doubtlessly have a few choice words to say about that.

Just then she heard the bedroom door open.

"Breakfast."

It was Agnes, her housekeeper of sixteen years. Serena took a robe from the back of the bathroom door and slipped it on. She looked out to see Agnes placing the tray on the table where Serena ate every morning.

"Breakfast already? What time is it?"

"The driver will be out front in exactly an hour, Mrs. B."

Agnes had called her "Mrs. B." since her first day on the job. Their relationship was warm, but not overly familiar. Serena treated the people who worked for her with respect, but never as intimate friends. She'd gotten that from her beloved father, who'd come from an aristocratic Southern family.

Alden Bouchard had been a throwback. He'd attended a military prep school and Virginia Military Institute, and knew the name and background of every regimental commander in every Civil War battle. But the best thing about him was that he'd positively adored his darling daughter. To her, he was a giant and would always be.

"Can I bring you a cup of coffee?" Agnes called to her.

"Please."

Serena started drying her hair. She'd recently had it cut in compliance with Monsieur Anton's dictum that for a woman of a certain age, less was more. She had luxurious hair, naturally dark and effortless to care for. Michael had always loved it, though he hadn't yet commented on the change of style.

Agnes, a small, round woman of sixty, entered the bath, placing the cup and saucer on the vanity. Serena put down the drier. She fluffed her hair with her fingers, then picked up the coffee. Agnes waited for instructions. Serena almost always had something for her to do to expedite her morning routine.

"Is Michael up?" she asked, examining her neck in the mirror.

"Yes, ma'am. He was having breakfast in the kitchen when I left. It was a welcome sight, I have to say."

Serena heard the lilt in her voice. Agnes adored Michael—he was popular, in fact, with the entire staff. Maybe it was his blue-collar sensibilities. At parties he'd spent as much time talking to the help as he did to the guests. "At least they're real people and not a bunch of stuffed shirts," he'd argued.

Serena had no doubt that if they'd had a vote, the help would have taken his side in the divorce. But they knew who was buttering their bread. The theory of money and loyalty was another thing she'd learned from her father.

"It is a little strange having him back in the house, isn't it?" Serena said, watching Agnes in the mirror.

"Yes, ma'am. Mornings are different since Mr. Hamlin went away."

"They've certainly been less bawdy," Serena said with a smile.

She recalled Michael's habit of waiting until she was dressed for work before deciding to seduce her. It was obvious why he did it: for power. Sex and power were flip sides of the same coin. That's probably what made him so good in bed.

Humoring Michael in the morning had cost her a small fortune in panty hose, but it also had done wonders for her day. Morning sex was better than a two-mile run and a hell of a lot more fun.

Seeing Agnes's blush, Serena knew it was time to change the subject. "Are the suitcases ready to go?" she asked.

"Yes, Mrs. B. Everything's downstairs in the hall."

"Good."

She sent Agnes off to deal with Michael. Serena had a lot to do before they left for the airport.

After finishing her makeup, she decided to call Walter Soloman. When he came on the line, she brought him up to date on the Happy Host deal. They discussed the pros and cons of giving class B, nonvoting stock in lieu of cash. Walter suggested she add a buy-back option and a first-right-ofrefusal clause to the contract. Serena agreed it was a good idea.

They finished their conversation about the London deal, and Walter asked if she'd heard from Roberto Cabral. "Before dawn," she told him. "But once I heard that voice, all was forgiven. If he looks as good as he sounds, and the judge is a woman, it might not even matter if Jeffrey's innocent."

"I don't know a thing about the man except that he has an excellent reputation and lots of clout."

That was Walter—literal and humorless. But he got results, and that was what she expected for her money. "Let's hope he's as good as you, Walter."

"Thank you, Serena."

"I'll be in touch after Blake confirms we've got a deal with Bumgardener."

After the call, she took her coffee to the bedroom, where she snatched a piece of toast from the breakfast tray Agnes had left. She wandered to the window. To her surprise, Michael was down in the garden. She munched her toast and watched him. He had the air of someone visiting a childhood home, gazing about as he moved through the yard, touching a blossom or a lounge chair with reverence.

It had been apparent to them both that Michael was not suited to life in Beverly Hills. Not really. As much as anything that was why they'd grown apart: he'd never fit into her world. Even their fabulous sex life hadn't been enough.

Michael was much more than a great lover, though. Oddly, he'd served as a moderating influence, keeping her excesses in check, though of course she'd never admitted it. And before becoming her lover, he'd been her champion, a family crisis having originally brought them together.

They'd met six months after her father's death, at a time when she was struggling to get control of the company. The lawyers and company execs were giving her trouble, certain she wasn't up to the job. They wanted her to be a constitutional monarch and leave the management to them. Her father had warned her it would happen, so she did what she had to do. She sent a few heads rolling to make sure they got her point.

Right in the middle of the bloodletting, some nutcase snatched Christina, thinking a kidnapping would be easy money. Serena should have foreseen the danger, but she hadn't. In retrospect, it probably wasn't as serious an incident as it had seemed at the time. But when your child is kidnapped before your eyes, nothing is more traumatic or more frightening.

The abductor was a screwball emigrant from Eastern Europe who worked as a busboy in their flagship property, the Beverly Bouchard. Brandishing a gun, he'd grabbed Christina, intending to demand a million dollars in ransom. But the bastard never made it out of the hotel. He was immediately cornered in the kitchen by the fleeing staff, who barricaded the service entrance.

When Serena had turned to see her child being carried off, she'd almost lost it. But she'd willed herself to appear calm, even though her heart was screaming in anguish and her instinct was to charge in after the sonovabitch.

Someone had the sense to call the police, and Serena had a secretary summon security. Michael, who'd been newly hired as number three in the department, was on duty that day. He took control immediately, ordering everyone away from the door. Her first impulse was to resist, but his commanding manner—not unlike her father's—made her back down.

That didn't stop her, though, from imagining the worst. Nor did it help when she heard Christina sobbing. Serena knew her daughter was terrified, but didn't know if she was being molested or tortured or what. It was the worst experience of Serena's life. She'd never felt so helpless.

Finally, it became too much to bear. She marched up to Michael and said she wasn't waiting for the police—she was going into the kitchen and getting her child.

"If anybody's going in there, it'll be me," he'd said. "You'd only mess things up."

No one had ever spoken that way to her before, but Michael was never one to shrink from his opinions. He always called a spade a spade.

"If you want to help, keep people quiet and away from the door."

And so he'd gone into the kitchen, unarmed. After a few angry shouts, it got very quiet in there. Serena's heart beat so hard it hurt. She recalled holding her breath, waiting for the sound of shots, wondering if she'd forced Michael to do something stupid.

But it had worked out in the end. By the time the police arrived, Michael was already negotiating with the kidnapper. A swat team and a police negotiator were on the scene as well, but their services were never needed. It took half an hour for Michael to convince the guy to give up, then the three of them came walking out of the kitchen like old pals. The police grabbed the busboy, Serena took Christina and Michael went off to get himself a beer.

She went looking for him after Christina had calmed down and they'd both gotten through their tears. She found him in the bar, watching a baseball game. He accepted her thanks with equanimity, but when she offered him a twenty-five-thousand-dollar reward, he refused it, saying it was all part of the job. *That* had impressed her even more than his physical courage, considering twenty-five thou was a lot at the time. When she'd asked him later why he'd turned down the money, he'd said, "To impress you, of course." She loved his honesty.

Michael did agree to let her take him to dinner, which they did a few days later, after she felt comfortable leaving Christina. They went to Scandia for champagne and caviar. He went home with her and they made love nonstop until Monday morning. Six months later they were married.

Michael was a charmer, all right, a cocky guy with shoulders, deep blue eyes and a grin that became indelibly imprinted on her soul. He was blessed with great hands—her mother would have said artistic hands—and he knew how to use them. Michael wasn't a sexual athlete; he had more savoir faire than that. And subtlety. In bed he was like an accomplished European lover, which was saying something considering he was just a kid from Bakersfield.

She'd asked him early on where he'd learned to make love, and all he'd say was that he had good teachers. For a while she wondered if maybe he'd had on-the-job training, picking up a few bucks making horny, bored, rich matrons happy, but he'd sworn he'd never been paid for his services.

Then once, after they'd been married for a couple of years, he'd told her about Yvette, a French journalist he'd met when he first came to L.A. He was twenty-three at the time and she was thirty-seven. Over the course of eighteen months, she taught him everything the French had learned about the boudoir since Louis XIV. Serena and quite a few other ladies in Los Angeles owed Yvette and her countrymen a tremendous debt of gratitude.

Michael was by the pool now. Serena sipped her coffee and watched him squat down and run his fingertips through the water, testing the temperature. She wondered if he was thinking about the times they'd sneaked out and gone skinny-dipping in the moonlight, high on champagne and each other.

Michael stood up and Serena watched him stretch. She liked looking at him. His days of five-percent body fat were over, but he hadn't slipped much. He was still firm and would undoubtedly wear his middle age well.

Serena wondered why she was feeling so charitable toward him. He was an ex-husband, after all. If things had been perfect, they'd still be together. Michael, for all his virtues, knew how to piss her off as well as turn her on. And he certainly hadn't lost a lot of sleep over the failure of their marriage. That had really galled her.

Within two weeks of leaving her, Michael had begun sharing his bed with a blond bimbo named Terri, an inflatable sex doll who could walk and giggle and, when prompted, make semi-intelligible sounds. The fling was his way of coping, Serena knew, but he could have at least given the marriage a respectable period of mourning, even if the divorce hadn't been his idea.

Part of it was bitterness, which probably explained what had happened at Tahoe a year after their divorce. Michael had almost gone into shock when he saw her skiing the bunny hill at Heavenly—slipping and sliding and cursing every foot of the way.

"Jesus Christ, I thought I'd see the Virgin Mary on skis before you," he'd said, leaning on his poles, that big lazy grin on his face and his goggles pushed insouciantly up into his browny blond hair. "Have you found religion on the slopes or what?"

"I'm doing it for love," she'd replied. "And believe me, I'm not proud of it."

"The guy must be a stud to lure you up here. God knows, I never could . . . something about being allergic to snow, if I recall correctly."

She arched a brow. "I got shots for the trip."

"So you're a snow bunny now, eh?"

"Actually, no. We're mainly here looking at property."

"A love nest?"

"No, a hotel."

"Then it's not all pleasure."

"No."

"Does *he* know that?" Michael asked, a cocksure grin on his face.

"He thinks I adore him. And I do, so I guess it's all right."

"Anybody I've met?"

"Cornelio Icardi, if you must know."

"As in Count Icardi, or as in Cornelio, the *paisano* from the hood?" Michael had quipped, annoyingly sure of himself. The man had seemed to be utterly without jealousy, much to her chagrin.

"Does it matter?" she'd asked, looking him square in the eye.

He shrugged. "No, I've never heard of him, so I guess it doesn't."

She'd glanced up the slope, knowing that Cornelio, who was neither a count nor a *paisano* from the neighborhood, but rather a hotelier from Milano, was up there somewhere doing snowplows or whatever it was the experts did. When she turned back, Michael was checking her out as though he was wondering if her body felt and tasted the same as before.

"I haven't put on a pound," she'd announced.

"So I see."

"You alone, Michael?"

"In fact, but not in spirit. I still fantasize about Michelle Pfeiffer."

"Would you like for me to arrange an introduction?"

"Thanks, but I'll struggle along."

"What happened to Terri? Get tired of her three-minute tape and her gum chewing?"

Michael grinned. "I'm flattered that you've paid such close attention."

"Every former wife is curious, Michael."

"Curious?"

"Your women not only say something about you, they say something about me."

"Oh, I see. Terri made *you* look bad."

"Don't act self-righteous. I had to contend with your dolly birds during our marriage."

"I never screwed anyone until we were separated and you were dating, too, Serena."

"Oh, bullshit."

"What's this?" he asked with mock surprise. "You didn't get your pound of flesh before? Still want a piece of me?"

"No, thank you. I got you out of my system, believe it or not." It was a fib, but how could she admit she still fantasized about him when things were slow?

It had amazed her how naturally they'd fallen back into the bickering that came with sexual tension. It had always been like that before they'd make love. She had no idea why, unless it was because sex was as much a form of combat as love.

"Nevada's just a few minutes away," he'd said, giving her a vaguely salacious look. "We could ski on over and get married so you can beat on me some more. After the honeymoon, of course."

"Go to hell, Michael. I'm sorry I brought it up. I don't even know why I did. It was a reflex reaction, I suppose."

"Old habits die hard, my dear."

"Maybe it's your after-shave."

"Christ, and all along I thought it was the way I was hung."

She flipped him the bird.

"Nice to know I still warm the cockles of your heart."

"Speaking of which, I'm going inside. I promised Cornelio I'd take one lesson and I have. That's my skiing for this decade."

"My lift ticket's about to expire or I'd buy you a drink," he said. "Maybe later, when I can buy one for Cornelio, too."

"I'm sure he'd love that," she said dryly.

"Love me, love my family. Isn't that the Bouchard philosophy?"

"Sorry to disappoint you, my sweet, but you've been excommunicated, remember?"

"Ah, yes. How easily one forgets."

He moved over to her, slipping his ski between hers, and gave her a kiss on the cheek. "*Arrivederci, mi amore.*" And then he headed off for the lift.

That night, after Serena got back from the hospital, where she'd left Cornelio in traction, she ran into Michael in Harrah's, where he was staying in a comped suite.

"Buy me a drink," she said to him. "I need cheering up." She told him about Cornelio's unfortunate accident.

Michael expressed his sympathy, then asked if she cared to join him in his suite for a bottle of champagne. She didn't bother playing games. She went with him, and they'd partied until dawn. When she was dressing the next morning, she told him that it had been mindless sex and that she hated him even more than before.

"As long as Cornelio's pals don't call him 'Godfather,' I'm cool," he said in reply.

"You're safe."

"It was a great skiing trip, Serena," he told her. "Thanks for the memories."

She'd hated him for that snide remark, but then she could hardly blame him. *She'd* divorced *him*. It was revenge of sorts. Still, she had pointed her finger at him threateningly before leaving. "This never happened, you sonovabitch. Don't you ever mention it to a soul. It *never* happened. Hear me?"

"My lips are sealed."

To the best of her knowledge, he had never said anything to anyone. Her relationship with Cornelio had petered out after that. It had to. Every time they'd have had sex she would have thought of his stand-in at Tahoe.

Serena moved away from the window as Michael turned and began strolling back toward the house. She checked the clock. Time had gotten away from her. She had to hurry. Rio and her poor little brother were waiting.

From the front porch Mike could see the Mercedeses and the BMWs, the Jaguars and the occasional Rolls or Bentley moving down Beverly Drive, headed for town. The early birds were leaving their châteaus in search of the golden worm.

It was hard to believe he'd once been a part of this game, this L.A. rat race, sparkling and alluring though it seemed. Vegas was even more glittery, but it didn't pretend to be bigger than it was. Las Vegas was a carnival, a show— though instead of packing up every few days to move on to the next town, people came to it. Los Angeles, on the other hand, took itself seriously. He'd learned that from Serena when she was tutoring him on the good life.

She owned one of the grand old Mediterranean mansions located just north of the commercial district. While the neighborhood was very expensive, it was easily two cuts below the sort of place she could afford.

She had been given the house by her father after her divorce from her first husband, almost two decades earlier. Having lived for so many years with her "Italian Bitch," as she called it, Serena had been unable to give it up. Besides, it was convenient for her corporate offices in downtown Beverly Hills.

It was strange to be under her roof again. It made him wonder how he could have been gulled into joining her crusade. What was he doing, flying off to Rio with her, for God's sake? Maybe it had more to do with self-indulgence than duty.

Being in the home they'd shared brought back memories, though. Many of them good. A part of him liked the place, even if it had never truly felt like home—not his home. He'd always felt like a guest, suspecting it had more to do with her attitude than his. For all her devotion to family, she'd never wanted a family with him.

Early in their marriage she'd made it clear there weren't to be any more children. Been There, Done That was her motto. "I love Christina more than life," she'd told him during their first serious conversation on the subject, "but I can't do that again. And I refuse to do a half-assed job. It wouldn't be fair to the baby and it wouldn't be fair to you."

If his own childhood hadn't been such a mess, and if he hadn't relished the notion of doing the job right, it might not have been such a big deal. But her intransigence on the subject left a raw wound. He'd felt it was a comment on how impermanent she wanted their relationship to be.

When he'd tried to point that out, Serena scoffed. "For crissakes, Michael, you don't have to get me pregnant for there to be a bond between us. It will either work or it won't." At first he'd thought she didn't understand how much it mattered to him. Ultimately, he'd decided that she did. Either way, it had been a bone of contention—one over which she ultimately had the final say.

Mike watched a long-legged blonde jog past the house. She had a ponytail, headphones, a skimpy pink tank top and pale blue shorts, and acted oblivious to the men rubbernecking from their luxury cars as they zipped by. He judged her to be somebody's daughter, rather than a wife or mistress. "Going out for a run before breakfast, Mom. I'll be back after I wrap a couple of Mercedeses around a lamppost."

Mike shook his head. Amazing what a little ass cheek could do on a city street. He checked his watch. Five minutes till the limo was due.

He turned to examine the array of luggage on the porch, counting seven full-size suitcases. This was a woman who'd rather charter an extra 747 for her luggage than be stuck without a dress she absolutely had to have. Serena's solution to travel-wardrobe problems was to bring her closet with her.

Amazingly, she used to be worse. When he'd asked Agnes why Serena had gone from ludicrous amounts of luggage to merely excessive, she'd told him that the new Bouchard theory of travel was go with seven bags, come back with ten, if necessary. The odds were pretty good one or two would get lost, anyway.

Mike himself had decided to make do with a single suitcase. That was all he needed for three or four days—a couple of dress shirts, a few polo shirts, some pants, bathing trunks. To pack more would have sent the signal he could be had, and he was determined to be on a plane back to the States as soon as he could leave in good conscience.

Their layover in Vegas the previous afternoon had been just long enough for him to go home for a shave, a shower and to pack. He hadn't invited Serena along, suggesting instead she wait at the airport, but she'd insisted on seeing his place. "A surprise visit to a man's den reveals the unvarnished truth," she'd explained.

"Wasn't five years of marriage long enough to figure me out?" he'd asked.

"I want to see how much you've evolved," she replied.

Just as he took another peek at his watch, a white stretch limo stopped on the street opposite the house to make a left turn into the drive. Because of traffic, it was half a minute before the driver could complete the maneuver. As he did, the huge wrought-iron gate swung open and the vehicle entered, moving slowly up the arc of the circular drive.

Serena didn't keep a chauffeur, but she did have an arrangement with a rental agency that a select group of two or three drivers would always be available to her. She liked to know everybody who worked for her or rendered personal service. Mike knew the system well.

It was hard to see the driver because of the sun reflecting off the windshield, but when the vehicle stopped, he saw that it was Eddie Brown, who'd done most of the chauffeuring for them during Mike's own years in the big house.

Eddie, a black man about his age, was a former junior-college football lineman. He was the sweetest guy in the world, always ready with a smile and a cheerful word. Serena said she didn't know how he could have played football, since he'd have apologized every time he hit someone. She was right.

Eddie popped out of the limo, though not quite as nimbly as he used to. It looked like he'd put on fifty pounds over the last five years. But Eddie had the same familiar ear-to-ear grin.

"Mr. H.!" he exclaimed, using his old nickname for Mike. "What a surprise!" He gave a whoop. "I can't believe my eyes. Is it really you or am I seeing things?"

"A ghost of Christmas Past," Mike said, descending the steps.

They embraced, giving each other a bear hug. Then laughed.

"No shit, what you doing here?" Eddie asked, looking up at the front door. "Miz Bouchard ain't made you a houseboy again after sendin' you off to the fields for all these years?"

Mike laughed and playfully slapped Eddie's beefy side. "Hey, big fella, you've been spending time at the table."

"It's one of these new diet plans. They take the after picture first, you do your eatin' second, then they take the before picture. I'm almost there."

They had a few laughs, then Eddie lowered his voice. "All kiddin' aside, what you doin' here? Or is it none of my business?"

"Believe it or not, I'm going to Rio de Janeiro on business with Serena. Jeffrey's got himself in a pickle."

Eddie said he'd read about it in the newspaper. "Goin' to Brazil's not a bad thing to have to do, if you're gettin' paid," he said. "Mrs. B. sure has got somethin' to offer besides her checking account. Woo-ee!" A sudden frown crossed his face. "I guess I can say that since you ain't married no more."

"It's a free country."

Eddie made his round face even rounder. "Don't suppose you'll be gettin' any of that sweet stuff this time around, though."

"It's strictly business, Eddie. I plan on being comfortably back in my little tract house in Vegas in five days' time, still a reconstituted virgin."

Eddie whooped. "That'll be the day you're a virgin anything."

"Now how would you know?"

"I can name three times without even thinking about it that you and the missus was makin' whoopee in the back of my limousine. One time we almost rocked right off the freeway."

Mike had to struggle to keep from laughing. "I guess we weren't as discreet as we thought."

"Just don't give me no bullshit about bein' some kind of virgin," Eddie chided. "I know better."

"Those days are over," Mike told him.

"But you're headed for Rio, ain't you?"

"For five days."

"A man can have some fun in five days, can't he, Mr. H.?"

"I didn't say I was adverse to having a good time." He winked. "It's only a question of who with."

"That's my man," Eddie said, squeezing Mike's shoulders with his beefy hands. "Well, guess I best be gettin' these cases in the trunk. Mrs. B.'s goin' to come flyin' out that door any minute, expectin' me to beam her straight to the airport."

"I'll give you a hand."

"No need, Mr. H. I got this down to a system. Since she's started travelin' light, it's a piece of cake." Eddie laughed.

Mike helped carry the bags to the trunk anyway, but he let Eddie load. The chauffeur put it together as neatly as a Fuller Brush man repacking his demo case. Then he closed the trunk.

"All we need now is the lady," Eddie said, dusting off his hands.

Just then the front door swung open, as if on cue, and Serena appeared, radiant in a white linen suit with a peach silk blouse, her short black hair shining in the morning sun. As usual, she caught Mike off guard. No woman he'd ever known had a better sense of presentation. Serena could enter a bedroom and make it look like a coronation procession, a stripper's first moment on stage or her wedding night, depending on her mood and her intention.

"Morning, gentlemen," she said, looking them over. "Have we gotten our boy talk out of the way?"

"We've discussed you at length, Serena," Mike said, "if that's what you mean."

She arched a brow. "I hope you haven't told him all my secrets, Eddie," she said, descending the steps.

"No, ma'am," he replied, stepping over to open the rear door of the limo for her.

Serena turned to the housekeeper, who was standing at the top of the steps. "Look after things, Agnes. You know how to reach me. So does everyone at the office."

"Yes, Mrs. B. Goodbye. Have a safe trip."

Mike gave the woman a wink. "No wild parties now, Agnes."

She blushed and gave him a go-on-with-you wave.

"Come on, Michael," Serena said, climbing into the car. "We're going to be late."

He went around to the other side of the limo and slid in next to her, instinctively inhaling her scent. "Damn, you smell good," he said, scooting closer.

"Don't distract me," she said. "My mind's already in Brazil."

"Glad you left your body here."

Serena pushed a button, closing the window that separated them from Eddie as the limo moved down the drive and into the street. "In case you've gotten the wrong idea," she said, "this trip is dead serious. I don't intend a replay of Tahoe."

"Me, neither."

"Promise?"

"As far as I'm concerned this is a job. You're paying me a thousand a day, and I intend to collect my paycheck. Just because the working conditions are pleasant doesn't change the fact."

"What working conditions are you referring to?" she asked.

"The boss smells good and she doesn't make me ride in front with the rest of the help. What more could a man ask for?"

Serena squeezed his knee. "Thanks for being supportive."

"It's all part of the service."

"No, you're being kind. And decent, when you could easily be a horse's ass. I want you to know I appreciate it."

They fell into a tentative silence, though tension hung in the air. After a couple of blocks they passed the little blond jogger. Serena saw Mike notice her, but acted oblivious. She had never been the type to give a man the satisfaction of her jealousy.

"Did I mention I've hired a lawyer for Jeffrey?" she asked, moving smoothly to the next topic.

"No."

"He called early this morning, waking me from a sound sleep."

"You must have liked that."

"It was all right. I was dreaming about you."

"Oh?"

"Don't jump to conclusions. Sex isn't the only thing I dream about."

"That's a relief."

She gave him a rebuking look. "I was telling you about the lawyer. His name is Roberto Cabral. And he has a set of lungs like you wouldn't believe."

"Lungs?"

"A voice, Michael. After listening to him for a minute, I wanted to have his baby."

"Nice to know somebody can bring out the maternal instinct in you."

"Please, Michael, let's not dwell on the past. This trip is going to be hard enough as it is."

Incongruously, she put her hand on his knee.

Mike glanced up and saw Eddie looking at them in the rearview mirror, his smile as wide and bright as a rainbow. It was obvious what the guy was thinking—that there'd be some R and R in Rio, after all.

There was no disputing the fact that in her white suit Serena was as delectable as the frosting on a cake—sweet, enticing and ready to be licked. But this wasn't going to be a replay of Tahoe. Serena had gotten herself into a high-stakes game, saddling him with special responsibility. Much as he'd like to play, there was the matter of honor, pride and common decency to be considered . . . not to mention self-preservation.

West Los Angeles

As they drove down Santa Monica Boulevard, passing the southern edge of the Los Angeles Country Club, Serena thought of her father, who had played the L.A.C.C. golf course with his business cronies in the fifties and sixties.

Occasionally, she'd gone along and watched him in action. But not all of her memories of the place were positive.

Her father had taken Jeffrey there under duress at age seventeen to undergo one of the rites of manhood—golf with the old man. Jeffrey and their father were one of the more tragic pairs in the Bouchard family history. And not just on the golf course. Poor Jeffrey.

Serena glanced at Michael, grateful for his reassuring presence. This was another of those times when she needed his look-trouble-in-the-eye brand of guts.

People did tend to pull together in an emergency, but she felt guilty pressuring him into going with her to Rio. The divorce had hurt him, and she couldn't quite put that completely from her mind.

Serena reached over and took his hand, intertwining her fingers in his. Michael, who was off in thought, regarded her with surprise. She gave him her warmest smile.

"Did you call your friend, Connie, last night to say goodbye?"

"No. Why?"

"I feel badly taking you away from her, if you must know."

"You're not taking me away from her. I'm not hers. I don't belong to Connie or anyone else."

"She cares about you, Michael. I could hear it in her voice when I spoke with her the other day."

"Serena, why the concern? You're my employer, not my romantic advisor."

"If I'd known you were going to be sensitive about it, I wouldn't have said anything. But I wasn't prying. I don't care about your relationship with her."

"Look, I screw Connie once or twice a month, when one or the other of us has to get our rocks off. There. That's the story of the relationship. Are you satisfied?"

"That wasn't what I was getting at," she said icily. "I was trying to show a little compassion. For *both* of you."

He stared out his side of the limo and said nothing. Serena let the silence hang. Then Michael shifted uneasily.

"I'm sorry I was testy," he finally said. "I'm still uncomfortable with this . . . what we're doing."

"Strange. Only fifteen minutes ago you were reveling in my discomfort."

"I know," he said. "This isn't easy for either of us."

"Would you rather not go?" she asked. "When we get to the airport, you can get on a flight to Las Vegas instead of coming with me. You don't even have to refund the ten thousand. Buy Connie and her kid a new TV. Take them to Disneyland."

"I wouldn't do that and you know it, Serena."

"Well, do as you wish. You're a grown man. God knows, it's not my place to tell you what to do."

"Thank you."

"I wasn't being sarcastic," she said.

"I know. I meant that sincerely. Thank you. Really thank you. It isn't something you'd have said five years ago."

"I never tried to make your decisions for you or run your life," she said, starting to feel defensive.

He seemed a touch bewildered. "Serena, I'm not saying you did. Not consciously. But you never respected me, which is all right because I probably wasn't deserving of your respect. But you do recognize that I'm deserving now, or seem to be, and I want you to know I'm grateful. That's all I was trying to say."

She took his hand again. This time he squeezed her fingers in return. Leaning over, she bussed him lightly on the cheek. "I'm glad we can put the past aside and be friends."

"That would be nice, if true," he said.

She looked into his eyes and felt the most pronounced sexual desire for him yet. There had been twinges earlier, but this was powerful and unmistakable. Ironic. Just when they were agreeing to be friends, she got an overwhelming urge to seduce him.

"Excuse me, Mrs. B.," Eddie said over the intercom, "but can I interrupt you for a second?"

Serena pushed the speaker button. "Yes, Eddie, what is it?"

"I was wonderin' if Mr. Hamlin would check that gray sedan a couple of cars back. He's been on our tail since Whittier Drive."

Michael and Serena both glanced back. Michael reached for the button. "Have you changed speeds and lanes, Eddie?"

"Yes, sir. Whatever I do, he do, too."

"Don't get on the freeway," Michael said. "Drive on down Santa Monica, then make a U-turn. Let's see what he does."

Serena felt her stomach clench. Michael's tone carried a hint of danger. Like anyone with money, she knew she and her family were potential targets for crackpots. What had happened to Christina was proof of that. The mere thought of the kidnapping made her shiver. She still woke up some nights crying as if Christina was being ripped from her arms.

"What do you think it could be, Michael?" she asked, trying not to appear overly concerned.

"I don't know. But we'll probably find out."

She scooted a bit closer. Serena didn't mind being protected, and God knew Michael didn't mind playing the role of protector. The process was as biological as sex.

He glanced out the back window of the limo. They'd gone down Santa Monica Boulevard a few blocks past the San Diego Freeway entrance. The limousine moved into a left-turn lane. Serena waited, not even certain what to fear. Michael was calm—that, at least, was reassuring.

He reached for the intercom button. "Is that them two back?"

"Yep, two cars back, Mr. Hamlin."

"Okay, after you make your U-turn, go a block, then pull over to the curb. Let's see what they do with that. Get a license number if you can."

"Check."

Serena pressed against his arm, her heart thumping. Michael remained calm. She checked the look in his eyes.

The light changed and they made their turn. Coming back they were able to see that there were two men in the gray car.

Serena only had a glimpse of them, but the driver looked rather seedy.

"Recognize them?" Michael asked.

"I didn't get a very good look, but no."

"Me, neither." He reached into his coat pocket, took out a pen and wrote the license-plate number down on his palm. Then he pushed the intercom button. "I got the plate, Eddie."

"Good, 'cause I didn't, Mr. H."

After a block they pulled over to the curb. Michael looked back. The other car pulled over as well, stopping a hundred feet behind, leaving a parked car between them.

"What now, sir?" Eddie asked.

Michael thought for a moment, then pushed the button again. "You don't have any bookies after your ass, do you, Eddie?"

"Shit, no!" Then his eyes rounded. "Oops! 'Scuse me, Mrs. Bouchard. I meant no, sir, I don't."

She pushed the button. "You can skip the niceties, Eddie. Personally, I'm ready to pee in my pants."

He gave an enormous smile into the mirror. "Yes, ma'am!"

Michael drummed his fingers on the door handle, then asked, "How much spare time did you work into the schedule, Serena?"

"Not enough for a gunfight."

After another look through the rear window, he said, "All right, we'll play it smart rather than brave." Into the intercom, he added, "Take us to the airport, Jeeves."

Once they were on the freeway, Michael got on the car phone. Serena listened as he tried to get through to the L.A.P.D.

"Joe Murdoch in?... Mike Hamlin... I see... No, it's a personal matter. I'll check back in half an hour or so. Thanks."

"What was that about?" she asked.

"I have a detective friend down in the Parker Center who I thought might be able to get a line on that plate, but he's not there and I don't want to fool with anybody else. If we have time, I'll phone later." He spoke into the intercom again. "Eddie, see how determined those fellows are. Do a little creative driving."

"All right, Mr. H."

Serena checked the rear window. "Why don't we just notify the police we're being followed?"

"It's not a crime unless it turns into stalking. Anyway, calling would be a waste of time. They wouldn't have much interest in this."

Though the traffic was heavy, Eddie maneuvered the limo from lane to lane, weaving up the freeway as fast as traffic allowed. Michael checked the tail.

"They're persistent," he said.

"They must know we're aware they're following."

"That may be the point."

"But why, Michael? I don't understand."

"I don't either, babe." He sat calmly, thinking, as Eddie continued his maneuvers. "Have you been getting bugged by the press over Jeffrey's arrest?" he asked.

"There've been a few calls, but I haven't talked to any reporters. All they could possibly get from me is a reaction."

"Yeah, you're too much on the periphery. I thought maybe our friends back there were enterprising reporters, but I guess that's not likely." He got on the intercom again. "Eddie, let's get off at Sepulveda south of the Marina Freeway and approach the airport that way. Once you're on the surface streets run some yellow lights, see how brave the boys are."

"Right."

"What's the purpose of that?" Serena asked.

"If Eddie hits an intersection just as the light turns red, our tail has a decision to make. He either comes through long after the light's changed or he has to get on our bumper. It's sort of like forcing them to play Russian roulette."

"Sounds sadistic to me."

"They can always obey the traffic laws and leave us alone."

Serena leaned back in the seat, though she wasn't particularly comfortable. "Well, I guess this is why I hired you."

He pinched her cheek. "Might as well earn my money."

They moved onto Sepulveda, the gray sedan a hundred and fifty feet behind them. Michael glanced back, shaking his head.

"What's the matter?" she asked.

"They're not being particularly subtle. It's almost as if they're making a statement."

"What kind of statement?"

"That's just it. I don't know." He stroked his chin. "Anything been happening in your life you haven't mentioned?"

"Like what?"

"I don't know. Jealous boyfriend. Gangsters trying to shake you down. Obscene phone calls."

"No, nothing. I keep myself pretty well insulated from the world. I haven't had any trouble at all."

"It must have something to do with Jeffrey, then."

"I can't imagine what."

Suddenly a loud horn sounded behind them, followed by the screech of tires. They both glanced back. The sedan was barely clearing an intersection.

"Those boys are determined, Mr. H." Eddie's voice came through the speakers. "I went through a full red and so did they."

Michael nodded. "Keep up the good work."

Serena was nervous and getting more uncomfortable by the minute. She wasn't sure if Michael was showing off or if what they were doing was necessary. But she felt helpless, knowing things were out of her control. This situation did prove one thing to her, though—she'd been wise to hire Michael.

They were coming to Manchester Avenue, and the limo lurched forward as Eddie accelerated. Serena saw the light turn yellow when they were still a couple hundred feet away.

As Eddie speeded up, she closed her eyes, gripping the door handle. Michael muttered, "Oh, shit..." An instant later the limo swerved, tires around them squealed, then she heard a tremendous crash. Serena whipped her head back and saw the gray sedan crumpled against a mail truck in the middle of the intersection, both vehicles encircled in a cloud of smoke and dust.

"Oh, Lord."

"Eddie," Michael said, "pull over."

The limo stopped. Michael had Eddie back up, then opened the door and got out.

"Sit tight," he said to Serena. "I'm going to check this out. I'll be right back."

She sat motionless, her heart pounding. Were they responsible for what had happened? It was like a bunch of teenagers playing games. Eddie kept looking at her in the mirror, consternation on his face.

"Sorry, Mrs. B.," he said into his mike. "Sorry to scare you that way, but those guys are crazy. There was no way they should've been comin' through that intersection."

"Don't worry about it," she replied. "Let's hope nobody's seriously hurt."

Eddie shook his head as he peered into his side mirror. "Nobody walkin' away from that, Mrs. B. Jesus."

After a minute Michael was back. He climbed in beside her, grim-faced. He signaled for Eddie to drive on.

"Is it bad?" she asked.

"You don't want to know."

"Shouldn't we do something?"

"There's nothing to do. We weren't involved in the accident. There were a couple of people on the scene with cell phones."

The limo was moving down Sepulveda again, this time at a cautious pace.

"I feel just awful," she said. "Sick."

"We didn't make them do it, Serena. The stupid bastards had no business following us recklessly."

She sat there dazedly, knowing they must be dead. "Who were they?"

"I don't know. It was pretty messy, but from what I could see one was a white guy, the other Latino."

"Anybody else injured?"

"The truck driver was shook up, but not really hurt. Thank God it wasn't a family," he muttered under his breath.

They could hear sirens in the distance.

"Were we wrong?" Serena asked, slipping her hand in his.

"It was my decision," he said. "I take responsibility. You just forget about it."

He stared straight ahead, sober but surprisingly calm. Serena remembered that day at the hotel when Christina had been kidnapped. When she'd found Michael in the bar, she'd hugged him. She was feeling the same sort of emotions now. Whether those men meant her any harm or not, she definitely had the feeling she'd been saved.

It took two porters and a dolly to handle the luggage. Serena stayed in the limo during the unloading process, and Michael and Eddie stood on the curb, chatting somberly. The accident had upset the chauffeur, and Serena could tell Michael was putting his mind at ease.

Michael was thoughtful that way. He could be gruff, he could be acerbic, he could be an bastard at times, but underneath he was a considerate person. He had humanity, a basic decency.

It was one of the reasons she'd married him. Michael was a real person in a world full of phonies. When she'd told him that during their engagement, he'd said her problem was she didn't know anything about the real world. She'd been raised in a bubble and had never so much as set foot on a public tennis court or wet her toes in a community swimming pool.

One of the things she'd asked him to do before their wedding was to take her to Bakersfield, where he'd grown up in the home of his aunt. She'd wanted to see what it was like at the local Dairy Queen on a hot summer night with the smell of alfalfa and cotton fields in the air. He'd warned her she'd find it far less romantic than she'd imagined, but he was only partly right.

He'd showed her the house where he lived, his schools, the intersection where he'd totalled his aunt's car after downing a few beers—the incident that led to his hitch in the navy—the steak house where he'd washed dishes, the home of the doctor's daughter who loved him but chose college over marriage, and the drive-in movie theater where he'd lost his virginity at sixteen. The poor boy from Bakersfield was unlike anyone she'd ever known. He was so real she'd almost felt guilty leading the life she had.

Michael opened the limo door and peered in at her. "Come on, babe, we're ready to roll." He helped her out of the car.

"I hate to sound like a grumpy old feminist," she whispered in his ear, "but that 'babe' crap was passé when we met. The showgirls might go for it, but I hate it."

"Sorry," he said under his breath, "I'll watch my tongue."

She brushed her cheek against his. "Your tongue was never the problem, lover boy. But I've got a public image to maintain."

"What do you prefer, Highness or Ms. Bouchard?"

She straightened his tie. "Anything but babe." Giving him a flirtatious look, she turned to Eddie. "You're the best," she said. "Thanks, Eddie." She offered her hand, slipping him a hundred-dollar bill. She patted his shoulder. "See you soon."

A representative from the airline showed them to the VIP lounge. Michael handed Serena his passport and went off to make a phone call. They had thirty minutes till boarding.

Serena sat in a comfortable chair and accepted coffee from a pretty hostess who reminded her of Christina. It occurred to Serena this might be a good time to try to reach her daughter in Rio. She'd tried the previous evening without success and hadn't had time that morning. She took her cell phone from her briefcase and dialed. Where, exactly, Christina was staying was a little murky. "With friends, the Monteiro da Silvas," was what she'd said when Serena first broached the subject, a couple of weeks earlier. "Things were tense between Uncle Jeffrey and Drake, so I'm staying with this wonderful family on their estate."

Serena hadn't liked the ambiguity and had called Jeffrey to find out what was going on. He was supposed to be looking out for his niece, and clearly wasn't taking his duties seriously. "She's of age, Serena," he'd said, "so causing a fuss will only make for resentment. Believe me, she's in good hands."

Serena hadn't particularly liked the sound of that, either, but Jeffrey had a point about resentment. She and Christina had been on uneasy terms since the end of spring, when Christina had announced she intended to drop out of college for a year or so and stay in L.A. Serena insisted she take the summer to think it over, but wanted her daughter out of town. The trip to Rio to visit Jeffrey was their compromise solution.

The problem with Christina staying in L.A. was the tennis pro at their club, a thirty-one-year-old lothario named Cameron. Christina had had a fling with him the previous summer, right before heading to the University of Virginia. They'd kept in touch during the school year, and over the holidays Christina had hinted that things were getting serious. Serena, dismayed, went to the club and had a talk with Cameron. Fifteen minutes of conversation and she knew the guy was after Mommy's money. Of course, she couldn't tell Christina that. More subtle measures were required.

At the beginning of the summer Jeffrey had reported that Christina was meeting lots of nice boys from good families and that Cameron was being mentioned less and less. Serena thought that was a good sign, but her last conversations with Christina made her wonder if she hadn't prodded the girl out of the frying pan and into the fire. Not much had been said about the Monteiro da Silva family, but Serena suspected there was a twenty-two- or three-year-old named Pablo or Raul or whatever somewhere in the woodpile.

This business with Christina had been moved to the back burner when Drake was killed, of course, but it had been gnawing at Serena. She hadn't said anything to Michael because he would have reacted like a father. But she'd have to brief him, just so there wouldn't be any surprises.

Getting through to Brazil was proving difficult. She shook the phone with exasperation and dialed again, this time making the connection. A young female answered in Portuguese, probably a servant.

"Could I speak with Christina Bouchard, please?" Serena said slowly, enunciating the words.

"Momento, por favor, senhora."

A minute later a man's voice came on the line. "Yes, may I help you please?" he said in sweetly accented English.

"Hello, this is Serena Bouchard. I'm trying to reach my daughter, Christina. Is she there?"

"Oh, *senhora,* it is indeed an honor to hear your voice. I am Joachim Monteiro da Silva. I'm sorry, but at this moment Christina is out riding the horses. Can I have her telephone to you?"

The voice was young—not a boy, by any means, but not the father of the family, either. "I see," she said, a vivid picture coming to mind. "Christina is aware that we're on our way to Rio. I just wanted to give her our schedule."

"Excellent, *senhora.* May I have the honor of giving her the information, or do you wish for her to telephone back to you?"

"I'm at the airport in Los Angeles now, so why don't I give you the information?"

"It would be my pleasure."

Serena gave him the details of their itinerary and he read them back. She decided he sounded like a delightful young man, rather charming. In one way she was pleased for Christina, yet in another she was wary. The girl had led a sheltered life—not that Serena had wanted that, but it wasn't easily avoided given their life-style. Money could be as limiting as it was enabling. She'd learned that the hard way.

"May I have a car sent for you?" Joachim asked.

"No, I've made arrangements. But thank you, Mr. Monteiro da Silva. I would like to see Christina though."

"May I suggest at your hotel, *senhora?* It would be most comfortable for everybody that way."

Serena told him they would be staying at the Atlântica in Copacabana. Joachim suggested she leave matters to him. Then he wished her a bon voyage and ended the call. For a minute she sat there, thinking about the conversation. Joachim exuded charm. He was exceedingly polite. What was it that bothered her? Then it hit her. He was the typical Latin male who smiled deferentially, but insisted on being in charge. Cornelio Icardi had been that way, too. Smooth as silk, but macho to the core.

"I appreciate your help, Joe," Mike said into the phone.

"I'm going to take you up on that room at the Desert Palms, Mike," the detective said. "The old lady and I get up to Vegas a couple of times a year."

"You got it. And a complimentary bottle of champagne."

"Geeze, maybe I ought to bring one of the dispatchers instead!" Murdoch laughed.

"Careful. Some gal will hear you joking about it and go to the *L.A. Times* with a sexual-harassment complaint."

"You got that right. Christ. A guy can't piss on his own shoes anymore without some broad...er, some *woman,* that is, getting pushed out of shape about it."

Joe Murdoch was from the old school, a generation ahead of Mike. While he was still working for Serena, Mike had had an opportunity to make Murdoch look good in a robbery incident at the hotel, which won old Joe's undying gratitude. Besides, the detective was originally from Delano, a little town up the road from Bakersfield, which made them practically cousins.

"You sound like a chap who's been burned, Joe."

"I came damned close. But I still got my pension and that's all that matters. Enough said. As regards that second guy in the accident, I should have the details in a couple of hours. Give me a buzz when you get to Brazil and I'll brief you."

"Roger. And thanks again, Joe." Mike hung up. He thought for several moments, then dialed his next call.

The phone in Connie's trailer rang and rang. He could picture it, sitting on the kitchen counter amid the clutter of notes and business cards. In his mind's eye, he saw the tattered menu from that Chinese take-out place taped to the wall. He could smell the breakfast coffee and the maple syrup. It made him vaguely sad. All of it. Connie was treading water and so was he.

He listened to the phone ring some more. Apparently she'd already headed for work. He was about to hang up when Connie picked up the phone.

"Hello?" she said breathlessly.

"Did I catch you going out the door?"

"Oh, Mike, hi!" She took a couple of breaths. "I was getting in my car and thought it might be you."

"I'm at the airport in L.A., about to leave," he said. "Thought I'd check to see if Jason's okay."

"That's thoughtful of you." She sounded touched. "I assume he's fine. At least he was when I talked to him last night at the motel. He was scheduled to leave at eleven this morning. I'm meeting him at the airport at noon. He told me you arranged for him to fly over the Grand Canyon."

"Serena said he could go anywhere he wanted, but I figured the Grand Canyon was good enough for a maiden flight."

"Yeah, no sense having a kid who's done more than I have," she said. "By the way, your wife is really nice."

"My *ex*-wife, Connie."

"She was nice, very considerate."

"Yes, she told me she'd spoken to you," he said.

"It was kind of strange."

"I imagine it was."

There was a pause. "Oh, yeah. Your car arrived last night. The deputy called and I met him at your place. We put it in the garage. The keys are in your kitchen drawer with the silverware."

"Thanks for doing that."

"What the heck. After what you've done for Jason . . ."

"I'm sorry our trip got messed up. I told him, but tell him again for me."

"Messed up?" she said. "He got to go fishing and ride in a fancy jet airplane. How many kids can say that?"

"All the same . . ."

"Oh, Mike, there is one thing. Something strange."

"What?"

"Last night at your place when I met the deputy, just before I left, your neighbor on the right . . . What's his name?"

"Mr. Able?"

"Yeah, him. Anyway he came out to the car and asked if you were having problems."

"You mean because of the deputy bringing my car back?"

"No, it wasn't that. He said there'd been somebody hanging around the neighborhood the last few days, watching your house—at least that's what he thought was happening."

"Who? Did he have a description?"

"It was a dark-complected man in what seemed to be a rental car. The man looked like he might be Mexican. Well dressed, but swarthy. Mr. Able said the guy hung around the better part of two days, coming and going. Sort of seemed like he was waiting for you."

"Hmm. Very interesting."

"Do you know who it might be?" she asked.

"No, but there's a few places I can check. Thanks for the information, Connie."

"Well, I've got to run. I'm late for work."

"Sorry," Mike said. "Tell the boss it was international business that kept you."

"Your ex is your business, Mike, not mine."

"Yeah, right. How easily we forget."

Mike could picture Connie Meyers clearly. She was in her mid-thirties, still with echoes of unblemished virginal enthusiasm in her soul. She was short and blond and cute. The few extra pounds the last twenty years had given her were noticeable because she was small. But if there was anything about Connie that stood out in his mind, it was that she was a victim—one of those people who suffered through life, even as she tried to smile.

Connie was on the down slope without realizing it. Divorce and a kid and bills could do that. But who was he to judge? Life had worn on him a little, too. If his relationship with Connie had taught him anything, it was that he didn't want to look into her eyes and see himself.

They said goodbye and Mike hung up. When he thought about somebody watching his house, a strange feeling went through him. Coincidence? he wondered. He shook his head in answer to his own question. He didn't believe in coincidences, but he sure as hell didn't know what to make of it. Maybe he was a lot more popular than he thought.

Mike checked his watch. Serena would be getting antsy. He made his way to the VIP lounge.

Sure enough, she was waiting impatiently, her crossed leg bouncing in a way that belied the calm expression on her face. "Get the information you wanted?" she asked.

He sat down across from her. "Yeah."

"What happened? Were the men in the accident killed?"

"Yes, one instantly. The other died in the hospital."

"Oh, dear God."

"The driver was a P.I. out of Long Beach, fellow named Wade Sims. He's a shady character, always walking the line. His license has been suspended a couple of times. He was the driver."

"What about the other man?"

"Eduardo Ribeiro. They don't know anything about him yet except that he was carrying a Brazilian passport."

Serena's mouth dropped. *"Brazilian?"*

Mike nodded. "Yep."

"It must have to do with Jeffrey, just like you said."

"You have to wonder."

She looked worried. "Oh, Michael, *what* is going on?"

"Wish I knew. I'm going to call Murdoch again when we get to Rio. He said they'd try and find out where Ribeiro was staying, et cetera. They have no reason to treat it as a criminal situation, but when I gave him a little background, his ears perked up."

"Just so the press doesn't follow us to Brazil."

Mike grinned. "If they do, we'll have to keep our sunglasses on, won't we, babe?"

She gave him a wry look.

"Sorry. Make that Mrs. B."

"Michael, be serious. My stomach's in knots."

"You're paying me good money to do the worrying, so why don't you let me handle it? Sit back and relax."

"You know me better than that," she said. "I'm incapable of sitting around. In fact, while you were making your calls, I made one of my own."

"Oh?"

"I tried to reach Christina, but got her boyfriend instead."

"Boyfriend?"

"It's a long story, Michael. I'll have to tell you on the plane. I see they want us to go to the gate," she said, nodding toward the hostess.

"Christina has a Brazilian boyfriend?" Mike asked.

She looked amused. "You should have found that girl and had your rug rats, Michael. You are a father, through and through."

"One nineteen-year-old stepdaughter is quite enough at the moment," he said, standing. "Thank you, anyway."

Serena gave him her hand and got up. "I don't know about you, but I have a feeling Rio is going to be quite an adventure."

They headed for the exit. Serena took his arm. Mike thought of his conversations with Joe Murdoch and Connie Meyers.

"For once you may be right, Serena. Maybe I sold my services too cheaply."

"A deal is a deal," she said.

"Yeah," he replied, "like 'till death do us part.'"

THURSDAY
September 14th

Rio de Janeiro

It was not yet dawn when the plane began its decent into Rio. Serena had been in the lavatory for twenty minutes, trying to repair the damage of twelve hours of travel. Notwithstanding the first-class pampering, she was feeling the rigors of a D-day landing—that's what it was like coming to Rio under these conditions.

"Throw some things in a suitcase and come down, Mom," Christina had said in that first conversation after Jeffrey's arrest. "Uncle Jeffrey needs you."

The last part was undeniably true, but what did Christina know about mounting a rescue operation? It was like mobilizing a country to go to war. It took planning. Energy. Flying off to Rio was not a walk in the park—not when you were forty-two, struggling with all the personal problems of midlife, and were the head of a multi-million-dollar corporation. But what could a nineteen-year-old possibly know about life, anyway?

Serena had been every bit as naive at that age. She'd just turned twenty when she met Eric Lorimer, and over her father's bitter objection, she'd married the man a week after her twenty-first birthday. What she hadn't realized was that she'd used the marriage to cause a break with her father, who'd adored her obsessively and tried to dominate her life.

When they married, Eric was the age Michael was now, which had seemed ancient at the time—to everybody. "He's closer to being my goddamned brother than your husband," was the way her father had put it. But that was exactly what she'd wanted. It made perfect sense that if she was going to replace a father figure, it should be with another.

And when she discovered she could manipulate Eric, she'd felt empowered for the first time. She'd reveled in it. Of course, Eric had an agenda of his own—having more to do with her money than with her—but she hadn't cared about that because she was defining her life.

Their divorce had been more a financial mess than an emotional one, but in the end Eric made things easier by getting killed while taking a flying lesson shortly before the settlement was final, much to the delight of her attorneys. She'd gotten what she wanted—her freedom, her child and a new beginning.

What Serena feared now was that Christina would make the same mistake. The girl was riding a wild pony of self-discovery, and there wasn't much to be done other than to watch, pray and be prepared to pick up the pieces. But that was easier said than done. She had a lot of her father in her—the bad as well as the good.

The irony was that Jeffrey's crisis, coming in the middle of it all, could turn out to have a silver lining. If nothing else, it was drawing the family together. But the twin burdens of her brother and her child still fell on her shoulders.

Soon after they were airborne, she'd called Blake Peters in London and given him her terms on the Happy Host deal. He wasn't sure about the buy-back option, but felt he could probably sell it to Bumgardener. She told him she'd gone as far as she was willing to go, so it was up to them. Blake got the message.

Having taken care of London, she'd had a heart-to-heart talk with Michael about Christina, giving him the details about her conversation with Joachim Monteiro da Silva. Michael had been surprisingly calm. "She's almost twenty," he'd said philosophically. "You can't lock them in their rooms." -

Taking that as her cue, Serena figured he might as well hear the whole story, so she'd brought him up-to-date on the business with Cameron, the tennis pro. Michael listened to that tale more glumly. Cameron's game did not please him at all.

"Why didn't she tell me about this?" he'd asked with annoyance.

"For the same reason I didn't tell my father about Eric until after I'd given him my virginity."

Michael blinked. "You were a virgin when you met Eric?"

"Figuratively speaking, Michael."

To her chagrin that gave him a real belly laugh. But they did have a constructive conversation about Christina, agreeing to work in concert and not allow her to play one of them off against the other. Divorced parents had to stand together, and it didn't matter that Michael was an ex-stepfather, because he and Christina were extremely close. Besides Serena knew *she* had the most to lose in the event that her daughter managed to drive a wedge between them.

Sighing with fatigue, Serena left the lavatory, only to find a young flight attendant sitting on the arm of her seat, chatting with Michael. He'd always been attractive to perky young women. For that matter, he'd always been attractive to sultry older ones. She didn't know if it was his phero-mones or his smile or his quiet unassuming strength, but whatever it was that appealed to women, Michael had it in spades.

What had made being married to him tricky was that he'd never flaunted his appeal. Michael wasn't an outrageous flirt. He'd let the women come to him, then gently rebuke them—at least in her presence. But watching women react-ing to him made her wonder how faithful he'd been, his protestations of fidelity notwithstanding. Of course, it shouldn't matter now, though it did.

When they'd met, Serena hadn't been accustomed to worrying about the man in her life. And he, for his part, had never been with a woman who had leverage over him. In that sense, their marriage was groundbreaking for them both. Truth be known, the only jealousy she ever experienced was in connection with Michael. She'd never admitted that to him, though. And God would have to strike her dead before she would.

The flight attendant got up when she saw her coming. Serena gave her the smile of an older and wiser sister.

"You can tell the captain I'm as ready for a landing as I'll ever be."

"We're nearing Rio now, Ms. Bouchard," the girl said, amused but deferential. "Not much longer."

"The hours are crueler than they used to be. But you'll discover that for yourself one day." Again she smiled conspiratorially.

The girl knew it was time to withdraw and, after asking if they had any last-minute requests for food or drink, she went away. Michael said nothing.

"Well, did you find out what the hot spots are in Rio?" Serena asked when the girl was out of hearing.

"Not really. It was just idle conversation."

Women were biologically incapable of idle conversation in the presence of an attractive man, but Serena saw no point in explaining that. Besides, he knew it.

"She's attracted to you," she said bluntly.

"Oh, I don't know."

"I do."

"If you say so, Serena."

"I only mention it as a point of interest. If you'd been traveling alone you'd have been given the name of her hotel."

"You think so?"

"If I were in her shoes, you'd have gotten it." She laughed. "Are you kidding? Rio de Janeiro and three thousand miles from anything that matters?"

"You paint an alluring picture," he said.

"I'm a realist, Michael. Always have been, always will be."

"That couldn't be the reason I married you."

"I'm sure it wasn't," she chortled. She listened to the changing sounds of the engines, reflecting on what she wanted to say. "There is something I want to tell you, Michael, and this is probably as good a time as any."

"Shoot."

Serena drew a long breath, preparing herself for the speech she'd been running through her mind. "I don't know how it's been for you being around me again," she said. "But this is the most we've seen of each other since, well, Tahoe, I guess. And I have to be honest, Michael. It would be very easy for me to hop in the sack with you. I'm sure I'd even enjoy it."

"Including the morning after?"

"I usually don't worry much about the morning after. That's not what I'm trying to say."

"What are you trying to say?"

"If something were to happen between us, it would only get in the way. That may sound prissy and moralistic, but we've got to be practical."

"I'm not one to argue against practicality," he said.

"The point is we need an understanding. Ground rules."

"Fair enough. What ground rules do you propose?"

"We both have to stick strictly to business," she said. "Specifically, no games, no titillation, no sex. Absolutely none."

He poked his tongue in his cheek. "No sex period, or no sex with each other?"

She laughed. "You can lay all of Brazil, for all I care. Just not me. And the reason I'm saying this is because I'm going to be tempted to let you have your way with me. I might as well admit it. I may be tempted even more than you."

He yawned. "How refreshingly candid of you to say so."

"But I also have more willpower than you, so it evens out."

"Uh-huh."

"I'd like your cooperation, Michael. As I've said, we're here for a deadly serious reason, and I don't want it screwed up by screwing."

"Interesting way to put it," he said.

"You know what I mean."

"Yes."

"There's one other thing. Neither of us will make a fuss or get jealous if the other . . . has a . . . social relationship. In fact, I think it would be easier for both of us if we felt perfectly free to do as we wish on this trip."

"I won't stand in your way," he said.

"I know that. Frankly, I was thinking more of you. I want you to do anything you want with any woman you choose. The truth is, I'd be relieved if I knew you were enjoying yourself—on your own time, of course."

"That's damned decent of you," he said.

"Take that little stewardess, for example. If you want to make a date with her, go ahead. Feel free."

"Thanks, but I'm not desperate to get laid."

"Really?"

"Really," he said.

"Well, do as you wish. The point is we've gotten the matter out in the open now. There won't be any misunderstandings."

Michael fingered the magazine on his lap. "Anything else?"

"No. I feel much better for having gotten that off my mind," she said.

"So do I."

Smiling, she offered him her hand. Michael took it.

"Who knows," she said, "maybe someday down the line, when this is over, we'll run into each other on the ski slopes and things will go differently."

"The ski slopes?"

"Well, maybe not there. But somewhere. Of course, it's just as possible it won't happen. I'm not proposing anything, please understand. I'm just letting you know I don't plan on being a hard ass for all time.''

''Just for Rio.''

''Yes, just for Rio,'' she said.

Michael looked past her out the window. The first hint of light was beginning to appear. She studied his face, feeling a whirl of conflicting emotions. She'd made her speech and already she was regretting every word she'd uttered.

''Be honest, Michael, would another Tahoe appeal to you?''

''I don't know,'' he said. ''I honestly don't.''

He sounded sincere and that gave her pause. ''At least we understand each other,'' she said.

''Yes.''

The plane gave a lurch as the pilot lowered the flaps. Serena stared into Michael's eyes, hating herself for being so practical, so rational, so right about what she'd done. And even though it was the wrong thing to do, she leaned over and kissed him full on the mouth.

Afterward, he gave her a wary look. ''What was that supposed to be? Proof of your sincerity?''

''No, something to remember me by.''

''Bitch.''

''I meant it lovingly, Michael.''

''Fine. You've got a heart of gold. So let me be.''

She leaned close to him and whispered in his ear, ''Lay the stewardess tonight. You'll feel much better.''

''Let me think about it,'' he said dryly. He was clearly displeased with her.

''One last thing,'' Serena said. ''Don't hate me for saying this, but in my way, I do love you, Michael.''

''Oh, thank you very much. And I suppose you divorced me to add poignancy to the statement.''

''No, I divorced you because I couldn't be married to you anymore.''

He grinned, shaking his head.

''What?''

"Somehow a thousand dollars a day doesn't seem like enough."

"Let's make it fifteen hundred, then. I was feeling a little guilty about getting you so cheap, anyway."

Michael laughed. "So even realists have a conscience."

The engines accelerated momentarily as the plane dropped. Seconds before the wheels touched down Michael pointed out the window at the dark hills covered with twinkling lights.

"Rio," he said.

It was getting light as the jet pulled up to the terminal building. Mike was peering out at the gauzy gray dawn, getting his first look at South America. He'd been to Mexico and the Caribbean, but this was the farthest south he'd ventured. What he hadn't realized was how far east they'd actually gone.

The flight attendant, Jan, had told him Rio de Janeiro was in the same time zone as Angmagssalik, Greenland, which was five hours east of L.A. and only three zones west of London. What it boiled down to was that back in L.A. it was 1:00 a.m., and Rio was getting ready for breakfast.

But for a man whose domain was a Vegas casino, time of day was just a function of the clock, certainly not tied to the rising and setting of the sun. At seven in the morning, the early risers were at the blackjack tables, shoulder-to-shoulder with the hangers-on from the night before. Meal breaks and bowel movements were the extent of nature's influence on the gaming crowd.

"Am I the only one who feels like hell?" Serena asked as the engines went dead at the gate.

"I'm here, but my internal clock only made it as far as Albuquerque," Mike said. "It's on a Greyhound and should be arriving around Monday."

Serena laughed. "Much as I travel, you'd think I'd adjust, but I don't. I'm sorry now I didn't ask Christina to come by the hotel this afternoon instead of this morning. As soon as we get to our room, I'm going to want to hit the sack.''

''You'll get your second wind.''

''At forty-two, honey, I'm grateful if I get a first one.''

Jan came along, cheerfully getting their carryons from the overhead compartment. When she smiled at Mike, she held eye contact an extra moment or two.

''Enjoy your stay in Rio, Mike.'' Then to Serena she said, ''It's been a pleasure having you aboard, Ms. Bouchard.''

Serena's brittle smile suggested she'd just as soon give the girl a pop in the chops. ''No doubt.''

Mike gave Jan's wasplike figure an admiring glance as she retreated. Serena was right—he probably could have found out where she was staying and bought her a drink. And from there, it might have led to her room. But what was the point? To please Serena? Or better still, call her bluff? Mike liked to think he was beyond that.

Serena had gotten up. She gave him a not-so-gentle poke in the ribs. ''Come on, *Mike,* let's get out of this tin can.''

Another airline representative was waiting at the gate to assist them. He was small, all teeth and mustache. Mike was glad—he had an innate fear of exposing his ignorance in front of a whole country of foreigners. Serena, on the other hand, was so used to people waiting on her that helplessness was an obligation she assumed. Like a queen, she didn't carry money except when she was traveling alone on business.

But to her everlasting credit, Serena did not feel she had a moral right to privileged treatment. It was a matter of paying for service. She was rarely unkind to a stranger, unless it was to a female interloper infringing on her territory. But Serena could be compassionate, too.

He remembered an incident at Santa Anita once, not long after they'd married. A boozy old geezer had gotten excited watching the ponies and had had a heart attack right in front of them. Serena had sat down on the cement with him, holding his head and calming him until the paramedics arrived. It was a genuine act of human decency and it had won his respect.

"Will this take long?" Serena asked the solicitous agent as they walked toward customs.

"No, *senhora*. We are more efficient than you might think." He gave her a piano-key smile.

During their layover in Miami they'd had a drink in the cocktail lounge, and Serena had briefed Mike on the arrangements her hotshot Brazilian attorney had made. And she'd told him about the private investigator, Pericles Kotomata, who'd be assisting them with the investigation.

"Kotomata. Unusual name for a Brazilian," Mike had noted.

"I know nothing about him except for the little bit Senhor Cabral told me. He said Kotomata was highly regarded. Frankly, I don't give a damn about his reputation, so long as he's able to help me get Jeffrey off the hook."

"I hate to bring up a sore subject," Mike had said, "but are you preparing yourself for the possibility that this thing could turn out differently than you expect?"

"You mean that Jeffrey will be convicted?"

"I mean that your brother's guilty."

That had incensed her. "What do you mean, guilty? My brother is innocent!"

"I know that's what you want to believe, and it's what you do believe, but what if—"

"You detective types always think you're scientists," she'd said frostily, "but I *know* the truth, Michael. Your job is to make sure it wins out."

That had been the end of that conversation. Serena had a blind spot the size of a 747 when it came to Jeffrey. Add to that the fact that she was used to lawyers whose primary role was to make the truth fit the will of their clients, and you had a slightly spoiled, very intractable woman who demanded and expected the result she sought. A good cop didn't work that way. A good cop didn't care about anything but objective truth. At least that was the theory.

Mike wasn't a cop, of course, but he thought like one. He had an investigator's mind, which tended to put him at odds with people who cared more about outcome than truth. Not that he didn't intend to help Jeffrey, but he wasn't there to be a "yes" man.

They hadn't walked far before he started getting his first sense of Rio. The building was artificially cooled, but distinctive smells and aromas were becoming evident. They hadn't seen much of the city from the air, save occasional glimpses of sepia-colored mountainsides twinkling with lights. There had been a view of Sugarloaf hunched against a pink-and-indigo sky.

From everything he'd heard, Rio came alive at night. Yet even at dawn, he sensed an energy. Samba was in the air, even without the music. There was a zest in the faces of the people, in the way they moved.

Serena hadn't said a word, but there was a subtle spring in her walk, too. She was responding to the smiling faces of the men, the languorous looks. Had the circumstances been different, Brazil, Mike decided, might even be good for her soul.

"Where is it that you are staying, if I may ask?" the airline representative inquired.

"In Copa," Serena replied, sounding like someone who knew what she was talking about. "I know Ipanema's the in place now, but I'm a traditionalist."

"Copacabana's always in, *senhora*. Me, I prefer it."

"Well, this is mostly a business trip, so what's hot and what isn't doesn't really matter."

"You can't go wrong," the man said.

He was too saccharine for Mike. These people saw it as their mission in life to spew propaganda for the tourist board. With the very real possibility of a bus being hijacked outside the airport gates, it was understandable they'd be conscious of first impressions. New Yorkers didn't appreciate that, but Brazilians apparently did.

Serena had talked about the danger during their flight. A friend of hers, who spent a month every year in Rio, had told her a platoon of marines wouldn't be overkill when it came to security. Of course, her friend had the habit of wearing expensive jewelry in public. She'd paid for it by getting rolled twice, costing her two expensive rings, a gold watch and a bracelet.

When they came to the passport booth, the official spent more time checking out Serena than her passport—an early morning treat for his sleepy eyes. When Mike's turn came, the passport was of greater interest.

Finally the man looked up and said, "Senhor Hamlin, please wait. Here, please." He pointed to a spot on the floor nearby.

Mike went to the mark, feeling like a schoolboy. He wondered what was up. Their escort exchanged a few words with the official, who dismissed his inquiries with a wave and got on the phone.

"We must wait," the airline man said unnecessarily, as he and Serena joined Mike in the designated holding area.

She appeared less than happy about the delay. "Brazil is beginning to lose its charm, Michael. You didn't do anything unsavory with the flight attendant, did you?"

"I didn't grope her, if that's what you mean."

"What could be the trouble, then?"

Before he could comment, another official approached. The fellow was in uniform and appeared senior, if only because of his girth. He checked out Serena, but addressed Mike.

"Mr. Hamlin?"

"Yes?"

"Will you please come with me," he said cordially.

"What about Ms. Bouchard?"

The official clicked his heels smartly, drawing himself up. "*Senhora,* if you would be so kind, there is a waiting room, just there," he said, pointing. He gave instructions to the airline representative, who took Serena off. The official stared after her admiringly. Then he smiled at Mike, gesturing toward the door she'd exited. "She is not your secretary, certainly."

"No, my employer."

The official's brows rose. "Indeed. Handsome woman, *senhor.*"

"She'd be flattered, I'm sure."

They entered a sparsely furnished office. The official signaled for him to sit, then retreated behind the desk. He picked up a slip of paper, studying it.

"We have received an urgent communiqué from the police in Los Angeles," he said solemnly. "A Detective Murdoch wishes for you to call him at once. I have the number of the international operator, if I may connect for you."

"Please."

The official dialed and, after a few words, handed the receiver over. "It is ringing in Los Angeles," he said.

The switchboard operator at the Parker Center answered. Mike asked for Murdoch.

"Glad you called, Mike," Murdoch said, coming on the line. "I was about to leave for the night."

Mike looked at his watch. It was after one in the morning in L.A. "What are you doing at your desk at this time of night?"

"Talking to you, earning a couple of bottles of Scotch."

"Sounds serious."

"To us it don't mean shit, Mike, but I thought you'd like to know what I turned up on Eduardo Ribeiro, our Brazilian corpse."

"I'm sure I would."

"Eduardo's got a record half a block long, according to our brethren in Rio. Mostly gangsterism."

"How interesting."

"Don't matter to us, like I say. As far as I'm concerned he was in a car that ran a red light. No reason to think he was involved in any criminal activity in the States, which means there's no need to investigate. But since it was your ass he was tailing, I thought you'd like to know his history before hitting the streets."

"Yeah, Joe, it does put a new perspective on things," Mike said, rubbing the stubble on his chin.

"A couple of other points," Murdoch went on. "We checked out the motel by the airport where he stayed last night. Found a slip of paper in the wastebasket with a Vegas address on it. *Your* address, Mike. I doubled-checked it."

Mike thought of the car his neighbor, Mr. Able, had seen. "Hmm. Sounds like I had a friend I didn't even know."

"Yeah. Well, your friend also had a slip of paper in his wallet with another number on it. We weren't sure what kind of number it was until one of our bright young things figured out it had the international telephone code for Brazil. A Rio number. We've got no use for it, but I thought you might. Could be the number of Eduardo's bookie, or could be something more interesting."

"You're very astute, Joe."

Murdoch gave him the number. Mike jotted it down on his hand.

"Well, that's it from the home front, pal," Murdoch said. "While you're watching all the snatch on the beach, you might want to keep an eye on your own ass, huh?"

"Yeah, looks that way, doesn't it?" Mike said.

"To be forewarned is to be forearmed."

"Maybe I owe you a *case* of Scotch, Joe."

Murdoch laughed. "Your ass is worth more than I thought! Have a good time."

Mike hung up and smiled at the Brazilian official. The man had been sitting with his hands folded on the desk, listening intently. He wouldn't have been able to glean much from Mike's side of the conversation.

"I hope the urgent matter is resolved satisfactorily," he said, his pudgy face duly solemn.

"Yes," Mike said. "Unfortunately, it complicates my stay."

The ambiguity was not lost on the official, whose English had proven to be good enough to catch subtleties. But since it was none of his business, he had to let the remark pass.

"I trust we have been of assistance, *senhor.*"

"I am most grateful." Mike wondered if some sort of gratuity was expected, but decided the risk of insult was worse than the possible disappointment of no reward. Anyway, the man appeared to be proud enough to disdain a gratuity even if appropriate.

The official rose, as did Mike. "Then, unless I can be of further assistance, I will send you on your way, Mr. Hamlin."

They shook hands and Mike thanked him.

"Perhaps I can advise your employer that your business is completed," the official said, apparently recalling Serena.

"Please," Mike said, seeing the man would have his reward, after all.

The official returned with Serena on his arm. He was beaming. Once the party was reunited, farewells were expressed and they proceeded to customs. Serena looked concerned.

"So, what was that all about?"

Mike summarized his conversation with Joe Murdoch.

She gave a sigh. "This is getting bizarre. And scary."

"Somebody apparently wanted to check me out."

"But who?"

"I may be able to throw a little light on the subject with a phone call." He showed her the number he'd written on his hand, explaining about the paper in Ribeiro's wallet.

Serena stopped, holding his hand and examining the number more closely. "Why does that look familiar?"

"I don't know. Why does it?"

"Wait a second." She opened her purse and took out a slip of paper. She compared the number written on it with the one on his hand. "They're identical," she said.

Mike took the paper and compared the numbers. "Where did you get that?"

"From Christina. It's the telephone number of that family she's staying with. The Monteiro da Silvas."

Mike's jaw went slack. They stood there, staring at each other, absorbing the implications. "What sort of people does your daughter associate with, Serena?"

"I don't know," she said, "but I intend to find out."

The Brazilian method of baggage management was labor intensive. It took three porters. As Serena and Mike exited customs, their bearers in tow, Mike felt like he was on safari.

The Rio de Janeiro beyond customs walls was teeming with a multiracial crush of humanity, a pastiche of accents and skin tones, a real hors d'oeuvre tray of people. To Mike it was like walking into a gigantic block party. Almost as if by magic, the crowd parted for Serena. There was wonder on some of the faces they passed. Most everybody, women and men, checked her out.

Serena stopped in the middle of the large room, the crowd swirling around them like uncoupled dancers at a Viennese ball. The porters stood behind them, quietly awaiting orders. Serena glanced around. "Where the hell do you suppose Mr. Kotomata is?" she muttered. "He's supposed to meet us here."

It was then that he saw her—Grace Jones, Shari Bellafonte and Iman all wrapped into one. She was tall, six feet or more, and she was standing near the doors opposite customs, holding a sign over her head that read Bouchard.

"Jesus," Serena said, seeing her at about the same time. "That girl is gorgeous."

Mike stared, transfixed. The face, bare shoulders and arms rising above the roiling sea of people was perfection—a graceful beauty that belonged in the lens of a camera, not the teeming lobby of an airport.

Only after several moments was he aware of the pansy-faced little man next to her. He was of Asian ancestry, in his middle years, paunchy without being fat, slightly rumpled in a white linen suit and open-neck shirt. He made his way toward them, his short legs moving in a determined whirl. The creature striding serenely behind him wore a pale pink tank top, white miniskirt and high-heeled sandals with straps that wrapped halfway up her calves.

"Mrs. Bouchard, I presume," the little man said as he reached them. He had a grin that seemed genuinely friendly. His eyes were mere slits on his puffy face. With some help from Industrial Light and Magic, Mike could imagine him transforming into Yoda.

"Yes," Serena said. "You must be Mr. Kotomata."

He extended his hand. "Indeed I am. But please, only my butcher calls me Mr. Kotomata. The rest of Rio knows me as Koto." His English was American, and it was almost perfect. There was only the slightest Latin tinge to it.

"I'm pleased to know you, Koto," Serena said, responding to his cheery manner. "I'd like to present my security consultant, Mr. Hamlin."

"Hi," Mike said, shaking Koto's hand. "America knows me as Mike."

Mike winked at the girl. She glanced away.

"Half of America, anyway," Serena said under her breath.

"And this is my assistant, Bebe," Koto said, presenting the girl. "My right-hand man, so to speak."

"Welcome to Brazil, Mrs. Bouchard," she said with the lightest, most musical accent Mike had ever heard.

"Thank you," Serena said, checking the girl's legs.

Bebe shook Serena's hand, then Mike's, her grip surprisingly powerful. She made real eye contact for the first time, but only briefly. Her smile was perfunctory and lacked even the tiniest spark of warmth. He wasn't sure whether she disliked him or whether it was generic hostility.

"If you don't mind me saying so, Koto," Serena said, "you're a bit confused about the difference between boys and girls. This gorgeous creature couldn't be anybody's man, right hand or left."

The little man laughed heartily. Bebe seemed embarrassed. She blushed as they all continued to regard her.

"Don't you agree, Michael?" Serena asked.

"A deft observation," he replied.

Bebe lowered her eyes like a shy child made to stand up before company. Serena and Koto began discussing arrangements, giving Mike an opportunity to admire the girl.

He estimated that Bebe was in her mid-twenties. She was flawless. She had the smoothest, silkiest cocoa-butter skin he had ever seen. There was plenty of Portuguese, or something, in her—probably starting with a sailor spending several balmy nights in Rio a hundred years ago. Her eyes were a startling shade of pale blue, giving her an exotic look that had no parallel on any human being he'd ever seen. An albino panther? A snow tiger?

Sensing his scrutiny, she gave him a look that registered unmistakable displeasure. He gave her a friendly smile, anyway. She turned her attention to Serena and Koto.

Now that Mike was standing next to her, he realized that in heels, Bebe was almost as tall as he. She had the longest legs he'd ever seen on a woman and well-shaped breasts that drooped slightly under the cotton tank top. Her nipples showed unashamedly. This was a girl-woman in her natural state, a female warrior with a face out of *Vogue*. There was something so unexpected about Bebe, so alien to his universe, that he couldn't help gaping.

Serena and Koto had finished their conversation regarding transportation to the hotel. Koto turned to Bebe and gave her marching orders in crisp, but politely issued Portuguese.

"Please, Mrs. Bouchard," he said, "Bebe will lead the way to the limousine. I'll see to your baggage."

Giving Serena a nod, Bebe headed for the door. They fell in behind her. The sweet curve of Bebe's ass was criminal, especially in the miniskirt. She had a nice rhythmic swing when she walked.

Serena was checking Bebe out, right along with Mike. "What does that do for your hormone level?" she asked out of the corner of her mouth.

"The young lady has admirable qualities."

"Does that explain the drool on your chin?"

"Am I being too obvious?" he asked.

"Michael, a sailor in a strip joint would've been more subtle. But if you seduce her, do it in your off-hours so it won't interfere with business. I'd be careful, though. Koto seems a bit proprietary about her."

Bebe glanced back to make sure they were behind her. She looked at Serena, but not Mike.

"Maybe he screws her," he said under his breath.

"Somehow I think not. The girl's interested in you, Michael."

He laughed. "She's been shooting darts at me since before we were introduced."

"Dear sweet Michael. The greater the hostility, the greater the interest. She's afraid of her own instincts, can't you see that?"

"She could be a lesbian."

"No chance."

"I'll defer to your superior judgment," he said.

"She obviously gets hit on more than a wounded fly," Serena said. "Be subtle, be sweet, and you'll bag her."

"I should have hired *you* as a consultant," he said, "not the other way around."

"Think of it as a fringe benefit."

"How is it you've waited so long to share your insights?"

"You stumbled along fairly well on your own," she intoned. "Got what you wanted behind my back, as I recall."

"Serena, you know that's not true!"

"At this point you might as well be proud of it," she said loftily. "I don't really give a damn about the past. And five years is a hell of a long time."

He gave her a sideward glance, but didn't respond. There was no point in arguing. Besides, he was having too good a time admiring Bebe's ass.

* * *

Copacabana

They had no sooner settled into the limo than Serena started questioning Koto about Jeffrey. She was not here for a shopping spree, after all, and wanted to learn everything she could.

"To my knowledge, Mrs. Bouchard, there have been no new developments since you spoke with Senhor Cabral. But he will be calling you this afternoon. Perhaps you can ask him if there is more news."

"Do you know anything he doesn't?"

"I have told him everything I know, which is very little, I'm sorry to say."

Serena was disappointed. She'd been hoping to find out what the hell was going on. Now she wondered if they were trying to spare her some painful truth. Maybe she'd have to find out from Jeffrey herself. "When will I be able to see my brother?"

"I've made arrangements to take you to the jail tomorrow."

Her frustration subsided. At least Koto was anticipating her needs. It was the sort of thing she expected from people on her payroll. "What sort of jail is Jeffrey in?" she asked, not sure she wanted to know. "Is it the kind of place I don't want to hear about?"

"Prisons are not pleasant places," Koto said. "But Senhor Cabral has made every effort to see that your brother's treatment is of the highest standard. Exactly what that means, I cannot say."

More ambiguity. She sighed and turned to Michael. "Ask some intelligent questions, Michael. I'm too tired to think straight."

He complied without hesitation. "What, exactly, do the police have on Jeffrey?" he asked. "Any physical evidence?"

The investigator's expression turned stone sober. "I have only the sketchiest details. Mr. Manville was shot to death in his rented villa in Santa Teresa. The body was found by the landlord, a Senhor Hector von Vehrling. A revolver was recovered at the scene. I understand it has been connected with Mr. Bouchard, I assume by fingerprints, though I can't be sure.

"Later the day of the murder the police found Mr. Bouchard at his apartment. He was taken in for questioning and admitted being at the villa that morning. But he denies shooting Mr. Manville. Nevertheless, formal murder charges have been brought."

"There were no witnesses?"

"Not to my knowledge," Koto replied. "But I am not apprised of all the facts."

"The case against him may be entirely circumstantial then," Michael said.

"Possibly, *senhor*. We should be able to learn more when we visit the jail tomorrow. I will talk to the investigators."

"When we get Jeffrey's side of the story, we'll know the truth," Serena said.

Koto nodded politely. Michael regarded her, his expression noncommittal. She could tell he was skeptical about Jeffrey's innocence. Michael had never liked her brother, and she'd always considered it unfortunate that there was no love lost between them. But whatever his prejudices, Michael was fair-minded. She had that to be thankful for.

"So what do you think?" she asked him.

"About Jeffrey?" Michael said.

"Yes."

"I don't have enough information to draw any conclusions."

"But you know him, Michael. Can you honestly say he's capable of murder?"

"Everybody's capable of murder, given the right circumstances."

His stubbornness did not please her. Why couldn't he give her the satisfaction of saying Jeffrey was innocent and that he was determined to prove it? "Well, I'm positive I'll be vindicated. Senhor Cabral told me Jeffrey vehemently denies murdering Drake. That means he's been framed. If necessary, we'll have to find the real killer—whatever it takes to exonerate Jeffrey."

"Yes, Serena, that's why we're here."

"You may not have the enthusiasm for this that I do, but I'd feel better if you'd at least give Jeffrey the benefit of the doubt."

"Serena, the U.S. Constitution may not govern here, but as far as I'm concerned Jeffrey's innocent until he's proven guilty. But what we need now isn't emotion, it's facts."

Facts! The word made her want to scream. But there was no point in arguing about what mattered and what didn't. They were going to get Jeffrey off, and that was that. If Michael needed facts, fine. They'd get facts.

There was an uncomfortable silence, and Serena turned to look at the traffic. They'd entered the city proper, but she didn't care where she was. She wanted to clear her mind and start over, to think about something besides Michael and his goddamned facts.

Before long the limo got stalled in traffic. Serena stared out the window, frustrated and depressed despite her desire to be positive and upbeat. Until this point, the tragedy had had an unreal quality. Now that she was in Rio, Jeffrey's suffering seemed more real.

She wedged herself into the corner of the seat, paying little attention to Koto, who was pointing out landmarks to Michael as they crawled through traffic. She did, however, turn her head to see the bright yellow trolley running atop the Lapa aqueduct. It was crowded. Men and boys clung to it like bugs on a stick floating down a stream. Jeffrey had mentioned the trolley in one of his letters. He'd said it was a fixture in Santa Teresa district, where he and Drake lived.

It was odd to think her brother had come here to meet his fate. Rio, a place overcrowded with the sons of the Portuguese, their African slaves and the indigenous peoples. Sun, music, sex—it was all here. Yet quiet, moody Jeffrey, so alien from all this, was languishing in a jail cell, his life in jeopardy.

The Brazil of her memory was so different. Serena's first trip here had been a family vacation nearly three decades ago. She'd been sixteen, off on a wonderful adventure. Rio hadn't seemed overwhelming then. Was the fact that it did now due to all the emotion, or was she getting old?

The little Latin cinnamon cookie sitting in the front seat didn't help matters. Bebe was a cruel reminder of how old forty-two was. She was heartbreakingly alluring—a deadly mixture of child and woman. And Michael was smitten. That was obvious.

It was easy to understand. He had arrived on the doorstep of middle age, and Bebe's zippy little mini had him wondering if he was ready to give all that up. He was like the old ballplayer saying to himself, "I'm good for one more season." Ironically, he didn't even know what was happening—Serena would have bet her life on it.

What the hell. She'd already told him that was exactly what she wanted him to do. She'd simply have to condition herself to accept the inevitable. That was even more important than conditioning Michael.

Serena listened as Koto told Michael to avoid the Lapa district at night. Along the Avenida Mem de Sá the transvestites could get aggressive, he said. Obviously the tour-guide role did not come easily to Koto, but the man had a sense of duty. He was diligent, if cautious. That was good. She liked dedication in an employee. Koto would be just what the doctor ordered.

She observed Michael. He was listening to Koto, but keeping one eye on Bebe, who was talking to the driver, a black man with gray hair. She couldn't hear them because of the glass, but her soundless laughter was as warming as the morning sun.

Maybe Bebe was what Michael needed at this point in his life—a girl to brighten his world. Rio had done that for Serena the last time she was here, though she'd experienced the teenage version of love Brazilian style.

It had taken careful planning to pull it off, but after she had done the tourist bit with her parents, she'd managed to get an unauthorized taste of Latin culture. By morning she frolicked in a string bikini on the Praia de Copacabana, and by night, once she was free of her parents, she got herself finger fucked by a Brazilian named Maximino, the most beautiful bronze boy-man that God had ever made. She'd sneaked out with him to lay on the beach under the stars, the waves off the Atlantic washing over their legs.

After their illicit lovemaking, Maximino had taken her to a soothsayer, an ancient woman who dispensed wisdom on the beach, sitting cross-legged at a campfire. The woman prophesied they'd marry and have many babies, an ominous prognostication. Even at sixteen, there had been limits to Serena's sense of romance, and she'd decided she'd been wise to only let Maximino finger her.

The boy had hung around the entrance to their hotel for days after that, but she never spoke to him again. Instead, she'd refocused her attention on Rio's material attractions. She and her mother had bought presents for Jeffrey, who was attending a macho boys' summer camp that their father had hoped would turn him into a man. But Serena'd had her thrill, had tasted the tropics and tropical men. Michael, the neophyte on this trip, deserved as much.

Koto, who was in a conversational hiatus, smiled cordially. "I'm sorry about the traffic, but we'll be at the Atlântica before too long, Mrs. Bouchard."

"I wouldn't mind if I wasn't so bushed," she said. "I'm sure I look as bad as I feel."

"You look fresh as a spring daisy," Michael said.

"Oh, shut up, Michael. You know I hate liars."

Outside the limo, only the motorbikes and pedestrians seemed to be moving. There were youthful, tanned bodies everywhere and, if Serena recalled the Rio life-style correctly, everyone would be heading for the beach shortly. The daily life of the *cariocas* revolved around the beaches. They did everything there—from exercising to courting to conducting business. The beach was at the heart of their culture in the same way the automobile was in L.A. or the cafés were in Paris.

She turned to Koto. "Senhor Cabral recommended you highly. If you don't mind me putting you on the spot, how did you come to earn such an illustrious reputation?"

"Thank you, Mrs. Bouchard, but I wouldn't describe my reputation as illustrious. I am honest. Perhaps it is my independence that separates me more than anything."

"What do you mean by independence?"

"I am my own man, Mrs. Bouchard. Nobody owns me. In the long run, it gives me the greatest power to do my work. Power without money is scarce in Brazil."

"It's scarce everywhere, my friend," Michael said, giving Serena a sardonic grin.

"To each his own," she said.

"I'm cool."

"Michael and I were once married," she explained to Koto. "We've been divorced five years. Long enough to be friends, short enough to still remember why we got divorced."

"I see," Koto said.

"You probably don't, but it doesn't matter." She nodded toward Bebe. "Tell us about your assistant, Koto. Is she an investigator, too?"

"Bebe is the best," he said, sounding like a proud father. "I have several men working for me, but she is better than any of them. She has a detective's mind and is afraid of nothing. In a fight I would want her at my back more than any man I've ever worked with."

"She's a beautiful girl," Serena said.

"Yes, and she has the heart of a lion."

Serena glanced at Michael. "What more could a man want?" Then she turned to Koto. "She isn't married, I take it."

"Oh, no. She has no time for men, though she is admired by all who see her."

"Now there's a challenge if I ever heard one," Serena said for Michael's benefit.

He gave her a sideward glance but not the satisfaction of a response.

"Bebe has had a hard life," Koto went on. "Her mother was a barmaid, her father a prominent man among the leading *cariocas*—that's what the people of Rio call themselves. Bebe never knew him, but she has his proud spirit. Her mother was a mulatta and, it is said, a very beautiful woman. She died years ago, and so Bebe and her younger half sister were raised by an aunt in Rochina, Rio's great hillside favela, or slum."

"You mean in one of those cardboard-and-tin shanties in the hills?" Serena asked with dismay.

"In Rio everything is relative. Rochina, which is on the mountainside overlooking the sea, is practically middle-class in comparison with other areas. Our grinding poverty is in the *baixada fluminense,* the flatlands to the north. There is no sewage, no sanitation for two-and-a-half-million people. Rochina is a step up."

"But still, her life has not been easy," Serena said.

"No, and it isn't today. Bebe has a daughter who is four. The father of her child was of the upper classes. Bebe thought that he would do the honorable thing, as you say, but he wanted only a mistress. He offered money, but she refused. She is still bitter. Bebe no longer believes in romance. Work is her only passion."

"Men *can* be shits," Serena said, "if you gentlemen will forgive my directness."

"I imagine Koto's heard it before," Michael said. "God knows, I have."

"Well, maybe you should do your gender a good turn and have a little chat with Bebe," she said. "See if you can undo some of the damage. Michael's very good with bruised female psyches, you see," she said to Koto. "Especially if there's a child involved. I bet the little tyke is adorable."

Koto nodded.

They passed through the Tunel Novo and came out the ocean side of the mountain onto the Avenida Princesa Isabel, which sloped down to the sea. To the east was Leme, the small district tucked under the Morro de Babilônia, one of the hills separating Copacabana from downtown Rio. Their hotel, the Atlântica, loomed up ahead on their left. A few blocks along the Avenida Atlântica was the grand old Copacabana Palace where Serena had stayed with her parents. She'd chosen the Atlântica this time because it was newer than the Palace, plus it was a high-rise, which she preferred for its majestic views.

Her travel agent had booked them an exclusive suite on the thirty-sixth floor overlooking the beach. Christina would be joining them, so they'd need lots of space. Besides, Serena liked the idea of having Michael close by. It would almost be like when they'd been together as a family.

"Here we are," Koto said, as they pulled under the portico of the hotel. "I'm sorry it took so long, Mrs. Bouchard. Traffic was unusually heavy this morning."

"If you could do anything about traffic, the mayor of Los Angeles would already have you under contract. Right now all I care about is a shower and cool sheets."

Koto acknowledged the comment, though she could see the poor man didn't quite know what to make of her. Few men did. It was the way she liked it.

Bebe was out of the limo before the doorman had pulled open the rear passenger door. She glanced around like a nervous secret-service agent. Beneath that pretty face Serena sensed there was a woman of steel, an Amazon willing to go toe-to-toe with men on their own terms. That was something every woman could admire. The sisterly smile Serena gave the girl was warmer than before.

Michael followed Serena out of the limo. Bebe ignored him. Koto alighted beside Serena and gestured toward the white-marble-and-gold entrance. "Please, Mrs. Bouchard, I will escort you in. Bebe will take care of things here."

"Michael," Serena said loftily, "will you help the young lady? I'll check us in."

They entered the casually elegant lobby. The floor was white marble, but the forest of lush potted plants and the fountains gave the space a tropical feel. The furnishings were modern, the colors aqua and earth tones, and the scattered carpets and art were inspired by native culture.

Serena was greeted by an assistant manager. The man was fair, but well tanned, his manner cordial. Serena paid close attention to these things. Her father had frequently said, "Tend your own shop first, but pay close attention to the competition."

Koto discreetly moved some distance off and stood with his hands folded in front of him, assuming the demeanor of a loyal and trusted servant. Serena would have to tell Roberto Cabral she approved of his choice.

The assistant manager was preparing the paperwork when Michael sauntered up.

"Well, well," she said glancing at him, "have we finished with the luggage already?"

"I was politely instructed to get my ass inside," he said. "Whichever way I turn some woman wants to give me an order."

"Poor baby. Well, after we've had our showers I'll give you a back rub."

"Under the circumstances that may not be wise."

"Afraid it might lead to something?" she asked offhandedly as she looked over a brochure on the desk.

"*You* evidently aren't."

"I keep things in perspective better now that I'm old. Besides, I've made my feelings clear. I wasn't suggesting a seduction."

The assistant manager politely ignored their conversation. Serena ignored him. "I certainly meant no offense, Michael," she said, taking the pen the man handed her. "You know I have the utmost respect for you. If I didn't, you wouldn't be here."

He looked away, unwilling to spar. Not that that surprised her. Michael had never liked public spats, but Serena knew some of the most effective communication could be made before a neutral audience. About half her public utterances to Michael were calculated for effect. She was often petulant, but she took care never to turn into a screaming bitch in public. It was so unrefined. Still, she didn't hesitate to speak her mind.

When she'd finished the paperwork, a bellhop who'd been hovering nearby was summoned.

"Pedro will show you to your suite, madam," the assistant manager said. He gave the keys to the bellhop.

Serena and Michael walked over to Koto. "Do we have further business?" she asked the detective.

"I will call this evening about arrangements for visiting your brother," Koto replied.

"You go on up to the room," Michael told her. "I have a few things to discuss with Koto. I'll be up shortly."

Serena took one of the room keys from the bellhop and handed it to Michael. "I'll probably be in the shower." She gave him a sly wink. "Kinda like the old days."

"Kinda."

"Bye, Koto," she said. "And thanks." Turning, she saw Bebe watching them from halfway across the room. She was beautiful. If another woman could admire those legs, those curves, those bones with such awe, how could a man help but be a slave to them?

Serena followed the bellhop, knowing damned well Michael wasn't staying behind for Koto. Bebe, in her little miniskirt, really had him by the balls. Well, Serena was in no position to complain. She was the one who'd laid down the rules. And it *was* her idea for them to have a good time, if the opportunity arose. Besides, a little suffering was good for her soul. If this was what it took to save her brother, then so be it.

"Can I buy you a beer, Koto?" Mike asked when Serena had gone off with the bellhop.

"I'll buy you one. You are, after all, the visitor."

"No, my friend," he said, putting his hand on Koto's shoulder, "I asked first. Besides, I thought we might invite your sidekick to join us."

Koto shrugged. "If you wish."

They made their way across the lobby toward Bebe, who drew herself to attention as they approached. She looked a bit self-conscious. Michael wondered if it was him or if she saw every pair of admiring male eyes as a threat.

He let Koto do the talking. They spoke Portuguese, so he wasn't sure what was being said, but Bebe's enthusiasm for joining them seemed less than overwhelming. It was obvious that she was leery of him—and probably every other man she met.

A woman wasn't hostile toward a guy without cause. Bebe was wounded. That would have been evident even without Koto's account of her life. And that attracted Michael as much or more than the girl herself. Challenges always appealed to him. That was why, as a twenty-seven-year-old hotshot, he'd set his sights on Serena Bouchard—one of the most desired women in California, even without her fortune—and had got her. Of course, she'd made damned sure he'd fallen in love with her and not her money, which he'd considered as much a curse as a blessing.

Since Serena, his romantic life had turned on friendships rather than challenges. He'd opted to switch gears and go for the quiet and commonplace instead of the inaccessible and exciting. Serena wasn't easily replaced.

Bebe walked on the other side of Koto as they made their way to the bar. The place was practically empty. Michael had forgotten it was morning, because to him it was the middle of the night.

They installed themselves in a quiet corner table. Koto ordered coffee and Bebe some kind of fruit juice. Mike was in the mood for beer, so he went with it, despite the hour. He asked Koto if he had a recommendation.

"Brazilian beer is good and it's cheap," the detective said. "Ask for draft. *Choppe* is the word. It's like asking for a brew."

"*Choppe,*" Mike said to the barman.

The man went off and the three of them looked at one another.

"I'm a babe in the woods when it comes to Brazil," Mike said. "I'm sure Senhor Cabral explained that's why your services are essential."

Koto nodded. "Our mission is to assist you. We understand that."

"Let's not kid ourselves. Mainly I'm here to hold Serena's hand, give her some perspective. She's a very shrewd woman, but she's also smart enough to know her limitations. One of them is her blind spot over her brother. When it comes to Jeffrey, she can be very emotional."

"I understand."

"But don't underestimate her. She's no fool when it comes to people, the possible exception being her choice of husbands." He laughed.

"That was true what she said about you being married?" Koto asked. "I thought maybe it was a joke."

"It was no joke, my friend."

"A most unusual situation."

"There's nothing usual about Serena." He glanced at Bebe. "She liked you, by the way," he said. "Both of you. And that's good if you're working for her. Serena can be a pain or a delight. It helps if she's favorably disposed."

"If you say so, *senhor,*" Bebe said, undoubtedly feeling she should respond.

He studied her mouth. "But since the investigation comes under my end of things, I thought it would be good if we talked philosophy. I tell the people who work for me back home that yes-men can't do me a damned bit of good. I want you both to feel free to tell me what you think at all times."

"Thank you," Koto said. "I prefer to work that way if possible."

"And being American," Mike said, "I tend to be informal. If I'm overly familiar, please don't be offended. I try to respect the people I work with and hope for the same in return." He was looking at Bebe as he said this, hoping she'd see it as a peace offering. "My friendliness can be misinterpreted as flirting, so please don't take offense if I seem too forward. It's my way and it's harmless. Does that make sense?"

She replied without hesitation. "The experts on love write columns in the newspaper, *senhor*. I have different talents." She gave him a long, steady look. It wasn't cold, but neither was it warm.

"Well said."

She did not smile.

"So, I guess we should deal with matters at hand," he said, moving on. "One of the reasons I wanted to talk to you two is because I need some advice."

"Sure," Koto said, "what kind of advice?"

"It seems one of your Brazilian wiseguys was poking around L.A. and Vegas, checking up on me over the past couple of days. Just as we were leaving the country he met with an unfortunate accident and got himself killed."

"What is a wiseguy?" Bebe asked.

Mike found the way she pronounced it so damned sweet he wanted to pinch her cheek.

"Gangster," Koto said.

"One of ours?" she said, surprised.

"He carried a Brazilian passport," Mike said.

"You say he was killed?"

"In a traffic accident, while tailing us."

"I see. Do you know the guy's name?" Koto asked.

"Eduardo Ribeiro."

The detective shook his head. Bebe did as well. "Don't know him," he said, "but we can check it out." He signaled Bebe, who opened her shoulder bag and took out a notepad.

As she was making her notes, Mike noticed a silver-plated automatic tucked in her bag. Somehow he'd pictured her leveling guys with karate kicks, using those long legs of hers to whack them on the side of the head. Evidently she could be even more lethal if the situation warranted.

The barman served their drinks. Bebe's came with a slice of pineapple perched on the rim of the glass. It made him think of the Shirley Temples Christina had drunk as a little girl. Christ. Now that he thought about it, Bebe and his stepdaughter were of the same generation. A depressing thought.

He picked up his glass. "Well, amigos, what do we drink to?" he asked. "D'Artagnan? Eduardo Ribeiro? Brazilian justice?"

"To your health and long life, *senhor,*" Koto said. "First things first, eh?"

"Yeah, no sense shooting for the moon first night in town." He raised his glass in salute. "To us all, then." He quaffed a quarter of the beer. "Not bad, this *choppe,*" he said.

Koto and Bebe each sipped their drinks. "Do you have any idea why this guy, Ribeiro, was checking on you?" Koto asked.

"No, but it seems that if somebody's interested enough to go all that way to sniff around, they'd probably find me even more fascinating now that I'm here."

"Yes, that makes sense," Koto said.

"One other thing," Mike said. "The police found the phone number of my stepdaughter's friends in Mr. Ribeiro's wallet. A prominent family. Monteiro da Silva."

Koto's brow rose. So did Bebe's.

"You've heard of them, evidently."

"Everybody knows the Monteiro da Silva family," Bebe said. "Zozimo writes about them once or twice a week."

"Zozimo?"

"A famous gossip columnist," Koto explained. "To be mentioned by Zozimo is better than being blessed by the Pope. Rio is very social. Celebrities, the rich, everybody wants to be in Zozimo's light."

"Your daughter must be the American millionaire that is the fiancée of the son, Joachim Monteiro da Silva," Bebe said. "Zozimo wrote about his American woman three or four times already."

"Did you say fiancée?" Mike asked, surprised.

"I do not know what is official," the girl said, "but in the papers it sounds like she is a fiancée. *Não,* Koto?"

"Perhaps."

"I think there's a misunderstanding," Mike said. "If Christina's engaged, I'm sure her mother would have heard."

"But not you, *senhor?*"

"Christina's not my daughter, though I helped raise her and we are close—close enough that Ribeiro's connection with the Monteiro da Silvas has given me pause. Do society types and the underworld rub shoulders as a matter of course down here?" he asked.

Koto took a sip of coffee, then put his cup down. "There are certain jobs that require certain kinds of people. When you have money you can buy whatever service you need, Mr. Hamlin. And in Brazil it is difficult to do wrong if you have money and a name. The rich scratch the backs of the rich. They are good at keeping the dirty linen in the closet."

"Anything goes. Is that what you are saying?"

"In Rio, the rich allow the poor the use of the beaches, *senhor,*" Bebe said. "This is the way they are kept quiet and happy. The only time there is talk of health care, of sanitation or of education is before the election. After the election, they give us a few more buses to take the poor to the beach."

"Sounds like we have a politician in our midst," Mike said.

"I will not speak of it if you prefer, *senhor.*"

"Say anything you like, Bebe," he said. "I'm here to learn."

He'd said the right thing, because for the first time the girl smiled. She actually seemed pleased.

"My favorite teacher in school used to say you find wisdom with your eyes and ears open and your mouth shut," he observed. "So feel free to enlighten me."

"Is this an American principle?" she asked.

"It's my principle, Bebe."

"Men do not say this in Brazil. Not to a woman."

Mike saw an opening and decided to take it. "Men usually make the mistake of thinking we know everything. But

there is wisdom in every human heart, Bebe. Don't let anyone tell you otherwise.''

She grew quiet. He could see he'd struck a chord, planted
a seed. Even if she wasn't a feminist, she wanted respect.
Everyone did, but with her it was a pivotal issue. He was
proud of himself for having detected it.

Koto cleared his throat and they both looked at him.

''Ah, yes,'' Mike said, ''we digress. Ribeiro and the
Monteiro da Silvas.''

Bebe shifted uneasily, perhaps realizing there'd been a
connection between them and not sure how she felt about
that. He was content to back off and let the seed take root.

Koto was thinking about business. ''The important question is why the Monteiro da Silvas need a guy like Ribeiro,''
he said.

''Is it reasonable to assume they wanted to check up on
me?'' Mike asked.

''Possibly.''

''But why? Are Brazilians particularly sensitive about the
family backgrounds of their friends?''

''In all countries the social elite are not like other people,'' Koto said, ''but I can't say whether in Brazil it is worse
or not. Perhaps you know better than anyone what they
might be looking for.''

''Seems like a lot of trouble to go to just to check up on
Christina's ex-stepfather.''

''Perhaps it is your qualifications, *senhor,*'' Bebe said.
''We are told you are a...*Como dizer?*'' She turned to Koto.

''Renowned criminologist,'' he replied.

Mike laughed. ''Who told you that?''

''Senhor Cabral,'' Koto said.

''I'm afraid it's a slight exaggeration.''

''You are not famous?'' Bebe asked, in a tone that fell
somewhere between surprise and dismay.

''Honey, I'm a hotel dick.''

''What is a dick?''

Both Mike and Koto had to fight back their smiles.

"Hotel security," Mike said. "I protect places like this. At the moment, I'm head of security at the Desert Palms in Las Vegas. It's a responsible job, they pay me damned well, but Sherlock Holmes I'm not."

Bebe acted disappointed. Mike felt like he'd let her down. "I hope you aren't disillusioned."

She shook her head. "It's better like this. I was afraid before you would tell us how to do our work."

Koto cleared his throat. Bebe looked at him, realizing she'd been too candid.

"Desculpe, senhor. Forgive me."

"We're just folks here," Mike said. "No need for apologies."

She seemed to appreciate his gentleness.

"Maybe Mr. Ribeiro was under the same misapprehension," Koto said solemnly.

"Wouldn't that be ironic." Mike considered whether Eduardo Ribeiro had gone to the States to convey a warning of some kind. "That brings me to my next request," he said, after reflecting a moment longer. "What are the chances of picking up a peashooter like Bebe's?"

"You need a gun?" Koto said.

"If Ribeiro was just an advance scout, it occurs to me there might be a few more bad guys hiding in the bushes around here. I like being prepared."

"No problem," Koto said. "Nine millimeter okay?"

"Perfect."

"I'll get it. How urgent?"

"How great is the danger? This is your turf, Koto, not mine."

Koto gestured with his head to Bebe. "Make a note. Something that can't be traced. Bring it to Mr. Hamlin this afternoon."

"Sim, senhor."

Bebe and Mike exchanged warmer looks. "I appreciate your cooperative attitude," he said to the girl.

"I try to do my duty, *senhor.*"

"It's all right if you call me Mike."

"If you don't mind, Senhor Hamlin, I prefer it if I call you by your formal name. This way there are no mistakes."

"As you wish."

"It is for you as much as for me," she replied. Then, taking her glass, she guzzled down all but a bit of her juice, the cords of her neck rippling as she drank. She put down the glass. "If you will excuse me, please," she said, rising to her feet, "I have many things to do."

Mike watched the hem of her skirt slip down those last critical inches. He looked up into her eyes. "By all means."

After a nod in Koto's direction, she said, *"Adeus, se-nhores,"* then headed off, her hips swinging gracefully but with unmistakable allure. Bebe had the long, slinky strides of a jaguar.

"Adeus," Mike called after her, watching until she was out the door. "Quite a pistol," he said.

Koto glanced discreetly down at his coffee cup.

"I hope my friendliness with Bebe isn't a problem for you, Koto," Mike said. "I prefer to know the people I work with. Maybe it's a Gringo thing, eschewing formality."

"No problem," Koto said.

"I don't want to step on anybody's toes."

"The only toes you must watch out for are Bebe's. She is very proud. And there are always men after her."

"It must be annoying to you, as well as to her."

"Yes, if there is a downside, it's that. But I admit it can also be an asset. In Brazil, sex is almost as important as money and influence, so Bebe offers advantages, too."

"I admire your objectivity. I'm afraid if I had that mini-skirt prancing around in my office, I'd never get any work done."

"When you are my age it becomes easier to ignore, *se-nhor.*"

"It's Mike, Koto. I'm much more trusting of people when I'm on a first-name basis." He took a long drink, finishing his beer. He signaled the barman for another. "This *choppe* is as enticing as your women, Koto. How about more cof-fee?"

"No, thank you. I sip it for flavor. My stomach does not like coffee as much as I do. But that's life, eh?"

"Tell me, Koto, where did you learn English? You speak it very well."

"Thank you. I lived in the States for several years. My father sent me to the University of Miami to study business."

"No kidding."

"Yes, I liked America very much and became a student of the culture, I guess you could say. And I have a natural aptitude for language. In addition to Portuguese I speak Japanese, Spanish, Italian and some French and German."

"Were you tempted to stay in the States?"

"Yes, but I love this country. It is my home, after all. I am married and have six children. The eldest is in the university."

"Interesting. You and Bebe aren't...more than employer and employee, then."

Koto shook his head. "No. I live by very strict rules."

"Yeah, I figured as much," Mike said, drawing on his new beer. "Normally I do, too. But away from home the professionalism slips some, if you know what I mean."

"Do not let it slip too far, my friend. I don't know what problems you will encounter working on this case, but it could be a mistake to underestimate the danger. The social elite are buzzing. Something serious is going on. I can smell it."

Mike braced his hand on the detective's shoulder. "We plebeians have got to look out for each other then, my friend."

Koto nodded. "Yes, I agree."

"All for one and one for all, eh?"

"You've read Dumas?" the Brazilian asked.

Mike chuckled. "Saw the movie."

As he stood waiting for the elevator to arrive, he thought about Bebe and sex and being in Brazil. In a way, he was tempted to test his and Serena's resolve. He wouldn't do anything overt, but if she gave him an opening he just might take it. He was perfectly aware that her so-called rules were intended to be provocative as much as restrictive.

Admonishing himself for the thought, he peered up at the floor-indicator lights. Jesus, an affair with his ex-wife was all he needed. Better to make a pass at Bebe and end up with a fat lip.

Just as one of the elevator doors opened, he heard a woman's angry voice across the lobby. "Joachim, just leave me alone! I don't want to talk to you now!"

Mike turned, for the voice was familiar. It was Christina, her tawny hair flowing, long tanned legs protruding from a little cotton sundress that was almost as short as Bebe's. The handsome young man at her side was trying to take her arm, but she jerked it away. He was persistent, talking to her in a low tone, but she was clearly more upset than fearful. Their spat had all the earmarks of a lover's quarrel.

Mike's paternal instincts took over. Between the adrenaline and the alcohol, the decision to intervene came easily. He walked toward the couple.

"I told you, I'm handling this my way!" Christina insisted.

He could not hear the response, but he noticed the argument had drawn the attention of others. As he neared them, Christina glanced up.

"Michael!" she exclaimed. A smile spread across her face.

The young man turned. Christina freed herself and threw her arms around her stepfather. She'd always been affectionate, but this struck Mike as more enthusiastic than usual.

Christina smelled like sun and shampoo and gardenias. She had her mother's sensuous figure, though she was an inch or two taller. She also had Serena's wonderful skin, and much of the same beauty, with slightly less delicate features. Christina's best asset was her mouth. She was fairer than Serena, having gotten her coloring from Eric Lorimer.

Because he, too, was fair, Mike was often taken for her father.

Christina, her arm still around him, turned back to the young man. Mike squeezed her waist, feeling protective and possessive as he stared the guy down.

The Brazilian was older than he'd thought at first—twenty-eight or thirty. He was only a few inches taller than Christina and was broad-shouldered and muscular, though his waist and hips were narrow. He was wearing a flashy gold watch, a dark green silk shirt and crisp white trousers. He had the look of an aristocrat—arrogant and smug, but in a charming, almost capricious way. At the moment, he did not seem pleased.

Christina took Mike's hand and led him to the Brazilian, who pushed his sunglasses up into his longish black hair. "Michael, I want you to meet Joachim Monteiro da Silva. Joachim, this is my stepfather, Michael Hamlin."

They shook hands. Monteiro da Silva's grip was quite firm.

"Welcome, Michael," he said, his brown eyes neither hostile nor friendly. He seemed faintly embarrassed. "We've been looking forward to seeing you and Christina's mother." He spoke grammatically correct English, though his accent was pronounced.

"And we've been looking forward to meeting you, Joachim."

Mike turned to Christina. "I didn't mean to interrupt, but I heard you . . . talking . . . and—"

"We were arguing, Michael," she said contritely, letting go of his hand. She, too, seemed embarrassed. "Joachim's very protective of me and, well, he doesn't understand I'm not used to . . . being looked after that way."

"It was my fault," Joachim said nobly. "I was too insistent. But I feel great concern for her safety."

Mike looked back and forth between them. "Is there a particular danger?"

"After all that has happened," Joachim said with a shrug. "I offered to stay, to drive her home, we disagreed and . . . well, I apologize for making a—how do you say?— a scene. It was not the way to make a favorable impression. I'm sorry, *senhor*."

"No need to apologize to me," Mike said. "Christina's the one to concern yourself with."

"I'm sorry, Christina," Joachim said dutifully. "Please forgive me."

She took compassion on him and stepped over, taking his arm. Her rapid change of heart was more telling than anything.

Mike again saw the telltale hint of smugness on Joachim's face and felt surprising contempt. It was probably his paternal instincts, but the animosity he felt was very strong. He'd been predisposed to dislike Joachim Monteiro da Silva because of the business in L.A. Now, having seen him in the flesh, his feelings were no less negative. In fact, he didn't like the guy at all.

"I've always admired a man who can admit to a mistake," he said lightly.

Joachim nodded, accepting the compliment, though he seemed to sense Mike's insincerity. The dislike might well be mutual. They evaluated one another. Monteiro da Silva was obviously a prideful man. Any retreat would be tactical.

Christina, on the other hand, was dazzled by her Brazilian Romeo. Blind as a bat and in love. And Joachim knew it, making it all the worse.

"Incidentally, Joachim," Mike said, "I ran into a friend of yours in L.A. He said to pass along his regards."

Joachim was taken aback. "Oh? Who would that be, *senhor?*"

"Eduardo Ribeiro." Mike watched closely to see Joachim's reaction.

A tiny flicker of awareness passed across his face but he quickly recovered. "Ribeiro? The name isn't familiar."

"He seemed to know you. In fact, I had the distinct impression you were business associates."

Joachim shook his head. "There must be a mistake, Michael. I don't know a man by this name. Perhaps he was confused."

"If so, he took his confusion to his grave. Poor Eduardo paid a visit to St. Peter after visiting me, unless maybe he went to the other place."

"Senhor?"

"Eduardo had the misfortune of getting a little too close to one of Uncle Sam's mail trucks and came a cropper. I'm sure his family will hear about it, if they haven't already."

Joachim was cool as ice.

"Well, I'm dying to see Mom," Christina said. "Are you sure you don't want to come up with me, Joachim?"

"No, Christina. This is a time for your family. When it is the right occasion, I wish for you all to come to meet my family. It is the Brazilian way."

She took his hands, looking up at him like a remorseful schoolgirl. "I'm sorry I got cross with you earlier."

Joachim drew himself up, but at the same time touched her hair, tenderness in his eyes. He was both bullfighter and poet. Mike felt a distinct sense of revulsion. Joachim trailed the back of his index finger across Christina's cheek. Then, turning to Mike, he extended his hand.

"I will leave her in your good hands, Michael."

"I've looked after her before, amigo."

Smiling thinly, Joachim turned on his heel and walked smartly, but with a controlled swagger, to the entrance of the hotel.

"Isn't he wonderful?" Christina said.

Mike could almost hear the patter of her heart. "Yeah, real macho kind of guy. Does he fight bulls for a hobby?"

She gave him an impatient look. "Are you being snide, Michael?"

He pinched her cheek. "The old man's a little jealous, that's all, pumpkin."

She sighed and they turned toward the elevators. Mike slipped his arm around her waist and she put hers around his.

"Joachim plays polo, actually," she said wistfully. "He's one of the top players in Brazil."

"Impressive. But I thought your game was tennis."

"Don't tease me, Michael," she said. "It was over with Cameron eons ago."

"I know people who haven't had a shower since Cameron was the love of your life, pumpkin."

"Don't give me a rough time," she pleaded. "Joachim is very special."

Mike wondered how special, but he almost preferred not to know. So he didn't ask.

They released each other as they came to the bank of elevators. They'd just missed a car filled with guests. Mike was glad—he preferred empty elevators.

Christina stared up at the lights above the door. "So, how's Mom taking Uncle Jeffrey's arrest?"

"Not well. You know how she feels about him. He's as much her child as you are."

"Yes, I know. It's terrible." She bit her lip. "I can't tell you how glad I am that Mother wanted you to come along. I'd have suggested it myself, but I was afraid she wouldn't be up to taking you on, on top of everything else. She always gets nervous when she knows you're going to be around."

Mike couldn't help laughing. So it hadn't been Christina's idea. He wasn't really surprised. Actually, he was glad. "She's bearing up for the sake of Uncle Jeffrey," he said.

"Don't tell her I told you about her getting nervous, by the way."

"It doesn't matter. The truth is I get nervous around her, too."

"At least you admit it."

An elevator car arrived and they stepped inside. He pushed the button for the thirty-sixth floor. Christina leaned against the side of the car, her shoulders slumping. She blew her bangs off her forehead and looked at him as the doors slid shut.

"What was that business about you meeting somebody in L.A. who knew Joachim?" she asked.

Mike leaned against the railing at the back of the car. "I was just testing Joachim to see how nimble he was on his feet."

"But why?"

"Mind games, pumpkin. Old-bull, young-bull stuff."

She let it pass. She watched the lights moving across the panel, a sad look coming over her. Her eyes began to tear up.

"What's the matter, Christina?" he asked.

Her eyes welled. "Michael, Drake's getting murdered is the worst thing that's ever happened. It's been a terrible week." She stifled a sob.

He held out his arms and she fell into them, the way she had as a child. He stroked her head. "It was a bad week for Drake, too, babe. Don't feel like the Lone Ranger."

She peered up at him through her lashes, the way her mother did when she was making a bid for compassion. "It's really not funny," she admonished. But she couldn't help laughing shortly.

"I know it's not," he said, "but a person's got to keep a sense of humor. Sometimes it's the only way to survive."

"What worries me," she said, sniffling, "is that it's going to ruin things between me and Joachim."

"Why would it?"

The elevator arrived at their floor and they stepped out.

Christina shook her head. "I don't know, exactly. But Joachim thinks Uncle Jeffrey is guilty. He's sure he murdered Drake. We've fought over it several times."

"Why would *he* get emotional about Drake Manville's murder? Jeffrey's *your* uncle, not his."

"I don't know why Joachim's so uptight about it, but he is."

"What, exactly, has he said?"

"That it's bad enough that there's a scandal, but for there to be a big to-do, a showy trial, all my relatives trooping down, will only make it worse."

They began walking down the hallway.

"Well, what did he expect?" Mike said. "That Jeffrey would plead guilty to avoid a little negative publicity for his niece's friends?"

"Joachim said that would be the best thing for everyone in the long run. That way, if it was handled quietly, Jeffrey could get a minimal sentence. Supposedly, the less notoriety, the easier it is to handle everything discreetly."

"Sounds like your friend has a lot of pull. Or thinks he does."

"Joachim's father died a couple of years ago, leaving him head of the family. That makes him one of the most influential men in all of Brazil. The Monteiro da Silvas are very wealthy, Michael."

Mike was checking the room numbers as they walked. "Let's hope he doesn't let it go to his head. It's always dangerous to play with other people's lives. I don't care what kind of money you've got."

"That's what I think, too," she said. "But how can I tell Joachim that?"

"He's not used to listening to women, I imagine."

Christina shook her head. "No, that's one thing we have to work out."

"Turn him over to your mother, if you want him straightened out quick. She'd chew him up and spit him out in little pieces."

The young woman rolled her eyes. "I can't tell you how nervous I am about them meeting. It's good that you're here. *Really* good."

That pleased Michael, but he didn't want her kidding herself. "Don't overestimate my influence on your mother. I didn't have much pull with her when we were married, and I have even less now."

"That's not true," she said. "You're the only man besides Grandfather that she really respected. She told me that once. I'm sure that's the reason she wanted you here."

"Serena always appreciated my ability to listen," he said. "And now that I'm an old guy she figures I won't give her much lip."

Christina laughed, giving him a playful jab in the stomach. "Mom still is hot for your bod, Michael, and you know it. She doesn't even pretend she's not."

"You're a hell of a source of intelligence, kid. I hope you know that."

"Well, don't say anything to her."

"My lips are sealed," Mike said.

The suite was at the end of the hall. They paused at the door so Christina could take a hanky from her purse to wipe her eyes.

"Don't worry about Joachim," he said. "You've got your mother to contend with now."

Christina took a deep breath and nodded. He put his key in the lock. Giving her a wink, he swung the door open, curious how this mother-daughter meeting would play out. Serena was sure to make it interesting.

Serena was out on the balcony in her bathrobe, staring down at the beach, when she heard the door to the suite opening. She took a last, languorous look at the Praia do Leme. Somewhere down there she had frolicked in the surf a thousand years ago with Maximino. They had played at sex like two children toying with a gun, titillating fate as they'd titillated each other. Lost youth.

"I'm out here, Michael," she called over her shoulder. She inhaled the surprisingly mild air.

"Pretty, isn't it?" came a soft feminine voice behind her.

Serena spun around. "Christina!"

They embraced, Serena instantly in tears.

"God, it's good to see you," she said, holding the girl's face in her hands, savoring the tears and the joy of reunion. "I've worried about you!"

"About me? You mean Uncle Jeffrey, don't you?"

Serena brushed a strand of hair off Christina's cheek. "Yes, Jeffrey, of course, but you, me, the whole family."

Christina glanced back at Michael, who was at the sliding glass door, watching them. "At least we're all together again."

"Yes, but I won't rest until I've gotten your uncle out of jail." Serena took Christina's hand and led her into the sitting room, an airy space with large plants, a tile floor and colorful, angular furniture that managed to be luxurious and institutional at the same time. They went to the big, off-white sofa, where they plopped down side by side. "Tell me what you've heard since we talked."

"Hardly anything about the case. Joachim said the police are investigating, but there's been almost nothing in the papers except hype about Drake. Postmortem, he's an international megastar."

"There's a lot of irony in death," Serena said. "But let's not talk about Drake. Tell me about this family that's taken you in. I want to hear everything."

Michael had drifted over and sat on the arm of an easy chair nearby. Serena and he exchanged looks.

"They're very prominent," Christina began. "There's three of them left—Joachim, his mother and grandmother. His father died a number of years ago."

"Where did they get their money?" Serena asked.

"Joachim's father was a big industrialist, and his father before him. I'm not sure what all they did. Mining, shipping, banking. About everything, I guess."

"Are they still active in business or did they sell and start living on the income?"

"They still own a lot. Joachim's mother seems to run things. She's not involved day to day, like you are, Mom, but she makes the big decisions."

"What about Joachim?"

"He's involved, but he's not in charge. I think there's tension between him and his mother because of it. They hardly ever talk about business around me. At least not in English, and my Portuguese is pretty basic."

"What does Joachim do besides play polo?" Michael asked.

Serena's head turned. "He's a polo player?"

"That's not all," Christina returned. "He does business, too. And he's involved in lots of things."

"The sort of things Zozimo writes about?" Michael asked.

Christina was surprised. "How did you know about Zozimo?"

"I'm not a renowned criminologist for nothing."

"Who's Zozimo?" Serena interjected.

"I'm impressed," Christina said.

"It turns out I'm even well known for my investigatory skills here in Brazil," Michael went on.

"Would somebody please tell me who Zozimo is?" Serena demanded. She was becoming annoyed.

"A society columnist," Christina said.

Serena was taken aback. "Michael, what do you know about society columnists in Rio de Janeiro?"

"If my stepdaughter is featured prominently in Zozimo's column, I make a point of knowing about it."

"What?" Serena said.

Christina's brow furrowed. "How did you know about that, Michael?"

"I make it my business to know everything when I'm working a case."

"Scary."

"Scary?" he said.

"Would you two stop talking to each other long enough for somebody to explain to me what's going on?"

Michael got up, stretching. He looked at Christina. "Do you want to tell your mother how the Rio society mavens have you practically engaged to Joachim Monteiro da Silva, or shall I?"

Serena's jaw dropped.

"That's just gossip, Michael," Christina said.

"But if your mother is going to be hobnobbing around Rio, I think you owe it to her to explain how things are between you and Joachim. There's no point in making her look like a fool."

"Engaged?" Serena demanded, gathering herself.

"I planned to explain," Christina said defensively.

"You're engaged?"

"Of course not, Mother. Like I said, it's gossip."

"Then what's the truth?"

Christina shifted uncomfortably. "Joachim and I care about one another very much."

"Care about one another? What's that supposed to mean?"

"Well, if you'd give me a chance to talk and stop asking questions," Christina snapped, "you might find out!"

Serena bristled but held her tongue. She crossed her legs, smoothing the robe on her knee. "I'm listening."

"I like Joachim and he likes me. I was having a wonderful time with him, a fabulous time, until Uncle Jeffrey . . . until Drake was killed."

"Liking someone and being practically engaged to him are two very different things," Serena intoned.

"Maybe we love each other, then," Christina said curtly. "And we have started talking about the future. Preliminarily."

"I should hope to God preliminarily," Serena said, getting to her feet. "How old is this boy, anyway?"

"Joachim's twenty-nine."

"Twenty-nine? He's not a boy."

"Of course not. And I'm not a girl, though to listen to you, you'd think I was sixteen."

"You're only nineteen, Christina. That's fifteen minutes older than sixteen." Serena started to pace.

"Mother, really. I'll be twenty in a few weeks and Joachim only just turned twenty-nine. It's not like we're decades apart or anything. Not like *you* and my father!"

Serena ignored the barb. "Listen to this, Michael," she said, pacing like a caged animal. "My daughter hasn't been in Rio long enough to be on her second pair of panty hose and already she's *preliminarily* engaged and planning to bear me grandchildren!"

Michael laughed.

"It's not funny."

"Mother," Christina said, "you're blowing this all out of proportion. I'm not engaged yet. And if I were you'd know about it, all right?"

"Maybe I am being a bit hysterical," Serena said calmly, matching her daughter's tone. "We've had a long flight and haven't slept. I guess I'm a little rummy."

"I just wish you trusted me," Christina said. "Then we wouldn't have these kinds of discussions."

Serena wanted to bring up Cameron. She wanted to ask if Christina had ever heard of falling in love on the rebound, of being in love with love, of letting herself be blinded by the erotic and the exotic, or transfixed by the sweet talk of a polo-playing Latin lothario.

"You're right," she said, taking the high road, "I should trust you. And, of course, I want to meet Joachim. I'm sure he's delightful. You wouldn't care for him if he weren't."

"Oh, he's wonderful, Mom. You'll love him."

"I'm sure I will. And Michael, as well. Right, dear?"

"I've already met him, Serena."

She blinked.

"Michael met him downstairs a few minutes ago," Christina explained. "He drove me here."

"Why didn't you bring him up to meet me?"

"I wanted to, but he didn't want to interfere. Isn't that sweet? He's so considerate."

Serena and Michael exchanged looks again.

"So when do I get to meet him?" Serena asked.

"He wants to have you over to meet his mother and see their place. It's a country estate with horses and everything. They have a nice condo in town, too, but they spend most of their time in the country. Brazilians really know how to live," she gushed.

Serena sat in a chair across from Christina. "Evidently," she said under her breath.

Michael sat on the arm of the chair next to her. Christina studied the two of them.

"What's happened to poor Uncle Jeffrey is terrible," Christina said, "but at least it's reunited the family."

"Your idea of asking Michael to come with me to Rio was an excellent one, Christina," Serena said.

"Too late, babe," Michael said. "I already know it wasn't her idea."

Serena refused to look embarrassed. "So it was mine," she said airily. "So what? You knew it was a little white lie the minute I told you, and you humored me."

"That's why I'm in Rio—to humor you?"

"Oh, shut up, Michael."

"The important thing is that you're both here," Christina said. "And getting along so well," she added with a smile.

Serena looked toward the door. "Speaking of togetherness, where's your luggage, Christina? Is it downstairs?"

"Mother, I'm not staying here at the hotel."

Serena was shocked. "Where do you plan to stay?"

"With Joachim."

"Darling, there's no need for that now. I arranged for a suite with three bedrooms."

"I'm very comfortable at the Monteiro da Silvas', Mother, and that's where I plan to stay."

Christina got up and went to the slider, gazing out at the sea. She was oblivious to any possible danger, Serena could see. So how did she voice her concern? Should she just come out and tell her about those men who'd died on the way to the airport in L.A., the gangster with the Monteiro da Silva phone number in his pocket?

"Christina, I'm sure Joachim's family is lovely, but how well do you know them? It was nice of them to offer you a place to stay when you needed it, but don't you think virtually living there is going a little far?"

"I'm not *virtually* living there, Mother. I *am* living there. There's nothing wrong with it. Joachim's mother is conscious of appearances—not that it matters."

Serena turned to Michael. "You're the one with rectitude. How do we convince our daughter that she belongs here with us?"

"I'm not sure that we do," he replied.

"I'm glad *someone* sees the point," Christina muttered.

Serena shot Michael a wicked glare. "You want to ignore what happened to that fellow Ribeiro?"

"Who's Ribeiro?" Christina said, returning to the sofa. "Michael, isn't that who you were asking Joachim about?"

"Yes."

"Who is he?"

"A Brazilian we ran into in L.A."

"We weren't *exactly* the ones who ran into him," Serena said under her breath.

Michael went on. "I thought maybe Joachim knew him. Apparently he didn't."

"So what's it got to do with me and Joachim?"

"Nothing, pumpkin. Your mother and I are having the normal concerns of parents. We'll be having them when you're fifty, so you might as well get used to it."

Serena bit her tongue. She hoped Michael wasn't being a fool. She didn't want to gamble with Christina's safety. But it was also true that if they were too honest, it could backfire. That was probably what Michael was thinking.

"It's good that we've had a chance to talk," Christina said. "Joachim's got a meeting, so I've got to run. Mainly I wanted to say hi and set a time when we can get together."

"The first thing I want to do is get some sleep," Serena said. "Tomorrow, I hope to see your uncle. Once I've done that, I'm at your disposal."

Christina paused. "I might be able to come into town and we can shop or something. Otherwise the two of you can come out to the house . . . if you still want to, that is."

"Of course we do."

"Then why don't I call you tomorrow afternoon and we'll set something up?"

"That would be great."

Christina got up and so did Serena. They embraced.

"I know this sounds crazy coming from me," Serena said, "but there are times when it pays to be conservative."

"Mom, there's nothing to worry about. Joachim adores me."

"You haven't married him yet," Michael interjected.

"Michael," Serena said, "you're supposed to be the diplomat. Are your stepfatherly instincts finally catching up with you?"

He smiled sheepishly.

"See?" Serena said to her daughter. "We're moderating influences on each other."

Christina looked back and forth between them, wonder on her face. "You two are really staying in the same suite?"

"We're not sleeping in the same bed, for heaven's sake," Serena rejoined. "Give us some credit."

"I think it would be a hoot if you did." Christina giggled.

"God. Brazil has corrupted my only child."

"Mother, I was corrupted long before Brazil."

Serena blanched despite herself. "I don't think I want to have this conversation right now. Not with this headache."

Christina laughed and kissed her again. "I'm going. I'll leave you two with your sexual frustrations."

Serena caught Michael's eye as Christina went over to kiss him goodbye. He seemed to be thinking the same thing she was—that their little girl was all grown up. Lord, for all they knew, their flirtations were child's play compared to hers.

"Bye," Christina said cheerily as she headed for the door.

"Tell Joachim I'm looking forward to meeting him," Serena called after her.

"You'll love him, Mom, I promise you."

Serena smiled. Christina smiled. Michael smiled. The girl blew them a kiss and went out the door.

Michael turned to face Serena. They stared at each other for a long moment.

"I don't think I'm up to discussing it," she said.

"Then maybe I'll have a shower," he said. "How's the water?"

"Wet, just like at home."

"Then we'll probably survive. Which is my room?"

She pointed to a door.

"And where's yours?"

She pointed toward the door on the opposite wall.

"Sturdy locks on the door?" he asked.

"I think so."

"Good, then I should be safe." He headed for his room.

"Dream on, Michael."

He stopped in the doorway. "I wonder what would happen if I tempted fate and left it unlocked."

Serena didn't reply. There was no point. She was thinking the same thing: sometimes the simplest and easiest way to get rid of an itch was to scratch it.

Mike was more tired than he'd realized. The hot shower told his body that he'd struggled enough; it was time to take a snooze. As he dried off, he glanced into his bedroom and saw bare feet and legs on the bed. Wrapping the towel around his middle, he went to the door. Serena, still in her robe, lay there, casually propped up on a stack of pillows, hands behind her head.

"I have a serious question for you, Michael," she said. "Here's my theory. In going the Puritan route, we're making the problem worse. We both want to get laid, but pride and common sense tells us it's a bad idea because we don't want short-term gratification to cause long-term problems."

"Yeah, that kind of sums it up."

"Okay, but we both know that sexual frustration feeds on itself. A small desire can become an obsession."

"What are you saying, Serena? That you want to screw so that you don't have to think about it anymore?"

"I want your honest opinion. If we make love, can you put it behind you and let go?"

"Lovers tonight, brother and sister tomorrow?"

"Something like that."

Mike sauntered over to the bed and sat on the edge, next to her. He ran his index finger lightly down the side of her face. "Can *you* do it and let go?" he asked.

"Yes. Women are far less sentimental about things like this, believe it or not."

"I think you're generalizing."

"Okay, *I* can do it, but I don't want to be unfair to you."

His mouth widened into a grin. "What do you have on under that robe, Serena?"

"Nothing."

"I'm supposed to ignore that and make like I'm buying a used car?"

"Really, Michael, couldn't you have said, 'a new Lexus' or something?" She grimaced. "Used car?"

"You get my point."

"No, I'm not sure I do. If you regard me as an old wife, I don't want you to do it. I thought if we could be modern about this—you know, get it on, have fun, then go about our business—it might be all right. But if the past and the future become issues, then we shouldn't even consider it."

Mike was amused. He ran his fingers down the side of her throat. Serena shifted. "Let me get this straight," he said. "Are you trying to talk me into having sex with you or talk me out of it?"

"I'm trying to find out if you can be mature about it."

He slid his hand inside the flap of her robe and cupped her full breast. It had been a long time, but the feel was familiar. And so was the scent rising from her warm body. He could feel the steady thump of her heart under his palm.

"We're going to do it without ever agreeing what it means, aren't we?" she said in a hoarse whisper.

Mike ran his thumb over her nipple, making it harden. "The uncertainty adds to the excitement, don't you think?"

"Just like a man. It's a power trip, Michael. That's what this is. You've got to prove you're in control."

He gently pushed her robe open, exposing her breast. Then he leaned over and took her rock-hard nipple between his lips, sucking lightly. "Think so?"

Serena closed her eyes. "You bastard. Why do I even try?"

He wasn't going to point out that *she* was the one who'd come to *his* bed, that she'd presented *him* with a foregone conclusion, not the other way around. He'd been married to her long enough to know that all she wanted deep down was to lessen her responsibility for whatever happened between them. That way, if things went wrong, she could remember that it was his hand that had found its way under her robe first. The sequence of events was very important to a woman. All women.

"Been skiing lately?" he muttered as he ran his tongue around the areola.

Serena grabbed two handfuls of his wet hair and jerked his head up so she could see his face. "Listen, Michael, if you make a joke of this, I'm going to kick you in the balls and walk out."

"God, you're beautiful."

She still had his hair in her fists. Instead of letting go, she pulled his face to hers and kissed him the way she used to when they were in lust. In the process his towel fell away and her robe slipped open.

Her skin was cool and dry and soft. His genitals had been full from the moment he'd seen her on his bed, but now he was hard as oak. Serena found his sex. When he touched her between the legs, she brushed his hand away. She was already wet.

"Just do me, Michael," she murmured, biting at his lips.

Serena was a woman who knew her mind and her body. She had never needed much prompting or encouragement when it came to sex. "I screw like a man," she'd told him once a long time ago, "and I am proud of it." It took awhile before he understood what she meant. "I'm never at a disadvantage," was the true meaning. But she knew how to submit. "Control in bed is knowing how to get the most out of your body." At that she was a master.

Serena knew how to be unselfish with her loving, especially when it was the second or third time a night. She could make erections out of mush. But that first time—that first orgasm—was usually hers. She loved to ride her excitement like a bucking bronco. Mike found that fearlessness, that greed, electrifying.

She hungrily took in his sex. Mike's instincts gained control. He submitted to the impulse to possess and dominate.

She came as quickly as he, her body rippling under him, mindless, but with a will of its own. Unbridled.

He could still feel her body pulsing. Her arms dropped to the bed and she lay there, absorbed in her pleasure. This was the payoff. The itch had been scratched.

"Dear God, Michael," she murmured.

Her feelings for him were the farthest thing from her mind—it saddened him that he couldn't say the same. Not that she was unaware of him, but he could tell she didn't want to think about what it might have meant.

It took awhile before she opened her eyes. When she looked at him, he saw her register his presence. She pushed his wet hair off his forehead in an affectionate, almost maternal way. Then she kissed him tenderly on the mouth. It was more loving than anything that had gone before.

"Thank you for indulging me," she whispered.

Mike smiled as if to say it was all right, she was welcome.

It was time to disengage. He rolled off her, able to relax for the first time. He savored the satisfaction of release, but not as thoroughly as he sometimes did.

In a gesture of kindness, Serena took his hand, intertwining her fingers in his. She sighed, unperturbed, fulfilled.

Oddly, he thought of Connie Meyers. He thought of her sadness in particular, the sadness that comes after sex. Rio was a long way from her trailer in Vegas, but he was there in a strange sort of way. Serena had nothing to do with the feeling. It was him, pure and simple.

She pressed his hand in hers. "Say you don't hate me."

"I don't hate you."

"Do you mean it?"

"No, I don't mean it."

"Really?"

"Yes, really," he said. "But I don't hate you a lot."

"Just a little?"

"Yeah, just a little."

"I guess I can live with that. If you can."

He smiled slightly.

"I feel a lot better. Thanks for indulging me," she repeated.

"My pleasure."

"I'd like to think you were feeling what I'm feeling."

"What are you feeling?"

She didn't answer right away. She was giving the question due consideration. "Free," she finally said. "I feel free."

"Free of what?"

"That monkey that was on our backs."

"Lust?"

"Yes." She turned toward him. "I feel as though we can be friends now, Michael. Does that make sense?"

"Yes, I suppose so."

There was a short silence in which the only sound was the hum of the air-conditioning and the muffled purr of the traffic on the Avenida Atlântica. She propped her head in her hand and rubbed his chest. "You okay?"

"Yeah."

"No regrets?"

"No, how about you?"

"I'm fine," she said. "More than fine, if you are."

"I'm cool." He knew they were talking around the thing without addressing it. "Ninety percent relief and ten percent sadness," he said. "To be completely honest."

"Yes, ten percent."

"It'll make the friendship nicer and easier," he said. "I'm glad we did it."

"I'm glad, too." She kissed the corner of his mouth. "Really glad." She got up, cinching the belt of her robe. "Now I'm going to get some sleep." She went to the door, where she stopped. "The best sleep is after sex."

"Yeah, but it can be addictive," he said. "It's bad to rely on it. Worse even than sleeping pills."

"Right," she said.

"Friends," he said.

"Friends, Michael."

She disappeared into the sitting room, her bare feet not making a sound on the tile floor. Before he went to sleep, Mike opened the window to let in the tropical air.

He crawled back into bed, and his head had scarcely settled onto the pillow before he drifted off. In his dreams he wasn't in Rio. He was up at Meyson Lake in the Sierras. Jason wasn't with him, though. Nor was Connie or even Serena. The only one around was that deputy sheriff in the sunglasses. He wasn't very friendly. In the dream he was a sonovabitch and he was coming after Mike with his gun.

Serena awoke before the telephone rang, though not completely. She fumbled for the receiver.

"Hello?"

"Mrs. Bouchard?"

"Yes?"

"It's Bebe. I have something for Mr. Hamlin. Is this a good time to come bring it to him?"

Serena had to gather herself. "Michael may be asleep . . . but he loves surprises, so why not?" She stifled a yawn. "Where are you, dear?"

"At a telephone in the street nearby."

That struck Serena as strange. Why didn't the girl come to the hotel and use a house phone? She was probably shy about big expensive hotels, perhaps even intimidated by them. Bebe had no pretensions whatsoever. Serena had spotted that right away. She told her to come on over, giving her their suite number.

The curtains were drawn, so Serena had no feel for what time it was. All she knew for sure was that it was daylight. Turning on the lamp, she checked her watch. It was early afternoon. That meant she'd had only a couple of hours sleep.

She started to get out of bed to rouse Michael, then wondered if she should. Bebe hadn't said she needed to speak with him, only that she had something for him. Serena wondered what it could be. The key to her apartment? No, fast as Michael was, he wasn't that quick. Certainly not with this particular girl under these particular circumstances. If anything, Michael would be *needing* help with Bebe. The sexy little fox had to be pushed in the right direction by an older, wiser sister.

It was remarkable that Serena should be plotting Bebe's seduction. But then, why not? She'd gotten what she wanted—this time. In Tahoe it had been different. Michael had had the upper hand. That had been his triumph. This had been hers. Besides, they both knew he still loved her.

Bebe, she realized, could be knocking on the door at any moment. Serena's vanity wouldn't allow her to look less than eighty-five percent perfect, so she went into her bath and splashed cold water on her face. She examined the results. Seventy percent would have to do. She slipped on a caftan and went to the sitting room to wait.

Serena had to admit that she found Bebe as fascinating as Michael did. There were times when one woman could appreciate another, and this was one of those times. Serena simply couldn't see Bebe as a competitor. It would have been like being jealous of a panther or an exotic bird.

The light knock came sooner than Serena expected. When she opened the door, she found Bebe, dressed as before, as aloof as she was shy, an icy chocolate shake on a steamy summer day. This was a woman a man surely wanted to drink.

"*Boa tarde,* Senhora Bouchard," the girl said.

It was all Serena could do not to gape. Such loveliness.

"Hello, Bebe," she said, feeling an uncharacteristic humility. "Please come in."

Bebe glanced around the suite with reverence. Serena wondered if she'd ever been in a hotel room three times the size of one of those hillside hovels. It appeared unlikely, judging by her demeanor. As regal as Bebe was, she seemed like a princess visiting her very first castle.

Serena gestured for her to sit on the sofa. "Michael, the poor dear, is sleeping like a baby," she said, "so I didn't have the heart to wake him. I'll let him sleep unless it's important that you talk to him personally."

Bebe lowered herself gingerly to the edge of the sofa cushion, her shapely legs curving under her like the sensuous lines of a Benny Buffano sculpture. "No," she said, "I don't have to speak to him." She lifted her purse to her lap. "He asked Koto for a gun, and I wanted to say to him with apologies that I will not have it until the morning. But because we have concern for his safety, I wanted him to have mine until the other one comes."

With that, Bebe reached into her purse and removed a silver-plated handgun, weighing it in the palm of her long, slender hand. Serena all but gasped. The shiny instrument seemed oddly malevolent, completely incongruous with the Valkyrie holding it.

"Oh," Serena said, eyeing the device like it was a serpent. "That's for Michael?"

"He said he wanted a gun, *senhora,* yes."

Bebe extended the weapon. Serena took it with about the same enthusiasm she'd have had for a dead mouse. Having grasped it by the top, she wasn't sure what to do with it until pride took over and she lay the grip in her hand, the way it was obviously meant to be held. The metal was unexpectedly warm and the weapon seemed heavy. And angry. She stared down at it, thinking that the shiny surface was somehow vulgar.

"This is the first time I've ever held a gun," she confessed.

Bebe seemed neither surprised nor amused. Her expression was nonjudgmental.

Serena had an urge to lift the gun and point it at something—the painting of the peasant women on the wall across the room, the window, Michael's door. Funny how it was heinous and alluring at the same time. She put it on the table.

"I'll see that he gets it."

"Please tell him I'm sorry that he will not have his own until tomorrow."

"I'm sure he'll understand."

"This gun is a good one," Bebe said, sounding as though she might be discussing the latest Judith Leiber handbag. She stared at it with due solemnity.

Serena couldn't resist. "Have you ever used this thing?"

"Me?"

"Yes, have you ever shot it?"

"Of course, *senhora*. Many times."

"At a person?"

Bebe hesitated, then a smile crept across her sensuous mouth. Teeth as white and strong and perfect as any ever made by God shone from between her lips. "Do you want me to say no?"

It struck Serena then, at that very moment, that Bebe was the perfect mate for Michael. Granted, it was an impossible match on the surface, but at the level of the soul they were as syncretic as any two beings could be. That phrase she'd used—"Do you want me to say no?"—Michael could have said . . . would have said.

"*Senhora*," Bebe continued, "never have I shot anyone who didn't deserve it."

Serena couldn't help herself; she laughed gleefully. *Adorable*. That was the only way to describe this child.

"Bebe, I'm sure you wouldn't, and neither would Michael."

The girl seemed confused. "*Senhora?*"

"I'm sure Michael would use your gun with pride, if he had to. And with the same spirit."

"Senhora Bouchard, I do not understand."

"Of course you don't. That's because I'm not making much sense," Serena said, more giddy by the moment. "Jet lag, dear."

"Oh. I see. *Compreendo, senhora.*"

"Listen," Serena said, lowering her voice conspiratorially, "I want to tell you something about Michael."

"*Sim?* Senhor Hamlin?"

"Yes, Michael is an exceptionally sensitive, compassionate, caring person. Do you understand?"

"Yes."

"I hired him as much for his heart as for his knowledge and skill. You see, I feel about Michael much like Koto feels about you, Bebe. He's trustworthy, honest, sincere, decent, thoughtful."

Sweet Bebe's expression turned serious. "These are not the usual things in a man. Very rare."

"Very rare, indeed."

"You are fortunate to have him as your employee."

"It's only temporary. Michael is helping me out of a sense of duty. His obligation to me is limited."

"I see."

"I'm telling you this, Bebe, because you and Michael will be working together, trying to get to the bottom of Drake Manville's murder. I think it is important that you know the man, that you know he can be trusted."

"This is important, coming from you, *senhora.*"

Serena smiled, feeling deep satisfaction at her generous deed. "I care about Michael, and I care about you. The more we can do for each other, the better it is for us all."

Bebe pondered that. "I am very happy for this conversation, *senhora.* I have much respect for your words and for your heart."

Serena reached out and took the girl's hands. They smiled into each other's eyes.

"It is best if I go," Bebe said. "I have taken much time."

"Don't worry, dear. I'm glad we've had this little chat."

They got up and Serena walked her to the door. Again they shook hands, and Bebe left with a little more swing in her step than before. Serena watched her go down the hall, then closed the door, leaning against it. She beamed the be-atific smile of a saint. "Michael, darling, you owe me," she mumbled. "Big time."

Serena was no sooner back in her room than Roberto Cabral phoned. Once again his resonant voice reached right out and seized her gut. He had a magnificent voice, the auditory equivalent of Bebe's sleek body. He probably looked like a cobbler, but it hardly mattered. He could make a fortune doing phone sex if the legal business ever dried up.

"Was your flight satisfactory, Senhora Bouchard?" His tone was between a rumble and a purr.

"Long, Mr. Cabral. Flights are either long or short, with or without food and sleep."

"Los Angeles is very far, no? But you are here now and so we must meet," he said. He could just as easily have said, "Come with me to the Casbah, my darling."

"Yes, we must," she said, mirroring his seductive tone, though she reminded herself she was speaking to someone who more likely looked like Gepetto than Cesar Romero.

"Would I be too impetuous to ask if you have plans for dinner, *senhora?*" he asked.

Oh, Roberto, she thought, I'd rather be in love with your voice than look at your gnarly little face and crooked teeth. She told herself it was unavoidable, though. "No plans," she said.

"May I ask for the honor of your company, then? I know you are eager for word of your brother."

"Very eager, Mr. Cabral."

"Perhaps a light meal in the hotel would be suitable," he said. "I imagine you have no taste for extravagance after your long day."

"That's true."

"Shall we say eight?"

"Perfect."

"Until eight, then. *Ciao, senhora.*"

Serena let the receiver slip gently into the cradle and sighed, hoping to God he didn't have too much hair growing out of his ears. A man didn't have to be beautiful to be attractive, but certain negatives had to be avoided.

But then she asked herself what she was doing thinking this way. Because of the man's voice? No, it probably had more to do with Bebe and Michael. She wanted to play, too, even if that was not why she'd come to Rio. Flirting was like breathing. It was the way she tested her vital signs.

"London?"

Serena glanced up at the sound of Michael's voice. He was standing in the doorway in his shorts, an instant reminder of their lovemaking.

"No, Mr. Cabral, my lawyer. We're having dinner at eight."

"Oh. I trust I'm not on the guest list."

Serena realized she hadn't even thought of Michael. "You aren't obligated, but you're certainly welcome."

"I'd prefer not to bullshit with a lawyer, if you want to know the truth."

"That's fine," she said, staring at his bare chest. "Do as you wish."

Michael had a wonderful chest. Rubbing together had been one of the things they'd relished. Seeing him and recalling what had transpired only hours ago gave her a sudden feeling of regret about Bebe. Serena was sorry now she'd been so magnanimous. But it was only a fleeting thought. She shook it off.

"What's with the peashooter?" he asked. "Were we visited by the gun fairy or is the Brazilian NRA even more zealous than the bunch back home?"

"Bebe loaned you her gun because the one you ordered won't be available until tomorrow."

"She was here?"

"In all her glory."

Michael smiled.

"I know it was painful to have missed her, but she'll be back," Serena said.

"And that's fine with you?" he asked.

"We have our agreement, Michael. As far as I'm concerned, the itch was successfully scratched. I hope you feel the same."

"I'm cool."

"Good."

"So, what's the plan?"

She contemplated him pleasantly. "You're free tonight. Rio is yours this evening. Tomorrow we go to work."

"Check," he said. After giving her a long, lazy look, he left the room.

Serena sat alone with her thoughts for a couple of minutes, then went to her bath to take a shower. After dressing, she went downstairs, thinking she'd have a taxi drive her up and down the Avenida Atlântica. The concierge, a heavyset man with a large mustache, dissuaded her, saying that if she wanted to venture into town, she would need a car and a trusted driver, not a common taxi. It wasn't safe.

Serena elected instead to browse through the hotel shops, spending quite a bit of time in a tony, touristy jewelry store called Gummel's. As she looked at emeralds she thought of her mother and their shopping spree in Rio all those years ago. A pair of emerald drop earrings caught her eye. They seemed overpriced, and the stones were small, but she bought them. If she didn't like them after a few wearings she'd give them to Christina.

When she returned to the suite she found Michael on the sofa in the sitting room, reading a paperback. Dusk had fallen and the soft light coming from the windows was iridescent. He was in jeans and a fresh shirt and looked...well, husbandly. She showed him the earrings.

"Nice," he said.

"I was thinking of wearing them tonight when I dine with Senhor Cabral, but I'm not sure what would go best with them."

"Maybe something green," he said.

"That's a thought."

He gave her an ironic look, then turned his attention back to his book. Serena sat opposite him, crossing her legs. He pretended to ignore her.

"What are your plans for tonight?" she asked.

He glanced up from his book. "I haven't decided."

"You should see something of Rio while you're here," she said. "It would be a shame to spend all your time in the hotel."

"I thought I might find a little restaurant in a while, then roam around Copacabana after dinner."

It struck her as a fun idea, the sort of thing she would have enjoyed doing with him once upon a time, but she could hardly say so.

"Do you think it's safe for you to go out alone at night? I mean, after what happened with that man, Ribeiro, in L.A.?"

"What do you suggest? That I hire a bodyguard?"

"Don't be cross. I'm concerned for your safety."

"I'll be fine, Serena. Just worry about dinner with the lawyer."

She stared at Michael, who was doing a good job of ignoring her. It irritated her that he did it so well. She checked her watch. It was past time to get dressed, so she went off to her room, wondering if Michael was looking at her backside. Not that it mattered. This was the first day of the rest of their trip, and she was determined that it would be celibate from here on out.

Mike tried to read, but he was having trouble concentrating. Serena—probably without intending it—had upset him. He knew having sex with her would be a mistake even before he'd given in to the temptation. But they'd done it, and he had no choice now but to deal with it.

After struggling to read for another twenty minutes, he was spared by a knock at the door. He put down his book and went to see who was there. The man standing in the hall seemed as surprised as he.

"Pardon, but is this the room of Mrs. Serena Bouchard?" he asked in careful English.

The man was darkly handsome and mature—perhaps fifty or fifty-five. He was in a dark blue double-breasted suit that draped perfectly from his broad shoulders. He wore a pearl gray tie and stylish black Italian shoes. He was neither tall nor heavy, but he had a substantial physical presence, the air of a man of consequence.

"This is the place," Mike said. "You must be the lawyer."

"Roberto Cabral, *senhor,*" he said, extending his hand. "And you are?"

"Mike Hamlin. Serena's . . . associate." He gestured for Cabral to enter.

"Business associate?"

"Security advisor," Mike said, anticipating the formulation Serena would likely have used.

"Ah, I see," Cabral said, his voice melodious.

They went to the sitting area.

"Make yourself at home," Mike said. "I'll just let Serena know you're here."

He went and rapped lightly on her door to let her know her guest had arrived.

"I'll be right out," she called.

Mike returned to Cabral, who'd remained standing. "She's about ready," he said, "but you might as well get comfortable."

Cabral unbuttoned his suit jacket and dropped into an easy chair. Mike could not recall ever having encountered anyone this suave before. The guy was so smooth he was almost a caricature of the old-school Latin lover. This was not someone Mike could relate to well, though there wasn't anything especially pernicious about him. Cabral wasn't oily—a little staged, maybe, but not oily.

They exchanged pleasantries and were chatting about Rio when the door opened and Serena made her entrance. She looked fresh and softly elegant in a pale beige silk dress and the new emerald earrings. There was nothing overtly sexy or provocative about the way she was dressed, but Serena always brought her own special brand of sexuality to every occasion.

Cabral was on his feet and appropriately in awe. Her beauty was obviously unexpected.

"Mr. Cabral," she said, offering her hand. "I'm Serena Bouchard."

The Brazilian took her hand like it was a flower, gently drawing it to him, his eyes lively and shining. "Senhora Bouchard, it is indeed a pleasure." He kissed her hand.

Serena took her measure of him, obviously impressed. Mike stepped back, aware that a mating dance was already in progress. Energy was flowing from both of them, Serena's electricity and Cabral's magnetism almost tangible. The realization made him vaguely sick.

"I've heard so many wonderful things about you, Mr. Cabral," she said, going straight for his ego like a radar-guided bomb.

"Rumor and exaggeration," he replied, deflecting nicely.

"Don't say that," she warned, "or I'll have to find a man worthy of his reputation."

Cabral laughed heartily. "You force me to be immodest, *senhora,* and that is unkind."

Serena shot Mike a tiny conspiratorial smile. "Mr. Cabral, I'm a woman who's very clear about what she wants. How can anything that honest be unkind?"

"I shall do my best to serve you, madam," the Brazilian said gallantly. "I can't promise you more."

"Oh, but you must. I want your word that you'll see that my brother is freed. And soon." Serena shifted gears. "You've met Michael and know he's here to assist with the investigation."

"Yes," Cabral said, "Mr. Hamlin explained."

"I don't suppose he mentioned he was also once my husband."

Roberto Cabral's brows rose, as did Mike's.

Serena continued. "We've been divorced for several years, but remain—as you see—on excellent terms. I trust

Michael implicitly and wouldn't undertake a mission this important without him." She looked back and forth between them. "I'm telling you this, Mr. Cabral, because I like doing business with all my cards on the table. You can help us best if you know the situation."

"I understand."

"So, with your permission," she said, "I'd like to spend a few minutes talking about my brother's case while we have Michael with us. Why don't we sit down, gentlemen?"

Serena took the other armchair, leaving them to take their previous places. Mike noticed Cabral checking out Serena's legs. The old Latin lover's wheels had been turning in his head from the moment she'd walked into the room—not that the guy was totally transparent, but his mind had obviously jumped from the pursuit of prospective fees to the contemplation of prospective conquests.

"Mr. Kotomata indicated this afternoon that you may have more current information than his, Mr. Cabral," she said. "Could you bring us up-to-date, please?"

"Certainly, *senhora*."

Serena settled back in her chair, crossing her legs. Mike leaned back into the cushions of the sofa, wondering how many women could climb into a guy's bed, screw him into submission and then, in the course of a few hours, treat him to the drawing and quartering of a rival. Only Serena Bouchard had the balls and the gall for that kind of emotional gymnastics.

There was a tiny, self-satisfied smile at the corner of her mouth that betrayed her game. But he had trouble identifying the exact source of her pleasure—Cabral himself, or the fact that she'd already taken the lawyer prisoner. If that wasn't bad enough, she refused to give Mike a clue.

"Michael," she said in her patented businesslike tone, "what do we most need to know?"

"I'd like to find out if the authorities have a case."

Cabral cleared his throat. "I regret to say that the latest information is not good. Senhor Bouchard's fingerprints were indeed found on the weapon. And it turns out there is a witness."

"A witness?" Mike said.

The timbre in his voice made Serena turn toward him. He saw fear in her eyes. That was rare.

"Not a devastating one," the lawyer said, "but one that most certainly does not help our situation."

"What kind of witness?" Serena asked, her voice smaller, less assured than before. "Who?"

"A neighbor saw Mr. Bouchard depart from the villa moments after a shot was fired. It is most troubling, I'm afraid."

Mike and Serena exchanged looks.

"There must be an explanation," Serena said. "What did my brother say?"

"Mr. Bouchard has said that as he arrived at the villa, he saw a woman run out, jump in a car and drive away. Unfortunately, he did not get a good look and cannot identify her."

"How about the car?" Mike said.

"Nor the car, *senhor*."

"What did Jeffrey do next?"

"Mr. Bouchard told me he went into the villa to find Mr. Manville shot dead on the floor of the study, a gun on the desk. He picked up the gun, not thinking it was a terrible mistake to touch the weapon. He had a panic and ran out of the villa, fearful he would be implicated."

"There's your explanation," Serena said. "The woman shot Drake, and Jeffrey's prints were on the gun because he foolishly touched it. The neighbor saw him when he panicked and ran away."

"This is Mr. Bouchard's story, you are right, *senhora*. But based on the word of the witness, there wasn't time from when the shot was heard until she saw Mr. Bouchard for these other events to occur. The neighbor said she heard a shot, went to her window and moments later saw Mr. Bouchard come out of the villa. This directly contradicts the story your brother has given."

"Well, this neighbor could be lying or mistaken. Is there a reason to believe she's more credible than Jeffrey? Maybe the shot that killed Drake happened earlier. The neighbor may have heard a car backfire. I can imagine several possibilities, and I haven't even studied the matter. My interpretation could be just as plausible as the conclusions the police are drawing. Isn't that right, Michael?"

He gave a half shrug. "Maybe, Serena. I'd have to look at the evidence before drawing any conclusions."

Her glare was withering. "Well, this has spoiled my mood. I've been feeling optimistic all day, and now this."

"*Senhora,*" Cabral pleaded, "please don't despair. The information is preliminary. The police admit their investigation continues. There may be undiscovered information that shows the innocence of your brother."

Mike couldn't help but be amused. What the bastard was angling for was a piece of ass, not a verdict of innocence. Serena had to be aware of that. She probably wanted reassurance. The trouble was, Cabral's opinion didn't matter. The authorities, the prosecutors in particular, were the ones who counted. And if the defense couldn't convince them of Jeffrey's innocence, it would be in the hands of the courts. If she was going to screw anybody for Jeffrey's sake, it should be the judge, not Cabral.

"I'm not a woman who likes to play games," Serena said as she stared straight into Cabral's eyes. "I want a direct and honest answer, if you don't mind. Do the police have a case against my brother, or is it just posturing and bravado?"

Cabral clearly did not like being put on the spot. "It's early," he said, taking another deft side step.

"Mr. Cabral," she said, her voice inveigling and vaguely accusatory, "any cobbler could tell me that."

"*Senhora,*" Cabral said, rising to the challenge, "it is foolish to fire one's weapon before the target presents itself. You are asking me if I can kill a stag I have not yet seen."

Mike had to admire the riposte.

"You have a point," Serena said.

"My dear Mrs. Bouchard," Cabral said soberly, his deep voice taking on an even more resonant tone, "I have promised you to do my best to secure the release of your brother."

"Yes, I know you have."

"Well, I must ask something of you in return."

"What is that, Mr. Cabral?"

"I would like your trust, but also a promise."

Serena leaned slightly forward, increasingly mesmerized, judging by her reaction. "What sort of promise?"

"That you will let me worry about your brother. I am paid to assume the burden and could not in good conscience serve you, knowing you are doubtful and unsure."

Mike would have stuck his finger in his mouth and gagged himself, but he knew Serena would never forgive him. So he held his tongue and waited for her reaction.

"Let's go to dinner, Senhor Cabral," she said. "The better we know each other, the better we can work together. Jeffrey is too important to me not to do everything within my power to save him."

She rose, Roberto Cabral rising with her. Mike didn't bother getting up. The Brazilian offered Serena his arm. She smiled. He smiled. Mike wanted to retch.

She did give him a brief glance, however. "Have a nice evening, Michael," she said as Cabral led her away. "And be careful. I'm going to be needing you."

They were at the door. Cabral opened it for her. Serena went out. The man looked Mike's way before stepping out.

"It was most enjoyable meeting you, *senhor.*"

"The pleasure was entirely mine, Roberto."

Cabral gave him a final, triumphant look, then went off with the woman Mike had been in bed with only hours before. Have fun, Serena, he thought sardonically. And don't let the bedbugs bite.

Mike had no desire to sit around alone, so he tucked Bebe's automatic into his belt, slipped on a sport coat, stuck about forty dollars' worth of cruzeiros in his pocket and hit the streets. The Avenida Atlântica was crowded with people and traffic, but the real action seemed to be in the narrow streets behind the hotel. He headed in that direction.

Once beyond the shadow of the hotel, Mike found the people of Rio. A couple of hookers had sweet words for him. Men leaning against building fronts watched him pass. Eyes engaged him with mild curiosity. Rio was a big, racially diverse city, but he couldn't hide the fact that he was foreign and therefore vulnerable.

A kid with a shoeshine box ran up to him, making imploring sounds and tugging on his sleeve. Mike continued on without breaking stride, figuring the routine he'd used in Tijuana would work in Rio. The kid shouted what Mike took to be an obscenity before he retreated.

The shoeshine boy did bring to mind Joe Murdoch's remark about watching his backside, and Mike immediately crossed to the other side of the street, dodging a motor scooter as he looked back to see if anyone was following. Ironically, he felt the most paranoid when packing a gun. It was as though in being prepared, one invited trouble.

Mike strolled along, studying faces that came in a variety of shades and colors. A pretty mulatto girl in a bright yellow skirt laughing with friends reminded him of Bebe. He felt a strange emptiness at the thought of the girl-woman who'd dazzled him so, perhaps as much because of what had happened with Serena that afternoon as his feelings about Bebe herself.

In a way he regretted coming to Rio, regretted screwing Serena, regretted wanting to screw Bebe. Over the years he'd discovered that there could be a lot of emptiness in sexual desire and precious little satisfaction in empty sex. Yet he looked at the ripe young bodies on the street and felt lustful, knowing there were certain things a man was almost powerless to deny.

The alternative, sad to say, was pizza and a night of TV with a woman like Connie Meyers. But how long could a guy be content with that? After a while the little dish at the bowling alley or the one in the shipping department would start to look appealing. It was a trap he wanted to avoid, which probably explained his inability to let go of Serena, the one woman who couldn't bore him if she tried.

He resolved not to think of her—not because it was painful but because there was nothing to be gained. She'd beaten him once on this trip—exacting her revenge for the revenge he'd gotten in Tahoe—and there was no point in giving her more. Not that Serena wanted to hurt him. She would never see seducing him, or anyone else, that way. She simply had a need to be herself and that meant being in control. Not just of events, but of feelings.

"*Boa noite, senhor,*" the prostitutes said as he passed by. "You want love?"

He continued along, ignoring the solicitations, taking in the vibrant atmosphere—the cheap perfume, the cooking odors, the laughter, the syncopation of the music, the pulse and throb of life.

The people, he noticed, were mostly young, not surprising considering the average age of the population was probably eighteen. He felt old here, which was odd because at home he felt young—perhaps because he identified with the hotel and casino staff rather than the gambling public, much of whom tended to be slightly gray, slightly tired and doggedly in search of their personal El Dorado.

Mike crossed the street again, checking his rear, then went around a corner onto a busy cross street, this one lined with bars. He'd stumbled on the red-light district, which, though not glittery, had the smell of sex-for-sale. Behind the shop fronts with discreet signs bearing names like Erotika, The Pussy Cat, and Don Juan, a commerce of love was in progress. Doormen in polo shirts with bulging muscles, tattoos, trimmed mustaches and gold chains around their necks purred a subtle invitation.

"Come, *senhor,* have a look at the girls."

Koto had told him to stay to the east end of the beach because the west end was populated by the homosexual clubs, where the atmosphere was convivial, but suitable only for men with the appropriate inclinations. Mike didn't have to be warned twice. Not that heterosexual prostitutes were all that alluring. Apart from a couple of obligatory visits to a whorehouse during his stint in the navy, he was a stranger to the scene.

But sex wasn't the reason he was out. He'd intended to eat, and the smells from the cafés had sparked his appetite. Wedged between two clubs, he found a small *churrascaria rodizio,* a barbecue house. Koto had told him *rodizios* were the best food value and were uniquely Brazilian.

It turned out Koto was right. The waiter kept bringing barbecued meat to the table, carving it there. Mike finally had to call it quits. After finishing, he returned to the street, feeling well fed and a little more at ease. For a minute he stood at the door of the restaurant, surveying the milling crowd. Then he proceeded to stroll.

A block or so farther along he succumbed to the inveigling of a particularly charming barker and stuck his head inside the door of a club called She. A girl in a bikini top and what looked like skimpy jogging shorts immediately came to escort him to a table, but Mike told her he wasn't sure he wanted to stay. Looking across the darkened interior, he saw a naked woman slowly dancing on an elevated platform. It was a strip joint, but not the usual variety. At least a third of the patrons were women, and the atmosphere was less sleazy than the typical American dive.

Having no particular desire to watch naked women dance after a day of Serena and Bebe, he returned to the street. Once again he surveyed the crowd, spotting a face he thought he had seen earlier. It was a guy in his mid- to late forties. He was leaning against a building opposite the club. He was small and thin, wearing a white shirt and baggy pants. A coincidence that the face was familiar? Or was he following him?

The guy, who had the look of a weasel, didn't appear particularly threatening, though he could have been some sort of lowlife—a pimp or a pickpocket, maybe. Mike started up the street. After thirty yards, he checked. The guy was following, keeping a distance. Maybe Mike had reason to be paranoid, after all.

He ticked off the possibilities again—hustler, pickpocket, mugger, pimp or another friend of Joachim Monteiro da Silva's. This little weasel didn't seem in the same league with the heavy who'd been flattened by the mail truck at the corner of Sepulveda and Manchester, but one never knew. It stood to reason that if Joachim had sent Ribeiro to L.A. and Vegas to check up on him, he'd be watching him here, in his own backyard.

There was a quick way to find out. Mike turned on his heel and walked directly toward the Weasel. The man's eyes rounded at Mike's approach. He turned and started walking briskly in the other direction, beating a hasty retreat.

Mike started after him. The Weasel speeded up. Mike did, too. The man began a slow jog; Mike did the same. Heads turned as they passed. The Weasel grew more alarmed, acting like a scared rabbit. Glancing over his shoulder, he almost knocked over a sailor coming out of a bar. He broke into a run.

Despite the meal and the beer, Mike was kind of enjoying the chase. It was good exercise, and it seemed to be putting the fear of God into the little mole who'd been tailing him. Mike figured the worse that could happen was he'd run into a cop and get a language lesson.

It was obvious the Weasel wasn't a jock. He was breathing hard, his gait labored. Fear seemed to carry him along.

Half a block farther, the Weasel made a sharp right into a narrow, dark alley that appeared to have no outlet. Mike stopped at the mouth. He could see the Weasel limping in the shadows. A streetlight lit the end of the cul de sac. The buildings were shoulder-to-shoulder, affording no discernable route of escape. The Weasel appeared not to realize he was trapped until he reached the end and stopped under the lamppost.

Mike was beginning to feel like a boxer in a mismatched fight, though he knew the Weasel was in home territory and had darkness on his side. Mike checked the gun at his belt and started down the alley, his heels clicking on the cobblestones.

The beauty of the scene pleased him. The Weasel looked scared shitless. Mike wondered why. What did he have to fear? The only explanation was that he'd been up to no good.

When Mike was maybe fifteen or twenty yards away he called out, "You speak English?"

The Weasel muttered an unintelligible response. Mike figured it was an expletive.

"*Inglés, amigo?*" Mike's voice echoed in the close quarters of the alley.

There was another muffled response, then another, sounding almost like a plea for help. Why was the guy agitated? It didn't seem like the Weasel was trying to communicate with him. Suddenly Mike realized the man's pleas were probably directed at someone else. But it was too late.

He heard heels clicking on the cobblestones behind him. He spun around and saw the silhouettes of three men outlined against the streetlight. These guys were bigger than the Weasel. In that brief instant Mike realized he'd made the same mistake as George Armstrong Custer. He'd been lured into a trap.

Traffic was passing by in the street, not a hundred and fifty feet away. The world was there, just behind the three menacing figures facing him. There was an ugly irony to what was happening.

It was one of those moments rich in sensory perception—like a glimpse of the other driver an instant before a head-on collision. "Hamlin, you fool," he muttered. He'd read about the Battle of Little Big Horn as a boy, wondering how Custer could have been so blinded by the illusion of his own invincibility. For the first time he truly understood.

"You talking to yourself, amigo?" one of the men said. Their faces were obscured in shadow, which was probably the way they wanted it.

Mike slowly slid his hand under the flap of his jacket and gripped the handle of the automatic. "Just reviewing history. Something I can do for you boys?"

"*Sim, senhor.* Maybe there is."

It was then that Mike saw the guys were packing more than bows and arrows. In the faint light he could see the glint of metal in their hands. He was both outnumbered and outgunned.

"What might that be, friend?" he said, resorting to false bravado. He quickly calculated his options. They most likely didn't know he was armed, which gave him the element of surprise. He could probably shoot one of them without a problem, two if he was lucky. From there the odds started going downhill rapidly. It made more sense to talk than to start shooting when he couldn't even be sure of their intentions.

The men were facing him, about twenty feet away, poised for action. The guy in the middle seemed to be the spokesman. "You the Yankee from Los Angeles? Your name Hamlin?"

There probably wasn't much point in denying it, but it was the next question Mike was more concerned about. He hoped it wasn't "Do you know Eduardo Ribeiro?" Mike had no particular desire to meet up with poor ol' Eduardo's friends. But at this juncture, he didn't have much control over events.

"I'm Mike Hamlin."

"Listen, then, Mr. Hamlin," the heavy said, in a tone worthy of George Raft but with an accent that was all wrong. "It's time you go home to America, *comprendes?* You had a nice dinner, maybe on your way back to your hotel you stop and have a nice fuck. But in the morning you go home. Brazil is a nice place, yes, but it's not nice for you."

"Says who?"

"Says me."

"You guys obviously aren't from the tourist board."

"Shut up, Hamlin! This is no comedy."

George was obviously losing patience. Mike quickly checked for an avenue of escape—a stairway, an open door—but there wasn't one. He had the Weasel behind him and three stooges in front. His options were extremely limited.

The buildings on either side of the alley were two or three stories high. There were few lights on. Mike doubted that a scuffle would draw much attention. And Bebe hadn't taught him the word for help.

"You understand what I say to you?" George asked. "Or do we have to make it more clear?"

Mike's eyes had grown accustomed to the darkness and he was able to make out their faces. George was dark but European, the shortest of the three. The guy on the left was black, the one on the right something in-between.

"I understand," Mike said. "But I want you to tell Monteiro da Silva something for me. I don't like strong-arm tactics. If he's got a problem with me being in Rio, he can tell me himself."

"I guess you don't understand, Mr. Hamlin," George said. "So we will show you we are serious." Giving a curt command, he and the two goons moved on him in unison.

Mike had decided this wasn't a hit or he'd already be dead. It was a game of intimidation, a show of rough stuff. So he didn't pull his gun, figuring a few bruises were preferable to a hole in his chest. But he wouldn't go down easily.

The guy on the right got to him first. Mike gave him a karate kick to the scrotum that made him double over. He caught the black guy with an elbow to the head as he lunged. The man went down, but at the same moment George caught Mike square on the cheekbone with the butt of his gun, dropping him to the pavement. Mike didn't lose consciousness, but he was too stunned to jump to his feet. He was rolling over when two hundred pounds of foot caught him in the solar plexus, knocking the wind right out of him.

Mike knew it was over. And there was less doubt when the second man lunged on top of him, smelling like it had been two weeks since he'd been in a shower. His chest drove Mike's head into the pavement. Mike managed to roll him partway off, but the guy whose tire he'd deflated came up and returned the favor, kicking him in the balls. A white-hot pain went clear through his insides and he lay limp, unable to move, knowing there was no point in continuing the fight even if he could.

George hovered over him, his gun in his hand. He bent down, putting a knee against Mike's chest, settling his considerable weight on him.

"Listen, you creep," he snarled. Despite the pain racking his body, Mike couldn't help being amused by George's poor imitation of a gangster. "If you want to leave Brazil alive, you'd better be on an airplane tomorrow morning. *Comprendes?*"

After hurling a couple of maledictions in Portuguese, George grabbed Mike's head, digging his nails into his cheeks. It felt like a dog was trying to bite off his face. Then George slammed his skull against the pavement and stood up.

Mike lay there, seeing stars, virtually every part of his body in pain. He was aware of George turning and walking away. The genital specialist, who was standing nearby, kicked him in the thigh as a parting shot. The black guy was content to limp off, much to Mike's relief.

For a few seconds he didn't move. He could feel blood running down his face. He lifted his head to see his attackers walking out to the street. With their backs to him like this, he could probably have pulled his gun and gotten all three. There would have been no point, though, apart from revenge. Shooting three guys in the back with Bebe's gun would take some explaining, even if they *were* hoodlums. So he let them walk away.

A second later he heard footsteps from the other direction. He turned to see the Weasel. The little man gave him a wide berth, but Mike heard him spit as he passed. He didn't feel anything hit him, but the little bastard had made his point. Mike figured he and the Weasel were even. The other three he owed.

Mirante Dona Marta

It was the most magical sight she had ever seen, which was saying a lot because Serena had seen most of the world—all

the major European cities, the plains of Africa from the top
of Mount Kilimanjaro, the big Alps from the Jungfrau, Ko
Phuket in the Andaman Sea, and countless other international wonders. But none compared to Rio from the surrounding mountains at night.

Roberto had said the view from Corcovado was even
more spectacular, but the perspective from the patio at
Dona Marta Belvedere was nearly as good and they could
enjoy it in private. He had telephoned from the hotel to
make sure it would be open, just for them. Roberto insisted
the proprietors were friends and it cost him nothing to get
access, but Serena knew he was fibbing.

When they'd first stepped out onto the patio, she'd
gasped. She'd had glimpses of the city and bay from the
road, but this was like seeing it from an eagle's nest. Botafogo was directly below, the white buildings a cool gray in
the night, sparkling with amber and teal points of light.
Small boats speckled the bay, which in that section was
nearly surrounded by land. On the far side, the profile of
Sugarloaf rose from dark waters like a mythological sea
creature, guarding rather than threatening the town.

It was odd to be seeing it from above, and it was breathtaking. From their vantage point the center of Rio was to the
left, Copacabana, Ipanema and the dark Atlantic to their
right. Despite the glorious panorama, they were actually in
a forest with lush tropical vegetation. It was an Olympian
perspective. It was magnificent.

"This is incredible, Roberto," she said, leaning against
the railing as she peered out at the view.

"I thought you would enjoy it."

He stood off to the side, in the shadows, giving her space,
obviously taking pride in the gift he had given her. But he
was also doing some admiring of his own. From the moment she'd first walked out of her bedroom at the hotel, it
was clear he'd been smitten.

During dinner they'd engaged in a ritual mating dance,
but it soon became apparent that to Roberto it was more
than a simple case of attraction and flirtation. The man had
been knocked back on his heels. Serena took the usual

pleasure in that, but as the evening wore on she could tell that he was not just in lust, he was truly in the grip of a siren. And that fascinated her.

This was hardly the first time a man had fallen in love with her so quickly, so she knew the pitfalls. People tended to delude themselves, fall in love with their own expectations. The irony was she was sort of smitten herself, even knowing Roberto was practiced in the role of Latin lover. But he did it exceptionally well, and she couldn't help but be intrigued by a man with talent.

Like most women, she was especially vulnerable to passion—not routine desire, but all-consuming passion. Though he hadn't verbalized his feelings in those terms, Roberto could not hide the fact that he was lovestruck. Part of his allure was the flattery, but another was that she was feeling more needy than usual. She rationalized that Roberto, for all his macho gamesmanship, was really safe—as long as she kept things in perspective.

They'd already had their getting-acquainted conversation and had tacitly agreed on what was possible and what was not. Roberto was prepared to have a love affair—that was clear. He had a wife, of course, but they'd been separated forever. This, after all, was the largest Catholic country in the world. Divorce in Rio was more a state of mind than a legal status, so Serena knew she didn't have to be concerned about the wife—unless she wanted to become one herself, which she most assuredly didn't.

Right from the start she knew her interest in Roberto Cabral was limited to having fun. All that was in doubt was what kind of fun, and to what degree. The outcome would depend on her mood and his skill. She was interested enough to have left the door open. The rest was up to him.

"Tell me honestly," she said as she continued peering at the lights, "do you bring all your women up here after your first dinner date or only the tourists?"

"I have come here before with a woman," he replied, "but not with the same feeling in my heart, and not with the same intentions."

"Was that a slip or a fit of honesty?" she asked.

Roberto moved from the shadows. He slowly reached out and took her arms in his large hands, holding her slightly away from him. There was an air of dignity in the gesture, something a woman might have expected from a priest expressing a depth of feeling. "It is utmost honesty," he said, looking into her eyes.

"Then what are your intentions, Roberto?"

"To do your bidding. To make you happy. To share my joy for this life and this place that is my home."

"Lawyers have a very different approach to their work in Brazil, don't they?"

"This has nothing to do with my profession, dear one," he said. "It is the devotion I feel."

"And why do you feel devoted?"

"Because I have a great feeling for you, and I cannot help but express it."

Serena knew not to respond to that. Instead she turned away and slowly walked across the patio until she was under the boughs of a large flowering shrub. She couldn't tell what it was in the darkness, but its perfume was intense and distinctive.

"I hope it does not upset you that I say that," he said from where he stood.

"I haven't decided."

"Tell me your concern so that I can reassure you."

"You are very charming, Roberto, but I didn't come to Rio to be charmed. My purpose in coming is deadly serious."

"And my devotion to your cause is no less serious, dear Serena," he said softly, the timbre of his voice more distinctive than usual, its effect on her inescapable. "Your brother's welfare I place first. Above all."

"Then why are we even discussing personal feelings?"

Roberto leaned against the railing. Serena liked that he hadn't followed her across the patio. The man understood restraint.

"Secret feelings can become a poison if they go long unexpressed," he said. "I owe you the honesty of what I feel."

"And if I'm not interested?"

"Then I accede to your will. And if you feel I cannot, under the circumstances, serve as your legal advisor, then I shall withdraw from the case and find you another counselor."

It was not exactly a bold move, but she liked the sentiment. She decided to test him. "Is that true?"

"On my honor."

"So, if you had to choose, which would it be?"

"If it cannot be both, then the choice would be yours."

It was a little melodramatic, but she liked it. "You don't care which?"

"I care that you are content."

She said nothing for a time, nor did Roberto. They stood thirty feet apart, she in shadow, he in the dim, ambient light from the city below, his hand resting on the rail. Roberto had made his stand and he was letting the silence press his case. Serena knew what was happening. This was a negotiation. The first person to speak, the first to break under the pressure, was the one who lost.

She had already decided to give him the victory—if he was man enough to claim it—but she was not going to give it to him easily. Men should have to work for what they got, she believed, or they didn't value their triumph.

Roberto didn't move and didn't speak. He was like a statue. The Chinese were masters at this game. Serena had done more than one deal in Hong Kong and Taiwan. She wondered if Roberto had, as well. She let another half minute pass, then she let him off the hook.

"I don't know how I feel, Roberto," she said, "and I'm not likely to make up my mind quickly. Maybe we can take things slowly and allow them to unfold in their own way."

"I cannot ask for more."

"Will you take me back to the hotel, then? I'm very tired."

"Most certainly. I've been inconsiderate to bring you here after your long day."

Serena emerged from the shadows of the flowering shrub and moved toward him. Roberto met her in the middle of the patio. He took her hand, and they turned toward the panoramic vista so she could imprint it on her mind. Then they went through the dark restaurant and out to his car. The big Mercedes was occupied by Roberto's chauffeur, a large man who doubled as a bodyguard. He got out as they approached, opening the rear passenger door.

She climbed in first, followed by Roberto. He sat closer to her than he had on the drive up. As the chauffeur went around to the other side, Roberto took her hand, kissing her fingers.

"I am breaking every rule I have," he said in a low, rumbling voice that made her insides quiver, "but I feel helpless not to be your intimate friend."

"I have rules that are important to me, too," she said, "but I'm not so confident I can allow them to be broken."

"Time will tell what is right," he said softly.

The chauffeur got in and started the engine.

"There's a note of confidence in your voice," she said to Roberto. "Or am I reading something into that?"

"There are certain things for which I cannot apologize," he said bluntly. And then, as the Mercedes started down the road, he kissed her hand again.

Copacabana

A single lamp was burning in the sitting room when Serena got back to the suite. She had said good-night to Roberto Cabral in the lobby, purposely denying him the kiss he wanted. What was it about suave, macho Latin men, she wondered, that made a woman feel virginal? Sexual polarity, perhaps—yin and yang, the attraction of opposites, complementarity, female vulnerability. It was hard to say.

She looked toward Michael's door, wondering if he was out, getting drunk or getting laid. His door was ajar and it was dark in his room, but that didn't give her the answer she sought.

She'd thought about him only a few times during the evening, but he'd been in the back of her mind. She'd worried about him. Michael, like most men, could be fragile when it came to love. And she was feeling guilty.

Curious, she took off her heels and silently made her way to his door. She carefully pushed it open and peeked inside. There was one lump in his bed, which told her he was there and alone. The poor thing. She felt sorry for him.

There was no objective reason for pity. For all she knew the man could have had a hell of a night, but her instincts told her he hadn't. Instead of leaving him alone as she should have, she crept into his room.

The light coming from the sitting room was very dim, but she was able to see his face. She was surprised to see a large white bandage on the side of his head. Moving closer, she sat on the edge of the bed and leaned over him for a better look. As she did, he opened a swollen eye.

"You're home," he mumbled, sounding a little more surprised than not.

"Michael, what happened to your face?"

"Oh, nothing, a little accident."

"A little accident?"

"Yeah. It was nothing."

He was being evasive and she didn't like it. "That's bullshit. Something happened and I want to know what."

Michael rolled onto his back, groaning. "It's no big deal, Serena. Just go to bed."

"I'm not going anywhere until I get an explanation. You look like you ran into a brick wall."

"I did."

"Michael . . ." she said, letting her annoyance show.

"Okay, a brick wall ran into *me*. I got jumped in an alley by George Raft and a couple of his buddies."

"George Raft?"

"I guess he was before your time. Make it Robert De Niro."

"Michael, you're not making sense."

"I got the shit beat out of me. Three guys jumped me in an alley. I was stupid. Walked right into a trap. I should have seen it coming, but I didn't."

"Good Lord. Do you think it had anything to do with those men who were killed in Los Angeles?"

"Maybe. I don't know."

"Did they say anything or just beat on you?"

"They not-so-politely suggested I get on a plane for home. It was a way of saying I'm not welcome in this town."

"Why would they say that? Who wants you to leave? Michael, you don't think this has anything to do with Joachim, do you?"

"They didn't mention his name, or anybody else's, for that matter. It was an anonymous threat."

He closed his eyes and pressed on his temples. She could tell he was hurting. She reached out and touched his face.

"If you want to play Florence Nightingale," he said, "how about finding me a couple of aspirin? I didn't have any and I didn't want to go back down to the hotel shop, so I ransacked your medical kit. Unsuccessfully."

Serena went to her bath to find some Advil. The place looked like it had been hit by vandals. She dug around until she found the container she wanted, removed a couple of pills, half filled a glass with water and returned to Michael's room.

"Thanks for reorganizing my bath, Michael," she said dryly as she turned on the bedside lamp.

"I was desperate."

"Here's your Advil."

"You mean you had some? How come I couldn't find them?"

She gave him the tablets and the glass. "Because they were in the Midol bottle."

He propped himself up on his elbow and took the pills. "Why the Midol bottle, for crissakes?"

"So that no man would tamper with my pills. I keep my jewelry in my tampon box for the same reason."

He handed back the glass and dropped heavily onto the mattress. "I'll remember that if I ever become a cat burglar."

With the light on she could see how badly his face was swollen. "You look like hell," she said. "I think I'm going to call the house doctor."

"No, let the Advil have a chance to work. I'll be all right."

She took his hand. "Are you sure?"

"Positive." He looked at her through his swollen lid. "So how was dinner?" he asked. "Did Cesar try to get in your pants?"

"Roberto."

"Maybe that answers my question," he said. "One date and you're already on a first-name basis."

She laughed.

"So that voice got to you, huh?" he said.

"He is easy to listen to. And the accent." She fanned herself. "If you must know, he kissed my hand. Three times, I think. There. Are you satisfied?"

"The more candid you are, the greater the chance you're hiding something. I learned that about you a long time ago."

It amused her that he was able to cut right through to the heart of things. He did know her, actually. Better than anyone ever had. "You need to get some sleep," she said, "and let those bumps and bruises heal." She patted his hand and got to her feet.

"Sweet dreams," she said, her heart aching for him. "Tomorrow will be a better day."

F R I D A Y
September 15th

Copacabana

The next morning the tire tracks on his body were still in evidence. It was sort of like having played tackle football without pads and having one hell of a hangover at the same time. Mike managed to shower, then put on a white, short-sleeve shirt and khaki pants. He dragged himself into the main room, where he found Serena eating breakfast.

"There you are, Michael! How's the head?"

"I'll live."

He'd replaced the bandage with an ordinary Band-Aid, figuring his injury would be less noticeable that way. Serena took a good look at him as he sat down at the table.

"You're going to have a shiner."

"I've endured worse."

She poured his coffee without bothering to ask if he wanted any, handing him the cup. She looked pert in a sleeveless taupe linen Valentino dress with a slim skirt and tiny buttons up the back. Mike liked dresses with buttons up the back or, for that matter, dresses with no backs at all.

"I've been thinking about what those men said to you last night," Serena stated. "There's no telling how serious they are or what lengths they might go to."

"I suppose that's true."

"Well, I don't want you seriously hurt. It isn't worth it."

"I've never run from a fight in my life."

"Yes, we both know you're brave. That's not the point. The question is if it's worth the risk."

He thought for a while. Then he took a big slug of coffee, knowing without a doubt he was getting Brazilian. It was strong and flavorful, maybe too strong and too flavorful. He added a dash of milk and took another sip.

"Serena," he said, putting down his cup, "I'm going to ask a question, and I'm only going to ask it once, so I want a straight answer. Would you *prefer* that I hop on a plane for home? What I mean is, would it be easier for you if I wasn't around, whether because of what happened yesterday or because of Cabral, or whatever? Shall I leave for your sake?"

"No. Not for my sake. It's *you* I'm concerned about."

"Well, forget that. The matter's settled, then. I'm staying."

He grabbed a pastry from the plate and took a bite, then washed it down with more coffee. Serena plucked a single grape with her long, perfectly manicured fingers and popped it in her mouth. She contemplated him, probably speculating on his motives. Mike saw no point in elaborating.

"Are you sure?" she finally said.

"Positive. Though to be frank, I don't know what I can do for you that Koto can't—of a professional nature, I mean."

She gave him a chiding look. "Speaking of which, he's made arrangements for us to see Jeffrey." She checked her watch. "He'll be here in half an hour."

"Good. I'm eager to hear what your brother has to say. We've been getting so much information secondhand, it'll be nice to get something from the horse's mouth."

"Michael, promise you won't judge him too harshly. Jeffrey is not good in crises, you know. He gets confused."

"Don't start making excuses for him, Serena. The man's life is on the line. If he can't help us help him, he's in a lot more trouble than we think."

"Just promise me you'll be gentle. I know he's at his wits' end and ready to snap."

"The question is has he snapped already?"

There was a knock, interrupting the conversation. It was just as well. It was impossible for Serena to be logical about her brother. She went to the door, looking out the peephole before opening it. She evidently had gotten a bit paranoid, too.

"Good morning, Mrs. Bouchard," came a greeting from the hall.

Mike recognized Koto's voice. Serena invited him in.

"Do you have time for a cup of coffee, Koto?" she asked.

"Thank you, but I've had my morning quota already."

She ushered him to the table. Koto noticed Mike's bruised cheek, the Band-Aid and swollen eye. The question was on his lips, but he withheld comment.

"Nice town you've got," Mike said by way of explanation, "but some of the neighborhoods aren't so friendly."

"What happened? You go to the wrong end of the beach?"

"No, I forgot the lessons of the Indian Wars."

"Pardon?"

"Michael has yet to learn that discretion is the better part of valor," Serena said. With a tiny smile she added, "I'll leave you two boys to chat. Please excuse me."

She went off to her room to freshen up, and Mike told Koto what had happened. The investigator listened solemnly.

"Sounds like you better not be running around by yourself at night," he said after Mike had finished the story.

"Got any theories?"

"It's hard to say. Your friends could be connected with that incident in Los Angeles."

"That's what I figured. I gave the boys a message for Monteiro da Silva. They didn't act like the name meant anything, but it'll be interesting to see what develops."

"I'd say somebody doesn't like you snooping around."

Mike grinned. "Maybe I should feel flattered."

"Tough way to get attention," Koto said.

Mike's coffee was getting cold, but he took a sip anyway. "Where's your assistant this morning?"

"Tying up some lose ends on another case. She'll be catching up with us later."

"She'll be wanting her pistola back."

"Keep it until she brings a replacement. But I don't recommend lugging it to the jail."

"No, I wasn't planning on it." Mike broke off another piece of pastry. "Too bad Bebe wasn't with me last night. We might have handled those boys."

"No offense, but she probably could have handled them alone."

"Thanks for the warning," Mike said wryly.

"That isn't what I meant, but it doesn't hurt to know she's not someone a guy can fool with."

"Unless she's willing, presumably."

Koto actually smiled. "Unless she's willing."

Rio de Janeiro

Pericles Kotomata drove a nice, crisp little Toyota. It wasn't elegant, but it was a couple of notches above most of the vehicles in the street. When Mike asked him about the duties on a car like that, Koto mumbled something about having connections in the crucial government bureaucracy, but didn't elaborate.

After going through the Tunel Novo to the other side of the mountain, they followed the route tracing the edge of the bay, passing first through Botafogo, then Flamengo and Gloria, finally coming to the center of Rio. Mike was in the front seat with Koto, Serena in back. She was unusually quiet and Mike knew why. Jeffrey, and this visit to the jailhouse, was weighing on her. If Mike had to guess, she was afraid her brother would break down and confess all. And she probably wasn't so sure she wanted to know the truth.

Mike glanced back, and Serena gave him a worried look. Her normally smooth skin was etched with tiny worry lines.

He reached for her hand, and she squeezed his fingers gratefully. The pendulum had swung again; this time she felt beholden to him. Relationships were funny that way.

They soon arrived at police headquarters, a massive stone building tucked in a maze of narrow streets in the old Centro section. The exterior looked like a cross between a Wall Street bank and a Hollywood dungeon. The main entrance was inauspicious, except for the oversize wood doors that were as symbolic as they were functional.

Koto led the way into the building. Serena took Mike's arm as Koto shepherded them through the honeycomb of offices, doing one little bureaucratic routine after another. It was clear he knew his way around both the place and the people.

For a time they had to wait in an anteroom outside the office of some bigwig while Koto massaged egos. The adjoining area was a squad room of sorts, with people working around old wooden desks crowded together.

Apart from the distinctive Brazilian style of the people— the short-sleeve, tieless attire of the men and bare legs of the women—Rio police didn't seem much different than the ones back home. Most of the people seemed to be in their twenties or thirties, which was either reflective of the demographics of the country or the high attrition rate in the ranks. Mike figured the gold-watch ceremony was an extremely rare occurrence in the good old Rio P.D. Rare indeed.

Koto reappeared after a few minutes with a uniformed officer in tow, saying they could see Jeffrey, but first they had to be searched. The man patted Mike down and peered into Serena's purse. Then, nodding to Koto, he went off. Koto asked if they wanted to see Jeffrey alone or if they wished for him to accompany them. Serena thought it would probably be better if just the two of them saw Jeffrey this first time.

A clerk was summoned. After uttering a few words in Portuguese, followed by "Come, please," he led them away. As they walked along a hallway, Serena took Mike's hand, clutching it tightly. Arriving at a nondescript metal door, the man stopped.

Serena began trembling. "If it was anyone in the world but Jeffrey I could handle this," she murmured.

The clerk opened the door and said, "The prisoner comes in a minute, *senhores.*"

"Prisoner," she repeated as she entered the room. The door closed behind them. Serena stared up at the small window high on the outside wall and rubbed her arms as if she was cold. "My little brother," she mumbled in a barely audible voice. Then she turned around and gave Mike an impulsive hug. "I've got to be strong for Jeffrey," she said, more to herself than to him. "I've got to be confident."

Mike inhaled her scent as he held her, experiencing a momentary confusion about what he was supposed to feel. Compassion? Sorrow? Love?

No, not love.

And yet the smell of her perfume reminded him of the heat of their bodies as they'd rubbed together the day before. It had been an aberration. Not an accident like Tahoe, but an aberration.

Serena sighed, pulling herself together. "Let's try to be professional about this," she said, slipping from his arms.

She examined the room. There wasn't much to see. A wooden table. Four straight chairs, two against the wall. A shabby metal bookcase stacked with old files and forgotten supplies.

The walls were thick with paint and the air dank enough for moisture to accumulate on the ceiling in dingy droplets. On one wall was a grimy, poorly done religious painting of a saint being tortured or crucified. Mike had heard about interrogations in Latin America and wondered if the painting was intended to give the prisoner solace or the interrogator inspiration.

"Beverly Hills it ain't," Serena said. She put her purse on the table and brought one of the extra chairs to the table. She turned to him, her face a mask of trepidation.

Mike had seen her this way only once before—the day of their divorce, as they'd waited outside the courtroom. She'd paced back and forth. "If I hated you, I might actually enjoy this," she'd said, walking past the bench where he sat, "but I don't."

"Go ahead and hate me," he'd replied. "You might as well get your money's worth."

She'd laughed, then turned away before he could see her tears.

"Let's sit," she said now, looking singularly unhappy with the jailhouse environment. "People standing seem more worried."

Mike sat in the chair next to her. She took his hand and he absently toyed with her fingers.

There was a rattling at the door and Serena tensed. It swung open and Jeffrey Bouchard appeared. He was in faded prison gray, a day's growth of beard on his delicate jaw, his light brown hair disheveled, his head jutting forward. There were bags under his eyes. He looked sallow and defeated.

Serena rose, the legs of the wooden chair screeching in protest. There was recognition on Jeffrey's face, but not the joy Mike had expected. Perhaps Jeffrey's fear wouldn't allow him to react.

A guard gently guided him into the room, and Serena started toward him. They embraced and were crying by the time Mike got to them. Jeffrey's blubbering rose over her comforting sounds. They rocked back and forth, holding each other.

"Oh, God, I can't tell you how wonderful this is, sis," he gushed, tears running down his cheeks.

The guards withdrew, much to Mike's relief. There was no telling what his former brother-in-law might blurt out. To say Jeffrey was eccentric would be an understatement. But seeing him, Mike could tell Serena's brother had been diminished. Gone were the Armani suits, the monogrammed pastel shirts, the Bally loafers and the effete, self-possessed manner. Gone was the arrogance and false bravado. Jeffrey Bouchard had been cut down to size by the angry hand of the social order.

He stopped blubbering long enough to take notice of Mike. Wiping his red-rimmed eyes, he said, "You're a saint to come. Thank you." Reaching out, he patted Mike's shoulder. The uncharacteristic gesture made Mike feel his first real compassion for the man.

Serena stepped back a bit to get a good look at her brother. She held his face in her hands. "Dear Jeffrey," she whispered, "what have they done to you?"

"It's been hell," he said meekly.

He went to the chair that was obviously reserved for him and dropped into it like a man who'd been on his feet for days. Serena took one of the other chairs and pulled it around the table so she could sit nearer him. She held his hands, and Jeffrey gazed at her, shaking his head as if to say his feelings were beyond words.

Serena took a tissue from her purse and pressed it into his palm. Then she dabbed at her eyes with a handkerchief, carefully so as not to smudge her makeup. Jeffrey blew his nose.

"Sorry," he muttered, "but for the first time in ages I feel safe."

"We're going to get you out," she assured him. "I promise. That's why Michael's here. We're going to prove you're innocent."

Jeffrey looked at him with surprise, noticing his battered cheek, the Band-Aid. "Is that true, Michael?"

Mike shifted his weight. "I'll do what I can, Jeffrey."

"We're definitely getting you out of here!" Serena said emphatically. The statement was directed at Mike. "Whatever it takes."

Jeffrey's lip quivered, his eyes brimmed. He stared at Serena like she was the Virgin Mary, an irony she would have appreciated immensely at a less sober moment. She pressed his fingers.

"Tell me if they've hurt you, Jeffrey," she said. "I don't need the details, but I want to know if they've hurt you."

"Sometimes the guards get a little rough, especially the homophobic ones," he said, "but nothing to write Amnesty International about."

"What about the other prisoners?" She said the words warily.

Jeffrey sort of wound himself up, drew a breath, held it, then said, "Serena, I don't care if I ever see another man as long as I live. If they'd let me out of this goddamn place, I'd happily go to a nunnery. Swear to God."

Serena didn't know what to make of the remark, nor did Mike. Jeffrey didn't appear overly stressed, so Serena pressed on. "Darling," she said, "they've only given us a little time. We've got to talk about your case."

"Shit, I don't even want to think about it," he whined.

She patted his arm. "Come on, dear."

"Serena, I can't tell you how much I hate this. I'm a dead man. I swear I am."

"Jeffrey," she intoned, losing patience, "we've got to talk about it, otherwise my next trip here will be for your body."

He glared at her. "Jesus, you certainly know how to get a person's attention, don't you?"

"I'm here to help you, but you've got to cooperate."

"Easy for you to say. *I'm* the one they're trying to lynch!" He made a dismissive gesture with his hand. "They've got their faggot. That's all that matters. Let's face it, Serena, there's not a goddamn thing you can do."

"Jeffrey, stop this blather. Right now!"

It was her "mother" voice. Mike had heard her use it with Jeffrey many times. Jeffrey, as usual, took exception.

"For God's sake, Serena, I'm not a two-year-old. On top of everything else I've been through, I don't need this."

She bristled. "Must I remind you I'm all you've got?"

"Is that a threat?"

Mike saw that Serena was losing it.

"Listen, you little twit, I flew all the way down here to save your ungrateful ass," she snapped. "The least you can do is cooperate!"

Mike was normally loath to interfere in the Bouchard family imbroglios, but he saw this could easily get out of hand. "Hey, you two," he said, "let's keep our eye on the ball. We've got important business to discuss."

Jeffrey was shamed into silence. Serena looked embarrassed.

"You're right, Michael," she said.

Jeffrey pinched the bridge of his nose between his fingers, lowering his head theatrically. "You can't imagine what a strain it is to be incarcerated like this. I'm not myself."

"I'll take that to be an apology," she said. "And I'm sorry if I was brusque. But time's awasting. Let's get on with this." She turned to Mike. "Ask him something, Michael. You said there's a lot you need to know."

He was glad to be getting down to business. "Jeffrey," he said, "I want the facts, every single detail. But whatever you tell me better be true. I don't want any soft soap, best light or little white lies. Understand?"

"God, Michael, you aren't going to harass me, too, are you? Hasn't it occurred to anyone that losing Drake has been the great tragedy of my life? I'm in pain! Or doesn't anyone care?"

"Jeffrey, for God's sake!" Serena had run out of patience.

"Look," Mike said, "we don't know much of anything, except that Drake was shot and they arrested you. Tell us what you know, what you saw and heard. Start at the beginning."

Jeffrey dropped his eyes. "It's my fault they think I did it," he said. "I picked up the stupid gun."

"No, let's go all the way back to when you came to Rio. I need to know the background."

Jeffrey shifted uneasily. "Drake and I became friends in L.A., as you may or may not know, Michael. Not much had been happening with his career, and Hollywood was beginning to get to him. He wasn't officially out of the closet and the pretense was a problem. Anyway, he had some money set aside and he knew it would go a lot farther in South America. So one day he said to me, 'How'd you like to go to Rio?'" Jeffrey's eyes lit up. "What's a guy going to say to an offer like that? I mean, Drake Manville wants me to go away with him to a romantic place like Rio... I was ecstatic! What can I say?"

"You can skip the hearts and flowers, Jeffrey," Mike said. "What happened once you got here?"

Jeffrey didn't appreciate the comment, but went on. "We needed a place to live, of course. Fortunately for us, Drake had friends willing to help. We found a wonderful villa atop Santa Teresa Hill. It was idyllic, our own paradise. We both felt so free. I couldn't have been happier. I thought Drake was happy, too. It was all so unfair... he never really explained."

"Explained what, Jeffrey?" Serena implored.

"That he'd found someone else."

Mike and Serena looked at each other.

"Who?" Mike asked.

Jeffrey's expression turned to disgust. "A woman."

"Go on," Mike said. "Tell us about her."

Jeffrey sighed, recrossing his legs. "Her name is Antonia. She's the sister of Drake's friend, Hector von Vehrling, the guy who rented us the villa." He shook his head. "I don't know what he saw in the bitch. A goddamn spinster. Forty-something, and never been married."

"So what happened? Did Drake tell you he wanted to end it?"

"No, that's the point. At first I didn't know what was going on. Drake started changing. He got cold. Began going out alone. Of course, I realized after the fact that he was fooling around with her, but I was too trusting to see it at the time. It went on for weeks. Oh, how I suffered. It was just horrible."

"How'd you find out about this Antonia?" Mike asked.

Jeffrey sighed again. "One day I saw her. I'd been suspicious that he had someone else, but I couldn't believe he'd actually care for a woman. I was hurt that he was playing games. I had my pride, though. I decided to call his bluff. So I left.''

"Where'd you go?''

"I took a room in a place down the hill. I thought Drake would eventually come to his senses and ask for me. He didn't.''

"Okay,'' Mike said, "what about the day of the murder? Tell us what happened.''

Jeffrey swallowed hard. "I got up early that morning. I'd tossed and turned all night long, thinking about him. I'd kept my distance, hoping he'd miss me. But then I figured maybe I should tell him I loved him.'' Jeffrey's voice quavered. "And I *did* love him. I couldn't have killed him. Never! Drake was the first man I've ever wanted to spend my life with.''

"All right, what happened next? Did you go to the villa?''

"Yes. I walked up the hill, praying that he wouldn't reject me. I got within half a block, then lost my nerve. I was just standing there, vacillating, when I heard a shot. I knew immediately that Drake was in trouble, that he needed me. So I started running toward the villa. With each step, the feeling got stronger. I knew something was terribly wrong.''

"And...''

"And as I neared, I had a glimpse of a woman through the foliage and I heard a car door slam. I ran up the walkway, but I was too late to see who it was. The vegetation is very thick. I saw a flicker of movement and a car speed out the drive.''

"You didn't see who was in it, what kind it was, the color?''

"No. I think it was black, but I'm not sure.''

"All right,'' Mike said. "Then what happened?''

"I had this sudden feeling of doom. I believe it's like that with people who love each other. When they bleed, you bleed. Do you know what I mean? Has that ever happened to you?''

Mike shifted uncomforta'ıy. "No, but let's stick to the story. What did you do after the car sped away?''

"Well, I went up to the villa, of course. When I got to the top of the stairs I found the front door wide open. The slut had obviously left in a hurry."

"Slut?"

"Antonia."

"What makes you think it was her?"

"Who else? It was the natural assumption. Jealous love." His hand trembled.

"What did *she* have to be jealous of?"

Jeffrey gave him a look of annoyance. "Antonia had to have known that Drake truly loved me. What had happened between them was only a flirtation. Why else would she have shot him?"

"We may be assuming facts not in evidence," Mike muttered.

"What?"

"Nothing. You found the door open. Then what?"

"I went in. The house was quiet. I poked my head in the salon. No one was there. Then I stepped into the library. The desk in there is early nineteenth century Portuguese, a massive piece similar to one I picked out for Ralph, a friend of mine in Beverly Hills. You know Ralph, Serena."

She nodded.

"Anyway, the desk was across the room. The gun was lying on the floor in front of it. I remembered the shot I'd heard . . . the car driving off. I picked up the gun. I don't know why, I guess I panicked. Then . . ." His voice faltered momentarily. "Then I . . . noticed Drake's body." He closed his eyes for several seconds. "It was on the floor behind the desk. That's why I didn't see it when I first came in."

"You were still holding the gun?"

"Yes, it was still in my hand. I knew he'd be dead." Jeffrey drew a ragged breath. "Then when I saw his face . . . there was no doubt." He began to sob again.

Mike looked over at Serena. She'd been caught up by the account. Tears ran down her cheeks as Jeffrey wept. After a while he recovered. He wiped his eyes with the tissue Serena had given him.

"I'm sorry to be such a sop, but you'll never know how much I loved that man." He blew his nose.

"Okay," Mike said, "you're in the library, hovering over Drake's body, the gun in your hand. What then?"

"Well, like I say, I knew he was dead. Then my head suddenly cleared. There were several moments of total clarity, peacefulness. It was strange. I knew my finger-prints were on the gun. Antonia had killed him, but I was standing where she probably had stood, and the goddamn gun was in *my* hand.

"When it sank in, I dropped the thing and ran back to the entry hall. I called out—I don't know why, I guess to see if anyone was around. But there wasn't a sound. I remember hearing birds out in the garden. The birds were singing and the man I loved was dead. It seemed incomprehensible."

"Let me get this straight," Mike said. "When you real-ized your prints were on the gun, you dropped it on the floor and left?"

"That's right. I was in a dither, I guess. So I ran back down the hill to my place."

"Then what?"

"I sat on my bed and tried to think. If I'd been in L.A., it would have been easier. But I don't speak three goddamn words of Portuguese. I knew I should call the police, but I'd never have made myself understood. There was no one for me to turn to. Drake had handled everything...he even made arrangements for the room I'd rented. I considered making a run for it, but I figured I'd get caught. I was afraid of jail, but I wanted to save my ass.

"When I finally calmed down, I got cleaned up and went out to look for a policeman. I walked until I found a taxi and had him take me to the police station. By then the crime had been reported. They already knew.

"At the jail, a guy questioned me for hours in pidgin En-glish. I kept asking for the ambassador and a lawyer. Then they booked me, and I haven't seen the light of day since."

"Didn't you tell them about the car?" Serena asked.

"Of course. I told them everything. But they didn't seem interested. I even told them it was probably Antonia I'd seen...that they should question her. At first I thought they didn't understand, or figured I'd fabricated the story. The next day I asked if they'd found her, but they wouldn't talk about Antonia. It was as though they had me and that was all they cared about.

"Then it began dawning on me. She's an important lady...she's Brazilian...she's got connections. Why worry about her if they've got me? After all, my fingerprints were on the gun, and there's only my word that she was even there. They hang me, and they've rid the world of one more queer."

"That's it?" Mike said. "That's everything that happened?"

"As best I recall."

Mike pondered the situation.

"Jeffrey has explained the evidence against him," Serena said. "Now we just have to get the police to open their eyes."

Mike nodded. He was running Jeffrey's account of events through his mind, searching for logical consistency. He tried to put himself in the place of an investigator reviewing the crime. Jeffrey had motive and opportunity. There was physical evidence against him and the testimony of a peripheral witness. How did Michael explain to Serena and her brother that exonerating Jeffrey would not be a cakewalk?

The door opened and one of the guards stuck his head in. He pointed at his watch. "*Senhores.*" Then he held up a finger as if to say one more minute. The door closed.

Jeffrey looked panicky. "So, what do you think, Michael?"

"It's too early to say."

"Can't you give me any hope?"

"Your innocence is your best asset," Mike said. "It's not a guarantee, but it's a lot harder to get somebody off when they're actually guilty."

"Well, I'm innocent," Jeffrey said curtly.

"That helps."

"You think there's hope, then?"

"You would know better than anyone, Jeffrey."

Serena took Jeffrey's hand again. "I know you're worried," she said calmly, "but I've hired the best lawyer in Brazil and an excellent private investigator to help Michael. We're going to beat this. Trust me."

Jeffrey kissed her fingers, then reached a hand toward Mike. "Thank you," he mouthed. Out loud, he added, "Oh, God, thank you."

The guards came and whisked Jeffrey away. Serena sat for a moment with her eyes closed. She seemed almost stunned. "What do you think?" she said eventually.

"It all comes down to if he's telling the truth. You'd know better than I."

"I know my brother, Michael. He's capable of lying, but I was listening to him very carefully. He was telling the truth."

Mike considered that. Serena was not above self-serving bravado. The truth probably didn't matter to her a whole lot, considering Jeffrey's life was at stake. But the quietness with which she spoke, the measured tones, told him she believed what she was saying.

Koto was waiting where they'd left him, obviously curious how things had gone. But Mike wasn't sure what to think. Serena's passion and Jeffrey's performance had left him wondering if he owed his former brother-in-law the benefit of the doubt.

Serena sat slumped in one of the wooden armchairs. "Thank God that's over." She glanced up at them. "What now?"

"Senhor Cabral has arrived," Koto said. "He is with the police commissioner and asked me to inquire on his behalf if you have plans for lunch. He would like to discuss the case."

Serena brightened noticeably, her posture straightening. "Oh, how nice," she said.

Mike saw the smile on her lips and realized this was the direction things were headed. It was what they had agreed to—freedom to do as they wished. He had reason to be glad. The quicker he got back to regarding her as his ex, the better.

"I'll show you to the commissioner's office," Koto said.

Serena was instantly on her feet. "Yes, perhaps Roberto could use help convincing him they've put an innocent man behind bars. We'll talk this evening," she said to Mike before she left. "I'm sure we'll both have lots of notes to compare."

"Check," he said.

She and Koto went off in search of Roberto, leaving Mike to ponder the situation. Serena seemed to think he intended to run a full investigation of Drake Manville's murder, but that wasn't the deal. Mike had agreed to come down, check things out and give her an assessment.

Maybe she'd assumed that the beating he'd taken had changed things, but just because he didn't intend to run away didn't mean he was set on becoming a resident alien. He owed Serena a reasoned evaluation of Jeffrey's case. After another day or so he would be in a better position to say where things stood, then he could go home.

Koto returned shortly, an inscrutable smile on his face.

"Did you get her safely into Don Juan's hands?" Mike asked.

"Mrs. Bouchard and Senhor Cabral seem to have an affinity," Koto said diplomatically.

"She loves to play and he's after a piece of ass, my friend. If that's 'affinity' then maybe you're right."

Together they walked down the hall, headed for the entrance.

"It must be difficult working for your former wife," Koto said.

"It falls somewhere between strep throat and a root canal. Otherwise, it's a gas."

Koto smiled. "You'll be interested to know that while you were interviewing Mr. Bouchard, I picked up some very interesting information from Carlos Mendonca, the detective handling the case.''

''Oh? Good news or bad?''

''I'll tell you when we get outside. I never have liked discussing a case with colleagues while in this place.''

They went back out into the Rio sun. It seemed warmer than when they'd arrived, though maybe only because of the dankness of the building.

''There's a coffee bar up the street,'' Koto said. ''Shall we have some refreshment while we talk?''

''Excellent idea.''

The made their way along the narrow sidewalk to the place Koto had in mind. It was not much more than a hole in the wall. The counterman, who'd just finished serving a take-out customer, wore a white tank top, white pants and a white hat, a uniform of sorts. He grinned, welcoming them to the empty establishment. Koto ordered two coffees, and they sat at one of the four tiny tables.

''So, what do the police have?'' Mike asked.

''The technicians say the gun that killed Mr. Manville had been fired twice.''

''Twice? How many holes did Manville have in him?''

''Only one. And a thorough search of the room revealed no evidence of the second shot. No holes in the wall or ceiling. Nothing. For the moment they are assuming the weapon was test-fired at another location, but there is some concern.''

''I imagine. It's something we should keep note of.''

''Another thing,'' Koto said. ''It turns out the print on the murder weapon is only a partial. The technicians say there was an attempt to wipe the gun, but the print of Mr. Bouchard's right index finger was apparently missed.''

Mike was surprised. ''That's strange. Jeffrey didn't say anything about wiping the gun. Just the opposite. He panicked when he realized he'd touched the thing, dropped it and ran.''

Koto stroked his chin. ''Curious.''

''Any other tidbits?''

"Mendonca told me the origin and ownership of the gun are at this time unknown," Koto said. "We have to hope it can't be traced to Mr. Bouchard."

"Right."

"But the worst piece of news is that there may be still another witness," Koto went on.

"Another one? What's with these cops? A new witness a day?"

"It's uncertain if this one will add much. It's a maid. Apparently she was in the house at the time of the shooting. Her name's Ana. Unfortunately—or fortunately, depending on your point of view—she is a deaf-mute and also somewhat retarded. The bottom line is she is unable to communicate effectively. This is what Mendonca told me."

Mike shook his head. "Something else Jeffrey didn't mention."

"It could be that he was unaware of her presence. I don't have much in the way of specifics. All I know is that she was the first to discover Mr. Manville's body. The employer, Hector von Vehrling, had an appointment with Mr. Manville, and when he showed up sometime after the shooting, the maid led him to the body."

"Did she report seeing anything? I imagine since she's deaf she wouldn't have heard the shot."

"That's true. But as to if she saw anything, I cannot say. The police are unsure, as I understand it."

"Bizarre case, Koto, or are they all like this in Rio?"

"I thought it was a strange case because the victim and the accused were Yankees," Koto said, poking his tongue in his cheek.

Mike laughed. "Maybe it's the clash of cultures."

"Or the tropical air."

Mike thought of Bebe. "Yeah, the air does things to a guy."

Koto sipped his coffee. "I have more news on a related matter, Mike."

"Lord, but aren't you Mr. Efficiency."

"Mrs. Bouchard is paying me well. I believe in giving value for the money."

"That's definitely how to stay in Serena's good graces. She can be an exacting boss, but she's fair."

"This really concerns you more than her brother. I took the liberty of inquiring about Ribeiro. It turns out he is well known by the police here."

"I'm listening."

"Mendonca told me he's the henchman of a local gangster named Victor Souza. This man is no Al Capone, but he makes some noise running a few rackets and doing jobs."

"What sort of jobs?"

"In Brazil it is necessary to do things outside of the law at times. Certain people make a business of providing these . . . shall we say . . . extracurricular services."

"You mean like collecting bad debts?"

"That's a good example."

"So what interest would Souza have in me?" Mike asked.

"I'm suggesting that the someone who hired him has the interest."

"Joachim Monteiro da Silva, for example?"

"It's possible. But it could be someone else. Monteiro da Silva might be a victim himself. Someone could be shaking *him* down."

"Things are not always as they appear, in other words."

"Especially in Rio, perhaps."

Mike drank the rest of his coffee.

"Another?" Koto asked.

"No, thanks. One of these is about equal to three or four of what I'm used to."

"What are your plans for the investigation?" Koto asked.

"I'd like to see the murder scene, if that can be arranged. And it might be interesting to talk to this maid you mentioned."

"Talking with her is the problem, I believe."

"That's right. Deaf and mute."

"Perhaps you will want to speak to the owner of the villa, Hector von Vehrling."

"Good idea, Koto. And his sister, Antonia. Jeffrey thinks she shot Drake, so we might as well cover that base, too."

"You're going to keep me very busy," Koto said.

"The pay's good, my friend."

Koto again ran his tongue through his cheek. "I keep reminding myself of that."

Mike thought of Bebe. "Does your assistant still plan on getting me a gun?"

"Bebe was taking care of that this morning. She will have it at your hotel. Perhaps even by the time we return."

Mike checked his watch. "No reason why we shouldn't be heading on back, is there?"

Koto smiled ever so slightly. "None at all."

Ipanema

The drive was not as relaxing as Serena would have liked. The electricity between her and Roberto was, if anything, more intense than before. Oddly, that might have been because he was more restrained. Apart from caressing her with his voice, he was the model of decorum. He titillated without touching. A man who reined himself in this way had to care a great deal, which only served to arouse her interest more.

Roberto rested his well-manicured hand on the leather seat between them. She had the strangest impulse to seize it, though for what reason, she had no idea.

"Give me your appraisal of what the police are thinking, Roberto," she said after a lengthy silence. "Do they believe Jeffrey is guilty, or is it merely convenient to say that he is?"

"The police are like dogs after a bone, as you must know," Roberto replied. "Sometimes it is more important to have any bone than the right one."

"Is that what's happening in this case?"

"I cannot say. The commissioner is dependent on what his investigators tell him." Roberto patted the leather seat affectionately, as though it were she. "I have other news that may have a bearing on what is in the minds of the police."

"What's that?"

"Before going to the police headquarters I called on the prosecutor. I thought we should know what their thinking would be on a plea bargain."

"And?"

"No decision will be made until the investigation is complete, but my sense is that they will—how do you say it?—deal."

"You mean they'll compromise?"

"Yes," Roberto said. "We might get by with a reduced charge and only a few years in jail. These are preliminary impressions, but your brother is not necessarily facing life in prison, even if the evidence is against him."

"Roberto, at this point, a month in jail is much too long. He no more belongs behind bars than I do."

"What I'm trying to say is that even if we cannot prove his innocence, we have hope."

"I'll keep that in mind."

They had passed the hotel and left Copacabana behind. Serena did not recognize where they were. She peered out the window.

"This is Ipanema," Roberto said. "Here you will find the true *carioca*. Those who are sophisticated are in Ipanema and Leblon. Here we have a culture of our own. The rest of Rio and Brazil can only follow."

"Ipanema is in, huh?"

"Most assuredly. But I'm not objective. This is where I live."

"And this is where your club is?"

"Yes, on the shores of the lagoon, the *lagoa,* as we call it. You will see."

They turned inland from the sea and, after a few short blocks, came to a beautiful lake surrounded by a park and tree-lined streets. The apartment buildings were elegant, and the houses on the surrounding hillsides were substantial. This, it seemed, was the Beverly Hills of Rio.

As the Mercedes made its way around the lagoon, Roberto told her about Ipanema's bohemian tradition, the mix of coffeehouse liberalism and nouveau-riche consumerism, the intellectuals, the artists and the moneyed class. What she couldn't tell was if it was his pride speaking or if he was doing some subtle selling.

"Ipanema is your kind of place," he told her. "I can tell."

"What makes you say that?"

"You have style, wit, beauty, money."

"You're not afraid to flatter, are you?"

"I have a compulsion to say what I think."

"That doesn't sound very lawyerlike, Roberto. I thought the name of the game was to dissimulate."

"Pardon?"

"To pretend."

"Pretending is for actors."

"My father used to say lawyers were actors, mostly bad ones," Serena said wryly.

Roberto caressed the leather. "Tell me what I must do to gain your confidence."

"What you're doing is fine," she said.

"Which is?"

"Slow dancing."

Roberto smiled, glancing out the window. "Oh, look! There across the *lagoa*. See the building with the red roof?"

"Yes."

"That's my club, where we'll dine."

"It looks nice."

"A wonderful place for slow dancing."

Serena decided she liked Roberto. At times he seemed so old-fashioned it was almost comical. It was as though he didn't know Latin lovers had gone out with the fifties. But his voice and the way he stroked the leather—it was enough to make a girl want to lock her NOW card away in the file cabinet. Not forever, perhaps, but for a week or two.

Serena put her hand on Roberto's as the Mercedes glided around the lagoon. Turning off the drive, they went through a small park to the club. A doorman in white livery greeted them. The building, which was colonial in style, was what she liked to refer to as California elegant—casual but classy.

Roberto, in a rich, dark brown, double-breasted Italian suit and cream silk tie, was overdressed. Serena decided it was more the ex-government minister in him than the lawyer. He was at the very tip of society and wore his mantle with pride.

A hostess greeted them, discreetly checking Serena out. Heads turned as they moved through the marble-floored rooms filled with tropical plants, fine old leather furniture and oriental carpets. Roberto parceled out greetings like a nobleman. Serena could see he was in his element.

On one side of the dining room was a great curving wall of glass, overlooking the lagoon. They were shown to the table at the center of the curve. Handsome young men held their chairs for them under the supervision of the hostess, who then withdrew. Whispers buzzed about the room. Serena knew people were wondering who the hell she was.

Serena always stayed in the finest hotels and ate in the best restaurants, but she rarely rubbed shoulders with high-society types, so this was a little different for her. She had never been a snob. If anything, she'd considered society a waste of time and, as a girl, had taken pride in defying convention. But on vacation, people were prone to eat desserts they never touch at home and to play games they normally abjured. Besides, there was a lot on her mind she wanted to forget—Jeffrey, Christina, Michael . . . above all, Michael.

"This is delightful," she said, checking out the people checking her out. "Do you come here often?"

"A few times a week, depending. The view calms my soul."

"It is lovely," she said, glancing out at the water, trees and sky.

She thought of Roberto's remark that Ipanema was her kind of place and wondered if he was suggesting she ought to settle here. She'd traveled extensively, but much as she enjoyed it she could never become an expatriate. Jeffrey had done it for love, yet even that wouldn't be enough for her.

She tested the notion of becoming Senhora Cabral, realizing without having to think twice that it could never happen. Not even if Roberto was twice the man in bed that Michael was—an unlikely proposition.

She watched the graceful movements of a handsome waiter, who, beneath the uniform, was as proud as those he served. Elegance was not made, it was a product of birth, as was character. All of which made her think of Michael. As was so often the case, when she got philosophical, his role in her life came to mind.

"What are you thinking, my dear?" Roberto asked, his voice rumbling.

She favored him with a smile. "Nothing you'd care to hear about."

"Are you sure?"

"Very sure."

The elegant waiter appeared, asking if they wanted a drink. Serena ordered a double vodka martini, the nectar of seduction. She never had them on the road, but there was something about Roberto Cabral that enticed her to danger.

She asked about the people who were there, and Roberto gave her a rough profile. The common element was money—some of it old, some of it new.

Their drinks arrived. There was too much vermouth in the martini, but Serena was willing to make allowances. Having been in the hotel business her entire life, she knew how to be a guest as well as a host. As they drank, Roberto caressed her with his voice. It almost didn't matter what he was saying, especially after the martini started taking hold. She listened, wondering if having an affair with him would, in the greater scheme of things, be a plus or a minus.

He'd been talking about society people, which gave Serena an opening for the question she'd been wanting to ask for some time. "Roberto, do you know the Monteiro da Silvas?"

"Yes, of course."

"Joachim?"

"Not well. He's a different generation. His father I knew well, though I can't say we were friends. His mother also."

"What kind of people are they?"

"The—what's the term?—upper crust. Without a doubt."

"My daughter is staying with them, you know."

"I'd heard, but only in passing. I myself am not so active in the social whirl. To my wife it's more important, which explains why I keep a distance. This is a small world. It must be much the same way in Beverly Hills."

"I avoid most of that."

Roberto gazed deep into her eyes and sipped his drink. "Then we are very much alike."

Serena took a healthy sip of her martini, knowing she was on her way to a pleasant high. Roberto, for all his affectations, was slowly enticing her.

"Ah!" he said, looking past her. "I see someone you must meet." He rose and waved his hand toward the entrance.

Serena turned to see a small but elegant woman speaking with an older couple. She was in her late forties, slim, wearing a navy dress and South Sea pearls, her hair a dark gold. Seeing Roberto, she waved, indicating she'd come over in a moment. He sat down.

"That's Elaine Risollo," he explained. "During the sixties she was one of the leading film stars in Brazil and was part of Ipanema's liberal revolution, a sort of Jane Fonda. She became a force in national politics. Some thought she might be a senator or even president one day. Then, with the military coup, she fled to Italy. Elaine lived in exile, making films and becoming a sort of Brazilian Eva Peron. When democracy finally returned here, she came back, but to the surprise of everyone, she gave up politics to marry a prominent industrialist, one of the five wealthiest men in Brazil. Now she is a social icon and devotes her time to charity and the arts."

"How interesting."

"I thought you should meet her because she was a good friend of Drake Manville's. I believe they even did a film together many years ago. And if you want to know about people in society, Elaine knows everything.''

''I *would* like to meet her.''

A few moments later Elaine Risollo made her way toward their table. Roberto got to his feet, performing the introductions. The women shook hands, and Roberto had a chair brought over. Elaine asked for a glass of champagne and listened as Roberto told her about Serena.

''Ah, but of course,'' Elaine said in a rich accent that had overtones of Italian as well as Portuguese. ''I know your brother. Drake's friend.'' She took Serena's hands. ''What a tragedy he's been put in jail. He could not have done this murder. No. Impossible. It is a great injustice.''

Serena felt a warmth toward Elaine. ''Thank goodness I've met someone who agrees with me. There *are* some things that are simply impossible, and Jeffrey being a killer is one.''

''Yes, yes, absolutely true,'' Elaine said.

Up close Elaine Risollo did look familiar. Serena probably had seen her on screen years ago, though she couldn't have said in what. It was apparent that the woman wasn't as young as she appeared to be from a distance. Elaine was likely in her middle fifties, but well cared for.

''So,'' Elaine said, ''Senhor Cabral is your champion, I understand.''

''Humble servant is more accurate,'' Roberto insisted.

''Listen to this,'' Elaine exclaimed, trilling with laughter. ''The man is a lion, an absolute lion.'' She pronounced the word ''lee-on,'' making her speech even more quaint. Then she leaned toward Serena. ''But be warned, my dear, he is irresistible. There are a thousand broken hearts to prove it is so.''

''You are spoiling my reputation, Elaine. What can Serena think of me now?''

''She knows, Roberto,'' Elaine said, dismissing him. ''She knows.''

Elaine's champagne arrived, and Serena asked for another martini, though she knew she shouldn't. "Tell me, Elaine," she said, "who do you think killed Drake?"

"I have no idea," she replied. "It could be a robber, it could be anyone."

"I understand you and Drake were friends. Did he mention he was having problems with anyone? Did he have enemies?"

"The biggest enemy of an actor is age," Elaine said with a chuckle, "and it can kill, but not so swiftly as a gun." Then her demeanor grew more serious. "But I do know what you are asking. Drake was troubled, and he made problems for others. For as long as I knew him, Drake was—how do you say?—confused about his sexuality." Elaine lowered her voice. "I was one of the few who knew of his bisexuality."

"There were women in his life at the end, weren't there?"

"You are speaking, of course, of Antonia von Vehrling."

"Yes."

"I must tell you, I do not know Antonia well. The last time I saw Drake, he spoke of her. He said she was—how do you say?—madly in love about him."

"And how did he feel about her?"

"Drake," Elaine said, "could be like a woman in his heart. I think it was your brother he loved, but he was very...uh, Roberto, *commo dize prático?*"

"Practical."

"*Sim,* practical. Drake was very practical, *senhora.* You know what I mean? He regarded women as safer for his reputation. He hoped still to work in films. And Antonia, like your brother, has very much money. To Drake...well, this was important to him. He had to think of his future."

"So could Antonia have killed him?"

Elaine shrugged. "It's possible, no?"

"My brother saw a woman run from the villa as he was arriving," Serena said. "Chances are it was the killer. Unfortunately, Jeffrey didn't see who it was."

Elaine turned to Roberto. "Do the police know this?"

"Yes," he replied.

"But don't seem to care," Serena added sullenly.

Elaine patted Serena's hand. "Justice will prevail. Sometimes she is very slow, but even in Brazil she must win eventually."

"I'd like to share your optimism," Serena said.

Her second martini arrived, which she decided to drink slowly. Elaine finished her champagne but refused another glass.

"I must tell you, *senhora,* your daughter is beautiful," Elaine said as Serena took a tiny sip of her drink.

"You've met Christina?"

"At a party. She was with young Monteiro da Silva."

"I haven't yet met Joachim," Serena said. "What can you tell me about him?"

"A thousand pardons, *mesdames,*" Roberto interjected, "but I must call to my office. Will you excuse me for a few minutes?"

"Of course, darling," Elaine said. "We can talk better if you aren't here."

"Then I take my leave," he said with a small smile.

After he was gone, Elaine's tone turned conspiratorial. "Except for music and film celebrities and soccer players, of course, Roberto is among the most admired men in all Brazil. In the wealthy classes, I mean. It is a great compliment that he admires you so greatly, *senhora.*"

"It's a business relationship," Serena said.

"Perhaps, but he adores you. It is on his face." Elaine saw she'd gotten too personal. "We were talking of Joachim Monteiro da Silva."

"I know his family is highly regarded, but what can you tell me of Joachim himself?"

"He looks magnificent on a polo pony. He is the Roberto Cabral of his generation. More, even, because he does not have a wife."

"Tell me the gossip about him and my daughter, Elaine ... may I call you Elaine, by the way?"

"Please."

"And I'm Serena."

"We shall be good friends," Elaine cooed. "I've always been fond of you Americans. Perhaps because of my time in Hollywood."

"When was that?"

"A thousand years ago. But never mind me. You ask about Joachim."

"Should I be concerned about Christina?"

Elaine thought for a time. "How can I say this?"

Serena felt her stomach clench. These were not words a mother wanted to hear.

"Joachim is handsome and dashing. Errol Flynn and Tom Cruise in one. But he is struggling to find his—how do you say?—manhood. His life is fast cars, polo ponies and women. But maybe I should say *was*. They say since Christina, he is a changed man. Very jealous and very much in love."

"I don't believe in eleventh-hour conversions," Serena said, "especially not when it comes to men."

"But usually they do grow up, Serena, and because a woman changes them. Joachim has much that is good. A thousand girls from good families would give their soul to have him."

"I'm not sure that's good enough, Elaine."

"You are a mother."

"Would you worry, if you were in my shoes?"

"About Jeffrey, but not Christina."

Serena sipped her martini and considered that. "How is Jeffrey's arrest affecting Christina's social standing?"

Elaine lowered her voice again. "This is the concern. People care about these things. If you want to know the truth, it is something the Monteiro da Silvas are struggling with."

"I don't think much of people who would hold an uncle's difficulties against a nineteen-year-old," Serena said pointedly. "In fact, I couldn't respect them if they did."

"Perhaps you are lucky then," Elaine said. "You will see what kind of man Joachim is. What better test of character is there?"

"What applies to Christina should apply to me, as well," Serena said. "After all, Jeffrey is my brother."

"I think you will find the good people of Rio are very openminded, whatever the Monteiro da Silvas may think. But you will see for yourself. I know Roberto wants this lunch for just the two of you, so I will go when he returns. But allow me to invite you to have lunch with me one day soon."

"That's very kind."

"Where are you staying?"

"At the Atlântica."

"Excellent. I will call you. I'm planning a gathering soon, so I will talk to you about that, as well."

"Thank you," Serena murmured, gratified by Elaine Risollo's warmth. Not that she cared what people thought of her; she didn't. But she did care about Christina. And if Serena was to exonerate Jeffrey, it would help if she didn't have all of Rio against her.

It occurred to her that Elaine's friendship might be just as important as Roberto's, maybe more so. First, it wasn't bought. Second, there could be no ulterior motives. Third, a woman sensed certain things going on that a man didn't notice. Serena knew nothing about Brazil, but she'd seen enough to surmise that the social movers and shakers of Rio might well know more about Drake's murder than the police ever would.

Copacabana

Koto's Toyota pulled up at the entrance to the Atlântica. Mike offered his hand to the detective. "Thank you, my friend," he said. "I think we're off to a good start. If what I've seen so far is any indication, we'll make a good team."

"I feel the same," Koto answered.

Mike gave him a friendly tap on the shoulder with his fist and got out of the car, his bruises and aching muscles objecting. He leaned in the open window. "You'll let me know about tomorrow, then?"

"Yes, I'll phone you about arrangements with von Vehrling."

Mike saluted and stepped back from the car. Koto drove off. Mike gazed over at the beach, wondering if he had time for a stroll. He knew there were acres of string bikinis there, but he asked himself if he really needed the torture. He answered the question by heading for the hotel.

Mike was crossing the lobby, wondering how things were going back at the Desert Palms in his absence, when Bebe popped up from behind a potted palm.

"Senhor Hamlin. *Desculpe.* Sorry. But I have what you wanted."

She was a lean and voluptuous child-woman, vulnerable and intimidating. He took her in, his eyes going from her strappy sandals to her blue eyes. Hard to be cool around such an imposing beauty, he thought.

"What I wanted?" he said, aware of nipples pushing through her skimpy, pale green cotton frock.

Bebe swung her tidy little shoulder bag around in front of her. "The gun, *senhor,*" she said under her breath.

"Oh. Oh, yes."

"I am sorry it took so long." She was looking at his battered face now.

"It's not long," he said. "Not long at all."

"I have also ammunition." She scrutinized his cheek.

Mike glanced around the lobby, more in reaction to her demeanor than any particular concern about being overheard. "Your gun is upstairs. Why don't we trade weapons there?"

Bebe considered that briefly. "Okay."

"Less public," Mike said, gesturing toward the elevator.

He followed her, admiring her body. There was no two ways about it, Bebe was an exceptional specimen. Poetry to the eye.

An elevator arrived almost immediately. They went up alone, Bebe leaning against the far side of the car, her eyes on the indicator lights so that she wouldn't have to look at him. Mike had no such compunction. He took in the angular lines of her cheekbones and jaw, her long neck and wide shoulders, her lithe limbs and curves. He was aware of her scent. She smelled of sweet fruit and flowers.

Bebe bore his scrutiny quietly, if not with aplomb. He knew he'd make an ass of himself if he didn't cool it, so he turned to watch the indicator lights.

The car stopped at the thirty-sixth floor and they exited. She followed him to the suite. Mike opened the door and she stepped in, then waited for him to indicate where to go. He pointed to the sofa.

"Make yourself at home. I'll get your gun."

He went to his room, retrieved Bebe's pistol from the rear of the shelf in his closet and took it to the sitting room. Bebe had removed a 9-mm automatic from her purse and set it on the coffee table along with a box of shells. Mike sat across from her, his aching leg giving out as he dropped into the chair. He placed her nickel-plated weapon next to his.

"Thank you," he said. "As it turned out, I didn't need it." Then, clearing his throat, he added, "Or, rather, I chose not to use it."

That gave her the courage to ask about his face. "You had a problem, *senhor?*"

"My biggest problem at the moment, *senhorita,* is being called *senhor.* It makes me feel like the president of the republic or somebody. But when a pretty girl calls me Mike it gives me a warm, friendly feeling inside."

"Better *il presidente* than warm and friendly, *senhor.* And as far as I am concerned, we are in Brazil, not Los Angeles."

He managed a hurt look. "I bet that deep down inside you there's a friendly person bursting to get out."

"What sort of problem gave you the color on your cheek?" she asked. "Was it a man or a woman?"

"Three men. Four, if you count the bait."

"Senhor?"

Mike gave her a brief account of his adventure with George Raft and company, though he didn't elaborate on the extent of his injuries—the fact that he couldn't take a deep breath without pain. Bebe listened with interest, her expressive face reflecting each blow as he recounted the details of the battle.

"You're right, Mike," she said when he'd finished. "You *are* stupid. But I'm sorry for this happening to you, just the same."

"I can be Mike if I'm stupid?"

"I have gave it another thought," she said. "Better Mike than *il presidente,* perhaps." She giggled like a schoolgirl.

He smiled at her adorable face. The fact that she felt sorry for him was almost worth a beating. Oh, he thought, the things a man was willing to do for a woman's favor.

"So how about I buy you a *choppe* and you can tell me how you'd have handled the Weasel, Brazilian style?" he said, feeling daring.

"I don't need *choppe* to say. It's very simple. Don't follow people down a dark alley."

Mike stroked his chin. "Hmm. Well, how about we discuss something that isn't simple over a *choppe*? Politics, say."

"I don't care about politics and I don't drink *choppe* while I'm working."

"Even if I have a note from Koto saying it's okay?"

"Do you have one?"

He thought for a moment. "We could telephone him."

Bebe shook her head. But she did smile. A promising sign.

"Okay," Mike said, "let's make it an ice-cream cone. That can't be against your religion."

Bebe's expression turned serious. "What is it you want, Mike? It's better, I think, if you just say it."

"You're a girl who likes the bottom line, I see."

"Pardon?"

"Let me answer you this way. Twenty percent of me is full of ulterior motives. But eighty percent of me is decent. The good wins out in the end, Bebe, especially if there's more of it. I think Plato or somebody once said that."

Bebe considered his response thoughtfully. She was apparently not an avid reader of Plato. "The eighty I can accept. It's the twenty that gives me doubts."

"Then what we need is somebody who'll sell us eighty percent of an ice-cream cone."

"I don't think this is possible," she said, sounding more innocent than she probably was.

"Then I'll buy you a whole one and take two bites out of it. How's that?"

Bebe giggled. Mike felt he was getting a glimpse of paradise.

She put her gun in her purse. He took his and the shells.

"I'll put this in my room."

He stashed his new automatic in a dresser drawer. Bebe was at the slider when he returned, her purse slung over her shoulder, her hip cocked with an air of defiance. Seeing him, she went to the door, sober faced. She seemed to have reconsidered the wisdom of accepting his invitation. He expected her to say she'd changed her mind.

They walked to the bank of elevators. When a car came, she moved to one side as she had before. He went to the other. This time she looked at him, the expression in her eyes bordering on accusatory. "You're wondering why I am going with you, aren't you?"

"Because eighty percent is more than twenty percent?"

She shook her head. "Because to trust you I must know you. It is not for a romantic reason."

"I can accept that," he said reassuringly.

Bebe was mollified by his response, though not fully at ease. He surmised that considerations from the past caused her to remain wary.

The elevator stopped on the sixth floor and an older Latin gentleman with strong cologne stepped between them, moving to the rear. He gave Bebe a long, appraising look. She raised her chin another notch.

When they reached the lobby, she stepped out of the elevator, pausing long enough for Mike to join her before they headed for the door. There was determination in her stride. He assumed she was bent on getting this date over with. Before they reached the outer doors, he took her arm, stopping her.

"If you feel uncomfortable about this, I'd rather you not go with me, Bebe. Fun is no fun if it isn't fun."

She gave him a quizzical look.

"Ever heard of Yogi Berra?" he asked.

Bebe shook her head.

"Then there's no point in trying to explain. Look, do you like ice cream?"

"Yes."

"Then let's go for the sake of the ice cream. Don't worry about me. We'll just eat and enjoy."

She nodded her agreement.

They went outside. Mike could smell the ocean. From the portico of the hotel he could see the mobs on the beach. He wondered if that was also the scent of suntan lotion in the air.

"So where's the nearest Baskin-Robbins?" he asked cheerfully.

He received another quizzical look. "Until I met you I thought I spoke English," Bebe said.

"It's an ice-cream store in America," he said, taking her arm. "I'm being flippant."

"I don't understand that word, either."

They started walking toward the boulevard.

"Serena would say I'm being a prick," he said. "Do you understand that?"

"Yes, but I don't think it's true. She is very fond of you. She says you are an honorable man."

"Oh? Does she?"

"It is the only reason I trust your. . . eighty percent."

Mike chuckled. "My bullshit, sweetheart. Let's call a spade a spade."

They came to the corner and waited to cross the boulevard. "There must be ice-cream vendors on the beach," he said.

"There is a refreshment stand two hundred meters," she said, pointing. "In those trees."

The traffic stopped and they crossed the street to the broad sidewalk bordering the beach. The wide expanse of sand started at the edge of the walk and sloped to the sea. Most people were crowded down by the water, thousands upon thousands of them, a band of humanity stretching several miles, from one end of Copa to the other. They were huddled under beach umbrellas or lying on blankets or beach chairs like shrimp on a broiler.

Mike looked down at the swirling pattern of the sidewalk and at the ankle straps on Bebe's sexy, sandaled feet. Because of his strong attraction to her he felt less than honest about luring her out with him. But he was also helpless not to give it his best shot.

"Can I make a confession," he said, "to clear my conscience?"

"What confession?"

"I invited you for an ice cream because I hope you'll learn to like me. You're so pretty, just looking at you is a joy."

"I see," she said, showing no surprise.

"I hope that doesn't upset you too much."

"Thank you for saying it honestly. It's better."

"The truth is usually safest. And the truth is I'm curious what you're like as a person. The detective part I've seen."

"I could save you a lot of trouble by telling you I am not so different from somebody else."

How terribly untrue, he thought. "The lovely of the earth carry a special burden," he said.

"I don't know what this means."

"It's not easy for a pretty girl. I feel sorry for you."

"Why don't I believe this?"

Bebe had a point. The fact was he wanted to go to bed with her, and on some level she knew that. But how could he explain that every once in a while a guy met a woman he simply had to have? Mike was no predator, but in this case his desire was uncompromising.

Undoubtedly, Bebe had encountered more than her share of that, which made him feel guilty. Yet this was about much more than sex or conquest. Ego had nothing to do with it. This was about unquenchable thirst. Desire of the most elemental variety.

If Bebe understood, she said nothing. She gazed out at the sea as they walked, reflecting. Mike did as well.

In the nearer stretches of sand there were volleyball nets erected at random intervals. Some were in use, others were not. The largest group of beachgoers was gathered around some body-building equipment. Girls in string bikinis watched muscle men pumping iron under the broiling sun.

Brazilians, Mike was discovering, celebrated their bodies. Most of them, like Bebe, for good reason, it seemed.

As they walked in silence, he mused about the fact that he was actually pursuing this girl, abandoning what dignity he had because of a compulsion he couldn't resist. Maybe it had something to do with age. Or maybe Serena. Whatever it was, he was caught up in it, riding the tide of his baser instincts.

Glancing up, Mike was startled by the sight of a familiar face. Seated on a bench thirty yards or so farther up the walk, smoking, was the Weasel.

The little man saw Mike at about the same time he saw him. He was instantly on his feet.

"Jesus."

Bebe looked at him.

"There's the Weasel, the little bastard who led me into that alley last night."

Mike hadn't gotten the words out before the shifty little guy turned and started running, nearly colliding with a woman pushing a stroller along the sidewalk.

"Come on, let's get him," Mike said. "I have a few questions I'd like to ask."

Mike went after him, only to discover his bruised legs weren't too thrilled with the notion of running. He glanced back at Bebe. She was bending over and removing her sandals. Ahead, the Weasel was scurrying away as fast as he could. Mike tried to pick up his pace, but his sore calf started cramping. He began to hobble.

The Weasel, meanwhile, looked back over his shoulder in panic, terror on his face. Mike pressed on, hoping the cramp would stretch out, but it started grabbing at him even worse. After another dozen strides he was forced to give up. As he came stumbling to a halt, Bebe went racing by, her skirt hiked up, her legs flying like a greyhound's.

Mike watched her go, dumbfounded. She closed in on the Weasel rapidly. He tried an evasive action, swerving into the street and nearly landing on the hood of an oncoming car. Correcting his course, he looped back toward the beach, this time crossing the sidewalk and heading straight for the sea like a lemming.

Mike continued limping along, watching the chase. The Weasel was flailing like a wounded boar caught in the mud. Bebe, by comparison, had the look of a cheetah, skimming the surface of the sand, her heels flying. The little man was no match for her. He hadn't gone thirty yards before she was on him, tackling him right in the middle of a volleyball game.

The Weasel put up no resistance, though he and Bebe did instantly draw a crowd. The volleyball players soon surrounded the pair, cutting off Mike's view.

Hobbling across the hot sand, he finally came upon the small throng and pushed his way to the middle. He found Bebe standing over the Weasel with arms akimbo, feet firmly planted astride his legs, looking like Artemis, triumphant over her kill. All that was missing were her bow and arrows.

Ignoring the hoots of the men, she glared down at her prey, letting his fear work for her. The Weasel was babbling something that probably wasn't much more coherent to the Brazilians than it was to Mike. But his sniveling brought laughter from the men.

Seeing Mike, Bebe decided to put an end to the charade. She leaned over and grabbed the groveling little man by the shirt, lifting him to his feet. The act elicited a roar of approval from the crowd. She picked up her sandals and, with her hand clamped firmly on the Weasel's collar, pushed her way through the crush of glistening brown bodies and headed for the nearest clump of trees. Mike limped along beside her.

"Bravo," he said. "I bet you ran anchor on the high-school relay track team."

"Mostly I ran from the older boys."

The Weasel, who was alternately pleading and lamenting, seemed positively terrified. He was soaked with sweat. Bebe had only a fine sheen of perspiration on her lip. She looked as cool as a glass of chocolate milk.

The Weasel began wailing more plaintively, and Bebe, who'd grown tired of his blather, gave him a firm shake, hurling a command to be quiet. He fell silent.

They came to the shade of the trees. The only people around were a few older women, sitting near the sidewalk. Bebe found an isolated place under a tree and kicked the legs out from under the Weasel, dropping him to the ground like a sack of potatoes. The man looked back and forth between them, his mouth hanging open with fear.

"Are you sure this is the one?" Bebe asked.

"The last time I saw him, he was close enough to spit on me, and he did," Mike said. "I'd recognize him anywhere."

"Não, senhor! Por favor. Por favor!" he pleaded.

"Perhaps I should ask your friend some questions," Bebe said.

"Be my guest."

She squatted down next to the Weasel. He shrank back as she got right in his face, grabbing his jaw much as George had taken hold of Mike's the night before. The guy's bloodshot eyes rounded.

Bebe questioned him. Mike couldn't understand much, but *não* seemed to be his favorite word. Bebe raised her voice, turning angry, but all it did was make her prey's eyes open wider in terror.

Losing patience, Bebe swung her purse around and took out her gun. Seeing it, the man began squealing desperately. Bebe pressed the muzzle under his jaw and repeated her questions in a low, firm voice. The Weasel's resistance collapsed like a cardboard box in a tropical downpour. He began sobbing as he spilled his guts, unable to get the words out fast enough.

Bebe listened, asking an occasional question. A couple of small children approached and older people watched from afar. Bebe sent the children away with a gesture and a pointed word.

Once the confession was over, she stood, looking Mike in the eye. They were very close, the scent of sweet fruit and flowers from her body fuller and richer than before.

"This guy is nobody," she said in a confidential tone. "A street criminal. He was hired by a man named Souza to watch the hotel and report when you left."

"Ah, Souza."

"You know him?"

"That's who the corpse in L.A. worked for. Koto told me."

"Oh."

"Did the Weasel here say anything else?"

"He claims to know nothing more. But the only way to be sure is if I beat him."

"I don't think that's necessary, Bebe. I wouldn't want you to bruise your knuckles."

She smiled. Mike stared at her mouth, fascinated by it. The Weasel tried to get up, and Bebe put her bare foot on his chest, shoving him back down.

"The question is, do you want to take him to the police?" she said. "They will put him in jail on your charge.

They could learn more. They are very strict on crimes against tourists."

"Ask him about Monteiro da Silva. See what he knows."

Bebe knelt again. This time her tone was gentle. She patted the man's cheek as she spoke. The Weasel listened carefully, but shook his head. Again Bebe stood.

"I think he knows nothing about Monteiro da Silva. He says Souza, the man who beat you in the alley, is the one he worked for. I believe this is the truth."

"Yeah, I do, too."

"What shall we do with him?"

"Let's make him an informer for our side. Tell him to keep his ears open. If he can find out who Souza is working for, or what he's up to, he'll earn himself a hundred dollars."

"A hundred?"

"Is that too generous?"

"For little more than that you can have someone killed."

"I'm not that desperate, Bebe. Make it fifty. He can leave a note with the doorman at my hotel."

Bebe relayed the message and, after a final warning, sent the Weasel on his way. The man scampered off like a fox set loose from a trap. Bebe watched him go.

"Don't expect anything of use from him, Mike. He is the kind who would sell his mother."

"So I gathered."

Bebe looked into his eyes. It was the most open and the least defensive he'd seen her. "Mike, if I may say something, I don't think you are hard enough for this work."

"What makes you say that?"

"Because you have a soft heart. Or are the criminals not so fierce in America?"

"I have a soft heart."

"Yes, I heard this in the words of Senhora Bouchard when she talked to me about you. For talking to ones such as that man, it is not so good to be soft. But for other things it is..."

"What, Bebe?"

"...Nice."

"I strive to be nice," he said, giving her a wink. He glanced around. "So where's the soda fountain? Is that little building where we get the ice cream?"

Bebe grinned, showing him her large, pearl white teeth. "You still want an ice cream?"

"Sure. Don't you?"

"Okay." Bebe turned and they headed for the sidewalk. "I think someday I will go to America on holiday."

"Why's that?"

"You are the first American I know so well," she said. "I wonder if they are all so nice there."

"Bebe, is that a compliment you just gave me?"

"It is the truth, Mike. And this is our relationship, is it not? We are very honest with each other."

"Yes, we are very honest with each other. But to answer your question, men are men everywhere, Bebe. Only the style changes."

"Perhaps I won't go to America, then."

He laughed. "You lucked out, sweetheart."

"Why?"

"No need to go to America. She sent her best to you."

Bebe laughed, rolling her eyes. "Yes, I see you are right that men are the same. Everywhere they have an ego."

She giggled, and Mike put an arm around her waist, bumping her hip against his as he squeezed her to him. She didn't object, but he decided not to push things too quickly. Releasing her, he pointed to the sign ahead.

"*Gelado*. I bet I know what that means."

Bebe gave him a shy look. "Sometimes you are very funny."

One small victory for mankind, Mike thought, smiling to himself. Please, God, let there be more.

As it turned out, they both liked vanilla. "Sometimes I eat chocolate," Bebe confessed as they carried their cones to a table, "but mostly vanilla."

"It's only vanilla for me," he replied. "I don't consider it a lack of imagination. I just found something I like, so I stick with it."

They sat at a small table on metal chairs in need of paint. Bebe asked him to hold her cone so she could put on her sandals. He watched her strapping them on. It was a curiously erotic sight. Was there anything this woman did that wouldn't arouse a man? He'd even found the rough stuff she'd used on the Weasel stimulating.

"I feel the same about women," he said, handing back her cone. "If you've got one you like, there's no need to look further."

"I don't believe you," Bebe said, swirling her tongue around the ice cream.

"No?"

"For a man this is not possible."

"I don't mean to say I'm not tempted. And it's conceivable I could even fall off the straight and narrow, but it wouldn't be without a tussle. The devil might be tougher than me, but he'd get a fight."

Bebe laughed. "You're very funny, Mike."

"I'm honest, sweetheart."

"Yes," she said. "I'm beginning to believe that part."

She watched him as she licked her ice cream. He'd seen sexy eaters in his life, but this one made his insides quiver. Bebe crossed her legs. Mike sighed like a schoolboy.

"Your ice cream," Bebe said, pointing.

He looked, but it was too late. A big drop ran down over his fingers. Drops started running everywhere. He quickly licked the melting cone. Bebe laughed again.

"You like seeing a man in distress, don't you?" he said.

"What do you mean?"

"First you ran past me chasing the Weasel, and now you sit laughing while my ice cream runs all over me."

"Is this my fault? I cannot say how fast you run."

"I had a cramp in my leg, you know. After last night I'm in bad shape. Normally I'd have given you a run for your money."

"What are you saying—that you want to race when you are healed?"

"Yes," he said, "I think I would. I can't have you thinking I'm a wimp."

"I don't care if you are a wimp. It's not so bad."

A grin crept across his face. "You know, that may be one of the nicest things a girl has ever said to me."

Bebe made an especially large swirl with her tongue. "Now I think you're lying again."

"No, actually it was the truth."

They ate in silence. Bebe was trying to decide how she felt about him, he could tell. It gave him heart. Nothing in the game of love was as stimulating as a little mutuality.

"So tell me, Bebe," he said, as he watched her eat the last of her cone, "do you like chasing bad guys and beating confessions out of them? Or is it something you just do?"

"It is my work. And it is also part of my world, Mike. In the favela I have known a hundred guys like that one, the Weasel, as you call him. They are many and the police are few. A woman must either have a man or know how to protect herself. Maybe both. But if it's either eating vanilla ice cream or putting a gun to a man's head, I like better the ice cream."

Mike studied her, licking his dripping cone as he did. "That's very nice poetry, Bebe."

She seemed to understand the compliment. He had an urge to take her hand. Only his fear of moving too quickly held him back.

"Hey, Bebe!" The voice came from behind them.

They both turned. A very large black man in a bright, multicolored shirt sauntered their way. He was perhaps forty or forty-five. Mike noticed Bebe tense. The man stopped at their table and stood above them, his hands on his hips. He was beaming a gap-toothed smile that wasn't at all friendly.

"It been a long time, man," he said in English strongly flavored by the Caribbean.

Bebe turned away, a look of disgust on her face. The man checked out Mike, who wasn't quite sure what to make of him.

"So, Bebe," the guy said in a singsong Jamaican accent, "what you doin' with white bread? Find a new way to feed that baby?"

With that, Bebe jumped to her feet and began screaming in Portuguese. Mike had no idea what she was saying, but judging by the way she was tapping her finger against the man's chest, there were threats involved. The man listened briefly, then grabbed her wrists, bringing her tirade to a sudden halt.

Helped by a rush of adrenaline, Mike got to his feet. Both the man and Bebe looked at him.

"Is there a problem?" Mike asked calmly.

"Mind your own business, white boy," the Jamaican said. There was no smile now.

"You interrupt a conversation I'm having, you make it my business, friend," Mike said firmly. "Now let go of the lady."

The man let go of Bebe and turned menacingly toward Mike. Bebe took the Jamaican's arm, saying something in Portuguese. The man hesitated, replying in a low tone. More conversation between them followed, then Bebe addressed Mike.

"Excuse me for a minute, please. I must discuss business with Arthur." With that, she turned and started to move away, pulling the Jamaican with her.

The man finally withdrew. Mike threw the rest of his cone into a nearby trash barrel and watched as Bebe and the Jamaican had an animated conversation. After a minute she returned, and Arthur sauntered off the other way, but not before sending a last dirty look in Mike's direction.

"Sorry," she said.

"Mind if I ask what that was about?"

"That was Arthur Kingsley. He is not a good man."

"So I gathered. What did he want?"

"I made a bad business deal with him once a long time ago and he doesn't let me forget."

Mike wondered what sort of deal and if it was his place to ask. And what was that comment about her baby? Koto had said the father of her child was a rich *carioca*. That didn't describe the Jamaican. Whatever it was Kingsley had said, Bebe was obviously trying to play it down.

They started walking back toward the hotel.

"Did your friend Arthur want money?" Mike asked.

Bebe looked at him with surprise. "How did you know?"

"There was something in his tone."

"Arthur is a bastard," she said darkly.

Mike decided to take a flier. "Is he blackmailing you?"

This time she looked shocked. "You *are* truly a detective."

"I'm a man with a caring heart."

"Well, don't think about Arthur," she said. "I don't. If I could, I never would see him again."

There was a finality to her tone. Mike accepted that—he didn't have a choice. But he was also coming to understand that Bebe was a good deal more than a ravishing innocent. She was a woman who'd lived life.

The Mercedes came to a sudden halt, and Serena looked out and saw that they were practically at the hotel. Roberto spoke to the driver, who responded, gesticulating and pointing.

"There's an accident," Roberto told her.

"Well, my hotel's right there. I can walk."

"Wait, my dear. The car is air-conditioned and comfortable. If the traffic doesn't clear, then we will walk."

Roberto squeezed her hand. He had been holding it since they'd left his club. A tiny step, but a meaningful one.

Serena glanced out at the crowd that had gathered. Then she saw Michael and Bebe, moving along the sidewalk toward the hotel. Her first reaction was pleasure. Michael needed a fling, and since she'd talked with Bebe, she was convinced that the girl could use one, as well.

Serena watched them. She detected a certain familiarity. Bebe seemed more engaging. Perhaps the seeds Serena had planted were bearing fruit.

The Mercedes inched forward, but Michael and Bebe were going faster. Then they stopped to face each other. Michael offered Bebe his hand. She took it and, going up on her toes, gave him a quick kiss on the cheek, then walked away. Michael looked after her. He had the demeanor of a schoolboy in love. Or in lust. In those few moments, Serena could see the whole story.

The driver managed to get past the wreckage. Serena glanced at the crumpled cars, recalling the accident in Los Angeles.

Once they'd gotten through the intersection, they made it to the hotel without any difficulty. Serena turned to Roberto as the driver got out of the car. "It was a delightful afternoon," she said.

"I can't say when I've enjoyed lunch more," he replied. He smiled a bit sadly. "I would insist you have dinner with me, but I must go to São Paulo this evening. It is unavoidable."

"It's just as well," Serena said. "I wouldn't want you getting tired of me."

"I know the saying that absence makes the heart grow fonder, but in this case it cannot be so," he replied with fervor.

Then, drawing her hand to his mouth, he kissed her fingers. The door beside her opened. Serena reached up and, slipping her hand behind his neck, gave him a quick kiss on the cheek.

"Thank you again, Roberto, and have a good trip."

She was out of the car and striding toward the door before he could say more. Glancing over her shoulder, she saw him looking after her wistfully, longingly even. She liked longing.

Serena gave Roberto a final wave before entering the hotel. As she made her way to the elevator, a bellboy came running to her with a message. Joachim Monteiro da Silva had telephoned and would call again. That was all the message said.

On the ride up to their floor she studied the note. There was no indication what the call was about and no suggestion of urgency. She put the slip of paper in her purse.

Entering the suite, she found Michael's door ajar. She could hear the shower. Under other circumstances she might have gone in to tease him, but it seemed wrong now.

Instead she went to her room and undressed. Had it not been for Michael, she would have walked around the suite naked. But since that was out, she slipped on a filmy caftan and went back to the sitting room. Michael came out the same time she did. He was in shorts and was toweling his hair.

"Have a nice cold shower, dear?" she said pleasantly.

The comment seemed to amuse him. "Think I needed one?"

"I saw you with Bebe."

"Oh?"

"You'd be smart to fall madly in love with her, Michael."

"I appreciate your blessing, but it was more business than a date," he replied.

Serena smiled to herself. "Really?"

He proceeded to recount the adventure on the beach and the encounter with the Jamaican. "I don't know what that guy Kingsley was about," he said, "but it didn't feel good."

"I think Bebe needs a friend, Michael, an understanding, sensitive man. You could be just what the doctor ordered."

He tossed his towel on a chair and sat down. "Why do I keep asking myself what you're up to, Serena?"

She sat on the sofa, elegantly spreading the skirt of her caftan. "The problem is you don't trust me."

She crossed her legs. Michael noticed.

"What do you have on under that?" he asked.

"Nothing."

"Hmm."

"Does that bother you?"

"No, I was just curious."

"It never crossed my mind that you'd care."

"I don't."

She smiled. "Michael, you have your hands full with Bebe. You don't have the time and energy to worry about me, too."

"Right, Serena. So tell me about your day."

"Well, I had a nice lunch with Roberto. Not so exciting as your ice cream with Bebe, but I'm picking up bits and pieces of information that might prove to be useful to us later on."

She was in the middle of telling him about Elaine Risollo when the telephone rang.

"I'll get it," he said.

He went to the phone. "Yo?... Ah, good afternoon to you, Mr. Monteiro da Silva," he said, glancing back at Serena. "Good to hear your voice.... How nice, but I think I'll have you speak to the *senhora*. She's the social director of the family." He put his hand over the mouthpiece. "It's your future son-in-law, dear. He'd like to invite us to dinner."

Serena went to the phone. "Keep talking like that, Mr. Hamlin, and you may end up with another shiner."

Michael grinned, handing her the phone.

"Hello, Joachim."

"Mrs. Bouchard. Am I calling at an unfortunate moment?"

Serena had to smile. What did he think—that the old folks spent all their time trying to get it on? "No, not at all. Michael and I were just chatting about the challenges of being a tourist. What can I do for you?"

"I want to invite you to dinner."

"How thoughtful."

"I would have called sooner, *senhora,* but my mother has obligations outside the country and cannot meet you. We'd hoped to arrange it before she left, but it was impossible.

However, my grandmother is here and I would like for you to meet her.''

"That sounds lovely, Joachim. When did you have in mind?"

"Would Monday evening be okay?"

"Yes, our calendar is clear."

"Then I shall send a car for you. Shall we say at six? Unfortunately, our estate is some distance, Mrs. Bouchard."

"Call me Serena. Mrs. Bouchard sounds so old. I was quite young when I had Christina, you know." She glanced at Michael, who broke into a broad grin.

"Yeah, you were precocious, all right," he mouthed.

Serena flipped him the bird.

"I would be honored to call you Serena," Joachim said. "And now, if I may, Christina would like a word with you."

Serena waited and her daughter came on the line. "Mom, isn't Joachim wonderful? I'm dying for you to meet him."

"He seems delightful."

"He's the best."

"I wouldn't want less for you, darling. But never mind Joachim for the moment. I've hardly had a chance to see you. Why don't you come into town so we can do some shopping or something? Do you have plans for tomorrow?"

"Mom, I'd love to, but Joachim and I are going riding with some friends and there's a party afterward."

"How about Sunday, then?"

"Can we make it during the week? Joachim goes into town and I can catch a ride with him."

"That would be fine, Christina. Whatever works for you."

"But we'll be seeing you Monday night, don't forget."

"Yes, I can't wait."

"Mom . . ."

"Yes, Christina?"

"Are you happy for me?"

"Of course, darling. I'm ecstatic. And so is Michael."

"Oh, I hope so."

They said goodbye, and Serena eased the receiver into the cradle. She stood there, contemplating the conversation.

"There's something wrong with this," she said to Michael. "I can't tell you what, but there's something wrong."

"His phone number in that gangster's pocket is what's wrong."

"No, it's more than that. I smell trouble."

"A man in connection with a nineteen-year-old girl is trouble by definition."

"That's not it, either," she said.

"What then?"

"I don't know. That's the problem."

"Well, let's don't borrow trouble. We've got enough on our hands with Jeffrey."

She returned to the sitting area, dropping onto the sofa beside him. She took his hand and put it on her knee. His palm was warm through the thin caftan. His fresh scent enveloped her and she felt a twinge of arousal. It wasn't what she'd had in mind.

"What about Jeffrey?" she asked. "Did you find out more?"

Michael recounted what Koto had told him over coffee. Serena listened solemnly, then told him what she'd learned from Roberto.

"So how is this going to sift out?" she asked when they'd finished comparing notes. "Is there hope?"

"I'll be in a better position to answer that after tomorrow. I'm anxious to talk to this Hector von Vehrling character and his sister. I have a hunch the ballgame is going to turn on them."

"I wish you hadn't said that. Now I won't sleep."

"I'm sure Cabral will be happy to distract you."

"Roberto had to go to São Paulo."

"Then you're on your own tonight."

"I was thinking of spending a quiet evening at home," she said. "Maybe I'll have a room-service dinner. How about you?"

"No plans."

"I suppose we could dine together."

Michael drew a long, slow breath. "Only if you put on some goddamn underwear."

She got up and swished off to her room. "You're absolutely right, Michael. Absolutely right."

SATURDAY
September 16th

Copacabana

Bebe arrived bright and early. Serena was in her room changing, having decided she didn't like what she had on. Mike let Bebe in.

"Bom dia," she said.

"Bom dia," he replied. He checked her out unabashedly.

Bebe wore long white pants, a skimpy orange top and the same sexy sandals. Her skin was as rich and smooth as the homemade butter-pecan ice cream his aunt used to make when he was a kid.

"You look terrific," he said, gesturing for her to come in.

"Thank you, Mike." She paused to inspect his cheek.

She smelled like orange blossoms. It made his mouth water.

"It looks better," she announced. "I guess you stayed away from dark alleys last night."

"Honey, I didn't so much as stick my nose out of the hotel."

She gave him a wide, happy smile. "Only a few days in Rio and already you are smarter."

"Yeah, and the body's healing. Give me another day or two and I'll be ready for that footrace." He gestured toward the table. "Will you have some coffee? Serena's in a clothes-changing mood and it could be a few minutes before she's ready."

"No, I don't need anything." She went to the windows for a look at the sea.

Mike studied her. He noted a change in her demeanor, an effervescence that he hadn't seen before. The little kiss she'd given him when she said goodbye the previous afternoon was perhaps the first sign of a change in attitude.

It had been a completely innocent gesture—suggestive more of friendship and camaraderie than love and affection—but it had stayed with him all evening. Bebe had certainly done wonders for his libido.

"It's so beautiful the ocean, isn't it, Mike?"

"Hmm. Gorgeous."

She glanced over her shoulder at him, laughing.

"What puts you in such a cheerful mood this morning?" he asked. He'd gone to the table and stood sipping his coffee.

"I don't know. Sometimes I just wake up happy. The world seems so beautiful on some mornings. Isn't it that way for you?"

"Yes, maybe so."

She gave him a lift, he realized. Just looking at her did something for him, if only make him feel young and alive. Maybe that's why God made fresh breezes and young, firm flesh.

Serena chose that particular moment to make her entrance, floating into the sitting room like a sailing yacht riding the wind. She'd changed from a tailored dress to linen pants. Seeing the way Bebe was dressed, she seemed pleased by her decision.

"Oh, you're here, Bebe! Good. Nice to see you."

"Good morning, Mrs. Bouchard."

"It's Serena, dear. I insist on that. Michael and I are virtually the same age, you know." She gave him a sideward glance. "You haven't said otherwise, have you, Michael?"

"I try not to discuss your age with anyone, Serena."

She beamed. "See how well trained he is, Bebe? It's the untrainable ones a girl has to avoid."

Bebe smiled politely.

Mike thought he heard uncertainty in Serena's voice, an edge. He'd never seen her less than completely confident around another woman, but there was something new at work here. Did a mature woman fall back on guile in the presence of a youthful competitor? he wondered. Or was Serena at war with herself?

"Michael tells me you were a true heroine at the beach yesterday," Serena said. "Single-handedly captured a bad guy."

Bebe lowered her eyes, blushing. "It wasn't much. The man was little and not so fierce."

"He apparently gave Michael a challenge the night before," she said, giving him a sardonic look.

"Brains and beauty triumph over sloth and stupidity every time," he said.

"Are we talking about you or your friend, the Weasel?"

"Mike couldn't run because of his injuries," Bebe said, springing to his defense. "And in the alley there were four against him."

Serena chuckled as she went to the breakfast table. "Michael, I think you've found yourself a loyal partner."

"Would that it were true," he said under his breath.

Serena tore the corner off a pastry. "I understand you also ran into an old friend at the beach," she said to Bebe as she popped the bit of pastry into her mouth.

"It was not a friend," Bebe said, her expression dour.

"Oh?"

"Please, Mrs. Bouchard, this is not something I wish to speak of. It has nothing to do with the murder of Mr. Manville."

"Sorry, Bebe, I didn't realize it was a sensitive issue."

An awkward moment followed in which no one said a word. Serena finally took the initiative. "Well, boys and girls," she said, "what do you think? Shall we go find Drake's killer?"

"I think Jeffrey would be pleased if we did," Mike said. "Just let me get my gun."

Santa Teresa

Serena didn't get nervous until they began climbing the twisting, cobblestone streets of Santa Teresa Hill. Located close to the center of Rio, it was one of the first suburbs, having gotten its start, according to Bebe, when the wealthy denizens of the city fled to higher ground during the eighteenth century to escape a yellow-fever epidemic. "Until then," she said, "it was a tangle of secret trails used by slaves to escape their masters."

For some reason, the comment made Serena think of her brother. But Jeffrey, and the precipitous terrain of Santa Teresa, were only part of the reason she felt squeamish. Visiting the site where Drake had been killed struck her as morbid. And the closer they got, the less certain she was that she wanted to be there.

Bebe, who was driving her dilapidated Renault, was pridefully giving her tour-guide commentary. Churches and art museums flashed by with the dizzy blur of a rock video on MTV. Serena didn't try to understand. It was all she could do to keep from falling over with all the twisting and turning.

Back at the hotel, the poor thing had apologized profusely for her modest car. "It's not beautiful, Mrs. Bouchard, but it runs and it's better in the narrow streets." The back seat was covered with a nice clean blanket and the interior appeared to have gotten a fresh dose of spit and polish for this outing. Had Serena thought about it, she could've hired a limo, but she wasn't about to humiliate the girl by suggesting it for future expeditions. Fortunately it was still morning and the lack of air-conditioning not so noticeable.

Michael, she surmised, was enjoying Bebe's common touch. He'd always abhorred pretension. For the first year of their marriage he'd kept the VW Beetle he'd owned when

she met him, eschewing the Porsche she had offered to buy.
Eventually he'd bought a Pontiac Grand Am with his own
money so as not to embarrass her too much. She'd always
felt badly about that, but what could she do? He'd been
fiercely proud when younger and, although he'd mellowed,
he still took great pleasure in being his own man. "Real
people," he liked to say, "have dignity because they lack
pretension."

Watching the two of them interacting in the front seat,
Serena could tell Michael had a thing for both Bebe and her
car. It was difficult to believe that somebody else's modest
life-style could make Serena feel inadequate, but that's what
was happening. Being with the two of them, she felt like a
spoiled bitch.

Bebe, to her credit, did not focus her attention exclusively on Michael. She spent as much time looking over her
shoulder at Serena as she did watching Michael and the
road.

"I must tell you, Mrs. Bouchard, that we are coming to
the villa of Senhor von Vehrling before the appointment so
that we can have a little inspection. And maybe Mike would
wish to speak with the neighbor who saw your brother leaving the villa."

"That's entirely up to you and Michael," Serena said,
gripping the badly worn door handle.

Bebe casually swerved to avoid an oncoming motor
scooter, hardly missing a beat. "It is important to smell a
place as well as see it," she said. "The less people around,
the better."

"Fine, Bebe. Whatever you think."

Bebe honked at some children who'd strayed onto the
pavement, but zipped around them without slowing.

Serena tried to take in her surroundings calmly, knowing
this had once been Jeffrey's home. Oddly, it had more
character than she'd expected. The elegant homes in California could be neat and tidy to the point of sterile. These
mansions of Santa Teresa Hill were anything but. The higher
the Renault climbed, the larger the villas became. Most of

them looked worn, many shoddy and a few positively rundown, but they all were distinctive.

The evidence of past grandeur remained. Fancy European ironwork was commonplace, and statuary was abundant. Everywhere Serena looked she saw elaborate staircases and ornamentation, flowers in profusion and picture-postcard views of Guanabara Bay. Most striking of all was the way the grand old Victorian Era homes clung to the steep hillside as if by their fingernails. It reminded her of Sausalito. She liked the views, but to actually sleep in one of these eagle nests was unthinkable.

Near the crest of the hill Bebe pulled over and stopped at an iron gate. She set the hand brake and turned off the engine. Turning to Serena, she said, "This is the villa, Mrs. Bouchard."

Serena peered past the gate, but couldn't see much. The banana and palm trees were so dense that the fronds of the taller ones virtually formed a canopy. She lowered her window. In the unexpected silence she could hear a chorus of birds. The air was rich with the scent of bougainvillea. On the surface it seemed a peaceful, tranquil setting, but she knew better. Drake had been killed here, scarcely more than a week ago.

"We can get out," Bebe announced unnecessarily.

Michael opened his door, as did Bebe, but Serena hesitated. Then, looking out the window at Michael, she said, "Maybe I'll just sit here a few minutes. I don't like encounters with people such as this von Vehrling unless I'm prepared."

He nodded understandingly. "Yes, I know."

"I don't believe in ghosts," Serena said, "but knowing what happened here, I'm a little . . . spooked."

Bebe came around the car and looked in with concern. The window framed both their faces, as if she and Michael were in a photograph. It was a remarkable sight. A god and a goddess, two beautiful people—Bebe with her little Renault, Michael with his little tract house in Vegas. Serena wanted to give them her blessing, say something nice, but the most unexpected thing happened. Tears filled her eyes and she couldn't speak.

Bebe seemed troubled by Serena's emotion, but Michael knew to keep his mouth shut. Serena blew her nose and thought of making love with Michael. She thought of Jeffrey in jail. She thought of Christina on the verge of marrying a polo player with connections to God only knew who, and she wanted desperately to sob.

Normally Serena was tough as an old boot and rarely shed a tear in public. But for some reason everything that had been happening caught up with her. Michael seemed to be slipping through her fingers, and that wasn't supposed to be a problem.

"You two play detective," she managed to say before blowing her nose again. "I'll rest a few minutes."

She could tell Michael was a little disconcerted, but he didn't make an issue of her uncharacteristic behavior. He turned and looked through the wrought-iron gate, then back across the road. "Why don't we go talk to the lady who saw Jeffrey?" he said to Bebe.

"It must be that house," the girl said, pointing.

Serena glanced at the old stucco mansion. It was nearer the road than Drake's villa. In fact, she could see the balcony where the woman must have been when she saw Jeffrey leave. She shivered at the thought that some stranger's testimony could send her baby brother to his doom. Under normal conditions she'd have charged in, ready to confront an accuser, but she just didn't feel up to it. She had to get herself together for Hector von Vehrling. Michael had said he and his sister would be the key to the case.

"You two go on," she said, taking a calming breath. "I'll sit here and meditate."

Michael and Bebe crossed the road and made their way to the door of the big house. They knocked. A minute passed before the door opened and they went inside.

Serena sat upright and closed her eyes. At first she became aware of Bebe's soft, clean blanket, then her mind turned to the fragrant smells wafting in the window. She thought she picked up a hint of incense. That made her think of the old fortune teller on the beach she'd gone to visit with Maximino all those years ago. She wondered if he'd ever gotten all his babies.

It had been awhile since she'd meditated. It took a few moments for her to clear her mind. Michael had to be banished. And Bebe. She heard Roberto's voice, the warm throbbing tones, but she sent that away, too. She began slipping into a deeper meditative state, letting her thoughts go. Under she went—deeper and deeper and deeper.

Mike sat in a musty old armchair, listening to the persistent ticking of the grandfather clock in the entry hall. And he watched Bebe, perched on the edge of an antique loveseat, the whites of her eyes showing as she glanced around in awe. He understood why. She couldn't have seen many places like this. It looked more like the set of a Sherlock Holmes film than a mansion in Rio de Janeiro. If there had been fog outside instead of tropical sun, he would have said they were in London.

According to the maid, the owner was an Englishwoman named Penelope Ingram, a spinster who'd lived in Santa Teresa for fifty years. She'd sent word that she would receive them if they would be good enough to give her a few minutes.

Bebe stared for a long time at the large oil painting that dominated one wall of the room. It was a portrait of a tall, white-bearded gentleman with a stern British demeanor who, judging by his attire, must have ruled some greater or lesser empire during Queen Victoria's reign. A revered Ingram progenitor, in all probability.

"Doesn't look too friendly, does he?" Mike said.

Bebe shivered. "Once as a child I went to the Museum of the Republic. There was a painting like that of an early president, I believe, with a big white beard. I thought it was surely God. And when I said my prayers at night I always imagined it was the man in the painting listening to me."

Mike laughed. Bebe's innocence was irresistible. But he also remembered the lioness who'd chased down the Weasel, an equally compelling image.

"This fellow looks like he thought he was God," Mike said, bemused.

"I assure you, young man, he did indeed."

The voice came from the entry at the other side of the room. A tiny old woman, rosy cheeked and hunched, sat in a wheelchair. Her maid stood behind the chair. He and Bebe got to their feet.

"That was my grandfather," the woman said. "He could roar like God, I assure you." She signaled for the maid to push her into the room. "I'm Penelope Ingram. And you must be the young American investigator who wishes to question me about the murder."

"Yes, ma'am. Mike Hamlin's my name. And this is my associate, Bebe."

The old women studied her. "Looks more like one of those girls in the fashion magazines to me. Very pretty indeed. These days I shouldn't be surprised if you were to tell me she was a nuclear physicist. Please sit down."

Mike and Bebe took their seats.

"You may as well ask your questions, young man," Penelope Ingram said, "because I haven't much time to give you. And I won't be offering you tea, because you hadn't the courtesy to warn me of your visit. So let's get on with it. What do you want to know?"

"I apologize for dropping in this way, Mrs. Ingram, but—"

"It's *Miss* Ingram, but never mind. This is an age of directness, which you know perfectly well, I'm sure, Mr. Hamlin, considering you chaps in America invented it. Do you want me to recount what I saw and heard? I assume that's why you're here."

"Please, Miss Ingram."

"Well, it's not much, but I shall tell you what I told the police. Only the facts. I don't embellish, Mr. Hamlin."

"I'd be grateful for whatever you can tell me."

"On the day in question I was upstairs in my rooms. It's a large suite and I spend most of my time there, you see. When I became wheelchair bound, I had a small lift installed in the back of the house, but I don't fancy the thing very much and prefer to stay upstairs. Anyway, I heard what sounded like a gunshot. That being an uncommon phenomenon in this neighborhood, I proceeded to wheel myself out onto the balcony. Upon arriving I saw the young gentleman who resided with Mr. Manville these past months leaving the estate by the pedestrian gate."

"You know Jeffrey Bouchard?"

"I've never formally made his acquaintance, Mr. Hamlin, but I knew who he was. Mr. Manville, rest his soul, I *did* meet on one occasion, though I don't claim it to be a particular honor. Artists I admire, mind you. Stage actors and musicians, as well, but not film stars."

"I understand."

"I'm sure you don't, but never mind. Do you have other questions?"

"You say you saw Mr. Bouchard leave the villa after hearing a gunshot. Are you certain it was a gunshot?"

"I'm not a munitions expert, but that's what it sounded like to me."

"How long a time lapsed from when you heard the shot until you saw Mr. Bouchard leaving?"

"I move very slowly in this chair, as you might imagine. I should say at least one minute, perhaps one and a half."

"I see. And what was Mr. Bouchard's demeanor?"

"He looked terrified, to be candid. And he was in a very great hurry. He ran down the street."

"I see you aren't wearing glasses, Miss Ingram. How is your vision?"

"At a distance I see well, though I presume you'd rather I didn't."

"I'm interested in the unvarnished truth, Miss Ingram, and the best way to get it is by asking direct questions."

"Stand across the room and ask me how many fingers you're holding up, if you should like an experiment, Mr. Hamlin."

"That won't be necessary, ma'am. But let me ask you this, did you see Mr. Bouchard arrive at the villa?"

"No."

"Did you hear more than one shot?"

"No, only one. It was just after I'd come into my room from the bathroom. It's well insulated, so there might have been a gun battle outside and I wouldn't have known. I'd been in there for some time because I was alone. Janete, my maid, was away at the market."

"I was going to ask if she heard the shot," Mike said.

"No, she wasn't here."

"Let me ask you this, Miss Ingram, did you see a woman at the villa the morning Mr. Manville was killed?"

"No, the only time I was on the balcony was when I went out to investigate the sound of the gunshot."

"Have you ever seen a woman at the villa, apart from staff?"

"Mr. Manville had various ladies and gentlemen calling on him, but I assume you are inquiring about an habitual visitor."

"Yes."

"I did see a particular woman arriving and leaving the villa on several occasions in the last two months, yes, Mr. Hamlin. Three or four times a week, I should say."

Mike glanced at Bebe, who was on the edge of her seat. He leaned forward. "Do you know who it was?"

"No."

"Could you describe her?"

"Yes, certainly. She was middle-aged, very aristocratic, always well dressed. She was tall and had dark red hair. She invariably arrived in a chauffeur-driven Mercedes automobile. Normally she stayed for an hour or two before leaving."

"Would you be able to identify the woman if you saw her?"

"I must say I didn't see her up close. Only at a distance. I have a general impression, but no more. I'm sure you'd prefer it were otherwise, but I must be honest, Mr. Hamlin."

"When was the last time you saw her at the villa?" he asked.

Penelope Ingram thought. "In the past month less frequently than at first. Of course, I was away on holiday for several days at the end of August...but I would say three weeks ago."

Mike turned to Bebe. "Do you have any questions?"

"I am wondering about the Mercedes, Mike. Perhaps the *senhora* can tell us what color it was and something about the driver."

"Certainly. It was black. The chauffeur was white, but I can't tell you more than that. I never saw his face clearly."

Mike considered the information, stroking his chin. "I have one last request, Miss Ingram. Would it be possible for us to have a look across the road from the perspective of your balcony?"

"Normally I'd say no on principle, considering I'm a lady and it's my bedroom we're discussing. But you American chaps make a person want to be modern, if only to show she's not afraid. I'll have Janete show you the balcony, if you promise not to linger."

"Thirty seconds is all we need."

"Very well." Miss Ingram turned to her maid and in rapid, perfectly fluent Portuguese, issued instructions.

Janete led them upstairs. Bebe immediately engaged the woman in conversation—to ferret what information she could, Mike assumed.

The bedroom suite was as old-fashioned as the downstairs. Mike had no idea what a Victorian bedchamber looked like, but he imagined this was probably it. The rooms were neat, if dark and ponderous. He spent no time checking them out, however, but went right out onto the balcony.

From this higher perspective he was able to see the roof line of the von Vehrling villa through the trees. It was set back farther from the road than most of the places they'd seen. Because of the configuration of the hill and the curve of the road, there were no structures nearby. The closest house was on the downhill side of Penelope Ingram's mansion.

From the balcony he could not see the front door of the villa, though much of the walk leading to the road was visible. He had a clear view of Bebe's car and Serena seated in back. Miss Ingram would conceivably have had a good view of Jeffrey leaving the property. The gate accessing the drive was on the uphill side, and the drive itself was pretty well obscured from view by vegetation.

Bebe joined him on the balcony, leaning on the railing and studying the scene. She gave him a sideward glance when she sensed he was looking at her.

"So what do you think?" he asked.

"I think the *senhora* is honest and tells the truth to us."

"Why? Because she speaks with a British accent and her grandfather looks like God?"

Bebe gave him an exasperated look. "No, Mike, I am not so stupid. I say that because the maid told me Senhora Ingram is a good and honest person who can see and hear well. Janete also told me there are two maids who work in Senhor von Vehrling's house, not one."

"Oh, really?"

"Mike, you should know the servants know everything. They are the first ones you must ask when you want to know something."

"I do my own dishes, Bebe."

"Doesn't Mrs. Bouchard have servants?"

He laughed with embarrassment. "Yes. I've talked to them myself to find out what's going on. I guess you're out-thinking me as well as outrunning me."

That pleased her.

"I'm glad I've got you for a sidekick. Two heads are better than one."

"What is a sidekick?"

"The pretty one on the team," he said, giving her a wink.

She blushed. But to cover her embarrassment she turned and headed back inside, where Janete was waiting. "Come on, Mike," Bebe called, "our thirty seconds are up."

Serena became vaguely aware that Michael was softly saying her name. She opened her eyes. He was at the window, peering in at her.

"How are you feeling?" he asked.

"Much better," Serena said, blinking. She took a long, slow breath to draw herself up from her meditative state. "Did you talk to the neighbor?"

"Yes. Interesting lady. A British spinster who came to Rio with her brother during World War II and has been here ever since."

"My, you charmed her life story out of her," Serena said, flexing her hands.

"Penny was cantankerous at first, but she warmed up a bit as we were leaving. Offered us tea belatedly, invited us back."

"I knew you'd be useful on this trip, Michael," Serena chided.

"I should put that on my business card—'Specializing in little old ladies.'"

"Why qualify it? 'Specializing in females of every description' is more accurate."

"Are you complaining or giving me a compliment?"

"I'm being cheeky," she said. "So tell me, did you get anything useful from the old dear?"

"A few tidbits, nothing that'll break the case, I don't think."

"Is she a credible witness?"

"Unfortunately."

"Oh." Serena looked past him at Bebe, who had gone over to the rusted pedestrian gate and was trying to open it.

"Want to get out and have a look around with us?" he asked.

"Yes, I feel much better."

Michael opened the door and she climbed out. Bebe had the gate open. Smiling at them, the girl started up the walkway, taking the steps two at a time.

"God," Serena said, watching her go, "I couldn't keep up with her if I was Jane Fonda. And I don't imagine you could, either."

"I've tried and failed."

"Have you?"

"At the beach."

"That's right, the day the hare outran the tortoise."

They started up the steps.

"It wasn't a fair contest. I was on the disabled list."

"If Bebe had been naked, you probably would have found the strength to catch her."

"Intriguing thought," he said.

"Yes, isn't it?"

They wound their way through the tropical vegetation and up the steps to the front porch. Serena's heart was pounding. She hadn't worked out in weeks. She peered around as she caught her breath. Bebe was nowhere in sight.

"Where do you suppose she went?" she asked Michael.

"She said she wanted to scout around."

Serena gazed back out at the garden. Off to the left was a view of the bay and, farther down the slope, snatches of red tile rooftops. They couldn't see the road. Though it was a densely populated area, there was a feeling of isolation about the place. Serena told herself that this had been Jeffrey's home, but she still wouldn't allow herself to think about what had happened inside.

"When is von Vehrling supposed to be here?" she asked.

Michael checked his watch. "In ten or fifteen minutes."

Just then Bebe came around the house with a wizened little man in tow. "This is the gardener," she announced. "I thought we could ask him some questions before Senhor von Vehrling comes."

"Good idea," Michael said.

Serena studied the curious little man, whom Bebe towered over by ten inches. His appearance and demeanor were elflike. He had exaggerated features, leathery skin and humble eyes that only occasionally made contact. He wore dirty work clothes and held his straw hat in his hands, his head bowed. He declined to come onto the porch, standing instead at the foot of the steps.

"This is Paulo," Bebe said. "He works at the house almost every day, but on the day of the murder he was at his family's, his off day. He tells me that Ana, the deaf maid, is in the house, but that the other maid is not here since Senhor Manville was killed."

"There's another maid?" Serena said.

"Yes, the neighbor's domestic told Bebe," Michael interjected. "Interestingly, the police are either unaware of that fact, or they didn't let Koto know."

"They didn't tell him," Bebe said. "I am sure. He would have said this to me."

Michael nodded. "Ask Paulo who the other maid is and if he knows what's happened to her."

The two had an extended conversation, then Bebe translated. "He says Maria is the sister of Ana. Maria is the main one. She translates with hand words for Ana. He says Ana is very upset because Maria is gone, but he does not know where or what has happened, because only Ana knows, and without Maria she has no mouth or ears to communicate."

Serena and Michael exchanged glances.

"That could be convenient for somebody," Serena said.

"My thought precisely. Bebe, ask Paulo if he can communicate with Ana at all."

There was more patter.

"He says yes, but only the simplest things."

"Maybe we can talk to the maid before von Vehrling gets here."

Bebe and Paulo spoke together again.

"The gardener and I will go to the kitchen to look for Ana," Bebe said. "We will let you into the villa in a minute."

They went off and Serena folded her hands prayerfully. "You see, Michael, there's a lot more to this than meets the eye. It can't be a coincidence that one of the maids disappears right after Drake is murdered."

"You're right about that."

"My guess is there's a conspiracy. The question is if the police are involved."

"We'll find out," he said, sounding more determined than he had yet.

The front door swung open, and both Mike and Serena turned around. Bebe admitted them into the cool interior of the house.

"Isn't it pleasant in here," Serena said, glancing around the sparsely furnished entry hall. "I hadn't realized how warm it had gotten...." Her voice trailed off as a round little woman with a fearful face appeared behind Bebe.

The woman's neck was badly swollen with what looked like a goiter. Her short-cropped hair was dry and lifeless. Mike's first thought was that she needed medical attention. The gardener, Paulo, his hat still in his hands, was beside her. They resembled a Brazilian version of *American Gothic.*

"This is Ana," Bebe announced, closing the door.

The maid was too shy to look at them, keeping her eyes on the floor. Mike saw they were facing an uphill battle. Serena sat on a bench, leaving him and Bebe to contend with the maid. For the next few minutes they played a game of translation and pantomime: Mike to Bebe in English, Bebe to Paulo in Portuguese, the gardener to Ana in hand signs and facial expressions, punctuated by grunts and groans. What a way to save Jeffrey's ass! Mike realized that if it hadn't been so pathetic, it would have been funny.

It was soon apparent they weren't getting anywhere. Maria was gone and Ana was sad. Ana didn't know where her sister was. That made her sad, too. It was all very, very sad. Five minutes and that was the extent of what Mike had managed to develop.

Bebe tried to get information about the day of the shooting, but it was clearly beyond the capabilities of their jerry-rigged system. Ana was growing progressively more distraught and finally went to an adjoining room, beckoning Bebe to follow. Mike looked at Serena, who rolled her eyes and patted her face with her handkerchief. Her expression seemed to indicate she'd rather be buying a hotel in London.

Mike went over and offered her his hand. "Come on, sweetheart, bear up."

"I know I'm being a twit, Michael, and I'm sorry."

They went off in pursuit of Bebe and the maid. Paulo took the opportunity to escape to the garden. Smart man.

They found themselves in the library. There was the massive desk, as Jeffrey had described, and behind it a bookcase with glass doors, which covered the entire wall. The ceilings were high and a large oriental carpet covered the floor. Mike's eye went to where the gun would have been. There was nothing there, of course—just the mental image of the murder weapon inviting Jeffrey to pick it up.

The desk was solid. Mike couldn't have seen a body behind it from where he stood. Ana had gone behind the desk and was pointing to the floor. There was horror on the poor woman's face and bizarre sounds of anguish came from her throat.

Then something very strange happened. Ana glanced up and, seeing Serena, opened her eyes even wider. She put her hands to her mouth, shrieked and went waddling from the room. They could hear her making hideous sounds all the way to the back of the house.

"What's wrong with her?" Serena asked.

Mike shook his head. "Who knows?"

"I'm sorry," Bebe said. "I don't think she is much help."

"Not without her sister," Mike said. "You're right, Serena, it's no accident that Maria is missing."

"Perhaps Senhor von Vehrling will know something of this," Bebe said.

"Yes, I intend to ask him."

Serena appeared queazy. "What on earth did Ana see that got her so excited?"

Mike took her arm and led her around the desk. On the edge of the carpet was a large, faded, rust-colored stain.

Serena gasped. "Jesus," she said in a hoarse whisper. "That's blood, isn't it? Drake's blood." She backed away.

"You okay?" Mike asked.

She gave a half nod. "I'll just wait in the other room." Turning, she walked briskly from the library.

Bebe, who'd observed everything, appeared distressed on Serena's behalf.

"She'll be okay," Mike assured her. "Serena's got a few soft spots, but when the chips are down, she's tough as nails."

"My sister is the same. If she sees blood, she faints. But if we wrestle with our arms, she wins."

The image of Bebe wrestling with another girl was compelling, but not one to be pursued at the moment. He examined the stain. An attempt had obviously been made to clean it, but blood could be a stubborn agent.

He pictured Drake Manville lying in a pool of blood, with Jeffrey hovering over him, on the verge of panic. Mike could envision the scenario going pretty much as Jeffrey had described. Nothing he'd seen cast doubt on the veracity of the story.

Bebe watched as Michael wandered about the room, recreating Jeffrey's movements. The views, the angles, the distances made sense. He stood where Drake had stood. He saw where the killer would have entered the room. Outside the doorway he could see a portion of the stairway leading to the second floor.

In the quiet of the villa he heard Serena's heels moving across the hardwood in the entry hall, probably into the salon on the other side of the house.

He glanced at the walls of the library. There was art, mostly oils. The volumes in the bookcase were hardcovers, many of them of collector quality. Through the glare of the glass he read several titles—most in Portuguese, but some in French and English, as well.

Bebe watched him carefully. He paused long enough to return her gaze. She did not look away as she had in the past. There was a hint of defiance in her. Pride, too. It was so hard not to like what he saw. The long, elegant lines of her neck reminded him of that painting he'd seen in Florence with Serena. What was the name of the artist? Serena would know. She liked art. Parmigianino's *Madonna*—that was it. At the Uffizi.

"Why do you look at me that way?" Bebe asked, more puzzled than offended.

"I was thinking you remind me of a painting I once saw."

"A painting?" she said. "Not of a man with a long white beard, I hope."

He chuckled. "More like a goddess than God."

Bebe blushed. She knelt down and ran her fingers over the stain in the carpet. "Senhor von Vehrling will be here soon, Mike. Is there anything else you wish to do before he comes?"

"No, not really."

She looked up at him uncertainly. He tried to put thoughts of seduction from his mind. "Do you like museums?" he asked.

She blinked. "Why do you ask this?"

He didn't know. Because he'd thought of the Uffizi, perhaps. To find out if they had common interests apart from what they might discover in bed. He shrugged. "Just curious."

"I would like to go to museums," she said. "But I work many hours and when I am not, I try to be with my child. There is little time."

"You haven't told me about your daughter," he said, not sure why they hadn't discussed her. He liked kids. "How old?"

"Four."

"What's her name?"

"Branca."

"I bet she's adorable."

"Yes, it's true. Her father was very handsome."

"Then, with you as a mother, she can't lose," he said.

Bebe got to her feet. She was close enough that he could smell the orange-blossom scent rising from her body. A strong physical desire welled up in him, so strong it was palpable. And the electricity wasn't emanating from him alone.

Bebe tilted her head slightly and stared at his mouth. A strong visceral sensation went through him. Her chin rose a fraction of an inch. She stood there for a long moment, then eased away. "This is dangerous, Mike," she whispered.

The word *dangerous* tripped off her lips in a most enticing way. *Yes,* he wanted to say, *wonderfully dangerous.*

"Danger's a part of life," he said instead.

"But you must want to choose it. What I want for us in my heart is friendship."

"Friendship," he said, testing the word, not liking it.

They heard the sound of a vehicle outside the villa, and both turned toward the window. Mike's stomach dropped. Why couldn't von Vehrling have been fifteen minutes late? This conversation needed more time, another turn or two at least.

"*Bem!*" Bebe said. "I think it is Senhor von Vehrling."

Serena was under no illusion about what was going on in the library. There might be blood on the carpet, but Michael and Bebe were a couple of kids at play. A crime to solve, a little titillation, maybe a lot of titillation... Good for them, she said to herself. Good for them.

Then she heard Bebe's heels in the hall. The girl smiled in at her as she passed the entry. "*O proprietário, senhora.* The landlord is here."

Serena realized that was a car she'd heard. Good. She was glad to be meeting this Hector von Vehrling. Michael had called him the key to the puzzle, and she was ready for a confrontation now. More than ready.

Serena had given the meeting some thought and had settled on a strategy. If von Vehrling was as pompous as she expected, she would give him a dose of his own medicine. She smoothed her pant legs, waiting for him to be brought to her. God knew, she'd faced down many a man with millions of dollars at stake. What kind of challenge could a petty little Brazilian aristocrat pose?

In the hall Bebe was welcoming the *dono de casa* to his own house. Serena couldn't understand what was being said, but she heard the deference in Bebe's voice. Michael joined them, and the conversation switched from Portuguese to English.

"How do you do, Mr. Bouchard," said von Vehrling in richly accented tones.

"No, it's Hamlin," Michael said, "Mike Hamlin."

"A thousand pardons, *senhor,*" came the response. "I was of the understanding that Senhora Bouchard was in the company of her husband."

"*Former* husband, my friend. It's complicated, but I won't bore you with details."

"I see."

Serena could scarcely keep from laughing.

"Senhora Bouchard is in the salon, *senhor,*" Bebe said sweetly. She played the role of mediator adeptly.

The trio appeared at the entry. Hector von Vehrling stopped and gazed at Serena, who was sitting regally in a high-back chair at the far end of the room. His mouth dropped open. He looked shocked, but swiftly recovered.

"I see our host has arrived," she said mildly, though unsure what his curious reaction to her meant.

Von Vehrling, a tall, slender, silver-haired man with an aristocratic bearing, drew himself up. "*Senhora,*" he said, clicking his heels, "it is indeed a great pleasure." He walked briskly to her chair, taking her proffered hand. "Madam."

Von Vehrling kissed her fingers, making it seem like a perfectly natural thing to do. He had a cold, expressionless face, except for the dark, animated eyebrows that arched over pale blue eyes. The man was handsome in the way that a Gestapo colonel in a Nazi war movie was handsome—full of yang and very Prussian.

"May I apologize for being in your house when you arrived, Mr. von Vehrling," Serena said, "but we thought you wouldn't mind since it's unoccupied at the moment."

"No apology necessary, *senhora*. To the contrary, I apologize for not being a better host." He glanced around. "I see you have no refreshment. Please allow me to have the servant bring something to drink."

Hector started for the door, but Bebe, who'd drifted over along with Michael, stopped him. "Allow me, *senhor*."

"You are very kind, *senhorita*."

He watched the girl move across the room just long enough to indicate to Serena that he wasn't completely without sensibility—not that she confused bona fide sentiment with glandular response. But it was good to know something about his sexual preference. Von Vehrling turned his attention back to Serena.

"May I offer my condolences, *senhora,* regarding your brother's misfortune."

"Misfortune hardly describes an innocent man being jailed for a crime he didn't commit, Mr. von Vehrling."

"Indeed." He glanced around again. "Please, *senhora,* allow me to draw a chair so that we can talk." He glanced at Michael. "Perhaps you will be good enough to assist me, *senhor.*"

"Sure, Hector," Michael said, intentionally playing the role of ugly American.

The two of them had gathered chairs for the entire party just as Bebe returned to the salon.

"Ana is bringing juice," she announced.

"Excellent," von Vehrling said. "My thanks."

"*De nada,*" the girl said, sitting in the chair Michael indicated.

They formed a nice little conversation group, taking measure of each other for a moment or two after everyone was seated.

"Have you been leasing the house long?" Serena asked.

"For many years. The property came to my father in the settlement of a business dispute. It has been convenient to rent to visiting friends. Most of the tenants have been foreigners."

His charmingly sinister manner made Serena distrust him. Perhaps it was the accent, which seemed as much Germanic as Portuguese. She asked about his family background, and von Vehrling explained that, although he was a native-born Brazilian, his parents were German, their language his mother tongue. Serena put his age at fifty-five or so, which had his father leaving Germany before the war, but after Hitler had come to power—meaning the elder von Vehrling couldn't have been one of the boys from Brazil.

Ana arrived with a tray of glasses of orange juice, but she wouldn't bring it all the way into the room, putting it instead on a chair near the door before scurrying off. Bebe went over and got it, probably wondering along with Serena what was wrong with the poor woman.

Serena asked von Vehrling how he knew Drake. Their host told her they'd met several years earlier in Los Angeles, when he'd been there on a promotional tour for the Brazilian fashion industry. Needing accommodations, Drake had contacted him when he got to Rio. Von Vehrling had rented the villa to him.

She watched the man, listening carefully as he spoke. His English was excellent, but his speech was choreographed and careful—too careful to have the ring of candor. He lamented Drake's death. "A terrible tragedy," he said solemnly.

"Who do you think killed him?" Serena asked, figuring she'd go for the jugular.

Von Vehrling faltered slightly. "That, it seems to me, is a matter for the police."

"Come now, Mr. von Vehrling. Surely you think my brother is guilty. Everybody else in Rio seems to."

"With all respect, madam, I draw no conclusions. Your brother's guilt is for the court to decide."

"You're a diplomat, Mr. von Vehrling."

"I honor you with the respect you deserve, *senhora*."

"I insist you're a diplomat, sir. But it doesn't matter. We asked for this meeting so that we can satisfy ourselves concerning the facts."

"That was my understanding, Mrs. Bouchard."

"Then you don't mind if we ask a few questions."

"Assuredly not."

"Michael and Bebe are my investigators, so with your permission, I'll have them speak on my behalf."

"With pleasure," von Vehrling said, turning to Michael. "*Senhor?*"

"Out of curiosity," Michael said in a transparently innocent tone, "was Drake acquainted with other members of your family?"

Von Vehrling gave him a level look. "I take it you are referring to my sister, Antonia."

"Did she know Drake?"

"Yes."

"Did she know him well?"

Von Vehrling carefully put his glass down on the table to the side of him. "I trust you will allow me to answer your direct questions with direct answers."

"By all means."

"If you are suggesting that my sister is somehow involved in Senhor Manville's death, Mr. Hamlin, you are wrong."

"I'm not suggesting anything, Hector. But people are not normally murdered without a reason. Evidence seems to indicate that Drake was killed because of jealous love."

"Do you know this, or is your evidence from the mouth of Senhor Bouchard?"

"I've talked to Jeffrey."

"Do I understand you to say that it is my sister's jealous love that explains Drake Manville's murder, not Mr. Bouchard's?"

The man's tone sounded discernibly Prussian. Serena managed to maintain an icy smile, but the temper she'd inherited from her father was boiling.

"I guess what I'm after," Michael said, "are your views."

"I assure you, *senhor*, my sister knows nothing of Drake Manville's death."

"Perhaps. But if they were . . . close, she might be able to shed some light on the situation."

"If you are suggesting that you wish to speak with Antonia, I must tell you that it is impossible. My sister is ill and can speak with no one."

"Ill?"

"She is a fragile woman. And yes, I will admit to you that she was fond of Drake. They were good friends. When she heard of his death, she had a nervous breakdown."

"Is she in a hospital?"

"She is under professional care."

"Is it really impossible to speak with her, Hector, or simply more convenient that we don't?"

Von Vehrling's faint smile turned sardonic. He glanced Serena's way. "With all respect, I understand why Senhor Hamlin is your investigator and no longer your husband." And to Michael he said, "My compliments, sir, on your skills of interrogation."

"Truth is an addiction with me, Hector."

"And with me a matter of principle, *senhor.*"

"Ah, but which principle?" Michael returned with a ironic smile of his own. "There is principle and there is principle."

"Am I to conclude the questions are over, Mr. Hamlin," Hector said airily, "or have we simply moved on to polemics?"

"Nicely done, Hector," Michael said, bowing graciously. "I do have more questions."

"Please, then."

"I understand you were the one who notified the police that Drake had been shot. Would you mind telling us how you happened to be on the scene?"

"Certainly. I've spoken with the authorities at great length, but I don't mind telling you what I have told them."

"We'd appreciate it."

"There is not a great deal to tell. I had an appointment with Drake. He called a few days before to say he wanted to discuss the arrangements for the villa. He said there was a chance he would be leaving sooner than he had planned. Since he had paid rent a year in advance, I assumed he wanted to question me about a refund."

"What time was the appointment?"

"Ten o'clock."

Michael turned to Bebe. "When was Drake shot?"

"At about nine-thirty."

"Yes," von Vehrling said, "the police told me the same."

"Surely they don't know to the minute," Serena said. "It could have been earlier or later, couldn't it?"

"They can never tell precisely," Michael said. He turned to Hector. "You say your appointment was at ten. Do you recall what time you actually arrived?"

"It was a bit after ten. I was a little late because I had been with a group of business associates, six prominent citizens, at my home. The meeting lasted longer than I expected." An amused smile lit von Vehrling's face. Clearly he and Michael had been jousting about the possibility of Hector's own involvement, and the Prussian took great pleasure in deflating Michael's balloon.

"You went to the villa directly, *senhor?*" Bebe asked.

"Yes, *senhorita.*" He picked up his glass and took a long drink of juice. "Let me put your minds to rest, *senhores.* My home is twenty-five minutes from here. I was in the company of half-a-dozen prominent business people until a quarter of an hour before ten o'clock. I could not have been your murderer."

"We aren't suggesting you were, Hector," Michael said. "Our problem is we don't know who the murderer is."

"Nor do I."

"Then it's not unreasonable that we might cooperate," Michael said. "To return to my questions. Could you tell us what happened when you arrived at the villa that morning?"

"I found the front door open. I was surprised, but hesitated to enter before ringing the bell. No one came, but as I waited I heard the maid, Ana, in the back of the house. She is a deaf-mute, as you know, and makes rather distinctive sounds when upset."

Serena could certainly relate to that.

Hector continued. "I went to the kitchen and found her at the table, weeping. When she saw me she became excited. She took me by the arm and led me to the library, where I saw the body. Drake was quite dead. I telephoned for the police to come."

"Could you describe the condition of the room when you went in?" Michael said. "Was anything amiss, apart from the fact that Drake had been shot?"

"No, everything seemed perfectly normal. There was a gun on the floor, but except for that, everything was in order."

"Did you examine the weapon?"

"No, I knew it was evidence of the crime, so I didn't touch it. I instructed Ana, as best I could, not to disturb anything."

"What about the other maid, Maria? Did you speak with her?" Michael gave Serena a half wink.

Von Vehrling seemed a bit taken aback, but continued smoothly. "Why no, Senhor Hamlin. Maria wasn't here."

"Isn't that strange? I understand Ana is dependent on her sister, that they are virtually inseparable."

Von Vehrling glanced at the others. Serena sensed that what was coming next would be telling. Bebe waited with anticipation.

"I think that would be an exaggeration," he said. "Maria goes alone to the market almost daily. That is where she was at the time Drake was killed."

"How do you know?"

"I gathered this from Ana."

"Where is Maria now?"

Von Vehrling held out his hands in a sign of helplessness. "I have not seen her, and no one knows where she is. I am distressed for Ana's sake. It is unlike the woman to be gone so long, without my consent, particularly."

"Did it occur to you that her disappearance may be connected with Drake's murder?" Michael asked.

"No. Do you think this?"

Serena could see the Nazi colonel had antifreeze for blood.

"Let me ask you this, Hector," Michael said after a time. "Did you discuss Maria's disappearance with the police?"

"No," von Vehrling replied. "I thought it possible she went to relatives. We are not so quick to make a case of missing persons as you are in the States."

"I wasn't thinking of that," Michael rejoined. "I was referring to the murder investigation. The police might find it interesting that a maid disappeared the day a murder occurred, making it impossible for the other maid to be questioned."

"If you think it is important, then by all means I will tell them. It is simply that Ana gave no indication of a connection. She would have been even more upset if Maria had been abducted by the murderer, for example."

"Perhaps. But I think you must have greater confidence in her ability to communicate than we do, unless, of course, you know her well enough to ask questions we were unable to."

"No, I'm afraid my experience is exclusively with household instruction—bring coffee, clean the floor, that sort of thing. And frankly, I haven't done much of that. Maria is the one I usually deal with."

"I don't understand why we don't just bring in someone who speaks in sign language," Serena said. "Why is this Maria so essential?"

"I'm afraid, *senhora,* that the sisters do not use the recognized system. It is one they devised themselves."

"Yes," Bebe added. "I asked the gardener this. He says the same thing."

Von Vehrling glanced at his watch. "I will mention the maid's disappearance to the detective, Mendonca. If there is a connection, as you suspect, naturally he should know of it."

"I think that would be wise," Michael said.

Serena noticed him catch Bebe's eye. The girl nodded slightly. Serena could see they were already communicating well. They were a team, perhaps in more ways than one.

"Senhor von Vehrling," Bebe said, "I have a question also."

"Yes, *senhorita?*"

"How long was it from when you called the police until they arrived here at the villa?"

Hector shifted ever so slightly. "Perhaps twenty minutes. I told them it was not an emergency. Drake was, as I said, quite dead."

"*Sim, senhor,* but the murderer was making his escape. Did this not give you concern?"

Von Vehrling eyed her. "You aren't suggesting I did this with intention, *senhorita?*"

"I'm curious about that myself, Hector," Michael said. "A murder is hardly anything to take casually."

Serena couldn't help feeling triumph. Bebe and Michael were nailing the Prussian to the wall.

Von Vehrling's expression grew grim. "Again this is sounding like an accusation, Mr. Hamlin."

"I'm trying to understand what happened the morning Drake was killed," Michael replied. "Nagging questions keep popping up. As an investigator, I don't like that."

"Perhaps you should share your concerns with the police."

"Not a bad idea."

Von Vehrling's expression turned smug. "Personally, I think you make much of nothing. I admit I find the absence of Maria perplexing, but if she was not in the house at the time of the murder, what difference does it make?"

"Maybe she wasn't gone, Hector."

"Ana told me that she wasn't here soon after showing me the body."

"She *told* you?"

"There is a sign for this that I know," von Vehrling said dryly. He held out his arm as though he was carrying a basket on it. Then he picked up some imaginary fruit or vegetables with his other hand and put them in the imaginary basket.

Bebe and Michael exchanged glances.

"Excuse me, *senhores,*" Bebe said, getting to her feet. She left the room, heading for the back of the house.

Serena realized at once what Bebe was up to. It was a bold move, perfectly timed. She and Michael watched von Vehrling, who remained placid. Antifreeze. Serena could see that the missing maid, Maria, was looming larger by the minute.

Von Vehrling checked his watch again. "As you can imagine, Senhor Hamlin, I am a busy man. But to avoid your suspicion, I will make myself available in the future. I am sure, however, that you will be able to confirm everything I have told you."

He got to his feet. "Please feel free to stay," he said. "And if you would like more juice, ask Ana." Then he grinned. "It is a simple sign. Point to the glass, then raise your hand to your mouth as though you are drinking."

"Ingenious," Michael said, rising in turn.

Von Vehrling took Serena's hand, kissing it again. "I regret that this unfortunate crime finds us, shall we say, on opposite sides. I would prefer that we could be friends."

"Presumably we both want to see justice done," she said.

"Undoubtedly, *senhora.*" The man turned to Michael.

"I'll walk with you to the door," Michael said.

They went off together.

"By the way," Serena heard Michael say to von Vehrling, "how did you feel about your sister and Drake Manville having an affair?"

"I will be candid," he answered as they went into the hall. "I did not approve. Drake Manville was a confused man. He didn't know who he was or what he wanted."

The voices faded. A moment later Michael reappeared. Bebe came up behind him.

"Senhor von Vehrling was right about the sign for the market," Bebe said. "Ana understood."

"Our friend is too crafty to make a mistake like that," Michael said, grasping the back of the chair he'd been sitting in. He leaned on it, looking at Serena.

She sighed, not knowing what to make of von Vehrling's visit. Her cautious optimism had faded to tentative gloom. And her unschooled mind told her they'd found more questions than answers. "What do you think, Michael?"

"I don't know. Our adversary is clever. That's about all I'm sure of."

"Was he lying?"

"Of course. That's the good news."

"What's the bad news?"

"He was lying, but I don't know about what."

Copacabana

They rattled along in Bebe's Renault, Michael and the girl speculating on the various possibilities of what had actually happened that morning in Drake's library. For the first few miles Serena had listened with interest, but as the heat began to get to her, her mind focused on her physical discomfort and her gloom. For the first time she felt truly pessimistic about Jeffrey's chances.

The missing maid offered a ray of hope, but her disappearance also showed that the conspiracy against Jeffrey was deep and complex. It was beginning to seem like Serena and her merry little band were up against all of Brazil. How could they overcome such odds?

When the Hotel Atlântica finally came into sight, Serena started feeling better. Away from home, her hotel was a place of refuge. She needed to revitalize herself, recharge her batteries, raise her spirits—if not for herself, for Jeffrey.

Michael, who'd mostly ignored her during the drive back, spoke to her as they drew within a block of the hotel. "Bebe and I are going to meet with Koto and map out a strategy, so we'll drop you off, if that's okay."

"Fine. Hector von Vehrling is about all the investigating I can handle in one day."

Mike gave her a crooked grin. "You're showing your age."

"Michael," she said sternly, "don't ever say that to me in the presence of a beautiful young girl. Besides, complaining is a part of my persona. You of all people ought to know that."

He chuckled. "Apologies extended."

"Never mind. I'm feeling discouraged."

He reached back and patted her hand. "Don't worry, sweetheart, the fight's only begun."

She looked at his familiar hand, appreciating the gesture and the reassuring words. It was a small-enough thing, but she was grateful, nonetheless.

Serena noticed they were stopped in another traffic jam. "I guess since I'm paying for your efforts I should ask what you plan to do, Michael."

"We want to check up on ol' Hector's alibi. And we also need to see about tracking down that other maid. I'd like to know just how much of what Hector told us the police are aware of. And we've got to find a way to get to the sister, Antonia."

"That ought to keep you busy."

"For a few hours, anyway."

"Me, I want to go back to the villa," Bebe said. "I want to investigate the neighborhood and talk again with Ana. Maybe if we speak when she is calm I can learn where Maria might be."

Serena liked the spirit of the dynamic duo. They were good for her and Jeffrey, and they were good for each other. It was odd how much that pleased her. And displeased her.

Traffic was moving again. "I'll leave it in your capable hands," she said to them. "As for me, I'm going to have a hot bath . . . or a cold shower, I'm not sure which."

"An odd dilemma," Michael said with a laugh.

"This is a very strange trip," she replied. "Very strange."

They pulled up in front of the hotel and Serena hopped out. "Good hunting, kids," she called airily, heading straight for the door. She heard the Renault sputter away. She didn't look back. There was no point.

Inside, Serena checked for messages. There were two, one from Roberto saying his trip was going well and he was looking forward to seeing her—that instantly lifted her spirits—and another from Elaine Risollo, asking her to call. Cheered, Serena went off to the elevators, her discomfort half-forgotten.

The suite had been cleaned. There was a vase of roses from Roberto on the table. That, too, gave her a warm feeling. She sniffed a bud and thought of his velvety voice.

After taking off her shoes, she decided to call Elaine Risollo and see what was up. A maid answered. It took a couple of minutes for Elaine to come on the line.

"Serena, I've been thinking about you ever since Roberto introduced us," Elaine said. "I called him this morning to see if he would bring you to a little party I am having this evening, but they said he was in São Paulo on business."

"Yes, he won't be back until tomorrow night."

"That's what they told me. But I ask myself, why should I wait for Roberto? We are friends, Serena, is it not true?"

"I'd like to think so."

"*Bom.* Then you must come. It is last minute, I know, but I did not know you until yesterday. And it is very much informal. A few friends. Not elegant at all."

"That's very sweet of you. I have no plans for the evening."

"There are people for you to meet. One in particular is a friend of Antonia von Vehrling. I thought perhaps you would be interested to meet her."

Serena's heart lifted. "Yes, that might be very interesting. But I have a question. Would it be too gauche if I brought along my former husband? He's assisting in the investigation."

"Do as you wish, Serena. If he is not a problem for you, how can he be a problem for me?" Her voice trilled with laughter. "My apartment is in Ipanema, so it is not far. I will send my car for you. Shall we say at eight?"

"Perfect."

The call got Serena's juices flowing. It was important for her to feel she was doing something constructive. Michael's detective routine made her feel inadequate, and with Bebe involved she felt like a fifth wheel. The social milieu was more down her alley. That and business. But there was no business to be done in Rio, other than saving Jeffrey's butt.

She was getting hungry, but it was early for lunch. She was idly perusing the room-service menu, trying to decide what she would do, when the telephone rang.

"*Senhora,*" a voice announced, "this is the front desk. A telegram has arrived. Would you like it brought up?"

"A telegram? From whom?"

"This I do not know, *senhora.*"

Serena wondered who in the world would be sending her a telegram. She couldn't remember the last time anyone had. A fax, yes. But a telegram? "Fine," she said, "have someone bring it."

She decided she'd have enough time to get out of her clothes and went to change into a caftan. She'd no sooner returned to the sitting room than there was a knock at the door.

Serena opened it. Instead of finding a bellhop, as she expected, a stocky man with an unpleasant grimace on his face stood there. He wore a beige linen suit badly in need of a press.

In the instant it took her to realize she'd opened the door to a stranger, two other figures appeared behind him. She tried to slam the door shut, but it was too late. The men pushed into the room.

"What are you doing?" she cried. "Get out of here!"

"Quiet, *senhora,* or you won't get your telegram," the stocky man barked.

It was the voice she'd heard on the phone. Her impulse was to run to the telephone, but the other men—one a mulatto, the other black—moved toward her quickly. Each grabbed an arm. Serena tried to jerk free.

"Let go of me!" she screamed.

The stocky man stepped forward and slapped her across the face. "Shut up!" he snarled.

For seconds she was stunned. The anger in his eyes made her heart race as much as the blow. What was this? A robbery?

The first man grunted instructions, and the other two dragged her to a chair, shoving her into it. Serena looked up at them. The mulatto seemed almost bemused. The other man was not. He opened a switchblade and laid it against her throat. She tensed, wondering if they were going to kill her.

The stocky man, clearly the leader, dragged a straight chair over and sat down in front of her. He had a pensive expression on his face as he leaned toward her, his eyes hard. Serena felt the cool metal of the blade against her throat.

"What do you want?" she muttered. Only then did she notice she was trembling. "If it's money, I'll give you whatever you want. Twice what you're being paid now."

He put a finger to his lips. "*Senhora,* I want for you to listen, not speak. *Compreende?*"

She nodded, the terror growing.

The man was silent for several moments, as though he was trying to decide how to proceed. As he reflected, he looked her over, really taking note of her for the first time. It was not anger she was seeing on his face now, but something much more personal. He stared at her legs. Serena's stomach tightened.

"I'm going to say something to you, *senhora,*" he said, with a curious patience, "and I want that you listen close. Okay?"

She nodded.

"You and Senhor Hamlin have come to Rio and you are making much trouble. All these things you are doing, they are not good. *Compreende?*"

"What...things?"

"These questions with the murder. Your detective husband, *senhora.* I asked to him once to leave Rio, but he did not listen. Perhaps he is stupid, I don't know. So I decide to talk to you. It is—how do you say?—the final warning. Go home to America, *senhora.* Leave Brazil. It's finished here." He dragged his gaze slowly down her body. "Do you understand me?"

The flat of the blade pressed more firmly against her throat. Serena was afraid to swallow, but she managed a weak, "Yes."

"Excellent," the man said.

Serena realized this was Michael's friend George Raft she was talking to. What was the name Michael had mentioned. Salsa? No, Souza, that was it. Souza had come after her.

"Okay, *senhora,*" he said. "Now I want to tell you a little story about what will happen if you don't leave Rio immediately." He glanced at the man holding the knife to her throat. "Julio is a strange man. He doesn't like beautiful women. They—how you say?—upset him. Sometimes when he is upset, he cuts on their face. Cut, cut, until there is blood. Some go to the hospital because of Julio. They must see the plastic surgeon. *Compreende?*"

Serena nodded again. Her heart was pounding so hard she had to remind herself to breathe.

Souza looked at her breasts. "*Senhora,* you are much more beautiful than I thought. Poor Julio, he must be very nervous about this. Such a beautiful woman."

The man put a beefy hand on her knee. Serena shook so violently she thought the blade would cut her throat.

"Yes, very beautiful," Souza said.

Then, using his thumb, he began gathering up the skirt of her gown, drawing the fabric to her knees. She clamped them together as hard as she could, afraid the brute would rape her.

Apparently liking what he saw, he pushed the skirt farther up her thighs, grinning. He ran his tongue over his lips.

"Very, very nice, *senhora*. You have beautiful skin."

He drew his palm along her thigh. Serena's stomach tensed.

"Very soft," Souza said, smiling at her. "Perhaps you are a woman who doesn't worry for her beauty. So let me make one other warning. If you and Senhor Hamlin could not care for your own safety, think of your daughter. She is pretty. I have seen her. But how beautiful would she be if Julio cut her nostril or removed the tip of her ear? That would be sad, *senhora,* would it not?"

It was too much. Serena couldn't help herself. "You'd better not even think of hurting Christina," she declared, her eyes full of hatred, "or so help me God, I'll cut your heart out!"

Souza jumped to his feet and kicked his chair aside. "No woman talks to me that way!"

Then he spat something out in Portuguese. His men immediately lifted Serena to her feet. Souza reached out and grabbed the front of her gown, ripping it from her with one violent jerk.

She screamed.

A large hand clamped over her mouth. The men holding her tightened their grips. Serena was naked except for her panties. She was certain she'd be raped. But Souza, red faced, turned away and walked across the room, shouting orders in Portuguese.

Serena was slammed back into the chair, and the next thing she knew ropes were produced and she was bound and gagged. Souza paced the whole time. His anger seemed excessive, but unless he had some awful trick up his sleeve, it looked like she might survive the ordeal.

Once she was securely tied to the chair, Souza approached. "You are very fortunate, *senhora,*" he said. "If the choice was mine, I would teach you to talk to a man as a woman should. But I was told this should be a warning only. For this reason, we will leave you.'' Then he grinned. ''But with a small reminder from Julio.''

Souza gestured with his hand, and the black man opened his knife again. Serena knew he would cut her. She strained at her bonds. She tried to speak, to plead, but all she could do was watch as the man placed the edge of the blade on the top of her breast. Then she closed her eyes.

She felt the pressure of the blade but not the cut. Opening her eyes, she saw Julio grinning sadistically. She looked down at her breast. There was an inch-long line where he had cut her. Blood oozed from it. It stung, but it wasn't really painful.

She couldn't watch herself bleed, though. She thought she might be sick, but she wouldn't let that happen. Not while she was gagged. She could choke to death. She had to pretend it hadn't happened. So she closed her eyes and didn't open them again until she heard the door slam. Glancing around the room, she discovered she was alone.

For the next few minutes she fought to calm herself. When she looked at her breast she saw the blood beginning to coagulate. She wasn't going to bleed to death, but for as long as she was tied up, she wouldn't be able to ignore the wound. That clearly was Souza's intent.

Serena told herself to relax. She tried meditating. She tried to calculate how long before someone would come along and untie her. The maids wouldn't be back until evening. What had Michael said? Had he told her how long he'd be?

She pictured him sitting in some café with Bebe, the two of them flirting and laughing. Jesus, why did he have to fall for the girl? Now Serena hated the fact that she'd encouraged them. What if he didn't come back for hours? What if she had a panic attack and lost it?

For the next several hours she'd be worrying about not only her safety, but Christina's, as well. The thugs had turned her against herself, pushed her to her emotional limits, made her her own tormentor. And she was helpless to do anything about it. Then it occurred to her—that was exactly the point. They wanted her to think about this for a long, long time.

Rio de Janeiro

Pericles Kotomata's office was in an old building in the Cinelandia district, not far from the Municipal Theater and the modern, cone-shaped Roman Catholic cathedral. There was an ancient elevator in the building that Bebe said hadn't worked in six months. Koto was the only one who complained, she said, because he didn't like climbing stairs.

After showing Mike to the cramped suite of offices, she took off for Santa Teresa, leaving him in a shabby reception area about two-thirds the size of Serena's closet at home. The secretary didn't work weekends, so Mike waited alone for Koto to arrive. He thumbed through three-year-old magazines while he passed the time, but mostly he thought of Bebe.

After dropping off Serena, they'd fought their way back to central Rio in her Renault, chatting about the case. Mike had decided not to return to that danger zone they'd flirted with at the villa under the theory that with Bebe, less was more. Slow and cautious was the best approach. He did, however, propose a late lunch, after she got back from Santa Teresa. Bebe hesitated only a moment before accepting.

He had pretty well exhausted his reading material—which was to say he'd looked at all the pictures in the magazines—when he heard the sound of footsteps. The door opened and Koto entered. He was breathing heavily from the climb.

"Get your morning workout?" Mike asked pleasantly.

"I would complain about the elevator, but I've lost five kilos since it broke. So maybe I should be glad."

"How do the people on the third floor feel about it?"

"They all moved out," Koto said, unlocking the door to his private office. He signaled for Mike to come in. "Sometimes I think the landlord has a death wish."

"For himself or the tenants?" Mike asked.

Koto chuckled. "Very good. I must remember that the next time I negotiate the rent."

He went behind his compact desk and plopped down in the chair. Mike glanced around as he made his way to the wooden visitor's chair. The place was neat, if austere. There was a small bookcase and a file cabinet. The decor consisted of a single Japanese watercolor and a few artifacts from the Amazon. The venetian blinds blocked out the midday sun. Through the closed windows, Mike could hear the steady hum of traffic on the nearby boulevard.

"How was your morning?" Koto asked after Mike sat down.

"An enigma wrapped in mystery... or whatever that expression is."

"Oh?"

Mike gave a rundown of his conversations with Penelope Ingram and Hector von Vehrling. The missing maid in particular made Koto sit up and take notice.

"I see what you mean. Nothing seems to go as expected."

"I'd like to check out von Vehrling's alibi."

"The police are ahead of you on that one, Mike. I saw Mendonca again this morning."

"So what did he say?"

"Von Vehrling was meeting with a group of businessmen until around quarter to ten the morning of the murder. He couldn't have arrived at the villa until twenty or twenty-five minutes later."

"How firm are they on the time of death?"

"They've ruled out von Vehrling, let me put it that way."

"What about the sister, Antonia?" Mike asked.

"She's hospitalized. Mendonca spoke to the doctor and has agreed to wait a few weeks before questioning her. He feels it will take that long for her to stabilize."

"A few weeks? I'll be back in Vegas and Rio will be last year's vacation by then."

"I know," the investigator said. "I tried to impress upon Mendonca that we think Antonia von Vehrling is the key to the case, but he said not to worry. She's not going anywhere."

"Yeah, but neither is Jeffrey."

"I don't think Mendonca cares about that."

"No, it's Jeffrey who cares. And Serena, of course." Mike stroked his chin. "Do we know what hospital Antonia is in?"

Koto shook his head. "Mendonca wouldn't say."

"If we find out, I wonder if we could arrange to pay an extracurricular visit to the old girl."

"There are quite a few ifs in that question."

"Right, but we don't have to labor under the same restrictions as the cops. I'm not above walking into a hospital room and having a chat with the patient."

"If you can find the hospital room."

"If," Mike said. "Let's make finding Antonia's hospital room and the missing maid, Maria, our two top priorities. If it means spreading Serena's money around, do what it takes."

"Check," Koto said. He glanced at his watch. "You have plans for lunch?"

"Yes, with your lovely assistant."

Koto's brows rose. "You're accomplishing what few men have managed in all the years I've known her. My congratulations."

"Lunch is a very small step."

"Is that the secret—small steps?"

"The secret is caring about her passions and being honest about my own. Maybe it's just another way of saying I like her, Koto. I hope that's not a problem. I want to be upfront."

"I try to keep my personal and professional lives separate," Koto said.

"Do you know what the story is with Arthur Kingsley?"

Again Koto's brows rose. "You know about Kingsley after only three days?"

"We ran into him at the beach. All I know is that Bebe's done business with him and that he's a sonovabitch. Do you know the particulars?"

"Yes. Under normal circumstances I would say that if she wanted you to know, she'd tell you. But I'm wondering if this may be an opportunity for somebody to give Bebe some good advice. I've tried, without success."

"This is starting to sound ominous," Mike said.

"It is an upsetting story," Koto replied.

"So let's hear it." Mike sensed this was not going to be pleasant.

"When Bebe was a teenager, she faced the problem all beautiful girls born in the favela face—do they use their God-given graces to raise themselves from misery or accept a life of poverty for the sake of virtue?"

"She became a hooker."

"No. There were many opportunities for that, of course, but Bebe also had a brain. She wanted to get an education to better herself, but she needed money."

Mike's stomach began to knot.

"When she was nineteen," Koto went on, "she met Kingsley. Among other things, he is a photographer. He told Bebe he wanted to hire her as a model. She thought for fashion photography, but he did not tell her that most of his clients were pornographers.

"To make a long story short, Kingsley asked her to pose for more-and-more-risqué photos, until he had her posing nude. Bebe was uncomfortable, but the pictures remained tasteful. She thought it was art. Kingsley was paying her well and nothing unsavory happened, so she continued to cooperate.

"Then one day after a few months Kingsley told Bebe he had a very wealthy client who had a fetish for intimate photographs of young women. She would be paid two thousand dollars, which for a girl in her position was a great deal of money. She agonized for a few days and, after being assured the photos would be treated with the utmost discretion, she agreed to Kingsley's proposal."

Mike shifted uneasily. "Then what?"

"Bebe arrived at Kingsley's studio. At first he treated her respectfully. The shots were very graphic, but she felt detached. Kingsley gave her some wine to help her relax. Things were going as expected, until a young man arrived, an extremely well-endowed male model. It distressed Bebe when Kingsley said he wanted to photograph them together. She refused, but he offered another thousand if she would simply pose with the man, saying there was no need for intimate contact.

"Bebe still refused. Not to be thwarted, Kingsley managed to drug her, and for the next few hours, he essentially photographed her being degraded and raped."

"Jesus."

"Afterward, he offered her more money not to make trouble. It was over, he told her. She could never prove to the police it was not consensual. The worst that would happen to him was that his materials would be confiscated. From the police vaults the photos would make their way to the streets."

"So she let him get away with it?"

"She had her money, and she wanted to put it behind her." Koto got up to stretch. "Bebe went on with her life. She used the money to educate herself. She got a good job in an office. The owner of the company, a prominent *carioca,* took a liking to her." Koto turned to face Mike. "Edson Escovao was a handsome man of about your age. He seemed to love her and they had an affair. Because Escovao was divorced, he was not adverse to being seen in public with Bebe. There was a photo of them in the newspaper."

Mike saw what was coming. "Kingsley saw it."

"Apparently. In any case, he contacted Bebe and…well, as you might guess, he blackmailed her." Koto returned to his chair.

"And of course she paid him off," Mike said, "thinking that would be the end of it."

Koto nodded. "Escovao was generous, giving her money and gifts. Kingsley got it all, every cruzeiro. But he didn't stop there. He tried blackmailing Escovao, too."

"What a greedy bastard."

"Needless to say, it did not help Bebe's relationship with Escovao. He dumped her. I guess he figured Kingsley was a cancer and that cutting out Bebe was the way to get rid of him. She was three-months pregnant."

"Did Escovao know?"

"I'm not sure when he found out. Bebe never said, but I suspect it was after the baby was born."

"So that explains the bad blood between Bebe and Kingsley."

"There's more."

"Why am I surprised?" Mike said. "What else?"

"After Bebe started to work for me, Kingsley contacted her again. He told her he was strapped for money and that he had to sell the photos to a pornographer. Bebe asked what it would take to buy the negatives. The long and the short of it is that they negotiated a deal. She buys the negatives, one at a time, out of her salary. So she's working for groceries, rent and Kingsley."

"Doesn't she know there are ways to make duplicates of the negatives?"

"Yes, but she told him this was it. If he tried to pull anything else, if more negatives ever turned up, she'd kill him."

"Doesn't sound like the world would be losing much."

"My sentiments exactly," Koto said.

"Why is she dealing with the guy, though? She could have him kneecapped and be done with it. He's nothing but a leech."

"I've told her that. But she feels partly responsible for taking her clothes off in the first place. Maybe paying Kingsley is a penance. By buying her way out, she's also ridding herself of the guilt. I can't explain it, Mike."

"It's no wonder she's cautious about men."

Bebe has learned to be mistress of her own destiny, and she likes her independence. She's handling Kingsley her own way and that's important to her."

Mike sighed. "That's the kind of woman who really turns men on—some, anyway."

"Maybe in your culture, Mike. Not so much in mine."

"Which culture are we talking about? Brazilian or Japanese?"

"Interesting question. In this area, I'm more Japanese than Brazilian. Maybe it's in the genes, I don't know."

Mike propped his fingers together, thinking about the story. The compassion he'd felt for Bebe was stronger than ever. He wanted to protect her. True, he admired her for fighting this thing the way she had, but it added to her vulnerability. He'd gotten a glimpse of her soft underbelly, and it made him feel sympathy for her.

Koto looked at his watch. "I think I'll have lunch before I get to work. Finding Antonia von Vehrling and this missing maid is no small challenge, so I'd better get started."

They both got up.

"Is Bebe coming back here for you or are you meeting her someplace?" Koto asked.

"She's coming back here."

"Do you want to wait in the reception area?"

"I've read all your magazines cover-to-cover. Maybe I'll hang out in the street. There must be a café nearby."

"There's a juice bar across the street and a few doors up," Koto said, going out the door.

After Mike stepped out in turn, Koto locked the door to his office. They went into the dark hallway together. Koto locked the outside door.

"Electricity expensive in Rio?" Mike asked.

"Yeah, but there aren't any lights because the landlord's cheap. He turns them off on weekends."

"Sounds like you need new headquarters," Mike chided.

"Yes, but the rent's not bad here." Koto chuckled. "You see, I'm cheap, too."

They descended the stairs and went out into the afternoon sun. They each checked the narrow street. Being a Saturday, it was fairly quiet. Koto offered his hand. "Have a nice lunch," he said.

"You, too, my friend."

Koto headed up the street.

"And good hunting!" Mike called after him.

Koto waved over his shoulder.

Mike spotted the juice bar. There were two tables on the sidewalk. One was occupied by a young couple, the other was empty.

He crossed the street and sat at the empty table. The couple ignored him. The young man had his hand on the girl's bare thigh and was stroking it as he spoke in whispered tones. It wasn't hard to imagine what was on his mind.

A counter boy with a very wide smile came out. Mike realized he hadn't the vaguest idea how to order. He peered over at the couple, who had two half-empty glasses of what appeared to be orange juice in front of them.

Mike pointed. *"Um,"* he said. *"El mismo."*

The boy smiled at Mike's fractured Spanish and went back inside. Mike watched the young man's hand playing games with the flesh at the edge of the girl's skirt. It was easy to see why the population of Brazil was burgeoning.

Moments later a glass of juice was placed in front of him. Mike handed the boy a large bill and took a sip. It was orange, all right, but had something else in it, as well. God knew what—a filler, probably. But the flavor was good.

Easing back, Mike turned his attention to the traffic. He wanted to keep his eyes open for Bebe's Renault. Two or three sips of juice later he noticed a white Impala round the corner and head his way. It attracted his attention because his best friend in high school, a banker's son, had had a car just like it. The approaching vehicle looked to be in mint condition.

Mike was admiring it, thinking of the good old days in Bakersfield, when he noted the car slow nearly to a stop as it reached Koto's building. The driver, a large mulatto, didn't draw Mike's attention until he noticed who was in the back seat. It was Victor Souza, the bastard he'd met in the alley that night.

Mike's jaw sagged as the car cruised past. None of the men saw him, despite being less than thirty feet away; they were all looking the other way. The Impala proceeded up the street as he got to his feet, adrenaline coursing through his veins. Mike clenched his fists—there was nothing he could do but watch as the car paused at the corner.

"*Senhor...*" someone said from behind him.

The boy was in the doorway, holding his change. Just then there was a honk. It was Bebe in her Renault. Mike glanced up the street to see the Impala disappearing around the corner.

Waving at the boy to keep the change, Mike dashed into the road, nearly getting hit by a small truck coming from the other direction. He went around to the passenger side of the Renault and jumped in.

"Souza just cruised by," he said to Bebe before she could ask him what the hell was going on. He motioned up the street. "Quick, let's follow them, see what they're up to!"

Bebe jammed the car into gear and took off. "It was Souza? Are you sure?"

"Yeah. Him and his two sidekicks."

"Sidekicks?"

"Not the beautiful variety, Bebe, believe me." He pointed. "Turn right at the corner. They're in a white Impala."

They rounded the corner, but a short block away they saw the rear end of the Impala making another turn.

"There they go!"

Bebe floored the accelerator, but the Renault was gutless. The Impala was a muscle car, and they wouldn't have a chance if it came to a chase.

They rounded a corner onto a busy boulevard, and Bebe had trouble finding a break in the traffic. Finally, she forced her way into the flow, eliciting an angry blast of a horn from another driver. Bebe issued an expletive—Mike had no idea what she said, but the sentiment needed no translation.

He tried to spot the Impala, but couldn't locate it. Bebe drove with more abandon than usual, weaving in and out, getting additional rebukes from her *carioca* brethren.

"Do you see it?" she asked.

"No."

"Is that it there?"

"Where?"

"In front of that truck. A hundred meters...no. Too small."

They'd lost their prey. "I think they've given us the slip," Michael murmured.

Bebe eased up on the accelerator. "Sorry."

"Not your fault. I'm not sure what we'd have done even if we had managed to tail them."

"We might have learned where to find them," she replied.

"No point in crying over spilled milk."

The aphorism amused her. "I like that."

On an impulse Mike reached over and brushed her smooth cheek with the back of his fingers. "There's more where that came from."

She looked unhappy all of a sudden.

"What's the matter?" he asked. "Did I offend you?"

"No. This is not turning out to be such a good day."

He wondered how she could say that. They'd toyed with danger that morning. They were going to have lunch together. Just seeing her made him feel happy. "Seems like a pretty good day to me."

"No, I have bad news. And it is my fault."

"What's your fault?"

She turned a corner and pulled to a stop. "I went back to the villa. The maid, Ana, has disappeared."

"What?"

"Paulo said she was in the house working, and the next thing he knew the house was locked up and she was gone. He didn't know when or who she'd left with, but it must have been with someone, because he said she never went anywhere except with Maria.''

''So they're both missing now.''

''Yes.''

''Curious it should happen within hours of us seeing von Vehrling.''

''Yes, Mike, very curious.''

''Paulo didn't see anyone around the villa after we left?''

''No. But I sensed something strange. He was not happy to talk to me,'' Bebe said. ''Maybe somebody said something to him.''

''Like his employer?''

''I don't know who else.''

''Damn.''

''I'm very sorry, Mike. I should have talked more to Ana when I had the chance. It was stupid.''

''Don't be ridiculous, Bebe. You've been wonderful. You're an excellent investigator, a very smart lady, and I like working with you very, very much.''

Bebe's eyes welled up. An odd reaction for such a gritty girl, he decided.

''You're a very nice man, Mike. Thank you for saying that.''

He took her hand, toying with her long, slim fingers. She neither looked upset nor objected to the familiarity. Instead, she seemed self-conscious. The shy little girl in her was coming to the fore. He had a strong desire to kiss her.

''As I recall, we've got a lunch date,'' he said. ''Where shall we eat?''

''There are many places, of course.''

''There must be someplace special.''

''That is where I ate for all the months when I worked, but had no money,'' Bebe said, pointing up the street.

Mike looked. ''Where?''

''In that park. Don't you see the big fat man with the barrel and the people gathered all around him? That is a street barbecue. He has a fire there and he cooks sausages and little bits of meat that he puts in bread which you can buy for a few cruzeiros. It is cheap and quick."

"Yeah, fast food. It's not quite what I had in mind, Bebe."

"But that's my world," she said.

"Not today. We're going to the fanciest restaurant in town. Where would a man take a beautiful girl to impress her?"

"I don't know."

"Surely some man has taken you someplace to show you off."

She bit at her lip. "Maybe the Colombo."

"What's the Colombo?"

"What you asked. A fancy restaurant, where a man might take a girl. There is a tearoom in the old style. It is very elegant."

"Have you been there?"

"Yes."

"Is it nearby?" Mike asked.

"Not far."

"Then let's go have some lunch."

Bebe looked reluctant. "Maybe it's not such a good idea."

"Why? Does it bring back memories?"

She first seemed surprised, then gave him a penetrating look. "You are very smart about women, aren't you, Mike?"

"I'm a detective, too, don't forget."

There was skepticism on her face. "Sometimes I feel like you know me very well."

"That's what makes me so dangerous, sugar."

He gave her a wink and she smiled, reluctantly.

"I know about Edson Escovao, Arthur Kingsley and everything that happened," he said, feeling the need to be candid.

That caught Bebe off guard. "And why do you tell me this now? To show your power?" Her voice had an edge.

"Just the opposite. I'm trying to be honest, to let you know I understand what you've been through."

"And you do not think less of me?"

"Of course not. More, if anything."

Bebe shook her head with disbelief. "Sometimes I do not think I know you at all, Mike. Always you surprise me."

"Maybe that's because you haven't asked me any questions. That's the quickest way to get to know someone, kiddo."

She nibbled on her bottom lip as she stared out the window at the passing pedestrians. After a minute she said, "Do you still love Serena?"

He couldn't help laughing. "Your ability to go to the heart of the matter never ceases to amaze me," he said.

"Does that mean yes or no?"

He chuckled. Not only because of her sweet innocence, but also because of her wisdom. He liked to be surprised by a woman. It was provocative. "The answer is yes and no," he said.

"That is no answer at all."

"A part of me will always love Serena," he explained. "But there is also this great gulf between us, and it separates us like death separates a person from life."

"But Serena is not dead."

"The relationship is. And not just because we're divorced."

She shook her head. "For all your wisdom about women, Mike, I don't think you understand Serena."

"Oh? And I suppose you do."

"An older woman has much wisdom, but sometimes she forgets that a younger woman is a woman, too. I looked into her eyes and I saw what was in her heart."

"What was that?"

"Love, Mike."

"Bebe, with all due respect, you're a shit disturber."

"A what?"

He couldn't help himself this time. Her refreshing innocence got to him. She was too adorable. Leaning over, he kissed her on the cheek. Her scent was so lush, so intoxicating, that he lingered.

Bebe didn't move. She seemed to inhale him as he inhaled her. Then she turned her face directly toward his, her lip sagging slightly open. He kissed her tenderly. Kissed her sweet lips.

Bebe slowly turned away from him. She stared up the street, as if trying to decide how she felt. He watched her and waited.

"The Colombo is where I went with Edson many times," she said after a moment. "He wanted other men to see me with him."

"I can certainly understand that."

"We would have champagne, and afterward, he would take me to his apartment and we would make love," she said matter-of-factly. "He liked to make love in exotic ways. He was very skillful."

"Did you love him?"

Bebe thought for a while before answering. "I loved the—how do you say?—the . . . fantastic?"

"The fantasy," he said with a smile.

"Yes, the fantasy. You see, when you are Cinderella, the fantasy means so very much. A girl in poverty is always a girl in poverty in her heart, even if she has gold and diamonds. Edson gave me a different world, one I never knew before."

"I've got news for you, Bebe—the same is true of boys born in poverty. You can take the boy out of the country, but you can't take the country out of the boy."

"How do you know this?"

"You're looking at the Bakersfield kid," he said, poking his thumb into his chest.

"What is this Bakersfield?"

He took her hand and rubbed it. "A place where there are ten thousand Cinderellas," he said, "both boys and girls."

"You are trying to say we are alike?"

He slowly nodded. "That's why our danger is nothing to fear. Danger can be a good thing between the right people."

She stared at his mouth as though she might be reliving their kiss. Then she, too, nodded. "Do you know what, Mike?"

"What, my dear?"

"I think I'm hungry."

He grinned. "Then let's go have lunch."

The Colombo was both a tearoom and a restaurant. The main dining room was on a splendid wraparound balcony overlooking the tearoom below. The belle-epoque decor featured jacaranda-wood cabinets and wall-length Belgian-crystal mirrors. Light filtered through a stained-glass skylight, and trilling piano music set the mood.

To suggest this was a far cry from Bakersfield would have been an understatement, though, of course, Mike had had more than his share of tinsel during his years with Serena. He'd become familiar with the hundred-and-fifty-dollar bottles of wine, the limos, the jets, the hotels and more hotels. Of course, for Serena it was business, not merely a lifestyle, but ultimately Mike had realized it wasn't truly him.

The Colombo seemed to affect Bebe the same way. Though she'd been there before, her body language revealed that the place was essentially alien to her. They were like a couple of kids from the wrong side of the tracks out doing the town.

Mike was clearly underdressed, but Rio made allowances for tourists, especially gringos. Bebe sat across from him, nervously reading the menu, not looking too happy.

"I hope I didn't twist your arm to come here."

"No, Mike, it's okay."

"Sure?"

"Yes. Really."

He didn't believe her. He'd put her in an uncomfortable situation, but she was being a good sport. He appreciated that, but he was sorry now he'd pressed her.

They ordered seafood at Bebe's recommendation, then she spent a lot of time looking down at the tearoom, as though expecting to see somebody she knew. He had the sense not to order champagne, but he did request a nice crisp Chilean white wine. Bebe sipped it rather eagerly.

"Can I be frank about something?" he asked.

"Sure."

"I don't like what you're doing with Kingsley. It's none of my business, I know, but that monkey should have been off your back a long time ago."

"You've been talking to Koto."

"Yes."

"He's said it all to me before, Mike, so there's no need for you to do the same."

"What was it Kingsley wanted at the beach?"

Bebe gave him an impatient look. "If you must know, he was giving me a hard time because I missed two payments. My sister, Nina, was sick, and I had extra medical expenses. But it's okay now. I took him money last night."

"Bebe, if you insist on paying the bastard, just buy back your negatives, lock, stock and barrel. Borrow the money. I'll loan it to you. You can pay me back at your convenience."

"It's not your problem, Mike."

"Listen, Serena's paying me fifteen hundred a day to run around town with you, have lunch and drink Chilean wine. It's not exactly hazardous duty. The money is a windfall, and the only reason I'm taking it is because Serena's rich."

Bebe stared down at her folded hands.

"Since we're partners, I'd like to share the wealth," he told her. "I can help you out, with no pain to me whatsoever."

She lifted her eyes. "No," she said. "Thank you, but no."

Mike sipped his wine. "Stubborn, aren't you?"

"Yes, very stubborn."

"You're lucky you're so damned cute."

"No, Mike, you're lucky *you're* so damned cute."

He laughed. Bebe was silent again, but her mood seemed to have lightened some.

"So tell me about your place in Rochina and your family."

"I don't live in Rochina. That was where I was born. Now I'm in the middle class. I have a car, which Koto got for me so I can do my job, and I live in Barra da Tijuca."

"Where's that?"

"Farther down the coast from Copacabana and Ipanema. I live in a very small two-room apartment with Branca, my sister and my aunt. We have a happy life. Like all *cariocas*, we go often to the beach. It is beautiful, not so crowded there."

Mike played with his wineglass, testing his next question in his mind before actually saying it. "Can I come visit you sometime—meet your daughter, your sister and your aunt?"

"You make it very hard for me," she said softly.

His lip curled. "Does that mean yes or no?"

Bebe blushed. "Yes, but maybe not for a while."

"What's your day off?"

"Sunday."

"That's tomorrow."

"Yes, it's tomorrow."

"Is tomorrow a while?" he asked wryly.

"You are very determined."

"I'd like to see you away from the office, sugar. Or do you have plans?"

"My family will go to the beach, like all of Rio."

"Which beach?"

"Recreio dos Bandeirantes. It is not so big."

"If I happened to be in the neighborhood with my bathing suit, would it upset you if I showed up?"

Bebe gave him a sly look. "If so, I wouldn't have told you where I'll be."

Mike took a card and pen from his pocket. "Would you mind writing down the name of that beach?"

She laughed. "Sometimes you are so funny."

"Not my first choice," Mike said, "but it'll do."

The waiter came with their lunch. The food was excellent. Mike liked watching Bebe eat, it was very sensuous.

After he paid the bill, Bebe wanted to visit the ladies' room, so he took the opportunity to phone the hotel and see what Serena was up to. He didn't get an answer, which he found odd.

"Did Mrs. Bouchard go out?" he asked the clerk.

"No, sir, I don't believe so."

He decided she was either in the tub or browsing in the hotel shops. "Tell her I'm on my way back to the hotel and I'll have an update for her when I get there."

"Yes, *senhor.*"

Mike knew that, considering all the side benefits he was realizing from this job, he couldn't forget Serena. She was having a rough time, and his investigative skills, such as they were, constituted only part of why she'd asked him to accompany her. Having his moral support was the major reason she'd insisted he come along. His regard for her, not to mention his professionalism, demanded she not be slighted because of Bebe. It was one thing to have an adventure, but another to neglect his responsibilities.

Bebe returned, and as they went down the staircase, she drew admiring glances from the men. It was easy to see why Edson Escovao had wanted to show her off. As they headed for her car, Mike slipped an arm around her waist and bumped his hip playfully against hers.

She giggled and put her arm around him, making his heart trip nicely. The prospect of bedding her was seeming more likely with each passing hour. But for a sexual relationship to work, Bebe would have to get into the spirit of it—be comfortable with the idea. Mike knew he had to be very careful. And lucky.

Copacabana

Mike got out of the elevator with the message slip of his call to Serena in hand, plus another for her from London.

She hadn't answered the phone and nobody had seen her leave the hotel. For the first time, he began to worry.

Unlocking the door, he was greeted with the overpowering scent of roses. "Serena!" he called. "I'm home!"

The sound had no sooner died on his lips than he saw her, naked, bound and gagged, her eyes as big as saucers. For the briefest instant he thought it was a joke. But then he heard the muffled cries and saw how red her face was. He rushed over and removed the gag.

"Oh, thank God," she gasped.

"What in the hell happened?" he asked, quickly moving behind the chair. He began loosening the knots.

"Hurry, Michael."

He had her free in seconds, and Serena dashed for her room. He followed her, but lingered at the entrance to the bedroom when he saw that she'd gone into the bathroom.

"You all right, Serena?" he called to her.

"I'm fine now."

"Who did this to you?"

"Your friend Souza," she replied through the door.

Mike was stunned. "Souza?"

The toilet flushed. A few moments later she came out and leaned against the doorjamb, as if she didn't have the strength to come into the room. Michael went to her closet and got her a robe.

As he approached her, he saw an inch-long cut above her breast. It was crusted with blood. "What happened?"

"One of Souza's men cut me. Julio, the black one, wanted to give me a token to remember them by." She shivered.

"Serena . . ." He helped her with the robe, then took her in his arms. She pressed her face into his neck, holding him as tightly as he held her.

"They forced their way in," she explained, her voice shaky. "After I foolishly opened the door."

"What did they want?"

"To slap me around and threaten me. Told me to leave Rio." She shivered again. "The same story they gave you."

"The bastards," he said, clenching his teeth. "What kind of security do they have in this place, anyway?"

He opened the robe to look at her wound. It wasn't serious, but the thought of them hurting her was enough to make him livid.

"It's more the idea than anything," she said.

He stroked her head as she clung to him. Serena wasn't sobbing, but he sensed she was in shock.

"I didn't know what to think when I saw you naked," he said, wondering if she'd told him everything.

She sniffled. "I said something to piss Souza off and he ripped my gown right off of me," she said, clearing her throat. "I think he was considering raping me, if you want to know the truth." Her voice broke over the last words.

"But he didn't . . . ?"

"No, thank God. Just the cut and a few slaps. Still, it was one of the worse experiences of my life. That Julio scared me to death." She suddenly stiffened. "Michael, we've got to get hold of Christina."

"Why?"

"Souza said that if I wasn't afraid of being hurt, then I'd better worry about my daughter, because Julio'd go after her next." Serena marched to the phone and picked up the receiver. "Shit, what's that bastard Joachim's number?"

Mike went over, took the phone from her hand and put it back in the cradle. "Hold on a second, sweetheart. Let's don't go off half-cocked."

"Michael, if those bastards hurt her I'll just die. No, I'll kill them!" She sank onto the bed, shivering. "We've got to get her out of this country! Now! Tonight."

He sat on the bed next to her. "I know you're upset, but it won't help to rush into anything. We've got to think how this'll affect Christina. She's not five anymore, you know."

"I have *got* to warn her, Michael! She must know that threats have been made against her."

"I agree, but let's get clear what we're going to do." He took her hand and pulled her to her feet. "Come on, let's go in the other room and talk this through."

They went back to the main room, but Serena wouldn't sit down until he'd gotten rid of the ropes and her shredded caftan. Once the place was in order, they sat on the sofa.

"I insist we call Christina immediately. I insist."

"If Souza's threat against her was sincere, it means he's not working for Joachim."

"I hadn't thought about that."

"And if Souza *is* working for someone else, maybe the thing to do is to tell Christina what's happened and let her decide for herself."

"I want her out on the next plane," Serena said firmly.

"With you?"

She hesitated. "No, I refuse to be intimidated."

"Well, I have a hunch your daughter will feel the same."

"Michael, why do you insist on being so logical?"

"Look, why don't you let me handle Christina? If you don't like what I say, you can always put in your two cents' worth."

"Okay, but I want you to call her now."

"Get me the number."

Serena went back into her room. While she was gone, Mike stared at the door, picturing Souza and his friends charging in and slapping Serena around. He remembered the way they'd been in the alley that night, their cruelty. The thought of them abusing Serena made him shake with anger. Another reason to make the bastards pay.

She came back with the number, and Mike dialed.

"I'll get on the extension," she said, heading back into the bedroom.

Christina came on the line almost immediately.

"We've had an incident, honey," Mike told her, "and your mother and I want you to be aware of it."

"What sort of incident, Michael?"

"Can you talk?"

"Yes, there's no one here but the help and Joachim's grandmother. What's wrong? What happened?"

"This morning some men broke into our room at the hotel and roughed your mom up a little. Somebody's trying to intimidate us into leaving Brazil."

"Lord..."

"Your mother's all right. She wasn't seriously hurt, but we're concerned about you. They threatened to harm you if we didn't leave Rio immediately. Naturally, we wanted you to be aware so that you can take steps to safeguard yourself. Your mother's very concerned about your safety."

"God," Christina said, "I can't believe that it's happened to you, too. Joachim's been getting threats."

"What sort of threats?"

"Nothing specific. His business dealings have been mentioned, but he thinks it's just a crank. He didn't pay much attention to it until my name came up. They told him they'd cut my face or something. Security guards go with us everywhere. I didn't say anything because I didn't want you to worry. Joachim says these things happen to people with money down here. It just means you have to be extra careful."

"Well, I didn't expect this," Mike said.

"I think you'd better get someone to look after Mom whenever you're out, Michael. Hire some bodyguards. When you know you're safe you can relax."

"Christina," Serena cut in, "are you saying you've been living under death threats and haven't told me?"

"God, Mom, are you okay? I didn't know you were on. No, not death threats. Joachim thinks it's probably someone who's jealous or bitter over a business deal or something."

"Honey, don't you think you could use a little vacation back home?" Serena said. "Just for a few weeks until the dust settles. Personally, I think this is somehow connected to what's happened to your uncle Jeffrey."

"Mom, Joachim's very careful with me. Too careful, probably. There's no need to worry. Honest. I've got more reason to worry about *you,* if you want to know the truth."

"Just fly home for a week," Serena said.

"Mom!"

"Our main concern is that you be alerted to the danger," Mike interrupted. "But it sounds like you're already well prepared. Joachim seems to have things under control."

"Michael!" Serena interjected.

"He's right, Mom," Christina rejoined. "Joachim wouldn't let anything happen to me, I promise."

"No need to belabor the point," Mike said. "We can discuss it Monday. I'd like to hear Joachim's assessment of the situation."

"I'm sorry you had a fright, Mom," Christina said, "but one good thing about it—everything's out in the open now. Having to hide has been bothering me."

"Promise me you'll be very, very careful," Serena said.

"I promise. And you promise me you'll do the same."

Mike laughed. "I guess we're all on the same page. We're all going to be careful."

They said goodbye and Serena returned to the sitting room. She looked beat, like her ordeal had finally caught up with her. "So what do you think?" she asked.

"We have to reconsider Joachim's involvement. Though, of course, it's possible he could have faked the threats to him and Christina to throw us off the scent."

"How can we know?"

"We can't. Not yet."

Serena inserted herself into Mike's arms again. "I need to cry for a minute," she said. "Just for a minute."

As she cried, he rubbed her back. The feel of her in his arms was familiar. So was her scent. He felt an overwhelming rush of love, a desire to protect her. He wiped her tear-stained cheeks with his thumb.

"I think what you need is a nice quiet evening at home," he said, taking her face in his hands.

Serena looked into his eyes. He recognized feelings similar to his own. It seemed she, too, was remembering.

"I'd love nothing better than to curl up on the sofa with you," she whispered. "But we can't."

"It wouldn't have to lead to anything," he assured her.

"I know. But we've been invited to a party tonight at Elaine Risollo's place in Ipanema."

"A party? Serena, after what you've been through, how—"

She put her finger to his lips. "It's not for pleasure. Some friend of Antonia von Vehrling is going to be there. I'm going to try to find out where the bitch is hiding."

"I've got Koto working on that," he said.

"Well, I'm not going to pass up an opportunity to get some crucial information. It could take Koto a week to find out where Antonia is."

"All right, Serena," he said, knowing there was no point in arguing. "Whatever you say."

Serena pulled her robe tight at her throat. Something flickered in her eyes and she shivered again.

"What?" he said.

"I was thinking of when Julio cut my breast."

Her words made him feel the cut right along with her. "You know, I wouldn't mind seeing you and Christina both back in L.A."

"Yes, but what happened today is very important," she said.

"What do you mean?"

"Michael, isn't it obvious? We're scaring the shit out of somebody. Our being here in Rio is making someone very nervous."

"You could be right about that."

"And another thing," Serena said. "Do you have any doubt at all now that Jeffrey is innocent? Drake's killer is behind this, Michael. Or someone very close to her."

Ipanema

The streets of Ipanema looked cheerful to Serena. People all around were smiling, and on one street corner a group was dancing to a bossa-nova tune. The world—at least this corner of it—was oblivious to her in her hired car, her former husband seated next to her with a gun under his coat, a driver and hastily retained bodyguard in the front seat, all on the alert for an attack.

Of course, Souza had given her until tomorrow to get out of town, so logic dictated that they were safe until sunset the next day. But Michael wasn't taking anything for granted. After some discussion, they'd decided to involve the police under the theory that it might make Souza's life more difficult. A detective who spoke poor English had showed up with a couple of officers. Serena gave them a statement of sorts and they went away.

Michael had phoned Koto's office while they were waiting for the police to arrive and had left a message on his machine. Then he had a long talk with the hotel manager and the chief of security, who promised to take additional safety measures.

When they were finally alone, Michael told her about seeing Souza that afternoon. That seemed to indicate the thug wasn't resting on his laurels. It could have been that he was checking up on Michael, or that he was looking to give him more grief. It was hard to know which.

By evening Serena was still upset, but a little less traumatized by what had happened. The wound was nothing—she'd gotten much worse scratches from a cat or a thorn on a rosebush. It was more the idea of someone intentionally scaring her that upset her.

Souza, she'd decided, was sadistic, the kind of beast who would have worked for the Nazis—which made her wonder if he might not be in the employ of Hector von Vehrling. Given Joachim's problems, it was possible that Hector was the bad guy.

She and Michael had talked about that. If Antonia was Drake's killer, Hector would have a motive for discouraging anyone bent on proving Jeffrey's innocence. There were the two missing maids and the unidentified woman leaving the villa the morning of the murder. The pieces of the puzzle were slowly falling into place. Whoever had sent those men to the hotel had to know the roof was getting ready to fall in—and was probably more worried than she and Michael.

That had been the gist of the pep talk Michael had given her as they got ready to leave. He'd been really sweet. After she'd cried in his arms, he'd asked if she wanted him to clean her wound. There wasn't much to do, but he'd rubbed alcohol on it and put on a Band-Aid. She hadn't been self-conscious about him tending her naked breast, but he'd done it so tenderly that it was slightly erotic, and she'd actually become aroused.

If Michael had noticed her nipple hardening, he hadn't said anything. He might even have been tempted to kiss it— at one point she sensed the notion might be going through his mind. But he'd played the role of virtuous doctor to the hilt. After ministering to her, he'd covered her breast with her robe.

"That ought to hold you till next time," he'd said, pinching her cheek.

They'd had a nice, quiet room-service dinner, with a single candle flickering between them. She had felt very close to him, perhaps even closer than when they'd made love. The feeling of intimacy was as strong as it had ever been.

And yet nothing had happened. He hadn't let it.

They were cruising along the Avenue Vieira Souto, which ran along the beach. Serena gazed out to sea, where a brightly lit ocean liner plied the coastal waters. She watched it absently, very aware of Michael beside her. When she turned to him, he was looking at her.

She took his hand, intertwining her fingers in his. "Thank you for being so good," she said.

He chuckled, not entirely pleased. "Good is not what a man aspires to be."

"It's better than being a prick, which is what most ex-husbands are. I was paying you a compliment, Michael."

He brushed her knuckles against his cheek. "I know. And what I meant to say was thank you."

There was something in his look that told her there was a problem. "Something's bothering you, Michael. What is it?"

"Nothing."

"No, tell me."

He stared out the window for a moment, then said, "It's something Bebe said this afternoon."

"About what?"

He hesitated, then said, "Oh, nothing really. It was a little-sister, big-sister comment."

"That doesn't seem the sort of thing that would bother you."

"I thought it was a nice sentiment," he said. "That's all."

Serena knew he was lying. She could always tell when Michael lied—it was one of the things she liked best about him. Men who could lie well were not pure of heart. By definition. But she couldn't imagine what Bebe could have said that would bother him.

"That's really all?" she asked.

"That's all."

She rubbed his hand. The poor baby.

Just then the car swung off the main boulevard and pulled up in front of the biggest, newest building facing the beach. There was a doorman waiting. It was obviously the primo address in town.

They got out of the car. Serena inhaled a breath of sea air. It was balmy, fresh enough to be invigorating. She took Michael's arm and they headed for the big, heavy glass doors—doors so thick they were probably bulletproof.

It was an older, urbane crowd, mostly people with money living on past glory. The most interesting guest was a painter, a woman in her fifties who went by the single name Katia. An older gentleman, a lion of Brazilian arts whom Serena had never heard of, was, along with Elaine, the most celebrated person at the party, but he spoke almost no English, making conversation problematical.

The penthouse was elegant. Elaine told Serena it had been decorated by a Roman interior designer named Cuzzoni, but there were also Brazilian touches—lots of sculpture and modern, angular furniture, exquisitely proportioned. The apartment occupied the entire top floor of the building and was the size of Serena's place in Beverly Hills, though the pool was smaller. The balcony offered an unobstructed view of the Atlantic and all of Ipanema.

Serena circulated, waiting for the arrival of Antonia's friend, a woman named Clarise Sutcliffe d'Orléans, who Elaine told her was the grande dame of Brazilian society and a distant relative of the last king of Brazil.

Upon their arrival, Elaine had taken Serena and Michael aside for a confidential conversation. "Clarise is elderly, but very intelligent, and she's au courant with everything that is going on. I'm sure she knows all about your brother, Serena. I say this because I wonder if you might get more information if you're not introduced as Serena Bouchard. Perhaps I should present you with the name of your husband. After all, he is here."

Michael hadn't been able to resist a droll smile. "Never thought I'd see the day you *needed* my name," he'd said under his breath. "That alone is worth the price of admission."

And so for the evening she'd become Serena Hamlin, their divorce having been conveniently forgotten. "Chances are you'll never see these people again," Elaine said, "so why not be smart?"

She'd gone off then, and Michael had displayed some of his trademark skepticism. "If these folks are her friends, why is she conspiring with you against them?"

"Because she was a friend of Drake's. And I think she liked Jeffrey, too."

"Still, she has to live with these people."

"Michael, she's not plotting a coup d'état, she's helping me save my brother's ass."

"Well, good luck."

After Michael got her a martini, they'd each gone their separate ways. She knew the poor darling would suffer, because he hated cocktail parties even more than shopping. Fortunately the youngest, most attractive woman there buttonholed him. She was a bottle blonde from Milan in a gorgeous red Valentino. Elaine said she was the daughter of one of her dearest friends, in Rio to recover from the divorce of her third husband, a French wine baron. "Bakersfield's the cotton capital of California," Serena told Elaine facetiously, "so they can compare agricultural notes."

Serena continued to work the crowd while Michael struggled not to ogle the ex-wine baroness's breasts. Serena could see he was uncomfortable, despite the attention and Elaine's tasty hors d'oeuvres. Serena had learned party skills from the time she was ten, so even with a language barrier this was just another day at the office.

Forty-five minutes after their arrival, Clarise Sutcliffe d'Orléans made her appearance. Serena hung back, waiting until Clarise had finished her first cream sherry before moving into range.

Elaine, maneuvering like a sister lioness in a cooperative hunt, converged on Clarise at the same time Serena did.

"Clarise, you must meet my dear friend from Los Angeles," the hostess said. "This is Serena Hamlin. She owns hotels."

Clarise offered her hand. "How very brave of you, my dear," she said. "Do you run them, as well?"

"Yes, I'm a working girl."

"She has hotels all over the world," Elaine said.

"I admire that," Clarise said, looking out from under false eyelashes. It was the woman's only excess. Her tailored dress was conservative but extremely expensive, the diamonds in her bracelet the size of pop beads. She was definitely more with it than the Queen Mother, but had that same staid look.

Elaine excused herself, leaving Serena to find her own way to Antonia von Vehrling.

"What brings you to Rio de Janeiro, Mrs. Hamlin,"
Clarise said, "if you don't mind me asking?"

"I'm getting the lay of the land," Serena said obliquely.

"I understand. Business. You're a huntress. Like the men.
They love to be obscure. Well, good for you. I think if I were
a girl, I'd have a career. Will you buy one of our hotels?"

Serena admired the adroitness of the old lady's mind.
"It's much too soon to say."

"You're an astute young woman. I can see that straight
away."

"You've obviously spent time in Britain," Serena said.
"Your English is lovely."

"Thank you, my dear. My parents sent me to school in
merry old England," Clarise replied. "I still spend three
months there each year. A few weeks at Claridge's, the rest
in the country. The rain is better for the skin than our
tropical sun, you know."

"I recently purchased a small chain of businessman's
hotels in Britain," Serena said, purposely sounding casual,
as though she were talking about a new set of china. "But I
stay at Claridge's myself. Where else in London can you get
a log fire in your suite?"

"Precisely," Clarise enthused. "I do love that!"

"And the orchestra in the sitting room."

"With a glass of cream sherry," the old woman added,
lifting her nearly empty glass as if to emphasize the point.

Serena caught the eye of a waiter and asked him to bring
Clarise another. The woman smiled at her deftness. Younger
women had to seduce their elder sisters, much as men did,
Serena had discovered long ago. That was a lesson her
mother had taught her.

She made surface conversation for the next few minutes
while trying to identify Clarise's Achilles' heel. No obvious
approach presented itself, so she decided to take a blind
plunge. When a brief lull in the conversation occurred, she
said, "A friend of mine in San Francisco asked me to look
up a friend of hers here in Rio, but I'm having trouble

tracking her down. You wouldn't know Antonia von Vehrling, by any chance."

"Heavens, yes," Clarise said. "I'm her godmother. But you won't be able to reach her, I assure you. Antonia is ill."

"Oh?"

"It's common knowledge the poor dear has had nervous problems, so I'm not betraying any confidences."

"Nervous problems?"

"This was a complete breakdown, I'm afraid."

"How awful. Margaret wasn't aware, I don't believe. She sent along a gift, a personal memento that Antonia was eager to have. Something from their past. I don't even know what."

"What dreadful luck," Clarise said. "It would cheer her."

"There must be a way I can get it to her. Is she hospitalized?"

"Yes, but the family's keeping that confidential."

"I suppose I could drop it at her home and trust she'll get it when she's released from the hospital. Margaret was eager to get it into Antonia's hands. Hmm. I wonder if Margaret was aware of the illness and didn't want to say anything to me. Is Antonia hospitalized nearby?"

"Actually, no."

"Then I couldn't get it to her, anyway."

"I was thinking of visiting her myself in the next fortnight," Clarise said. "In which case I could deliver it for you. But that may not be soon enough."

"I wonder if I should risk sending it?" Serena said innocently. "Of course, Margaret could have done that herself."

"The hospital's just in Petrópolis, which, as you probably know, is our celebrated mountain resort. Only a day trip from Rio," Clarise added. "You know Petrópolis, surely. Some call it our Versailles."

Behind Serena's placid smile her heart was leaping for joy. How many mental hospitals could there be in the place? "Of course," she said, "Petrópolis."

"Listen, why don't you telephone Antonia's brother? He'll be seeing her before I do. Perhaps you can leave the gift with him."

"Wonderful idea."

Clarise paused, then continued, "I don't know Hector's number offhand, but you can get it from Elaine."

"I'll do that."

Clarise sipped her sherry. "Now, which gentleman is your husband, dear? If I had to guess I'd venture it's the handsome young fellow whom the blonde seems so enamored with."

"Yes, that's Michael."

"You must be very confident, considering the way she's been going after him."

"I have the utmost faith in Michael," Serena said. "He's utterly trustworthy."

"How many wives can say that these days?" Clarise murmured. "Is he a hotel man, too?"

"Mental health," Serena replied. "Family counseling. The man has a remarkable bedside manner."

"Indeed?"

"Indeed."

SUNDAY
September 17th

Petrópolis

Serena wasn't fully awake until they were halfway there. Maybe it was the bridges soaring over the breathtaking tropical gorges that finally brought her to life. Or maybe it was Koto's strong Brazilian coffee, which he shared from his huge thermos. Whatever it was, her engine was humming now.

Michael was in the front with Koto, while she'd sacked out in back. Lord, they'd left Copacabana at dawn. Civilized people didn't even have their eyes open at that hour. And if that wasn't bad enough, the men had kept her awake talking. They'd spent most of the time discussing the Hurricane season. It was five minutes before she'd realized they were talking about the University of Miami football team, not Caribbean weather patterns.

She couldn't complain, though. Koto was being a trooper to devote his Sunday to Jeffrey's cause. Michael had called the investigator the night before, when they got back from Elaine's party. "How hard can it be to find her in a town the size of Petrópolis?" he'd asked. Koto was sure it would not be difficult.

When Michael told him about the thugs breaking into their suite, Koto suggested he talk to Carlos Mendonca about putting some heat on Souza. Strictly speaking, it wasn't Mendonca's bailiwick, but the possible connection to the murder might be justification enough to get things moving.

An hour later Koto had called back to report Antonia von Vehrling could only be in one place, the Sanatorium Alba-Dora. They decided on an early morning assault. Koto reasoned that her doctor would not likely be there on a Sunday, and the place would be minimally staffed. Serena and Michael discussed strategy before going to bed and decided she'd have the best chance of getting in to see Antonia. A woman alone would seem less threatening.

They were high up in the mountains when Koto glanced at her in the rearview mirror and said, "How are you feeling, Mrs. Bouchard?"

"Better. The coffee helps."

"I wanted to say I'm sorry for what happened yesterday at your hotel. I should have foreseen it and urged precautions."

"You aren't remotely responsible, Koto," she told him. "I have to learn to be more careful."

"With luck, this Souza will be arrested," Koto said, "but from what I understand he is hard to find."

Serena asked if he thought Christina was in any real danger.

"My feeling is that the greater danger is to the Monteiro da Silvas. They are sure to employ all necessary security measures."

"You're assuming Souza doesn't work for them."

"If he does, the fox is already in the chicken coop."

"Not a very reassuring thought," Serena said darkly.

Michael reached back and touched her knee affectionately. "You had it right yesterday, sweetheart. It's the other side that's nervous." She smiled to thank him for his support. Michael winked.

"I never did ask you about that peroxide blonde at the party last night," she said. "Did she ever get around to propositioning you?"

"In a manner of speaking."

"Oh?"

"She gave me the name of her hotel and suggested we go to the beach this afternoon."

"How brazen! Didn't she know you were with your wife?"

"Wait a minute," he said disingenuously, "when did we get into the time machine? I thought we were divorced."

"Michael, being married was our cover last night, remember?"

He chuckled.

"So, what happened with Ms. Bazooms?"

"She was a hot-blooded Italian coming off her third divorce and didn't care a whole hell of a lot about my marital status. According to the Pope, she was already going to hell."

"That explains *her* motives, Michael. What about yours?"

"I said I wasn't Catholic and that we had an open marriage."

"Great. An open marriage. With me twenty feet away."

"Serena, I was under the impression our divorce meant I was free to be unfaithful."

She gave him a pointed look, even though she knew he was right. Why was she jealous, anyway? She'd spent a lot of energy trying to get him and Bebe laid, so this fit of pique was hardly logical. "So, are you going to the beach with the blonde?"

"No, I had to turn her down. I've already got a beach date for the afternoon."

"Bebe?"

Michael smiled.

"Do you believe this man, Koto? At the rate he's going Bebe will be pregnant before Jeffrey even goes on trial."

"I hope not," Koto said, "for the sake of us all."

"Amen," Michael said.

Yeah, Amen, Serena thought. But she didn't say it out loud.

* * *

The Sanatorium AlbaDora was located on the outskirts of Petrópolis in a pine forest interspersed with banana *fazendas*. The town looked like something Walt Disney might have come up with. Koto explained that King Dom Pedro II had had the town built by imported German craftsmen. It looked like it.

After they got directions, Koto found the road leading to the sanatorium. Coming to an outlook affording a splendid view of Rio, he stopped so they could admire it for a minute or two. Over the years, he told them, many people had made the arduous drive on the old cobblestone highway just for this view.

They climbed out of the car. It was a bit hazy, but Serena was able to make out the city in the distance, even the statue at the top of Sugarloaf. Koto was right. It was magnificent. And the air was fabulous—much lighter than at sea level.

"You know," she said, staring at the panoramic view, "I didn't bring a camera. Did you, Michael?"

"No, I didn't expect to stay in Rio long enough to need one."

"I guess it doesn't matter. Neither of us has a photo album. Unless you've started one."

Michael shook his head. "I have just a few pictures of me and Christina. And some of her alone. They're in a drawer."

"None of me?"

"Oh, maybe a couple at the bottom."

"The lot of ex-wives," she said solemnly.

"There aren't any dart holes in them, Serena. Take solace in that."

"A left-handed compliment. But better than none. Thanks, Michael."

They got back in the Toyota and drove the last half mile to the sanitorium. It was set on a hilltop, an attractive building that had the feel of a French château. The grounds were nicely maintained and there was a sweeping mountain vista. Koto pulled into a shady parking place not far from the entrance. They both looked back at her.

"Sure you want to go in alone?" Michael asked.

"If I'm not back by sunset, you can come for me."

He gave her a reassuring smile.

"Well, wish me luck, boys." Serena climbed out of the car. She'd worn a linen suit and pale lavender blouse, businesslike without being intimidating. She carried the most modest handbag she owned. She smoothed her skirt and started up the steps.

She was nervous because she knew the next few minutes could prove to be pivotal. Inside was the woman Jeffrey was sure had murdered Drake. With no other suspects, she had to damn well hope he was right.

There were no guards, just a well-appointed lobby complete with Persian rugs and soft couches. There were a couple of pieces of antique furniture, several original oils—undistinguished but authentic—and tons of potted plants. The receptionist, a pleasant-looking woman, was seated at a desk nearby.

"*Bom dia,*" she said. "*Posso ajudá-lo?*"

Serena strode right up to her. "I'm here to visit Antonia von Vehrling."

The woman's brows rose. "I see," she said.

"I don't have an appointment or anything, but I was in Rio and called Antonia, as I always do. I was distressed to find that she was ill. I'd looked forward to seeing her."

"I'm afraid it won't be possible to see Senhora von Vehrling without the permission of her doctor."

"Is he in?" Serena asked.

"I'm afraid he is not in the hospital, *senhora*. It is Sunday and only Dr. de Carvalho is present."

"I'd like to talk to him, then."

"Let me call him, *senhora*. Please, have a seat."

Serena went to one of the flouncy couches, her heart pounding. Staring down some self-important hotel mogul over a multimillion-dollar deal didn't make her half this nervous. She waited, wondering why there were no insane shrieks in the halls or orderlies with straitjackets in hand running to and fro.

A few moments later a small, cherubic-looking chap came down the hall, the click of his heels on the marble floor preceding him. He was balding and nicely dressed in what on a taller man would have been an elegant Italian suit. She had only to observe him for five seconds to know he was a player.

Serena greeted him and launched into her story, turning on the charm, using every trick in her arsenal. Michael had once observed that she knew exactly when, how and what part of a man's anatomy to stroke when she needed or wanted something. And of course, it was true.

The good doctor, who, as it turned out, spent three days a week in Rio, was finally convinced that it might not be so bad for Serena to visit a few minutes with Antonia, provided she shared her observations with him. He suggested a suitable place to share notes might be the cocktail lounge at the Hotel Atlântica. Serena assured him she'd be positively thrilled to confer with him.

"You're such a clever man, Dr. de Carvalho," she said, touching his arm.

He refused to accept the compliment unless she agreed to call him Jorge. Serena gave him a coquettish smile. The deal was struck.

"Follow me, please," he said. "The *senhora* is in the garden."

They trooped through the facility, which took on a more hospital-like flavor in its inner sanctum. There were people in white uniforms, and Serena had a glimpse or two of inmates with less-than-lucid expressions. She saw no straitjackets, but she didn't see any caviar, either.

De Carvalho stopped at some French doors that opened onto an expanse of lawn. Several patients were seated on chairs scattered about, while uniformed attendants kept watch. The air was cool enough that some of the patients wore sweaters.

"There's Senhora von Vehrling," the doctor said, pointing, "in the chair by herself at the far end of the garden."

"Poor, poor Antonia," Serena murmured.

To her relief he let her go into the garden alone. The nurse supervising Antonia was seated off a way, knitting. Antonia was sitting on the edge of her chair, her back to Serena, staring into space. Nodding at the attendant, Serena stepped up to Drake Manville's onetime lover, without the vaguest idea what the woman looked like.

Antonia, she discovered, was a pale woman who wore no makeup, yet there was a cool Germanic beauty about her. Her eyes were blue, like her brother's. There were touches of gray in her dark red hair. She was slender, and despite the simple cotton dress, she did look aristocratic.

"Hello, Antonia," Serena said, bending over so the woman was compelled to look into her eyes.

Antonia stared blankly. She was off somewhere in Never-Never Land. Serena reached for a lawn chair and pulled it over to sit facing her.

She took Antonia's hand. "I'm Serena, dear," she said softly. "I've come to visit you."

Antonia regarded her a bit strangely, but without particular concern. Then she quickly returned to whatever distant place her mind had been inhabiting.

"I'm a friend of Drake's," Serena said.

Antonia stared at her, then shook her head. Serena didn't know whether she was indicating she didn't understand or that she didn't want to talk about him.

"You do speak English?" Serena asked.

"Yes," Antonia said in a whisper.

"I want to find out what happened to Drake," she said.

"He's dead," the woman whispered.

"Yes. I want to know how it happened."

"I don't know. He's dead. I loved him, and he is dead."

"Were you at his villa when he was shot?" she asked.

Antonia looked at her queerly.

"Did you go to the villa?"

"I loved him."

"Did you shoot him, Antonia?"

Her eyes rounded in horror. "I would never kill my Drake. I loved him!" she cried.

The attendant glanced up from her knitting. Serena patted Antonia's hand. "Of course you loved him."

The look in Antonia's eyes grew full of hatred. She jerked her hand free. "You killed him, Mimi! You! I know it was you!" Then she clutched the collar of her dress over her throat and shrank back in her chair.

Serena reached for Antonia's hand again, but the woman pulled away, horrified. "Get away, Mimi, get away!" Then she screamed something in Portuguese. Whatever it was, it got the nurse's attention. The attendant tried to calm Antonia, but without success. By then she was hysterical. An orderly came running toward them.

It appeared Antonia would be unable to communicate again for some time. But at least she'd managed to say a few semicoherent words—she was adamant she hadn't killed Drake and she had accused somebody named Mimi.

Serena figured it was time to retreat. She headed back toward the main building, encountering Jorge de Carvalho at the edge of the lawn.

"Antonia's upset," she said, glancing back at the raucous scene. "I thought I'd better leave before it got too bad."

He shot a worried glance in the direction of Antonia, who was screaming. "Well, she has wild swings of emotion. I wouldn't worry about it."

"Perhaps, if she gets better, I can come back," she said.

"Do call first," de Carvalho said. "Senhora von Vehrling's doctor may be reluctant to allow more visits."

Serena couldn't help smiling. Jorge was stating the obvious: the other doctor's fly wasn't so easily unzipped. Despite de Carvalho's concern, he elected to walk her to the front door.

She offered him her hand. Jorge, his mind clearly on what favors he might yet gain, drew her fingers to his lips. "I will telephone you in a few days' time, *senhora*."

"Wonderful."

Serena started to turn away, but de Carvalho wouldn't let go of her hand. She regarded him questioningly.

"A thousand pardons, *senhora,*" he said. "I am embarrassed, but in the excitement I have forgotten your name."

"I'm so sorry, doctor. How rude of me." She smiled sweetly. "It's Connie. Connie Meyers."

Serena patted the good doctor's cheek, then went bouncing down the steps. He was still standing at the door as she climbed into the car.

Michael and Koto looked back at her.

"Well?" Michael said.

"The only thing I know for sure is that your girlfriend, Connie, has a date with Dr. de Carvalho."

"What?"

"You'd have to have been there."

"But did you see Antonia?"

"Yes." Her expression grew solemn. "Either she's nuts or she didn't kill Drake."

"That isn't much help."

"No, but she does have a theory who the killer is."

"Who?"

"Somebody named Mimi. And apparently she looks quite a bit like me."

"Mimi, huh?"

"Yes. All we have to do is find her."

"Great," he said. "Think she's in the phone book?"

"Don't be so sarcastic, Michael. I did the best I could. Anyway, the Mimi we want may not be hard to find. She had to know Drake and have a motive for killing him."

"You're assuming Antonia isn't stark, raving mad. Mimi could be an alternate personality or something."

"Or she could be Drake's killer."

Barra da Tijuca

It was midafternoon before Mike made it to the beach community where Bebe lived. Contrary to Koto's advice, he'd rented a car and taken on Rio's traffic—a brave act considering it was a weekend and the entire population would be going to the seaside.

Recreido dos Bandeirantes was on a natural cove protected by a breakwater, making it an ideal beach for swimming. When Mike saw the crowds he wasn't sure he'd find Bebe. The first thing he did was change into his trunks, then locate a vantage point where he could survey the crowd, hoping she might spot him. He was drawing lots of stares, probably because of his North American looks. To the sun-soaked *cariocas* he had to look like a polar bear.

After several minutes of surveillance, he spotted Bebe in the water. At first she was visible only from the waist up, but then, as she emerged, her legs came into view. Hollywood couldn't have done a better presentation. There wasn't a curve or line that could be improved. She was a living, breathing fantasy. A dream.

Seeing him, she waved and ran toward him, smiling. When they met she gave him a friendly hug. "Mike, you came."

"I wouldn't miss it for the world."

She took his hand. "Come on, you can meet my family."

Bebe's aunt was a taciturn woman of about fifty-five who looked even older than she was and spoke no English. There were traces of Bebe's grace in her, but not her elegance or beauty. A simple woman, a maternal figure worn down by time, the aunt was installed under a big red beach umbrella when they arrived.

Bebe's sister, Nina, was nearly a carbon copy, though at nineteen she didn't have Bebe's refinement and maturity. They were in matching string bikinis—Bebe's white and Nina's powder blue. The younger girl was, if anything, shyer than Bebe, looking at Michael only long enough to shake his hand and say, "Good afternoon," before retreating to her beach towel.

Branca, Bebe's daughter, was precious. She was in a topless suit, playing in the sand. Her skin tone was lighter than Bebe's, as was her hair. For the first few minutes she clung to her mother's leg, looking up at Mike through long, silky lashes.

After he'd joined the family, Branca returned to her play. Nina listened to her sister's conversation while pretending indifference. Bebe wanted to hear what had happened at Petrópolis, so for a while they talked business.

Mike was acutely aware of Bebe's near nakedness, though she seemed perfectly at ease. After he'd been in the sun awhile, she lathered him with sunblock. It was one of the more-sensual experiences of his life. Despite the precautions, though, he burned some.

He and Bebe played with a Frisbee for a while, then took a swim together. Afterward he bought them all an ice cream.

"Sad to think how easy it is to win a woman's heart," Bebe said as they watched Branca eating her cone.

"Think so?"

"I've tried very hard in my life to avoid temptations," she said, "but I haven't done very well."

It wasn't until then that Mike appreciated the tragic depths of Bebe's soul. It also gave him pause. Here he was on a mission of conquest, trying to quench that unquenchable thirst, and Bebe had the cheek, the audacity, to present herself as vulnerable.

"What, Mike? What are you thinking?" she asked.

He hesitated, then spat it right out. "Do you consider lust a sin?"

"Pardon?"

"Oh, never mind."

Bebe reached over to wipe a smudge of ice cream from her daughter's cheek. "No," she said, "tell me. I want to know. What are you asking?"

"If you'd hate me if I turned out to be selfish."

Bebe shook her head with disappointment. "You're talking as a professor of philosophy," she said. "I don't understand questions like this."

How did a man ask a woman for permission to exploit her? he wondered. It wasn't in him to be insensitive. He needed to know it was all right.

When she saw he wasn't going to respond, she said, "Maybe you think too much, Mike. Maybe instead of worrying you should see what happens."

If that meant what he thought it meant, it was indeed music to his ears. He smiled. Bebe did as well.

After a while Mike had to take refuge from the sun under the umbrella. As he watched Bebe and Nina play with Branca, he lost himself in idle musing. What would it be like to make love with her? Could they forget everything and enjoy themselves sexually, the way he had with Yvette, the woman who'd taught him the meaning of pleasure? Could Bebe detach herself that way? For that matter, could he, now that he was getting old and soft?

While he watched Bebe and Nina kicking a soccer ball back and forth, he tried to imagine the aftermath, the part where he said goodbye and got on a plane for home. It was odd how Bebe had focused on Serena, as though that was what this was really all about. Did Bebe realize that he had this need to purge himself of his ex-wife?

After the sun dropped behind the mountain, he drove Bebe and her family to their flat on a dusty back street in the older part of Barra da Tijuca. It was on the second floor of a concrete structure reminiscent of those he'd seen in Tijuana. The furniture was worn, but the place had a homey feel. Bebe agreed to go to dinner with him, but they both needed to clean up first.

They each had a shower. Mike suggested they dine at one of the nicer hotels in Barra, but Bebe insisted they have a Brazilian-style date. She took him to a place specializing in pizza. He chided her that it wasn't exactly Brazilian, but Bebe said it was the sort of place a young, middle-class *carioca* would take her.

The atmosphere was better than the pizza, but the *choppe* was cold. They drank most of a two-liter pitcher.

Leaving the restaurant under the starry sky, they were just tipsy enough to slip their arms around each other. She laughed, matching her long, swaying strides to his. They headed for the beach in town, where all the nighttime action was.

As they stood on a corner, waiting to cross the boulevard, Bebe put her arms around his neck, pressed her bare thighs against his pant legs and kissed him on the mouth.

"You are like nobody I've known before, Mike," she said. "Is that good or is it bad?"

"I don't know, sugar," he said, feeling wickedly lustful. "But I'm willing to find out."

Along the avenue bordering the beach a series of trailers sold food and drink. And there was music. Each trailer was lit with strings of lights, attracting crowds in a carnival spirit. Bebe said they were called *pagodes,* open-air samba bars, with young people dancing and singing to the rhythm of the music.

Bebe led him to her favorite trailer, where, she told him, the best samba "outside the northern neighborhoods" was played. For a while they watched the dancers as surf pounded in the background. Bebe swayed her hips to the music, her smile a bit wider, her cheeks a bit more flushed with each passing minute.

Finally, she took him by the hand and dragged him out to dance. He wasn't a bad dancer by most standards, but it was clear that here he was a Little Leaguer in a major-league park. Bebe didn't let that slow her down, though. Enticed by the music, she made moves that could have gotten her arrested back home. The woman not only had a body, she knew how to use it. After a while he stopped dancing and watched, literally in awe.

Samba, it seemed, had its own etiquette, because the next thing he knew a broad-shouldered samba god with ebony biceps had upstaged him and stolen his partner. Bebe and her new musical mate were soon at the center of the gyrating throng. People stopped to watch them. It was impressive: two perfect specimens in perfect syncopation. Bebe, the goddess in every man—long shapely limbs, bare midriff, ripe, full breasts swinging under her skimpy top, flawlessly curved hips arching between waist and thigh.

Opposite her was Othello, the god in every woman—a man with powerful legs and a chest so solid it seemed carved of wood. Yet he twisted and undulated in perfect rhythm to the sound of the music, his movements strong and graceful, even poetic.

Mike fell into it, as well, his blood pulsing to the beat of the drums. The tune had been lost in the passion of the dance, and it wasn't until the music began to fade that Bebe and her partner came down.

Bebe and Othello lightly slapped their right hands together as they swayed their final sway, turning from each other like a couple of panthers who'd brushed up together in the moonlight, then went on their way. Her face sparkling with dew, Bebe slipped her hand in Mike's and led him through the crowd and out onto the dark beach. She didn't slow down even when they were beyond the noise of the *pagode.* She walked until they came to the white, tumbling surf, where she stopped and removed her sandals. After handing them to him, she waded into the water alone, lifting her skirt to allow the water to creep up to the edge of her panties.

He thought for a moment she might swim away into the night, but she didn't. She stood motionless for several moments with the sea lapping at her legs, then turned and waded back to shore.

Even with the ocean breeze he could smell, taste, almost feel the heat of her body. Bebe took his face in her hands and kissed him. It was a sexual kiss. They pressed their bodies together, the friction making him hard.

"Mike," she said, kissing his chin, "I have to go home now. Do you mind?"

And so the game ended. They walked the few blocks to her apartment, neither of them speaking. A few of Bebe's neighbors were on chairs outside their doors, talking softly in the night, their features invisible.

At her door Bebe put her hand to his face and slowly dragged her palm across it, as though memorizing the feel of him. *"Boa noite,"* she whispered. Then she turned and climbed the stairs to her apartment, leaving him frustrated and unfulfilled, his cock hard, all dressed up with no place to go.

Copacabana

It was ten o'clock before Mike got back to the hotel. He wasn't quite sure what had happened that afternoon and evening. The relationship was showing promise, but there were no guarantees. Bebe was as illusive as she was irresistible.

Stepping out of the elevator onto the thirty-sixth floor, he saw no sign of hotel security. That upset him. The arrangement was that someone would be on duty when the suite was occupied. Was Serena out? Or had there been a breakdown?

Approaching the door to their suite, Mike felt a clutch of anxiety. He slipped the key in the lock and slowly pushed the door open. The sitting room was dark except for the light of a candle. A bossa-nova tune played softly on the radio. It took a moment before he saw them in the shadows. Serena was wrapped in Roberto Cabral's arms, their foreheads pressed together as they danced, swaying in half time to the music.

They were so engrossed in each other they hadn't noticed him. When he slammed the door, they both turned.

"Michael," Serena said, looking like a teenager caught necking on the porch.

"Where's the security?" he asked pointedly.

"I sent them away," she replied. "I thought it would be all right with Roberto here. What are you doing home? I didn't expect to see you until morning."

"Obviously." He headed for his room. "Don't let me interrupt. I'm going to bed."

"How was your day?" she called after him, apparently unwilling to allow his intrusion to gracefully end.

"Fine."

"Good evening, Michael," Cabral said, joining in.

Mike gave him a semipolite nod. "Hi, Roberto." He reached for his door handle.

"How's Bebe?" Serena asked, stopping him again.

"Fine," he replied. "Fine." He noticed an ice bucket by the sofa. A bottle of champagne peeked from under a white cloth.

"Did you meet her family?" she asked.

"Yes."

Serena seemed frustrated by his cryptic responses. "Well, what were they like?"

Cabral had his arm around Serena's waist, and they were both looking at him, shadows from the flickering candle playing on their faces.

"I'll tell you tomorrow," Mike said. "No reason to interrupt your party now. Good night."

He stepped into his room and closed the door. The image of Serena in Cabral's arms was burning his brain. He felt a white-hot jealousy. Funny that he should return from a date with one woman, still tormented by a hard-on, only to be inflamed with jealousy over another.

It disappointed him that Serena would be so taken with the guy. That right there said a lot about his marriage and why it had gone wrong.

Mike kicked off his Top-Siders and removed his pants. He turned on the lamp and plopped onto the bed, aware of the tenderness of his skin. For a while he relived his afternoon at the beach and the evening of dancing. Then, through the open window, he heard Serena laugh. They had apparently gone onto the balcony. He could hear the low rumble of the man's voice, but not his words. Good old Roberto was whispering sweet nothings in her ear.

How could Michael fault Cabral for trying to get laid when he himself had spent the day trying to do the same thing? Was he less cynical than Cabral? Or more? Was he morally superior—or less corrupt? Was Bebe? Or Serena?

Of course, Serena and Bebe had their own agendas. Women weren't any less involved in sexual machinations than men. They simply approached things differently.

Again he heard the trill of Serena's laughter. Michael had to resist the temptation to go to the window. If he did, and saw Cabral putting his hand down Serena's dress, what would he do? Why in the hell had they chosen the suite to play their little games? Despite Serena's protestations, they'd known he would be coming back eventually. On the other hand, maybe that was what Serena wanted—the protection of his presence.

Bebe hadn't used her family in quite the same way, but she had found ways to fend him off without exactly rejecting him. That, he realized, was the crucial dynamic between the sexes. Women wanted the game, men the payoff. They each had to give in order to get, and that made for potential problems—tension at best, resentment and animosity at worst.

By the sound of things outside, Serena was feeling the champagne. There were times when a woman had to get laid, when she needed to make a statement, if only to herself. He wondered if this was one such time for Serena. He hoped not. Of course, it didn't matter. Over the last five years he'd learned to let go. Or thought he had.

He went over to shut the window anyway. Sure, he was curious, but he didn't look out. He wouldn't allow himself the pleasure or the pain. He wasn't going to get sucked in. He wanted a reprieve, that was all. A reprieve.

The music from the next room became a little louder. It was more bossa-nova than samba, but it took him back to his last hours with Bebe, the dancing on the beach. Just thinking about it made him hard again.

Mike wondered if it wasn't just as well he suffer a little frustration. It seemed that occasionally the game ought to be enough. A lesson learned.

He held his wrist to the light and checked the time, deciding it was late enough to go to bed, if not to sleep. He went to the bathroom and was in the middle of brushing his teeth when he looked in the mirror and saw Serena standing at the bathroom door.

He spit out the toothpaste and rinsed his mouth. Wiping his face with a hand towel, he turned around.

"Well," he said, "come in."

Serena gave him an intoxicated smile. "I knocked, but you didn't answer."

"I was brushing my teeth. I guess I didn't hear."

"So I see."

"Where's Roberto?"

"He went home."

"Took his erection and left, eh?"

Serena smiled again. "Yes."

"Tell me, why do women derive so much pleasure from that?"

"Getting a man hard?"

"No, sending him away hard."

"Sex is so unequal to begin with, Michael, that women need to take every opportunity we're given."

"Opportunity for what?"

"To be in control," she said. The corner of her mouth quirked and she laid her head against the doorframe. "You didn't get any tonight, either, I see."

He couldn't help being bemused. "That obvious, huh?"

Serena nodded. "You can usually tell looking into a man's eyes...though not so easily as with a woman. For some reason sex stays with us longer."

Mike looked at her closely. He could see the whisker burns on her chin. Her hair was mussed, her dress slightly rumpled.

"I know you know this," he said, "but I'm going to say it anyway. We're not screwing tonight. It would be like getting the booby prize. We'd both feel like shit afterward."

"I know, Michael. I didn't come for that. I came to see if you came home with a hard-on, too."

"Well, I did. Are you satisfied?"

She beamed drunkenly. "Sad to say, but I couldn't be more delighted." After giving him a seductive look, she turned and slinked off to her room.

MONDAY
September 18th

Copacabana

Michael was gone by the time she awoke. He left a note saying he'd be spending the day with Koto but would be back in time to go with her to the Monteiro da Silvas'. Serena was glad not to have to face him. The events of the night before had left her feeling uneasy, and having to look at Michael over a cup of coffee would only have made things worse.

Not that her evening had been a flop. Roberto could kiss—Serena had to hand him that. And he knew how to do things to a woman, whether she was dressed or not. But even inebriated, she had found him too practiced, too intentional to be irresistible. Michael was accomplished, even masterful, in bed. And his love had a ring of sincerity that Roberto's lacked. At least that's the way it used to be.

Serena went to the door and looked out the peephole to make sure her security was in place. The guard on duty was a stocky, bald man. He was seated opposite the door, reading a newspaper.

She ordered breakfast. Shortly after it was delivered, she had a call from Walter Soloman in L.A. "How's Brazil?" he asked.

"Brazil's shitty, but that's another story. What's up?"

"I've reviewed the Happy Host contract."

"And?"

"There are a few nitpicky things I want to change, but basically I recommend you sign it."

"Courier it to me then, Walter, and tell Blake to get Bumgardener's approval to your changes. I'll hold off signing till everybody's on board."

"Check."

"Anything else?" she asked.

"I'm curious. How's Roberto Cabral working out?"

Serena rubbed the chafed skin on her chin. "He hasn't gotten Jeffrey out of jail yet, but otherwise he seems to be doing all right." She shivered as she said it. Nearly being seduced by one's lawyer would, under normal circumstances, be as humiliating an experience as one could have. It certainly wasn't anything she wanted going back to L.A. with her.

"He's only had four days," Walter said. "The wheels of justice can't turn any faster in Brazil than they do here."

Lord, Serena thought, had it only been four days? It seemed like weeks. If the wheels of justice didn't turn quickly in Rio, the wheels of love certainly did. "There are cracks forming in the case against Jeffrey," she said. "And with luck we'll soon find out who really murdered Drake Manville. But I'm not paying you to worry about that. Get the Bumgardener contract to me."

"Consider it done."

"Oh, Walter, one other thing. Are my personal affairs in order?"

"You mean your estate?"

"Yes."

"That's not my department, but as far as I know everything's in order. You changed your will after your divorce. Everything goes to your daughter, I believe. Why? Do you want me to talk to Ed Draper about it, have him do a review?"

"No. I'm just talking out loud. It's nothing."

"Serena, you don't feel you're in danger down there, do you?"

"Rio's a wild and dangerous place, Walter. Of course I'm in danger. In several respects."

"Oh, I see."

He didn't. But it didn't matter. Walter wasn't paid to understand that sort of thing. Serena said goodbye, then sat sipping her coffee and brooding.

During the hour before she'd fallen asleep, she'd thought about Christina and Joachim. Was the boy innocent, just a victim like the rest of them? There was no real reason to think he was connected with Drake's murder, but could Joachim have another motive for hiring Souza? If, say, he was serious about Christina and wanted to marry her, he might have decided she'd be an even *bigger* prize if she already had her inheritance. But if that was Joachim's game, he wouldn't have hired people to intimidate her family, he'd have had Serena killed. No, greed couldn't be his motive. He was either innocent or had something else in mind. Serena decided she'd know better that evening.

Antonia von Vehrling had also been in Serena's thoughts. The look in the woman's eyes when she'd called her Mimi and accused her of killing Drake...was it madness? Or was there truth behind it?

Mimi. Serena wondered if the name might ring a bell with Elaine Risollo. She got Elaine's number and called her.

"No, my dear," Elaine said in response to her question, "the only Mimi I can think of is French and lives in Monte Carlo."

"Well, I thought it was worth a try."

"I can ask around," Elaine volunteered.

"If you can do it discreetly."

"Why not? I am as eager for the discovery of Drake's murderer as you are."

There was a knock at the door. "Someone's here, Elaine. I've got to run. Maybe I can take you to lunch one day soon."

"I would adore it."

"Talk to you shortly."

"*Ciao.*"

Serena went to the door and peered out through the peephole. The guard was there with another man. A first she couldn't make out who it was because of the distortion of the lens. Then she recognized Hector von Vehrling. She opened the door a crack.

"*Senhora—*" the guard began, before being cut off by von Vehrling.

"Mrs. Bouchard, I'd like a few words with you."

"Mr. von Vehrling, I'm not dressed. I'm on the phone to L.A. and I don't appreciate having someone drop in uninvited."

She saw him flush. "Neither does my sister. I demand to know if it was you who tricked your way into her sanitorium."

Serena could see the situation had to be dealt with. "Give me a minute or two to dress, Mr. von Vehrling."

She closed the door and went to her room, slipping on slacks and a blouse. She didn't take the time to do her face, but put on eyeliner, a little mascara and lip pencil. After running a comb through her hair, she went to the door. Through the peephole she saw Hector pacing back and forth. She opened the door.

"Sorry to keep you waiting. Come in, Mr. von Vehrling."

He walked past her, giving her a hard look. Stopping in the center of the room, he turned to face her, ignoring her gesture to sit. He didn't have to tell her he was upset.

"I hope you appreciate the fact that by imposing on my sister yesterday, you have put her health in jeopardy," he began. "It was most irresponsible. I give you fair warning. Should you make another effort to see Antonia, I shall request sanctions—through the police, the courts, whatever is necessary."

"Yes, I did visit your sister. And if I upset her, I'm sorry. But you made it necessary by refusing to cooperate and by hiding witnesses, not to mention your dissimulation."

"What are you saying?" he demanded, drawing himself up.

"I'm saying you hid your sister and you're doing everything you can to keep the police from her. It's also interesting that Maria has disappeared. Curious timing, don't you think?"

"I assure you, I have no knowledge of that," von Vehrling said, sounding defensive. "But in any case, you try to divert me from the question at hand. The deception you used to get to Antonia was irresponsible. She is fragile. Now, thanks to you, she has had a setback. The police will hardly appreciate that."

"Look, Hector," Serena said, her own anger building, "if I upset Antonia, I'm truly sorry. I had no intention of hurting her. But I've got a brother in jail for a crime he didn't commit, and there's no doubt in my mind that you're doing everything in your power to hide evidence that would free him. In other words, I'm calling you a liar. So before you come in here, all-indignant, I suggest you take a close look at your own behavior."

Von Vehrling's expression grew even more steely. "I've given you the courtesy of a warning, madam. I trust, for your sake, that you have taken my words to heart, because if you haven't there will be consequences." With that, he headed for the door.

"Hector, before you go, let me ask you something."

He stopped at the door. "Yes?"

"Does the name Victor Souza mean anything to you?"

He pondered the question briefly. "No."

She gave him a thin smile. "Well, Souza tried warning me, too. It didn't work. I don't scare easily, Hector. You might as well know I'm going to find Drake's killer. And neither you, nor Souza, nor anybody else is going to stop me."

Hector von Vehrling glared at her a final time and left.

The car Joachim Monteiro da Silva had sent had already arrived and was waiting in front of the hotel when Michael came flying in the door. Serena, who'd been pacing for half an hour, was pissed off.

"Where in the hell have you been?" she asked, following him to his room.

"Earning my keep, sweetheart," he said, as he peeled off his shirt. "We located the missing maids."

"Both of them?"

"Yep. At von Vehrling's ranch. Their native village is nearby. Bebe went out there this morning and snooped around, talking to people. Finally tracked the maids down at the ranch."

He'd kicked off his shoes and was taking off his pants. Serena hardly noticed.

"So what's going to happen?"

"Bebe managed to hustle the maids off the ranch, and Koto's making arrangements for a place to hide them."

In his shorts, he headed for the bath. Serena followed him.

"Did Bebe get to talk to them?"

"I don't know. It was a rush thing." He turned on the water in the shower stall. "Koto talked to her on the phone. The plan is to interrogate them in the morning." He faced her, his hands on his hips. "I thought I'd take my shower now. Do you care to join me?"

"Go ahead, Michael. I've seen everything before."

He gave her a lazy smile. "What is it about crime that loosens the inhibitions?"

Serena did notice as he stripped off his shorts. Michael had great buns. She'd always liked his buns. He stepped into the shower stall without looking at her, closing the door.

"You'll be interested to know I had a visit this morning from Hector von Vehrling," she called out over the sound of the water.

"He came here?"

"Yes. In a snit over us going to see Antonia."

"No kidding."

She watched his bleary image through the frosted glass.

"Koto had a call from the detective, Mendonca, about that," Michael called back. "He was pissed, too. Told Koto to butt out or else."

"Did Koto tell him about the maids?"

"No, we thought we'd get what we could out of them first."

He turned off the water. Serena got a bath towel and handed it to him as he came out of the shower stall.

"Thanks," he said, wiping his face.

Leaning against the marble vanity, she watched him dry himself, with only half prurient interest. Mostly she was listening to his story.

"In fact," Michael went on, "Koto and I thought it might be interesting to spring the maids on Hector tomorrow. Invite him over, then hit him between the eyes. Shocking the truth out of somebody is often the most effective way of doing it."

"Are you sure von Vehrling is lying?" she asked.

"Yes." Mike vigorously toweled his hair. "What was your impression talking to him today?"

"He was indignant about me sneaking in to see Antonia. Said he was concerned about her health, but I couldn't tell if that was his true reason or not."

Michael plugged in his hair dryer. "I have a hunch we'll find out in the morning." He looked at her in the mirror. "I'll be ready in five minutes."

Her smile was a trifle embarrassed. "I suppose I should give you a little privacy."

"At fifteen hundred a day, you're entitled to a strip show."

Serena gave him a quelling look. "I'll be waiting in the sitting room. But make it snappy, Michael. We're running late."

"You know," he called after her as she made her way through his room, "I think this is the first time you've ever had to wait for *me.*"

"I'm either getting more responsible or you're getting less."

"That's one I'll have to think about."

His last words were drowned out by the sound of the hair dryer roaring into action.

* * *

Nova Iguaçu

It was dark by the time they made it to the Monteiro da Silva estate. With Joachim's driver and their own bodyguard in the front seat, Serena and Michael hadn't talked much. Mostly she worried about Christina, knowing her daughter had really fallen for this Brazilian polo player.

Her prejudices wouldn't serve her well, Serena told herself. Being nonjudgmental was important. But it was difficult to let go—and not only because Joachim might be mixed up in Drake's murder. Something about her daughter's boyfriend didn't feel right.

The fact that Christina was so naive about men didn't help, either. "Mom," she'd once complained during an argument about Cameron, "what's so wonderful about being *practical?* Were you being practical when you married my father? Or Michael?"

Serena had come to realize that nobody could be told about love. Experience was the only teacher that counted.

The car slowed and they turned off the road, into what appeared to be the gates of the estate.

"Don't forget," she whispered, "if you get the slightest inkling the situation's dangerous, I want Christina out of here tonight, even if we have to drag her, kicking and screaming."

Michael nodded, though she knew he didn't share her passion for the plan. Christina might be over eighteen, but Serena didn't give a damn. Sometimes a parent had to be despotic.

She gazed out the window at the moon rising beyond the mountains. As best she could tell, the estate was set in an open valley. The drive to the house was about half a mile from the gate. The home was well lit and had the air of a country estate—it was more than a ranch house, though not overly elegant. The two-story structure was mostly stucco, with a red tile roof and dark wood trim. The front was covered with flowering vines. The garden and surrounding vegetation were mature and well cared for.

When they got out of the car, the first things Serena noticed were the verdant, country smell and the plethora of stars overhead. In the city one wasn't so aware of the stars—especially in places like Los Angeles and Rio de Janeiro. But this was truly the countryside. Pleasant—lovely even—as it was, this estate did not seem like the place her baby belonged. Serena shivered at the thought.

The front door swung open and Christina emerged, followed by a handsome young man who had Dashing Heartthrob written all over him. This, Serena saw instantly, was the quintessential playboy—the kind of guy who was too pretty, too suave, too irresistible to help himself. This was Roberto Cabral without the mileage or the élan. One blink and Serena could see there wasn't a girl on the continent who wouldn't want this man. And worse—he knew it with undying certainty.

Serena embraced her daughter, but her eyes were on the young man as he approached. Christina stepped aside to present him. "Mom, this is Joachim. Joachim, my mother."

Young Monteiro da Silva took both Serena's hands in his, holding them as though he was going to kiss them, though he didn't. His dancing eyes looked straight into hers, giving her a taste of his magic. Joachim knew the importance of flirting with older women.

"Serena, it is indeed an honor."

"I'm glad we've finally met, Joachim."

"I welcome you to our home," he said airily.

Serena did not like him. He was concerned only with himself. His honor was phony, and so, too, was his love for Christina; Serena was sure of it. But she knew it hardly mattered what she thought. He was Christina's to worship. Serena's only recourse was to hope for the best.

Joachim greeted Michael, shaking his hand and tossing a pleasantry his way. Serena could tell Michael didn't like him, either. That was reassuring.

They went into the house and were presented to Joachim's grandmother, an aging madonna in a black satin, high-collar dress worthy of Whistler's mother. Her bearing, set jaw and thin smile screamed Catholic propriety. She had a few lofty-sounding words for them in Portuguese, which Joachim translated, but everything about the woman said she'd died many years ago. She was simply playing out her cards.

"My grandmother is most regretful that my mother could not be here," Joachim explained. "She apologizes for that."

"I'm sorry, too," Serena said.

"Mercedes is wonderful, Mom," Christina chimed in. "You'd love her. In fact, I've told Joachim that you're a lot alike." She turned to him. "Now that you've seen Mom, don't you agree?"

"Yes, most definitely," he said.

Serena noticed Christina slip her hand into his. Their fingers interlocked. Serena knew she was facing an uphill battle.

Joachim offered sherry and an assortment of aperitifs. Serena would have preferred a martini, but accepted the sherry.

The salon where they had their drinks was enormous. The ceilings were high, the furniture a mix of Portuguese antiques and modern pieces. The tapestries and oil paintings gave the room an Old World feel.

The grandmother went off to rest before dinner, leaving them to chat. Serena and Joachim got into a discussion about various businesses, prompting Christina to take compassion on Michael and suggest she show him the garden and the polo ponies.

Serena watched them go, then turned to a smiling Joachim. "Christina's a sweet girl, isn't she?"

"I love her very much, Serena. I hope that's okay to you."

"Okay? How could it not be? Christina deserves a nice young man who loves her. I want her to be happy, Joachim."

His quiet smile contained a trace of larceny. She could see it would soon be a lost cause. The relationship was set in concrete—freshly poured and still wet, perhaps, but about to be fixed for all time. Her only hope was to expose Joachim for what he was.

"Perhaps I could share a concern," she said to him.

"Certainly."

"I worry about Christina's safety. She tells me you've received threats, some aimed at her."

Joachim frowned, indicating his own concern. "Yes, this is true," he said. "I don't believe it is serious, but still I take all the precautions. I will not risk her security."

"I'm glad of that, naturally. But I have to tell you I don't like it. Don't you think it would be good if Christina spent a little time back home in California?"

He seemed uncomfortable with the question. "I think that is something you must discuss with her, Serena."

"Yes, you're probably right." She let him pour her more sherry.

Joachim, she could see, was not being diplomatic; he was running from the issue. But what did that mean?

Christina took Mike's arm as they strolled in the moonlight. They'd gone beyond the garden and were walking by the paddocks. He glanced at the horses grazing quiescently under the silvery moon and wondered if this life really appealed to her.

She steered him over to a rail fence. "Watch," she said.

Christina made a clicking sound with her tongue. A white stallion tossed his head. She clicked again and the horse trotted over to them.

"This is *Pago,*" she said, holding out her hand for the horse to lick. "It's short for *relâmpago,* which means lightning. He's Joachim's favorite pony."

Christina seemed especially young to him just then. She was dressed in a simple cotton dress and her hair was pulled back with a bow. How many times had he taken a smaller version of her to the movies or a museum or the beach?

How many times had he wondered if there'd ever be a man worthy of her?

"Mom doesn't like Joachim, does she?" she said unexpectedly.

"I don't think that's a fair statement," Mike said. "Your mother has to deal with an awful lot right now. A new boyfriend for her daughter is just another worry."

"Why should anyone I care about be a worry?"

"You'll understand when you have kids of your own."

Christina put her chin on the top board of the fence and stared across the paddock. "What do *you* think of Joachim?"

"In my eyes there isn't a man alive who's good enough for you, pumpkin. You know that."

"You've got to admit he's awfully special, though."

"He's one of a kind," Mike admitted somewhat disingenuously.

"I never thought there'd be anyone like him."

Mike stared at the moon, enjoying the balmy air without relating to it. As nice a place as this was, it felt foreign. He imagined that deep down it had to be the same for Christina, whether she admitted it or not.

"It must be a challenge to have a relationship, considering all the adversity you're facing," he said.

"If you mean Uncle Jeffrey, the answer is yes," she said gloomily. "Joachim and I try not to talk about it."

"What, exactly, is the problem? The fact that he's your uncle?"

"I think it's got a lot more to do with Mercedes's feelings than Joachim's. She is a dear and I love her, but the Drake-and-Jeffrey business was definitely a problem for her."

"Is she homophobic?"

"I don't know," Christina said. "Maybe it's a social thing. Maybe my family is an embarrassment to her."

"But not to Joachim?"

"He loves me too much to let it interfere."

"That's a good sign."

"After the murder things were pretty chaotic, though."

"Yeah? How so?"

She took his arm, and they started walking back toward the house. "It seemed everybody was telephoning in the first day or so after it happened. Joachim was on the phone constantly. I was a little ticked. It was *my* uncle in jail and people were acting like it was their tragedy. Mercedes was hysterical. Joachim apologized when he saw how upset I was."

"Who was he talking to on the phone? The police?"

"I don't know. It was in Portuguese. I don't understand too much yet, but Joachim and his mother did have one heated argument after a call from somebody named Hector something-or-other."

"Hector? Hector von Vehrling?"

"Could be. I'm not sure. Why, Michael? Do you know somebody by that name?"

"That's the name of Drake's landlord."

"Oh. I wonder why Joachim would have talked to him."

"Do you remember hearing the name Antonia von Vehrling?"

"No, I don't think so. Is that his wife?"

"His sister."

"What does she have to do with it?"

"They're just names we've heard bandied about," Mike said. "We've gotten the impression the Brazilian upper crust is not only rarified, but small and inbred."

"I guess you could say that."

"Maybe you can keep your ears open for me. The more I know about what people are saying, the better my chances are about helping Jeffrey."

"What should I watch for?"

"Listen for the name Mimi."

"Who's she?"

"Possibly somebody mixed up in Drake's murder."

Christina seemed pensive as she walked. "I suppose I could ask Joachim if he knows anybody by that name."

"Only you know how much you want to involve him."

She sighed despondently. "We do sort of have this agreement not to let the murder get between us."

Mike wondered if the impetus for their agreement had come from Christina or Joachim. "Whose idea was that, pumpkin?"

His stepdaughter hesitated before she answered. "It was mutual."

He didn't have to inquire further. But he wasn't surprised. If he was in Joachim's shoes, he wouldn't want to have to explain himself, either. The question, of course, was what did he have to hide?

After a hearty meal Joachim suggested they return to the salon. His grandmother excused herself and went off with her maid, leaving the two couples.

In the salon Joachim offered cognac. Serena had never been a fan of brandy, but she felt the need of fortification. She and Michael both accepted. Christina declined.

After serving the cognac, Joachim joined Christina on a big fluffy sofa. She immediately took his hand. Serena and Michael settled into matching leather wing chairs. Michael had been largely silent that evening, though she sensed not so much out of boredom as contemplation. She wondered if Christina had said something when she'd taken him off for their walk.

"You seem to be happily settled in with Joachim's family," she said to Christina when no one else appeared inclined to carry the conversation.

Christina looked up at her champion with girlish innocence. "Oh, I am, Mom."

"So finishing college is definitely on the back burner."

The girl bit her lip. "For now. This is where I want to be."

"I can see that, but it wouldn't be a bad idea for you to spend a little time back home, Christina," Serena said, taking a large sip of brandy. "In fact, maybe Joachim would like to come along. Couldn't hurt for him to see *your* home."

The girl leaned over and whispered something in Joachim's ear.

"It's up to you," he replied softly.

"Mother," Christina said, her voice a bit tremulous, "Michael—we—Joachim and I—have something to tell you...."

Serena's heart dropped.

"We weren't going to say anything until Uncle Jeffrey's case was resolved, but I feel like a sneak not telling you when we're sitting here like this...."

Serena waited, her breath wedged in her throat.

"Joachim and I have decided to get married."

Serena had known it was coming. Still, tears filled her eyes. "Darling, that's...wonderful!"

Both women got up.

"Are you really pleased, Mom?"

"Yes, of course. If you're happy, I'm happy."

They embraced. And while they hugged, Michael and Joachim shook hands. Serena reached over and took Joachim's face in her hands, kissing each cheek in turn. She could no longer dislike the boy, she told herself. That was something to put behind her.

Christina had received a big kiss from Michael, whose eyes were glossy. Serena went to Michael and they embraced. She had a sudden, overwhelming urge to cry. Michael rubbed her back.

"Our baby, Michael," she murmured in his ear.

"Time marches on, sweetheart."

That gave her pause. "But I'd like to think not as quickly for some of us as for others."

She wiped a smudge of Christina's lipstick from the corner of his mouth. Feeling clingy, she took his arm. Christina hugged Joachim and cried happily. Serena smiled through her tears.

"Love conquers all," she murmured. "Love conquers all."

Christina nodded enthusiastically.

"So, have you given any thought to when?" Serena asked.

"We thought maybe in the spring. May or June."

"The wedding will be in California, won't it?"

"We hadn't decided. What do you think?"

"Well, you can have parties both places so that nobody will have to fly halfway around the world to celebrate with you."

"That sounds good," Christina said. "Don't you think so, Joachim?"

"Yes, perhaps."

Serena looked at him. "So what does your mother think?"

"Actually, we haven't told her," Christina replied.

"But we will as soon as she returns from abroad," he added.

"When will that be?"

"Soon," he said, looking uncomfortable. Then he brightened. "We have champagne in the cellar, *senhores*," he enthused. "This is a suitable occasion, no?"

"*Sim,*" Serena replied, being the best actress she could be. "It's a perfect occasion. Let's celebrate."

Her words were upbeat, but her heart was breaking.

Copacabana

It was three in the morning and Serena still hadn't fallen asleep. She got up and went out onto the balcony to watch the night. Even at that hour there were people roaming the streets, although there wasn't much traffic. It was quiet enough to hear the surf, but she was only vaguely aware of it. Her baby was marrying a Brazilian polo player, a man who might well have been involved in a murder, and Serena was helpless to do anything about it.

It had been a trying evening, to say the least. The drive home had been tough for both her and Michael—because of the men in the front they couldn't talk. But as soon as they got out of the car, she'd said, "I refuse to let her marry that man."

"Good luck."

"There are ways." But the truth was she wasn't as confident as her words.

"We've got another problem," Michael said. He told her about Joachim's conversations with Hector von Vehrling in the days following the murder.

"Lord, do you think they're both mixed up in it?" she asked.

"Who knows? Nothing makes much sense right now."

"It's a conspiracy," she'd told him, "I know it. I thought that even before we left Los Angeles. But now my baby is engaged to one of the coconspirators!"

"Don't go off half-cocked. It could have been innocent."

"Oh, Michael, why deny the obvious?"

Of course, it made no sense to take her frustrations out on him. She would have liked to sleep in his arms, but even in a time of great need, like now, she knew that was out of the question.

When they'd returned to the suite they found the message light blinking. Michael called the desk. Roberto had telephoned and asked Serena to call him back. That it didn't matter if it was late; he had important news. She phoned him at home.

"I thought you'd want to know the police arrested Victor Souza tonight," he said.

"They did? Wonderful!" She related the message to Michael.

He was clearly pleased, giving a thumbs-up. Roberto had no information other than that, but the prosecutor promised an update in the morning. When the call turned personal, Michael went off to bed, emphatically closing the door to his room.

Roberto was in the mood to chat, so Serena decided she might as well get some commiseration. She told him about

Christina's engagement and asked if he thought Joachim would be a good husband.

"He's young," Roberto replied, "but then everyone under forty seems young to me."

She'd wondered why he couldn't have said everyone under forty-five, but her own fading youth hardly seemed worthy of concern, given her list of problems. She'd been tempted to tell him about their discovery of the maids, but Michael had warned her not to tell a soul, so she held her tongue.

"I know you have much on your mind, and I hope you won't think me insensitive," Roberto said, "but I wish to entertain you in my home. Can I entice you to come to dinner tomorrow evening?"

Her first impulse was to say no. Then she wondered if the diversion wouldn't be good for her. Her reaction to Christina's news had been to turn to Michael, even flirting with the idea of calling off their moratorium on sex. But misery was a lousy excuse for intimacy, and he'd have hated her for being selfish. Rightfully so. An evening with Roberto seemed the lesser of evils.

"Yes," she'd told him, "I'll let you entice me tomorrow evening."

He'd been more than pleased, making her wonder what he thought she'd agreed to. But he could be dealt with when the time came. The important thing was to keep her mind on the business at hand.

In the street far below she watched a young couple walking, their arms around each other. They were singing, of all things, their voices carrying to her balcony. Whether they were drunk or in love was hard to say. Maybe there wasn't much difference.

"So," came a voice from behind her, "another insomniac."

Serena spun around, realizing it was Michael just as he emerged from the shadows. "Lord, you scared me to death," she said, clutching her hands to her breast.

"Sorry. I saw you out here and . . . can I join you?"

He was in undershorts, acting as though modesty was the furthest thing from his mind. Serena hadn't much on herself—a filmy gown, that was all. Michael leaned on the railing and watched the few scattered pedestrians far below.

"There's something about the air this time of night that's different," he said. "Sometimes when I can't sleep I walk a few miles under the stars. That usually does it."

"I remember when you use to treat your insomnia with middle-of-the-night sex," she said. "It always put you right to sleep."

"I remember being awakened from a sound sleep on a few occasions to take care of your insomnia, too, Lady Bouchard."

"We did take care of each other in ways, didn't we?"

"In ways," he said.

His tone of voice spoke volumes. "You're still bitter that I wanted the divorce, aren't you?"

"*Bitter*'s the wrong word. I'm annoyed that we keep trying to seduce one another. You know how I hate hypocrisy."

She bristled. "You say that like it's my fault. Nobody's twisting your arm, Michael."

"That's not exactly accurate. You've been twisting my arm since the day you came up to the mountains looking for me."

"That's not true!"

"Bullshit."

"I suppose that's why you went to bed with me. Because *I* twisted your arm."

"Serena, you've been talking out of both sides of your mouth ever since we got here and you know it. One minute you're making oaths of chastity, the next you've got your hand in my pants."

"And you're the poor innocent. Is that it?"

"I didn't say that."

"You might as well have! Michael, you're the hypocrite! Your problem is you can't decide if you want to lay me or Bebe."

"Look who's talking. You can't decide between my cock and Cabral's. At least you narrowed it down to two."

Fury consumed her. She slapped him, and Michael was momentarily stunned. He rubbed his jaw.

"Got a little too close to home, did I?"

Serena started to swing again, but he grabbed her wrist and wrenched her around, hurting her.

"I think one shot is enough."

"You bastard," she snapped.

Michael glared. She tried to jerk her arm free, but couldn't. He was pulling one of those macho, brute stunts.

"Amusing," she said.

"You swung first."

"You deserved it!"

Michael tightened his grip.

"Ow."

"It's not fun to be on the receiving end, is it?"

"Okay, that's enough."

He squeezed harder, making her flinch. It was then she realized this wasn't about pain. She searched his eyes for understanding. He loosened his grip slightly.

Though her teeth were still clenched in anger, she felt the first twinges of desire. Slowly lust displaced her hatred, until they became indistinguishable. Michael seemed to be making the same transformation. He pulled her closer.

The adrenaline in her blood made her heart pound. She could feel the heat of his body. Still he wouldn't release her.

"You like hurting me, don't you?"

He didn't respond.

She ran her hand over his stomach. "I'm sorry I hit you."

He maintained an icy silence.

She inched closer. "It galls you that you want to make love with me, doesn't it, Michael?"

The grip on her wrist loosened a bit more.

She wanted to feel his body, so she leaned against him, touching her hard nipples to his chest. He didn't move as she slowly twisted back and forth, rubbing her chest against his.

Serena slid her fingers under his shorts, taking his swollen sex in her palm. "Somebody's glad to see me," she purred.

She caressed him, making him harder. Michael still hadn't let go of her wrist. She kissed his chin.

"You are a first-class bitch," he murmured, his arousal reflected in his voice.

She continued to stroke him. "That's what you love about me. Admit it." She kissed his neck, drawing the tip of her tongue down the side of it.

He shivered as she continued moving her hand up and down his shaft. She felt her juices begin to flow.

"Jesus," she muttered as her nipples grew harder. She wanted him very badly. "Let's go inside."

She led the way, pulling her nightgown over her head and tossing it aside as she went to the sofa. She threw herself down on it, waiting for him.

But Michael just stood there. What she could see in his expression in the darkness was aloofness, defiance, maybe even disgust. She was shocked at first, then grew embarrassed.

"Christ," she said, "you aren't going to fuck me, are you?"

"You know, Serena," he said, "sometimes what a person doesn't do is more important than what he *does* do."

He walked away, going to his room and closing the door. She lay perfectly still, her anger and her embarrassment competing. Part of her wanted to rage at him, scream every filthy word she knew, but the other part wanted to sob. In the end, the weaker part prevailed. Tears filled her eyes and she began to cry.

TUESDAY
September 19th

As soon as they arrived at the villa and were admitted by the new maid, Mike and Koto went into the library so Koto could examine the crime scene. Serena headed straight for the salon. The drive to Santa Teresa had been the second chilly engagement in what was proving to be a cold war of heroic proportions. Nobody had to tell Michael that Serena was royally pissed off. He knew from experience that she could be an accomplished ice queen when she chose, but this morning she'd outdone herself.

When he hadn't seen hide nor hair of her from the time he got up until he'd finished breakfast, he'd considered knocking on her door, just to make sure she was awake. Then he wondered if it wouldn't be better to let sleeping dogs lie. Confronting Hector von Vehrling without her would have been fine with him.

But a few moments after Koto had called from the lobby, she came out of her room, girded for battle, looking elegant but cool in a yellow dress with cap sleeves. She scarcely glanced in his direction.

"Was that our ride?" she asked with icy formality.

"Yes, Koto's downstairs."

"Is there anything I need to know before we see Hector?"

"Not that I can think of. I suggest you let me and Koto handle him."

"I wouldn't think of interfering," she said pointedly as she poured coffee. Serena hadn't sat, hadn't even looked at him. She took a few perfunctory sips, then put down her cup. "All right, let's go. No point keeping Koto waiting."

When they'd gotten into the Toyota, Serena was cordial, but as they'd fought their way through the traffic, she'd brooded. Now that she was in the other room, Mike finally relaxed. Koto was squatting behind the desk, looking at the bloodstain. Glancing over the top of the desk toward the doorway, he said in a low voice, "Is something bothering Mrs. Bouchard this morning?"

"Yes, my friend. Me."

Koto's brows rose in question.

"It's a long story," Mike explained.

"One I shouldn't ask about, I suppose."

Mike stared at the glass bookcase behind the desk. "Yeah. You'd find it boring, I'm sure."

Koto looked around the room. "Not a lot here that's helpful," he said.

"It's what's *not* here that's most interesting."

"What do you mean?"

"The two shots have me puzzled. I'd like it better if Miss Ingram had heard them both. I also wish there was a bullet hole in the ceiling."

"You don't like the test-fire theory?"

"I suppose everybody in the world doesn't reload after test-firing, but it seems the natural thing to do."

"Maybe that tells us our killer isn't meticulous, Mike."

"That, or doesn't know anything about guns."

Koto turned at the sound of a vehicle. He went to the window. "It's Bebe . . . with the maids."

Mike brightened. In his idle moments over the past couple of days the image of Bebe in a string bikini had often come to mind. She had him thinking and acting like a teenager. Joining Koto at the window, he looked out to see Bebe in one of her skimpy outfits, coming up the walk with two peasant women.

Bebe glanced up as she passed under the window on her way around the house to the back door. She gave them a little wave. Mike felt the warmth of her smile. It was in stark contrast to the frosty demeanor of the woman he'd spent the morning with. But then, Bebe hadn't been scorned.

Every woman had her dark side, he knew, as did every man, yet a sunny disposition could block out a lot of the negative. He couldn't resent Serena, though. If anything, he felt guilty about last night—not because he should have accommodated her, but because he could have been kinder in refusing to do so.

"I'm glad they got here before von Vehrling," Koto said. "I've been eager to see his reaction when we march them out."

"Me, too."

"I think I'll go back and see what frame of mind the maids are in," Koto said.

Mike would have liked to go along, but he figured he should give Serena an opportunity to throw a few darts his way—after all, she'd been utterly humiliated and she needed to salvage her pride. He found her seated by the window, her legs crossed as she gazed out at the morning sun. She was sitting erect, more rigid than normal.

"Bebe's here with the maids," he said.

"That ought to make you happy."

He took the shot in silence. He had to allow her a few zingers if her hostility was to dissipate. Going to the other window, he gazed out.

"Von Vehrling ought to be here soon," he said after a while.

His comment was met with silence. Then she announced, "Michael, I have something I want to say to you." Her voice had an ominous ring.

"Yes?"

"About last night. I hate you for what you did, but I still owe you an apology."

"No, you don't. I was an asshole."

"I won't argue with that, but I was out of line to try to seduce you. I'm not going to say any more than that."

"So, all's forgiven."

"No," she snapped, "nothing's forgiven. I still feel like scratching your eyes out, but that doesn't change the fact that I was wrong to have done what I did. I'd like this to be the last we discuss it, though. Ever."

"Whatever you want, Serena."

"That's exactly what I want."

"Fine."

They heard footsteps. Koto and Bebe entered the room. Serena changed expressions.

Bebe walked toward them just as she had that first morning at the airport. "Good morning, Mrs. Bouchard. Mike."

"Hello, dear," Serena said with a cheerfulness that would have been inconceivable only moments ago.

"Bebe has news," Koto said.

The girl beamed. "There was a message at the office from Mendonca," she said. "Two things. First, they arrested Souza."

"Yeah," Mike said, "we heard last night from Cabral."

"Oh?"

"News travels fast."

"Mendonca will be asking to you and Senhora Bouchard to come to the police station to identify that Souza was the one who attacked you."

"Gladly," Serena said.

"The second news is just as good," Bebe said. "The gun that killed Senhor Manville has been connected to Souza."

"You're kidding!" Serena said, getting to her feet. "It was Souza's gun?"

"I'm not sure how, but some way they know this through the criminal records. They only discovered it yesterday afternoon."

Mike and Koto looked at each other, smiling.

"The noose around Jeffrey's neck may have loosened a tad," Mike said. "Unless he had something going on the side with the boys in the underworld."

The words were no sooner out than Serena gave him a withering glare.

"So to speak," he added. But the damage had been done.

"Now, how does this fit in with the woman Mr. Bouchard saw running from the villa?" Koto asked.

"And Senhor von Vehrling and the maids?" Bebe added.

"And Antonia and Mimi," Serena said in turn.

"Not to mention Colonel Mustard, Miss Scarlet and Mr. Green," Mike said.

Nobody laughed, though Serena could have. She pointedly refused.

"Who are *they?*" Bebe asked with childlike innocence.

"Suspects in one of Michael's previous cases," Serena said dryly. "His list of accomplishments extends far beyond policing hookers and card counters."

Bebe shook her head. "I need more English lessons."

"And Michael needs more tact," Serena said under her breath.

He could see he would be paying for his sins for a long, long time. "So," he said to Bebe, "have you asked Maria what happened?"

"We only had a little conversation because she is very upset and not so much smarter than her sister. It was Senhor von Vehrling who took her to the country. He told her she must never speak of what happened. It is for this that she is not quick to talk to me. I get a little more each time, but it comes slowly."

"Don't worry. Hector won't know what we've got and what we haven't. The maids are good for shock value. And I'm sure he isn't eager for the police to talk to them."

"Hold on," Koto said, going to the window. "There's a car in the drive. I think it's Hector."

"Places, everyone," Serena said. "The show is about to begin."

"I'll go be with the maids," Bebe said, running from the room.

Michael decided to play butler. He went to admit von Vehrling.

"Well, my dear Mr. Hamlin," Hector said, looking up from the bottom of the front steps, "we meet again."

Mike offered his hand. Von Vehrling shook it perfunctorily.

"We're assembled in the observatory," Mike said. "Please join us."

Von Vehrling's smile was wry and slightly malevolent. "With Miss Peacock and the candlestick?"

"Hector, you're a man after my own heart. We should do lunch sometime."

"Somehow, I think not."

Mike shrugged and followed von Vehrling into the salon. Hector marched with the same crisp bearing as the last time. Approaching Serena, he shook her hand, clicking his heels. "A pleasure to see you again, Senhora Bouchard. I hope this encounter won't be quite so unpleasant as the last time we met."

"You're very generous, Mr. von Vehrling. I hope your sister is doing better."

"Thank you. The doctors tell me she's improved."

"That's good to hear."

Hector did not exactly signal forgiveness, but he had done better than Serena in that regard. Mike introduced Koto, and as everyone but Mike sat down, Hector glanced at Serena.

"Here we are once more," he said with a supercilious smile. "Only the young lady is missing."

"Actually, we've got several young ladies waiting to see you," Mike said. "Let me get them."

He went to the kitchen to fetch Bebe and her charges. As she passed by him on the way to the salon, she ran her fingers across his cheek. "Good morning, Mike," she said in a sultry tone. It was their first private moment.

"Good morning to you, sugar."

"How's the sunburn?" she asked.

Mike eyes were on the sweet curve of her ass. "Much better."

They entered the salon. When Hector, who had his back to the entrance, glanced over his shoulder and saw the maids, he jumped to his feet. Stunned, he looked at everybody with dismay.

"What—what is the meaning of this?" he sputtered.

"Why, Hector," Mike chided, as he put his arm around Ana's shoulder, "we thought you'd be pleased to see your missing chicks—sort of like Hansel and Gretel safely home."

"You're amusing, *senhor*," von Vehrling rejoined, "but I have no time for this. If it's a circus you want, then you won't have it with me." He started for the door.

"Then you prefer that we take these ladies to Mendonca? I'm sure he'd be pleased to see them, if you aren't."

Von Vehrling slowed, then stopped. He was only a few feet from where Mike stood. The maids recoiled.

"You brought them directly here?" von Vehrling asked.

"Hector, we're friends. And friends stick together."

The landlord lowered his eyes. "What is it you want?"

"The truth about what happened the morning Drake Manville was murdered."

Von Vehrling sighed wearily. In the passing of just a few minutes he looked older. Much older. He returned to his seat as Bebe ushered the maids to some straight chairs in the corner near the door. He glanced over at them, shaking his head. Mike went to the chair he'd occupied earlier and stood behind it.

"I had a call from my ranch manager this morning, saying they were gone. I had no idea they'd end up here," von Vehrling said.

"Surprise parties fascinate me, Hector," Mike said. "Let's hope they put you in a loquacious mood."

"For all your cleverness, you can be a very unpleasant man, *senhor*."

"I can be an asshole," Mike said with a sly glance at Serena. "Murder, especially, puts me in a foul mood."

"Not to mention ex-wives," she said under her breath.

Mike slipped around his chair and sat. "Would you care to give an amended version of your story? I'm interested to see how closely it corresponds to what Maria told us."

"Don't worry," von Vehrling said with another weary sigh. "You will get the truth."

"Please."

Von Vehrling took a handkerchief from the breast pocket of his jacket and mopped his brow. "I gave the police a false report," he said. "And you, as well."

Mike saw Serena lean forward. "We're listening."

"I came to the villa that morning, as I told you, but both the maids were here, not just Ana. Hysterical, they took me to Drake's body. I saw immediately that he was dead. I asked Maria what had happened. She said that while she was at the market Drake had had a visitor. Ana told her this, of course."

"Did she say who?"

"A woman. She didn't know the name. Only that it was a woman of refinement."

"Somebody rich."

"Yes."

"Go on."

"Well, I asked what Ana saw, exactly. Maria said the woman came to the door with a few books. Drake met her in the entry, where they chatted. Then they went into the library. At that point Ana returned to the kitchen. That was all she saw. Later, when Maria returned from the market, Ana told her Drake had had a visitor. Maria went to the library to see if they wanted tea and found the body. I arrived a short time later."

"The mysterious visitor was your sister, Antonia, wasn't it?"

"I thought so, yes," von Vehrling replied. "I'd learned a few weeks earlier that Antonia and Drake had a friendship. They'd met at a social gathering, a multilingual literary group. They were both surprised to discover a connection with me. Drake did not know I had a sister, and Antonia wasn't aware I'd rented the villa to an American actor. Anyway, their friendship bloomed, interfering in the relationship Drake had with Mr. Bouchard.''

Mike glanced at Serena, who was listening with rapt attention.

''Naturally, I was greatly distressed that my sister might have committed this murder,'' von Vehrling went on. ''Antonia has been very unstable emotionally for many years. The only violence she has taken has been against herself. As a young woman she cut her wrists. I thought perhaps this time she had turned against another.

''My first instinct was to protect her. I sent the maids to the back of the house so I could consider the problem. The gun was on the floor. I assumed it must have Antonia's fingerprints on it because if she was foolish enough to leave the gun, then she would not have thought to wipe the prints away. I knew it was a serious matter to destroy evidence, but Drake was dead and my sister's life was at stake. I looked around to see what else I might find. On the desk I found a letter in Antonia's writing. With the maids in back and a dead man on the floor, I knew I had little time. I stuffed the letter back in the envelope and put it in my pocket. Next I took my handkerchief and wiped the gun clean of prints.''

''This explains why the gun didn't have complete prints,'' Koto said, ''but not why the partial print was Mr. Bouchard's.''

''Obviously because Mr. Bouchard touched the gun, not my sister.''

''They both could have touched it,'' Serena interjected.

''With all respect, *senhora,* more than one person could have touched it, I agree. But as you will see, one was not my sister. But let me continue.''

''Please do,'' Mike said.

''Having removed all evidence of the woman's visit from the house, I knew it was safe to notify the police. But I could not allow them to talk to the maids because Ana had seen the woman—the one I then thought was Antonia. At first I planned to take them both away, but then I realized this would seem suspicious. Ana could remain, since she is dim-witted and unable to communicate. The plan nearly worked, because the police did not pursue the matter.''

"Until we came along."

"Correct."

"All right," Mike said, "so you sent Maria away and you called the police. What happened then?"

"As soon as I could I went to my sister's apartment in Copacabana. I found her reading one of her French novels. She was not the least bit distressed. I asked if she was aware that Drake had been murdered. She was astounded and became hysterical. I could not calm her. She had a nervous—what is the word?—*breakup?*"

"Breakdown."

"Yes, a nervous breakdown. I took her to the hospital. At this time I was beginning to think perhaps she was not guilty. I questioned her maid and her chauffeur. To my great relief they both said that Antonia was in her apartment all morning. It was then I realized that she was innocent."

"So who was the woman at the villa?" Serena asked.

"This, *senhora,* I do not know. I telephoned the police with the intention of telling them what had happened. But I was also afraid, because I know it is a crime to disturb evidence. Then I learned that Senhor Bouchard had been arrested for the murder and that his fingerprints were on the gun. I realized that my action did not harm the case. To the contrary, it very nearly destroyed the evidence against Mr. Bouchard."

"Yes, but there was still a woman here," Serena insisted. "The maid saw her. She was obviously the killer, not Jeffrey."

Von Vehrling shrugged. "About this, I do not know. The only certainty is that the woman was not Antonia."

"What about the letter, Senhor von Vehrling?" Bebe said. "The one in your pocket."

Hector shifted uncomfortably. "When I arrived at Antonia's, I threw it in the trash. Then, in the excitement of her breakdown, I forgot about it. It wasn't until the next day that I remembered. By then it was gone. I didn't see how it could matter, though. My sister was not at the villa on the day of the murder, so to bring her name into the affair served no purpose."

"Even assuming what you say about your sister is true," Koto said, "any evidence at a murder scene could bear on the identity of the killer."

"You are right, *senhor.* I did not behave properly. But there is no reason to think what I did will change the outcome."

"Unless my brother hangs because of it," Serena retorted.

"I did not put your brother's fingerprints on the gun."

"There's no point in quibbling over spilled milk," Mike said, rising. He moved behind his chair again and once more looked down on Hector. "The key, as far as I'm concerned, is to find out who this mystery woman is." He stared intently at the Brazilian. "Tell me, Hector, do you think it could have been Mimi?"

Von Vehrling blinked. "*O quê?* Pardon?"

"I was wondering if you thought the mystery woman was Mimi."

Hector shifted again. "I don't know what you mean."

"Why, Hector, I'm surprised. Surely you know Mimi. Your sister does."

"Antonia is mad, *senhor.*"

"That's unfortunate," Mike rejoined, "in more ways than one."

Hector crossed his legs. He began bouncing his foot. "Tell me, Mr. Hamlin, what do you plan to do about this?"

"You mean your involvement with the evidence?"

"Yes. Do you plan to go to the police?"

"My associates here would like to speak with your sister's maid and chauffeur. We'll be talking further with Maria and Ana, as well, to confirm your story. In the meantime you might pay a visit to Antonia and find out what you can about Mimi for us. If you could do that, and if we get positive results, perhaps the police won't need to find out about your tampering with the evidence.''

"In other words, you're blackmailing me, Mr. Hamlin."

"The truth is what we're interested in. Just the truth."

They traded long, unpleasant looks.

"Have you finished with me?" the Brazilian asked.

"You've been very helpful, my friend. Our thanks."

Getting up, von Vehrling said, "I've got some phone calls to make. You have no objection if I use my telephone, I assume?"

"Be my guest."

He arched a brow. "You're so very kind, *senhor*." He strode from the room, casting a hard look at the maids as he passed. He continued on to the library and closed the door.

For several moments the rest of them were all silent.

"Michael," Serena said at last, "sometimes I actually like it when you're a prick."

Mike smiled despite himself. "I tried to make it as unpleasant for Hector as I could."

"Your talents in that regard are boundless, dear."

"Coming from anybody but you, that could be a compliment."

"Just keep earning your money, Michael. In that department you're doing fine."

"Thanks." He glanced toward the entry. "Listen," he said, lowering is voice, "Hector's had a shock. It might be interesting to see where he goes in a time of crisis."

"Do you want one of us to follow him?" Koto asked.

"Maybe that's a job for Bebe and me." Mike turned to Serena. "You wouldn't mind Koto taking you home, would you?"

"It would be a welcome change, Michael."

"Somehow I thought you might say that."

There was a clatter in the corner where the maids were sitting. Ana was making one of her lamenting noises. Bebe went to see what the excitement was all about. After conferring with Maria, she reported that the maids were upset about being around Hector. They didn't want to stay there. Koto told his assistant to assure them they'd have a safe place to stay for as long as necessary.

"What's your reading of von Vehrling?" Mike asked Koto.

"If he's lying we can find out easily enough."

"We'd better. A bluff could be all he has left."

"Want me to go by Antonia von Vehrling's place?" the investigator asked.

"Yeah, after you drop Serena off. And somebody needs to thoroughly debrief the maids to see if von Vehrling's account is accurate and complete. Hector may not have lied, but he may not have told the whole truth, either."

"Check."

"Mike," Bebe called from where she was huddled with the maids, "I think you should hear this." She brought the two women across the room.

"What's up?"

Bebe glanced over her shoulder toward the entry hall. "I asked about the mystery woman, what she looked like. I asked if she had red hair."

"And?" Mike said.

"Ana said the mystery woman doesn't have red hair. It's dark and short. She said the woman is beautiful and she's right here."

"What?"

Bebe pointed to Serena. "You, Mrs. Bouchard. Ana said you were the one who came to the villa the morning of the murder."

"Me? I was six thousand miles away."

"Ana was sure you were the one when we came to the villa last time, but she couldn't say anything because she didn't have Maria and she was afraid."

They all peered at Ana, who was cowering behind Bebe.

"That's right," Mike said. "Remember how she went running from the library when she saw you? We all thought she was strange, but the truth was she thought she was seeing Drake's murderer."

Serena shook her head. "Michael, what is going on?"

"I think we just found out that Antonia isn't so nuts, after all. Mimi does indeed look like you, sweetheart."

The door to the library opened, and they heard Hector von Vehrling's footsteps. Pausing at the door, he said, "Goodbye, ladies and gentlemen. I wish you well on your quest."

"Don't forget to let us hear from you," Mike called to him.

Von Vehrling acknowledged the request with a wave of his hand. "Count on it. *Adeus, senhores.*"

Mike pointed at Bebe. "There goes our rabbit, sugar. What say we get on the scent?"

Koto stood up. "Don't worry. I'll take care of things here."

Bebe had already started for the door. Mike gave Serena a long, friendly, peacemaking look. "We're making progress."

"Thanks for what you're doing," she said. It wasn't quite friendly, but there was an air of conciliation in her voice.

"A guy's got to be good at something," he replied.

He gave her a wink and took off after Bebe. When he got to the door, she had it open a crack and was peering down at the road.

Mike put his hand on Bebe's waist. "Where is he?"

"About to leave. Be ready to run to my car."

Mike left his hand on her waist. She smelled sweet, like honeysuckle, and the flesh under her dress was firm and taut. She seemed to enjoy his proximity.

"He's starting the car," she said. A few seconds later she cried, "He's pulling away. Let's go!"

Bebe dashed out the door and down the steps. The hem of her miniskirt flew up just enough to give Mike a glimpse of her ass. It was a nice sight, an inspiring one. And it made it all the easier to go running after her.

* * *

Flamengo

Serena and Koto drove through a tawdry section of town on their way back to Copacabana. She'd wanted to sit in front, but Koto insisted she stay in back. "It's safer, Mrs. Bouchard."

"Do you think there's still danger, considering Souza's been arrested?"

"He has friends, as you may recall."

Serena thought of the man who'd cut her breast. "Don't remind me."

Koto, she discovered, could be talkative. As she gazed at the sleazy bars lining the street, he told her how Bebe had spirited the maids off von Vehrling's ranch. "We wouldn't have gotten the truth out of him if it weren't for Bebe," he said proudly.

"I'm grateful for the efforts both of you are making," Serena told him. "Jeffrey and I are very fortunate."

"Mike may not specialize in criminal investigation, but he has a good mind for it," the detective said.

She could see that Koto was lobbying on Michael's behalf. That amused her. "He has his talents," she said.

It never ceased to amaze her how well liked Michael was. Nearly everyone thought he was wonderful. But why was she having charitable thoughts about the man when she still felt like scratching his eyes out? The smart thing to do was to forget about him, but she hated being humiliated. Especially by a man. Especially by one who was a former husband.

She tried to concentrate on the revelations of the morning. Before leaving, Koto had questioned the maids at length. Once the sign-language conversation was over, he'd reported that von Vehrling's story was holding up.

"You don't suppose Hector could've brainwashed them, do you?" Serena had asked before they left the villa.

"They aren't smart enough to lie, Mrs. Bouchard. The only confusion is that they think you're the mystery woman."

"That doesn't make them very reliable witnesses."

"Maybe we can't rely on them completely, but neither can the killer," Koto replied.

"You have a point."

After the interrogation was complete, Koto had decided to send the maids off in a taxi. "You've got better things to do than run around Rio with me and the women," he'd told Serena, "so I'll take you back to your hotel."

At the moment Koto was in the midst of telling her about a case he'd handled involving a wealthy socialite who feared her husband was leading a secret life as a transvestite. "Her suspicions were well founded," Koto said. "I tracked him to a fleabag up the street from here, where he kept his wardrobe. He came out of the place each night looking like a hundred-dollar hooker. Great legs."

Serena smiled. "I wonder what it did for his marriage."

"Not much that was good," Koto said. "In fact—whoa," he said, interrupting himself. He gazed into his rearview mirror. "We may have a problem, Mrs. Bouchard. There's a white Chevy Impala that I just picked up a few cars back."

"Isn't that the kind of car Michael saw Souza driving?"

"Yes, *senhora*. That's why I'm concerned."

Serena had a sudden sick feeling. She looked out the back window, but couldn't see the Impala. Koto speeded up, but the traffic was heavy enough that he couldn't do much more than weave from lane to lane in an attempt to gain some ground.

"What do you suppose they want?"

"Who knows?" Koto replied. After a moment he said, "Could be they aren't too thrilled with the prospect of you fingering Souza."

"Oh, shit," she said under her breath as the realization of danger began sinking in.

She glanced back. The Impala was right behind them now. Because of the glare of the sun on the windshield, she couldn't see who was in the vehicle.

"Maybe you should get on the floor, Mrs. Bouchard," Koto said as he swung into the right-hand lane.

Just as he said it, a large truck pulled in front of them from the side street. Koto slammed on the brakes. Serena turned to her left as the Impala came up beside them. She stared right into the face of Julio, the man who'd cut her. His window was down. A sawed-off shotgun was in his hand, pointed directly at her.

Serena screamed and ducked at the same time. As she hit the floor, the window exploded, peppering the inside of the car with glass. She felt the car swing violently to the right, followed by a stream of expletives in Portuguese from the front seat.

"*Senhora! Senhora!*" Koto screamed. "Are you all right?"

She was terrified. "Yes," she managed to gasp, "they missed me."

The Toyota roared along and she peeked up over the front seat, seeing they were going down a side street. Nobody was behind them.

"Are we safe?"

"I left them on the boulevard. But we've got to get out of here. They could come around the block."

Serena slipped back up onto the seat as the Toyota careened around a corner. The rear side window was gone and the one on the other side badly shattered. When she realized her head had been between the two she felt sick.

"Jesus," she said under her breath, only then aware of the glass on the seat. She brushed it away as wind whistled through the car. Koto made another sharp turn.

"I think we've eluded them," he said, "but if you don't mind, I'll take you directly to the police station."

"Sounds like a good idea," she mumbled.

"Somebody wants you dead pretty badly, Mrs. Bouchard."

Serena swallowed hard. "I have the same impression."

São Conrado

Hector von Vehrling led Mike and Bebe on a merry chase through the hills and forests outside Rio. Were it not for the girl's driving, the Renault would have had no chance of keeping up. As it was, they nearly lost Hector several times.

At first they weren't sure where he was headed. Then, as they came out of the mountains at the coast near São Conrado, Bebe figured it out. "He's going home the back way," she said.

"He lives out here?"

"In a house on the golf course."

"Just like the fat cats at home."

"Fat cats?" she said.

"My proletarian roots are showing, Bebe. Rich bastards."

She shook her head. "Mike, you can be very strange."

"Sometimes I am, sugar."

They made their way along the coastal plain for a short distance, then, as they entered the development, Bebe dropped back. They kept von Vehrling in sight, but when the Mercedes pulled into a gated estate, she stopped under some trees, turning off the engine.

"All that racing around mountain curves and passing on hills, only to find out he's going home," Mike lamented. "We could have been killed for nothing."

"That's life, Mike. It can be dangerous to get out of bed."

"Honey, it can be dangerous to *go* to bed these days."

She laughed and touched his face in a friendly way, just as she had in the kitchen at the villa. "You are unlike any man I have known before," she said. "Is it because you're American?"

"No, sweetheart, it's because I'm strange."

She shook her head, amused. "I don't know why Serena is not still married to you. She must wonder if it's a mistake."

"You're sweet to say that, but if Serena once had doubts, I think it's safe to say she doesn't anymore."

"Why are you divorced?" she asked. "Or should I not ask?"

"Sometimes when people come from different worlds the gap is too great to bridge," he replied.

"I think I understand. It was like that for me and Edson."

"Life can be painful," he said, "but it's also interesting."

"You think this is true, Mike?" She studied him, perhaps reading with her Afro-Latin eyes the melancholia in his white-bread soul. "Suffering is good?"

"Suffering is unavoidable. So we're left with two choices—bemoan our fate or try to find the good in it."

"That is something a priest might say."

"You think so?"

"No, maybe not. The priests want you to believe it is better in heaven."

"They could be right," he said, "but personally I think we should live this life as if it's all we'll ever get. It'd be a shame to find out there's nothing else when it's too late."

"You aren't afraid of hell?"

"I believe that hell is what we make here on earth, and so's heaven. I try to find a way to live for today, as well as I can. I don't succeed all that often, but I keep trying."

"Perhaps that explains it," Bebe said.

"What?"

"What my fortune-teller has told me about you."

He was surprised. "You talked to a fortune-teller about me?"

Bebe nodded. "*Sim*. Yesterday. After you came to the Barra and we went to the *pagode* on the beach. I asked about the future."

He saw an odd sadness in her eyes. "What did she say?"

"She said you are good, very good. You bring excitement, but also danger."

"The excitement part sounds promising."

Bebe smiled and touched his arm affectionately. Then a thought came to her. She turned away.

"What's the matter?" he asked.

"Nothing."

"No, tell me."

She sighed. "I am sorry it will not be better for us, Mike. I could see in Curima's eyes there was evil in our future."

"Evil?"

"Yes, but it's not your fault. I'm sure of that."

"Bebe, you don't take fortune-telling seriously, do you?"

"Curima is very wise. She warned me also about my future with Edson, but I didn't listen."

"Maybe your fortune-teller got her wires crossed about me. Maybe you should get a second opinion," he said.

"No, I have tried others. She knows me best."

It amused Mike how Bebe took everything literally. He found it endearing. But he also found it inconvenient that she was letting herself be guided by irrational, unseen forces. It was like trying to argue with a priest.

"To you it sounds crazy, maybe," she said, evidently sensing his dismay. "But in Brazil everyone has a fortune-teller. It is a way of life. My mother was a firm believer of the *umbanda*—a cult that is part Indian, part African, part Christian."

"What about Buddhist?"

She laughed. "Who knows, maybe there is that in there, also."

"Are you *umbanda?*"

"Not like my mother. She was a fanatic. Before she died she consulted the spirits about me. They said I would never find a husband. That I would die an old maid."

"You believe this?"

"There are signs. We have a custom here. On St. Anthony's Day the unmarried women write the names of the three men they care for most on a small slip of paper, which they fold and put in a glass of water. The name on the paper which is open the next morning is the man the woman will marry. I did this first when I was seventeen, and I did it for three years after that. Not one time did a piece of paper ever open. My aunt said I am the only girl in Brazil this has ever happened to."

"Maybe you folded it too tightly. Or maybe you used the wrong kind of paper. Or maybe there were too many minerals in the water, Bebe. You can't let something like that control your life."

"No, Mike. It is a sign. Science cannot explain the future."

"So, because of the paper and the water you've given up?"

"No, I just don't think about love like most girls. I live the life I want for myself—one full of danger and excitement. Curima has talked to me of danger in my life before I asked about you." She blushed. "So you see, Mike, maybe you are my special danger."

"Frankly, Bebe, that's not what I had in mind."

"What *do* you have in mind, then?"

"Something more friendly."

"You mean exciting?" she said with a little smile.

"Yes, I want to walk with you in the moonlight, drink some champagne, dance, do what our instincts tells us to do."

"You're saying you want to make love with me."

Her directness delighted him. "Yes. Very much."

Bebe considered that. "You are like Exu, Mike."

"Who's Exu?"

"The *umbanda* god. He brings both good and evil. You scare me the way Exu does, but I love you, too. There is good and evil in your desires. Do you understand?"

Her insight amazed him. "I believe nature planned it that way, Bebe. Good and evil go together. And so do fear and love."

"Yes," she said thoughtfully, "I've been thinking the same. Maybe from the first time I saw you. It made me want for Curima to be wrong. You are special. Even Curima knows this."

There was a tenderness in her words that touched him. "I can't tell you how good that makes me feel," he said. "Truly."

She leaned over and kissed him sweetly. "But I must tell you, Mike, there can be no ideas of love. Since Edson, I no longer think of these things."

"What are you saying?"

"If we are together, it must be for the adventure, the excitement. If you expect more, then we must not do it."

"Sugar, I agree completely."

She touched his face affectionately. "Besides, I know it's Serena you love."

"Serena and I are quits, kiddo."

"Perhaps for the moment. But she wanted us to be together now. Did you know?"

"You really think so?"

"She told me this. She is a very good person. Not everybody can be so generous."

Serena did have her virtues, he had to admit. Generosity was certainly one, though her current feelings about him weren't as charitable as Bebe thought. "Sounds like a win, win, win situation to me," he said.

Bebe smiled. Mike put his finger on her bare knee, drawing a little circle.

"You are very sexy, Mike," she said. "I thought it from the minute I first saw you. But you already know this, don't you?"

"Sugar, you and I have been on a collision course from day one. At least that's the way it seems to me."

"And to Curima, too," Bebe said a bit sadly. She and Mike kissed, and she looked at him longingly. Her eyes told him there would be more. Much more.

*   *   *

Copacabana

Serena paced back and forth in the suite, glancing over at Koto from time to time. He sat very still, almost as though he were meditating.

"Now that I've identified Souza, maybe his friends will realize the game's over and leave us alone," she said.

"If they know, perhaps. It's possible they think you're dead. In either case, we must be careful."

She stopped pacing. "And it's not just me who's in danger, Koto. Michael is as much a threat to Souza as I am. There's no point in killing one of us and not the other, since either of us could put him behind bars."

"True."

"We have to warn Michael and Bebe," she said, "if it's not already too late."

"I've thought of that. My office has been notified. If Bebe calls, she will hear. But until she does..."

"Where could they be?"

"Probably wherever Senhor von Vehrling is."

Serena dropped into a chair with a heavy sigh. She looked around the sitting room, recalling what Victor Souza had done to her there, feeling his presence.

"The waiting is difficult," she said. "I feel so helpless."

There was a knock on the door, giving her a start. Koto got to his feet. "I'll see who it is."

Serena began trembling again, as she had been regularly since that shotgun blast nearly took her head off. Nobody'd ever tried to kill her before.

Koto went up on his toes to look through the peephole. "It is Senhor Cabral," he announced. He opened the door.

Serena got up as Roberto swept into the room. "My darling," he said, taking her into his arms. "When I heard, I came here directly. Are you all right?"

She nodded, the little girl in her coming to the fore. "A bit shaky still, but otherwise I'm fine."

Roberto took her face in his hands. "You aren't staying here a minute longer. You're coming to my condominium. I have a guest room. My building is secure." He looked at Koto. "Perhaps you will be good enough to accompany us to Ipanema, Senhor Kotomata. We cannot take too many precautions."

"Está bem, senhor."

"No," Serena said, "I'd rather Koto do what he can to find Michael and warn him of the danger. He's out there somewhere, a sitting duck, and doesn't even know it."

"As you wish." Roberto checked his watch. "You'll want to pack some things, I presume."

Serena wasn't sure she wanted to go with Roberto. A part of her said no, but another part wanted to curl up in the safety of a strong man's arms—only she knew she'd rather it be Michael's.

There was no reason to stay at the hotel, though. Should Michael call, the desk could alert him of the danger.

"Yes," she said, "I'll pack. Give me a few minutes."

"Senhora, with your permission I'll go to work," Koto said.

"Of course. And the minute you find Michael, let me know."

"Gladly."

Serena went to her room and packed. When Roberto saw her come out with two bags, he smiled.

"For me, this is traveling light," she said, knowing what was going through his mind. "Don't make anything of it."

"Your safety is my only concern," he replied politely.

"I'll remind you of that, Roberto," she said. "It's only fair that you know romance is the furthest thing from my mind."

Roberto did not look pleased, but how could he object? To Serena it was another example of the advantage of being a woman. God knew there were disadvantages, but in the card game of life, half the value of a hand was in the skill of the player. Her father had taught her that, and she'd never forgotten.

São Conrado

They'd been up the road from Hector's estate for a couple of hours. Mike figured there was no point in continuing the stakeout. Hector was undoubtedly enjoying his afternoon siesta while they sat in the heat, swatting insects and taking turns getting out to stretch their legs.

They'd talked a lot, and somehow that made their physical discomfort tolerable. At one point Mike had asked Bebe if she wanted to chuck it in and go to the beach. "Or one of those love motels in Barra da Tijuca."

Bebe had given him a jab with her elbow, but she'd laughed. "Never while I work," she said. "It is dishonest. You should feel the same. Senhora Bouchard is paying us very good money."

"Virtuous women can be a joy, but also a pain," Mike said.

"You are like all men," she chided. "You only think of sex."

She was right, of course. "I plead guilty to being a man."

"It's more than most are willing to do." She yawned and stretched her long arms as best she could, once again caressing his cheek as she drew her hand back. "I am sleepy. Would you mind if I went in the back seat for a nap?"

"No, I'll guard the fort."

Bebe got in back, handing him a couple of magazines that were on the seat. Then she curled up, looking like an oversize child in a crib. She gave him a smile before closing her eyes.

Mike stared at her flawless, perfect face, wondering at his luck. She was no child, he told himself, rationalizing. She understood perfectly well what he was proposing. He had not lied, nor misrepresented his feelings. He had proposed nothing more than mutual pleasure. Sex, yes, but sex with tenderness and regard and respect.

Incredibly, Bebe seemed to fall asleep immediately. He pictured her sleeping in his arms after they made love. He wanted very much to know the taste and feel and smell of her. Bebe was like a wonderful dessert—he couldn't resist her, but he also knew a steady diet of her would be impossible.

Mike started leafing through the magazines. They were in Brazilian, of course—some of the same periodicals he'd seen in Koto's office, though more-current issues.

He paged through one that seemed to cover celebrity and society features, a sort of Brazilian *In Style*. Coming to a society pictorial, he stopped dead at the sight of a large photo of three women in formal attire. One of them he immediately recognized: the older woman standing in the middle was Clarise Sutcliffe d'Orléans. One of the other two truly gave him pause. For a second he thought it was Serena, but this woman was older and probably smaller. The face, though, could have been Serena's in, say, ten years.

"Jesus Christ," he muttered, as he recalled Ana, the maid at the villa, insisting that the mystery woman was Serena.

He looked at the caption. *Mercedes Monteiro da Silva.* Joachim's mother! He checked the name of the third woman, a redhead with aristocratic features: Antonia von Vehrling!

"Bebe," he said, "look at this."

She groaned. "Oh, Mike, I was falling asleep."

"I found our girl, right here in your magazine."

"What girl?"

"The mystery woman at the villa the morning Drake was killed, the one Ana saw in the entry with some books."

"What?"

He pointed to the picture. "Who does the woman on the right look like?"

"Deus!" Bebe sat upright. "Mike, it is very much like Senhora Bouchard."

"Enough that Ana could think it was the same woman."

"It says in the writing that it is Senhora Monteiro da Silva! Do you think it is she who killed Senhor Manville?"

"If she's who Ana saw with Drake, and who Jeffrey saw running from the villa, there's a good chance she's the murderer." He stroked his jaw. "Things are beginning to fall into place, Bebe. Remember Antonia accused Serena of killing Drake. She called her Mimi, but Serena said she behaved as though it was Mimi she was talking to."

"So Senhora Monteiro da Silva is Mimi, even if it says here her name is Mercedes."

"Could be a nickname. They're friends, judging by the picture. It shouldn't be hard to find out if Mercedes' friends call her Mimi. And this also explains Hector's reaction when I mentioned the name Mimi this morning."

"If his sister knew Senhora Monteiro da Silva, he might, as well," Bebe said.

"Yeah. My guess is he not only knows her, he's mixed up in this. Christina told me Joachim and Hector spoke on the phone in the hours following the murder. Serena may be right. The murder may have been a conspiracy, or they may have conspired to cover things up after Joachim's mother shot Drake. One way or another, these people are all in bed together."

"It also explains why Senhora Monteiro da Silva has left the country."

"Yeah," Mike said. "I'm not surprised now that Drake's death upset her so much, not if she pulled the trigger. It also explains why Joachim has been behaving strangely, and his connection with Souza. He's been protecting his mother. At least that's a plausible explanation."

"Mike, should we go to the police? This is very important."

"Yes, but I don't think we have enough to be absolutely sure Mercedes is our woman. And without being able to pin the murder on someone else, we may not be able to get Jeffrey off the hook. This is a start, though, Bebe. A very good start.''

"Then what do we do?''

"I'll talk to Koto to see if we'll be able to count on the police cooperating. And Roberto Cabral will be able to tell us how this will cut legally. In any case, I don't see any point in hanging around here any longer.''

"Mike," Bebe said, pointing up the road, "look.''

He turned, seeing the gate of Hector von Vehrling's estate swing open and the Mercedes appear. "Hector's going out. Shall we see if hc's headed for the supermarket?''

"Couldn't hurt," she replied. "But we'd better duck. He's coming this way.''

Serra dos Três Rios

Twenty minutes later, deep in the Tijuca Forest, they saw Hector's car enter another gated estate, this one more isolated than his own. It seemed to occupy the entire mountain valley. The house wasn't in view, though the two guards at the gate suggested there was much behind the walls needing to be protected.

"Don't tell me this is the presidential palace," Mike said as they watched the huge gate close.

"I don't know who lives there," Bebe replied.

"It might be interesting to find out."

"I can ask the guards.''

"You mean just drive up and ask?''

"Why not?" she said with a laugh. "It can't be a secret.''

She put the car in gear and drove closer, pulling off the road within clear view of the entrance. Through the gate Mike could see a long, palm-lined drive meandering through a parklike setting, with forest at the edges of the broad, grassy corridor. It was like a fairway cut through the jungle.

"Not bad," he said.

"There are not many people who live like this," Bebe said, getting out. "The name of the owner will probably be familiar."

She strode across the road, having already attracted the attention of the guards. Mike realized her strategy was to use her miniskirt and those fabulous legs to lower any resistance she might encounter.

As Mike watched, she carried on an animated conversation with the guards, cocking her nicely rounded hip just so. One of the men reached out to pinch her cheek, and Bebe brushed his hand away. Finally, she came back to the car, looking pleased with herself.

"Any success?" he asked unnecessarily.

Bebe chuckled. "With men who have more *testículo* in their pants than brains in their heads it is not difficult, Mike. It is the estate of Senhora Clarise Sutcliffe d'Orléans."

"The older woman in the picture." He smiled. "Well, Bebe, it seems our circle is getting tighter and tighter. Unless this is a coincidence and he's just driven out here for tea, we've tied Hector into our merry little group, as well."

"It's no coincidence," Bebe replied. "While I was talking with the guards I learned that Senhora Sutcliffe d'Orléans has had a guest for the past week. A lady. They do not know her name, but she has short dark hair and she is perhaps fifty years or so in age."

"Mercedes Monteiro da Silva?"

"This is what I think, but we can't be sure. They said this lady does not leave the estate."

"Bebe, you're amazing. How did you find that out?"

"I told the guards the wife of the gentleman who just arrived is curious what ladies he calls on. Sexual scandals are the sport of all *cariocas,* Mike. We love to gossip."

"It couldn't have hurt that you're easy to look at."

"They invited me into their guardhouse for conversation...even a visit to the main house, if I wished to earn it."

"Serena pays well, but not that well, eh?"

"It is better to take advantage of the stupidity of a man than allow the reverse. Money has nothing to do with it. Anyway, what more do we need to know?"

Mike stroked the back of her neck. "I don't know if you're aware of this, Bebe, but you can make a man feel truly humble."

"This is not something a man wants to admit, even if it is true," she said.

"I can and I do. But then, maybe I'm humbler than most."

"You are very honest," she said. "It is perhaps the reason I like you."

Mike couldn't help himself; he leaned over and kissed her. Bebe drew her fingers over his cheekbone and along his jaw.

"The longer we are together the more I want to be with you, Mike," she whispered, sounding wistful.

Her words were enough to make his loins swell. God, the agony of wanting her...

"I think we've done enough for one day," he said. "We've earned some time off, don't you think?"

"Ever since you suggested it, I've been thinking about the possibility, Mike," she said, looking at his mouth. "I do not often feel this way."

He swallowed hard and his heart started to trip. His erection was so firm it hurt. "Let's get out of here."

Bebe reached for the ignition. Just as she started the engine, they saw a Jaguar coming down the road. Slowing, it turned into the drive and stopped at the gate. They saw the face of the driver. It was Joachim Monteiro da Silva.

"Jesus," Mike said as the gate swung open.

"Monteiro da Silva, too," Bebe said.

"Right. We happened along at a fortuitous moment, honey. I think the tribal chiefs are having a powwow."

She looked perplexed. "They're having what?"

"A powwow. A big meeting. The Hole-in-the-Wall Gang is gathering to plot strategy."

Bebe shook her head. "America must be a very strange place."

He laughed. "Forget it. I know I'm not making much sense. Maybe I'm tired."

"Me, too."

"Then I've got a proposal. Let's kick back and have us a party. We've earned it."

"Okay, but first I must call the office. At the end of every day I must check in. It is Koto's rule."

"Fine," Mike said, "but if he suggests an overtime assignment, tell him you've had a better offer."

Bebe laughed and put the car in gear. "It is no lie, Mike, I would much rather make love with you."

Ipanema

Roberto's apartment was not as luxurious as Elaine Risollo's, yet it had charm. It was on an upper floor of one of the high-rises surrounding the Lagoa Rodrigo de Freitas. Standing at the huge plate-glass window with a panoramic view of the water and the mountains beyond, Serena watched the last of the twilight fading.

It was a shame that all this beauty was before her and she couldn't enjoy it. She was far too nervous. Taking another sip of the martini Roberto had made, she sighed, wishing she could calm the anxious beat of her heart. Koto had called twice. The news that Michael and Bebe were safe had come as a tremendous relief. She was glad they were on their way over to discuss events.

It had been a day from hell. She wanted to see Michael, to give and receive the mutual reassurance that was so much a part of their relationship. Every time she imagined the side of her head being blown off, she'd begin trembling. The martini was supposed to calm her, but she didn't want to drink too much, too fast. She had to be clearheaded for their strategy session and sharp enough to handle Roberto. He'd proven to be a gentleman, but a gentleman with designs.

The news that Michael, Bebe, Koto and Mendonca were all converging on his apartment had not pleased Roberto. But being a professional, he had put the seduction he'd planned on the back burner. They would leave eventually, and he'd have her to himself.

Serena was still struggling with her feelings. Normally, she wasn't this ambivalent. Men didn't seduce her so much as she put them through their paces. Few, very few, qualified. Roberto had been a maybe right from the start, and she wasn't completely sure why she'd been unable to decide about him. It probably had more to do with her state of mind than anything.

Just then he came into the room, having gone to his study earlier to make some phone calls. "Ah, there you are, my darling," he said. He spoke with the confidence of a man who knew he'd be sleeping with her that night.

"I was admiring your view," she said as he came up beside her and slipped his arm around her waist.

"I adore it," he said in that soft, rumbling voice of his, "but not so much as you." He breathed into her ear. "Your beauty is all I see anymore."

"That accent is all that saves you from being corny, Roberto," she said, drawing her fingertips along his face. "I hope you realize that."

He'd put on more cologne when he'd changed after their arrival. She had to admit it was an enticing aroma. Roberto had his virtues, though they mainly related to his allure.

"Corny," he said thoughtfully. "I think I know that word, and as I recall, it is not a compliment."

"Can't you tell, dear? I'm trying to keep you off-balance."

Roberto turned her toward him, holding her waist in his large, warm hands. Serena had changed into a hostess gown, a modest but comfortable affair that was ambiguous in what it suggested. She still held her nearly empty martini glass.

"You are more fearless in speaking your mind than any woman I've ever known, Serena."

"Really?" The comment amused her.

"Yes, and it is one reason why in only a few days I have fallen in love with you." His voice resonated through her.

"*Love* is not a word to use lightly, Roberto," she said.

"I know the feeling in my heart."

"Yeah," she said ironically, "so do I." She put her glass down on a small table nearby. Then, taking his hand, she led him to one of the caramel-colored, leather sofas. They sat. She kept hold of his hand, allowing it to rest on her knee. "I think we need to have a candid conversation, Roberto."

There was uncertainty on his face. "Of course. What is it you wish to say?"

"I want you to know that I'm not going to have an affair with you. I've given it a lot of thought. I admit I'm tempted. Very tempted. But I've decided against it."

He was momentarily taken aback. "But why?"

"You'd think I'm crazy if I told you."

"No," he insisted, "I must know."

"All right. I owe you that." After taking a fortifying breath, she went on. "The fact is, I still love Michael."

"What?"

"I know it sounds bizarre, but it's true. It didn't fully sink in until today, after Souza's men tried to kill me. All I've been able to think about is Michael."

"You're worried about him. This is natural, Serena."

"No, it's more than that. I've been running from my feelings for years, denying them. Today they finally caught up with me."

Roberto withdrew his hand, looking sullen. He didn't speak for a long moment. "Naturally, I must take you at your word and respect your feelings. But I confess I am surprised."

"I am, too, Roberto."

He reflected for a while. "So what do you plan to do?"

"About what?"

"About Michael."

"Nothing. There's nothing to do. Michael already knows. And at some level I think he feels the same way I do."

"Then you'll be together again."

"No. Love helps, but it's not a reason for people to be together. Our marriage proved that."

"You're saying you cannot live together," Roberto said.

"I guess that's what it boils down to."

"By outward appearances he is not a gentleman in the same sense that you are a lady. I can understand that life together would be very difficult."

"I'm not the snob people think I am, Roberto. And Michael, for all his down-home honesty, is not a hick."

"Then what's the problem?"

"I've been giving that some thought. I used to think I understood why we couldn't make a go of it. Michael resented me for who I am. I resented him for the same reasons. Tension drove us apart."

"Does he understand this as well as you?"

"I don't know. The last five years we haven't had many chances to discuss it. We've been too busy justifying the past."

Roberto reflected on what she'd said. He was calculating what it all meant, how he was affected. His calmness suggested he might be considering the high road.

"Perhaps you should tell him how you feel, Serena," he said, confirming her analysis.

"Even knowing Michael as well as I do, it wouldn't be easy."

"But if you truly love him . . ."

She thought about that, her eyes filling as she pictured Michael's face. She tried to wipe the tears away, but they continued flowing. Roberto plucked the silk handkerchief from his breast pocket and handed it to her. She dabbed her eyes. "Sorry, I don't usually get this emotional."

"My advice," Roberto said, his voice sounding very lawyerly, "is to honestly express your feelings, no matter the cost."

She tensed. "You want to know why I don't, Roberto?"

"Why?"

"Because I'm afraid."

"Afraid?"

"I know that doesn't sound like me, but when it comes to Michael, I'm not myself. I can't handle the way he gets under my skin. Maybe that's the problem. I never learned to surrender to my feelings. I could do it in bed, but not at the breakfast table."

Roberto shook his head. "This all sounds very American. A Brazilian woman would never say these things."

"I don't think most American women would, either. I'm an odd duck when it comes to romance."

He smiled at the allusion.

"It's a compliment to you that I've bared my soul," she told him. "I wouldn't have been this candid even with Sergei Rosenkrantz."

Roberto gave her a questioning look.

"My shrink."

"Oh."

She leaned over and gave Roberto a kiss on the cheek. "I'd go to bed with you out of friendship," she said, "but neither of us would enjoy it."

He didn't dare contradict her, though it was obvious he didn't share her skepticism. He drew her hand to his mouth and kissed her fingers. "You can say what you want, but for me, what I feel for you is love."

Serena found herself wanting to believe him. She was about to tell him so when a buzzer sounded, interrupting them. Roberto glanced toward the entry as the maid appeared from the kitchen to answer it.

"Our visitors have arrived." He peered deeply into Serena's eyes. "What is it you Americans say? Never say never."

She gave him a questioning look.

"One never knows when one's heart will change." He went off to greet his guests.

As soon as Bebe and Michael walked into the room, Serena knew they were lovers. Bebe didn't look at her the same way. What was it on her face? Not guilt. It was a quiet joy — a touch self-conscious, perhaps, but there was a peacefulness about her that comes only with acquiescence to one's desires.

And Michael... With this beautiful girl on his arm, there was something extra in his eyes, a hint of self-satisfaction—triumph even—that fell just short of gloating. It was as if to say his love for Serena hadn't stopped him from living. He was his own man. He'd taken her challenge and he'd proved himself. He'd won.

No sooner had Roberto invited them to sit than the buzzer sounded again. He went off with a groan, leaving Serena to face Michael and Bebe. Serena had wandered over to the window, where she'd been watching the color in the sky fade into night.

"Koto said you two tracked the gang to their lair," she said, trying her best to make her pleasantness genuine.

"The case is coming together, Serena," Mike replied. "You're close to having what you came for."

He didn't have to add that he was getting what *he* wanted, as well. Bebe was his prize and they both knew it. Michael had Serena's blessing, but he was also perfectly aware that her generosity had not come without sacrifice, which was why he wasn't rubbing it in. Michael was considerate that way. He'd never turned against her, even in his bitterness over their divorce.

In the entry Roberto was conferring with the new arrivals. Serena could hear them, but the Portuguese made the conversation unintelligible. Roberto's maid, an older black woman in a crisp white uniform, brought hors d'oeuvres. Mike popped a canapé into his mouth and Bebe followed his lead. Their arms and knees touched as they repeated the ritual.

Michael glanced up at Serena. "This is lunch. We were staking out Hector's pad all afternoon and weren't able to make it to McDonald's."

"Poor babies. Why don't I have Roberto's maid whip you up a light meal? There must be something she can feed you."

"That's all right," Michael said, "this will tide us over. We're going to eat later and celebrate the break in the case."

He subtly nudged Bebe, eliciting a tiny smile. Serena watched him take a handful of nuts, realizing this was harder for her than she'd thought. Bebe had another canapé, her long fingers graceful, almost poetic. Serena felt her jealousy gnawing at her and tried to fight it.

She recalled the meals she and Michael used to have in bed, the way they'd take in each other's bodies along with the food. The time he'd plopped dollops of chocolate sauce over her chest and abdomen and thighs before proceeding to lick her clean, using his tongue to bring her to orgasm. Watching him now as he licked salt from his fingers, her body quivered, even knowing full well that later it would be Bebe who benefited from his masterful lovemaking, not she.

But Michael was looking at her again. "We got a message that Souza's boys tried to harass you," he said, popping an olive into his mouth. "What happened?"

"Julio took a shot at me in the car. Fortunately, he missed."

"A shot? You mean he tried to kill you?"

"Blew out the side window with a shotgun blast. I guess that qualifies as trying to kill me."

Michael's mouth sagged open. So did Bebe's.

"*Senhora...*" the girl said, an olive poised in her fingers, inches from her mouth.

Michael cocked his head. "Serena, you're kidding."

"No, that's why we were urgently trying to reach you. We figured they'd be after you, too, since either of us could have identified Souza."

Michael got to his feet, the gravity of the news having hit him. But before he could ask his next question Roberto came into the room with Koto and a short, slender, Latin-looking man with wavy hair and bad skin. Carlos Mendonca reminded Serena of Luis Gonzales, the fellow who'd serviced her pool for years, except that he was carrying a briefcase instead of a water-testing kit.

Koto handled the introductions. Mendonca, the man who'd masterminded the case against her brother, showed no special recognition when he shook her hand.

"Since the hour is late and Senhor Mendonca has many things to do tonight," Roberto said, "perhaps we can begin immediately. *Senhores,* shall we go to the table in the dining room?"

Roberto's eating area was off the salon and slightly elevated, surrounded by windows on two sides. A huge chandelier hung over the table. Roberto sat at the head of the table, the others arrayed around him. Serena stood behind the chair next to Roberto, saying she was too nervous to sit.

"Senhor Kotomata," Roberto said, "perhaps you would be good enough to summarize the day's events."

Koto began with the meeting with Hector. Most of it he'd already told Mendonca, but the detective took notes anyway, interrupting several times for clarification. At one point Roberto, Koto and Mendonca conversed in Portuguese before reverting to English.

"My pardons," the police detective said, bowing to Serena and Michael, "but my English is not so good and I must be sure."

"The important thing is that we get things right," Serena said. "The fate of an innocent man depends on it."

She could not stand still, so she paced as Koto went on with his account. After he'd finished, Mike recounted what he and Bebe had learned. His story about Hector's visit to the Sutcliffe d'Orléans estate brought Serena back to the table. When he mentioned Joachim's arrival, she could no longer hold her tongue.

"Michael, we've got to get Christina out of that house. I don't care what she says."

Mendonca, whom Serena felt had the look and demeanor of a rat, spoke again in difficult English. "I, too, have news, *senhores.* A little time ago Senhor Souza finally decided it is time to speak. He confessed of his attacks and also he said who is his—how do you say *empregador,* Senhor Kotomata?"

"Employer."

"Yes, employer."

Michael looked at Serena. "Who is it?" he asked.

"Senhor Joachim Monteiro da Silva."

"I knew it!" Serena said, turning on her heel. She took a few steps, then abruptly returned to the table. "Michael, I mean it, let's go get Christina. Now!"

"Hang on, sweetheart. We need to know more." To Mendonca he said, "What exactly did Joachim hire Souza to do?"

"He insists the violent actions were from the circumstances. Souza was to scare you away, but not to do great harm."

"Anything short of decapitation is obviously just a love bite," Serena said bitterly.

"I'm more interested in Joachim's motives," Michael said. "Intimidation makes sense. Especially if the mystery woman, Mimi, is his mother."

"Yes," Mendonca said, "I would like to know if Senhora Monteiro da Silva is known by this name Mimi."

Michael turned to Roberto. "Do you know?"

"I know Senhora Monteiro da Silva, but this nickname is not familiar. It may be only in the family and among close friends."

"How can we find out?" Michael asked.

They all pondered the matter.

"*Senhores,*" Bebe said, "if Antonia calls her friend by this name, it is reasonable that Hector would, as well. Or at least he knows her by this name."

"So?"

"Perhaps if someone posing as Hector von Vehrling calls either to the estate of Clarise Sutcliffe d'Orléans or the Monteiro da Silva ranch and asks for Mimi, we will know."

The whole group smiled in unison.

"Brilliant, Bebe," Michael said.

From where she stood, Serena saw his hand move under the table, undoubtedly finding Bebe's bare knee. Serena smiled at the warmth and camaraderie passing between them, but it made her heart ache with sadness.

"Who will do it?" Roberto asked.

"Either you, Koto or Mr. Mendonca," Michael said.

They decided Roberto was best suited for the task, but only if he modulated his voice. He went off to attempt the ruse. In his absence the others regarded one another. Serena took her seat.

"Mr. Mendonca," she said, "what will it take to get my brother out of jail? If Mimi is Mercedes and the maid can identify her as the mystery woman at the villa the morning of Drake's murder, will that be enough for you to release Jeffrey?"

"I must be honest, *senhora,*" Mendonca replied. "A woman at the villa does not mean she, and not Senhor Bouchard, is the killer. I would need her confession."

"Confession?" Serena exclaimed. "You're going to keep my brother in jail until someone else admits they're the murderer? All you've got is a fingerprint, and that's been explained."

"All you have shown today, *senhora,* is that there was a woman at the villa before Senhor Bouchard arrived. That proves nothing, even if it is Senhora Monteiro da Silva. Don't forget, the neighbor saw your brother leave the house moments after the shot."

Serena looked at Michael pleadingly.

"Don't worry, sweetheart, we're making progress," he said. "I've got a suggestion for Mr. Mendonca, but first I want to hear what Roberto has to say."

After a minute Roberto returned. He was grinning. "I spoke with the mother of Mercedes Monteiro da Silva, asking for Mimi."

"And?"

"She asked me why I was calling there when I knew perfectly well where she was."

Everyone cheered except for Mendonca, who only nodded.

"Michael," Serena said, feeling a surge of desperation, "what's your idea?"

"Carlos," Michael said to Mendonca, "what if you were to arrest Joachim in a showy manner as a conspirator in the murder of Drake Manville? You have proof he hired Souza, and a gun traced to Souza was the murder weapon. Also we know evidence related to the murder has been suppressed. There's ample reason to arrest him, isn't there?"

"*Sim, senhor,* but what will this accomplish? His crime is a minor one compared to the murder of Senhor Manville."

"Yes, but his mother may not appreciate that. If she thinks her boy is going to take the rap for a murder she committed, she may think twice about getting off at someone else's expense. She might be willing to let Jeffrey hang for her crime, but her own son may be a different matter altogether."

Mendonca pondered the suggestion. "You are saying arrest Senhor Monteiro da Silva for murder to scare his mother into confessing her crime?"

"Yes. I don't know the woman, but her maternal instinct may be stronger than her instinct for self-preservation."

Mendonca conferred with Roberto and Koto in Portuguese. When they'd finished, he said, "All right, *senhor,* I will agree. We will put Senhor Monteiro da Silva in jail, but only for a few days. If his mother, she does not confess, then I can bring the charges only for the evidence I have."

Serena felt a wave of joy. Maybe the day would end well, after all. Then a thought crossed her mind. "Michael, what about Christina?"

"Now that Souza and Joachim have been tied together, we know she's not facing the same danger we were. Joachim obviously faked the threats against her to throw us off track."

"Yes, but he's still involved in the murder conspiracy. I won't allow her to stay in that house under any circumstances."

Michael hesitated, then turned to the police detective. "Carlos, could you arrest my stepdaughter along with Joachim?"

"*Arrest* her?" Serena said.

"That would be a way to get her out of the house. Then the police could bring her here. Joachim doesn't have to know."

Michael's plan was discussed in both Portuguese and English, and it was decided it was worth a try. Serena felt genuine elation. She wanted to hug Michael until she remembered he probably had other forms of celebration in mind, and not with her.

Mendonca got up. The group repaired to the salon, but Mendonca excused himself, saying he had much work to do. Koto hadn't been home yet and he, too, wanted to leave. First he called Bebe aside, speaking quietly with her while Roberto showed Mendonca out. Serena and Michael were left alone.

"Again, thank you, Michael," she said. "I owe you so much."

"Hey, I didn't do anything. Bebe and I happened to be in the right place, that's all. The best ideas were hers."

"Well, you know what I always used to say. There's a man behind every good woman."

Michael laughed. "Seems to be my lot in life, doesn't it?"

There was sadness in his voice. Serena went over to him, taking his arm. She'd already thanked him. What was left but to apologize for the torment she'd put him through, the mixed signals, the confusion? But she knew that wasn't what he cared about. They both looked at Bebe.

"She adores you, Michael."

"Oh, I don't know about that."

"No, she does. Take it from an expert."

"She's quite a woman," he said, sounding almost wistful.

Serena checked out the girl's lean, sensuous body. "I'd like you two to go out and buy yourself the most expensive bottle of champagne you can find," she said. "On me."

"Thanks," he said, "but if I go that route, I'll pay for it myself. I'm making damned good money, you know."

Serena nodded, understanding him perfectly. Bebe's laugh, carrying across the room, cut right through her soul.

Yet Serena didn't have it in her to be truly jealous of the girl, at least not in a resentful way.

"I don't envy you having to deal with Christina," Michael said. "If it helps, tell her this was my idea."

"Always the knight errant, aren't you?"

"That, too, seems to be my lot in life."

She sighed. "I'll be relieved when this is over. All that matters now is getting Jeffrey and Christina safely back to the States. I swear to you, Michael, I'll kiss the ground at LAX if we manage to get home with both of them under our wing."

He gave her one of his grins. Then he leaned over and kissed her cheek. "Don't worry. We'll manage it somehow."

The gesture made her eyes glisten. He noticed.

"What's the matter? You aren't going soft on me, are you?"

She bit her lip, shaking her head. "No. Family's always been my weakness. You know that."

He rubbed her back the way he used to when they were parents fretting over Christina's adolescent antics.

Koto and Bebe had finished their conversation, but the girl saw they were talking so she waited, giving them more time.

"Go on, Michael," Serena murmured, knowing there was nothing more to be said. "Bebe is waiting."

"Stiff upper lip," he said.

She nodded. "Stiff upper lip."

He started toward the girl.

"Michael?" Serena called after him.

He turned. "Yeah?"

"Be careful. Souza's friends are still out there, you know. And they're probably more pissed off than ever."

Michael lifted the flap of his jacket, revealing the gun wedged in his belt. She gave him a thumbs-up sign. When he and Bebe headed for the entry, arm-in-arm, Serena wandered over to the expanse of glass overlooking the black lagoon. She stared out. Tears began to trickle down her cheeks. She dabbed at them with the silk handkerchief that she still clutched in her fist.

This day would prove to be a turning point in all their lives. How, she couldn't say, but she knew it was true.

Copacabana

Bebe drove Mike back to the hotel. Before he had a chance to speak, she turned to him and said, "Can I buy you a drink?" When he smiled, she added, "That's how American girls do it, no?"

He took her hand. "I don't much care what American girls do, sugar. Especially not now."

"Does that mean I can buy you a drink or not?"

He laughed. "The matter's open for discussion. Come on."

They got out of the car. The doorman regarded him questioningly. Mike took the car keys from Bebe and gave them to the man, along with a couple of bills.

"Keep this vehicle safe until the young lady needs it."

"Sim, senhor."

They went into the lobby hand-in-hand, then to the bar. It was mostly empty, but the ambiance wasn't what Mike had in mind. Bebe started to sit at the nearest table, but he stopped her. "I've got a better idea."

He went to the bar and asked the bartender if he had any champagne on ice. The man held up a bottle of Dom Perignon.

"We need two glasses."

The man produced the glasses. Mike paid for the champagne and added another ten dollars' worth of cruzeiros, eliciting a broad smile from the barman.

Bebe carried the glasses and Mike the bottle. As they waited at the elevator he popped the cork and poured a splash into each glass, summoning a giggle from Bebe.

"They do this in America?"

"Honey, they do this wherever you and I happen to be, trust me."

The door to the elevator opened and they stepped into the car. Mike stared at the control panel.

"Odd. There's no button marked Heaven. Shall we make it the thirty-sixth floor instead?"

Bebe trilled with laughter, and as the door closed, she leaned against him, kissing him deeply. The smile she gave him afterward was as wide as the Amazon.

"Damn," he said, as the car began its ascent, "who needs champagne?"

"Champagne gives the best orgasms," she said, draining her glass.

Mike refilled it, and his, as well. "Sure glad you told me." He touched his glass to hers. "To you, Bebe, and all the sunny mornings of your life."

She kissed him again, more deeply and passionately than before. They both spilled some champagne, but scarcely noticed. What was happening had become urgent. He was getting hard. It was a good feeling, as sweet as her kiss.

"Jesus," he muttered as the doors slid open. "Or maybe I should say—what was his name again?—Exu! That's it!"

Bebe drained what was left in her glass. "Mike, you are so wonderful."

The comment—spontaneous, giddy and gleeful—brought a surge of emotion in him. Joyful lust. A warm, happy feeling.

Bebe was too intoxicated with joy to notice. She snatched the bottle, refilled her glass and drained it like a frat boy at a beer party. Then she led the way toward the suite, swinging her ass, as devilish now as she'd been angelic before. She was singing softly, her long strides evolving into a dance before his eyes.

She filled their glasses as he fumbled for his room key. Bebe stopped him from unlocking the door, her expression turning serious. "Mike, I know this is not about love," she said in her soft, musical accent, "but does the person inside me make you happy?"

"Doll, I feel like I've died and gone to heaven."

"For me it's the same," she purred, kissing his chin. "For a long time I have not felt alive like this."

She rubbed the bulge in his pants and moaned. It made him all the harder.

Mike turned the key and let the door swing open. Bebe entered ahead of him, the song returning to her lips, the dance to her step. She tilted her head back, drinking from the bottle.

When he closed the door, her song and dance became more animated. He saw her more plainly in the ambient light. She was the goddess who'd danced in the moonlight that night in Barra da Tijuca.

She handed him the bottle. He took a long swig, and even before he'd swallowed, Bebe had her top off. His heart beat nicely at the sight of her full breasts. He stared. Bebe unzipped her miniskirt and let it fall to the floor.

Taking the bottle from his hand, she gently pushed him onto the sofa.

"Before a man makes love to a woman, he should see what she has to offer him," she said as she twisted and swayed her body in rhythm. "It's important that you want me very badly, Mike."

"Sugar, if you only knew."

He took the bottle back and guzzled some champagne. When his eyes focused on her again, she was fully naked, except for her strappy sandals. God, he thought, is this really happening?

After she'd danced for him for a few minutes, she moved behind the sofa, leaned down and said, "If you want me, I think you know where you can find me." With that, she slinked off to his room.

Mike was numb. This was an experience that would stay with him for a lifetime. There was no doubt about that.

He found Bebe lying on the white sheets of the bed. Her hands were between her legs and she was caressing herself. He moved to the edge of the bed. Her eyes were closed. She seemed unaware of his presence, though she did run her tongue around the edges of her lips, moaning softly.

Mike watched her pleasure herself as he undressed. God, what a sight.

He lay on the bed and Bebe took him in her arms. Their mouths met and they began exploring each other with their tongues.

Bebe took his cock in her hand, muttering a few words in Portuguese. He was surprised by the warmth of her silky skin and the firmness of the muscle underneath. Except for her breasts and the insides of her thighs, her body was hard, strong.

He touched the moist place between her legs, provoking a moan. They kissed again and she opened her legs wider, inviting him to take her.

As he positioned himself between her knees, he heard a sound. In retrospect, he realized it was the closet door opening, but at the moment—the glorious moment when he was about to enter her—he was unaware of the implications.

The first sign of danger came from Bebe. She lifted her head and gasped, jarring him. Her distress scarcely registered before she threw him off her, onto his back.

The shots came at almost the same instance—three in rapid succession. It must have been the last that nicked his shoulder, but in the excitement he hardly felt the bullet.

In that long moment between perception and understanding, the world seemed to stop. Their assailant, a black man, struggled with his jammed weapon, the fury of his deadly attack suspended. Then, flinging the gun aside, he reached into his pocket for a knife.

Mike sprang instinctively, landing on him with his full weight. The unopened knife went flying over his head and through the open door of the bedroom, skittering across the tile floor of the sitting room.

The assailant, stunned, scrambled to his feet, but Mike grabbed him by the leg. The man managed to kick free and went scurrying after the knife.

Mike charged after him, tackling him and driving him into an armchair with such force that it tipped over backward, the two of them landing on the floor with a thud. Mike felt a sharp pain in his shoulder as he tried to get to his feet.

The intruder became disoriented and ran toward the balcony, arriving at the doorway before realizing his mistake. He spun around, but it was too late. He was trapped.

In the faint light Mike got his first clear look at the assailant. It was Julio, Souza's man. His eyes were filled with terror.

Mike gained his feet, aware of the pain in his shoulder. He knew that in the bedroom Bebe was hurt, but the adrenaline in his blood drove him mindlessly. He wanted to tear the bastard to pieces. As he advanced on him, Julio feinted first one way, then tried to dodge the other. But it was hopeless. Driven by rage, Mike was lunging forward, smashing his head into the guy's solar plexus and knocking him out the door.

Julio went flying backward, the small of his back catching the top of the railing. Perhaps it was the bulk of his upper body—the broadness of his shoulders and muscular arms—that was responsible. Whatever it was, his high center of gravity carried him back. He teetered.

It appeared for a moment as though the man might recover his balance, but he didn't. The only sound Mike heard was a grunt as Julio's legs flipped upward toward the sky. The last thing Mike saw was the soles of his shoes as Julio did a backward somersault and disappeared from sight.

Mike staggered to his feet and peered over the railing. Thirty-six stories below he saw the body, splayed out like a gingerbread man on the floodlit lawn. People were running toward the corpse from the street. After a last emotionless look, Mike reeled back into the suite, afraid of what he'd find.

Turning on the light as he stumbled into the bedroom, he saw her. Bebe was on the bed, motionless, her perfect body scarred by two ugly holes oozing blood, one at the base of her neck, the other just under her ribs. Her eyes were open, but until he saw her chest rise ever so slightly, he thought she was dead.

He rushed to her side. Bebe blinked slowly, but the blood flowed from her, soaking the bed. "Hang on, sugar," he whispered, "help is on the way."

He called the desk and told them to get an ambulance there pronto. "Like now!" he screamed. "Immediately!"

Returning to Bebe's side, he checked her wounds. There wasn't much he could do. The dangerous bleeding was internal. Still, he went into the bath and got a handful of towels. He covered her with a large bath sheet and pressed a hand towel against the wound in her torso. Except when she coughed up blood, she hardly made a sound. Mostly she stared at the ceiling.

He got dressed quickly, then moved as close to her as he could and kissed her cheek. "You're going to make it, honey, just hang on. Help is on the way."

After a while they heard the sirens.

Bebe tried to speak for the first time. "I—I'm...sorry, Mike," she wheezed.

Tears flooded his eyes and started running down his cheeks. He could take her wounds, even her pain, but not her being sorry.

"It's not your fault, honey. It's mine. You saved my life."

Her eyelids fluttered. She wanted to speak, but couldn't.

"As soon as you're well, Bebe, I'm taking you to Las Vegas," he said. "I want you to stay as long as you like."

A slight smile touched her lips. "Maybe—maybe you were...right. Maybe I folded...the paper...too tight."

She closed her eyes, and he was sure she'd stopped breathing. But Bebe was hanging on. Maybe she wanted to see Vegas. Maybe she wanted to finish what they'd started. Or maybe leaving was harder than staying.

W E D N E S D A Y
September 20th

Copacabana

Mike rode in the ambulance with her. She stopped breathing twice, the last time as they were wheeling her into the emergency room. For twenty minutes he paced, feeling helpless. Finally, a sweet little nurse with soulful eyes who spoke some English told him Bebe was in surgery, but her condition was grave.

With the nurse's help Mike reached Koto at home. Twenty-five minutes later he arrived wearing shorts, a T-shirt and thongs. They got an update from a nurse. The prognosis was not good. The damage to Bebe's liver seemed irreparable, and her spleen and right lung were badly ripped up, as well.

A couple of hours later, when Carlos Mendonca arrived, Bebe was still in surgery. The police detective asked for an account of what had happened. Mike gave a statement with Koto's help.

Mendonca told them Souza's lieutenant, the mulatto, had been taken into custody. Between that arrest, and the death of Julio, they were probably no longer in danger, but it wouldn't hurt to be careful.

"It's too late," Mike said, pain stabbing at his heart. "The damage has been done."

Before leaving, Mendonca told them Joachim would be arrested later that morning. Given the polo player's relationship with Souza, the police could add the charge of assault on Bebe to his list of crimes. It probably wouldn't stick, but it would increase the pressure on Mercedes Monteiro da Silva, which, after all, was the point.

"Shit," Mike said, dropping his head into his hands, "after what's happened to Bebe, it's hard to give a damn about Joachim and his goddamned mother."

"If by chance you are right about their guilt, *senhor*," Mendonca said, "then they must pay."

Mike watched the man pop an antacid. Never had a cop's perception of justice seemed so perverted, so skewed from what really mattered in life. "Whatever you say, Carlos."

The police detective left. Mike and Koto looked at each other helplessly, the weight of the tragedy more evident than ever. "I'm sorry, Koto," Mike said, tears welling in his eyes.

His words and tone parroted those Bebe had uttered as she'd lain bleeding in his bed. Sorry. Sorry was all anyone could be. Sorry for things done and not done. Sorry for selfishness and blindness. Sorry for not being on God's good side.

"It's all my fault," he went on. "If I hadn't been so damned cavalier, more interested in getting laid than paying attention to business, this wouldn't have happened."

"You can't blame yourself," Koto said. "You didn't pull the trigger. You had no way of knowing."

Koto was being generous. If Bebe were to die, his loss would be greater than anyone's, other than her family's. She was his friend, as well as an integral part of his professional life. Compared to that, this case was nothing.

"I keep thinking of those damned pieces of paper she put in the water," Mike told Koto.

The investigator nodded, understanding. "To Bebe the spirit world was important. She consulted Curima, her fortune-teller, about everything."

"I know. Curima told her to stay clear of me," Mike said. "Good advice not followed."

"Me, as well, my friend. She chose this work even knowing it was dangerous, that the omens were not good."

"Why? Why did she do it?"

"It was important that what she did was her choice. And she took pleasure in breaking the faces of evil men whenever she had the opportunity."

"She'd have been better off breaking my face. Instead she went off with me to get blitzed on champagne and walk into a trap."

"Bebe never did other than what she wanted, Mike. That was very important to her." Koto clasped his shoulder, the one that had been nicked.

When Mike flinched, Koto noticed the blood on his shirt. It wasn't much more than a scratch, but the detective insisted he let the nurse clean the wound and bandage it.

"I'm too damned miserable to care," Mike told Koto.

"Then I'll care for you."

The two men embraced. "I think I'll step outside and get some air," Mike said.

It was dawn. He could smell the sea. It was not cold, but he felt a chill, anyway. Within moments the first rays of the sun angled down on the bench where he sat. An odd feeling of relief passed over him, but it wasn't a happy sort of relief. It was the kind that called for thought and attention.

He went back inside to find Koto weeping. He told him that Bebe had died.

It was more Christina's voice that awakened him than Serena's. For a moment or two he thought he was back in L.A., still married, the stepfather of a teenager. Then he realized it wasn't one of their Sunday-morning spats, and the man they were arguing about wasn't Christina's beau of the week. It was Joachim Monteiro da Silva, her fiancé.

"I don't care if his mother ran a concentration camp," Christina screamed. "That does not make Joachim bad. I love him and you're trying to destroy our lives! I've got news for you, Mother. It won't work!"

"Oh, Christina, don't be such a fool. The police arrested Joachim, I didn't."

"How stupid do you think I am?" the girl retorted. "You could have the president of Brazil arrested if you wanted. All you have to do is throw around your damned money!"

"Well, I've got news for you, too. Joachim is as attracted to your family fortune as he is to your sweet little ass. One look at him and that's obvious."

"Oh!" Christina shrieked. "How can you say such a thing?"

Mike heard her dissolve into tears and start sobbing hysterically.

"Christina, I'm sorry," Serena said in a stricken voice. "I didn't mean that. It just . . . slipped out. But I can't stand seeing you victimized."

"I hate you," the girl sobbed. Her voice was muffled, her face probably buried in a pillow.

It was not the first time he'd heard this sort of thing, each of them digging in their heels, preferring to march off a cliff rather than give any quarter. He felt sorry for them both.

Mike rolled over and looked at the clock. It was after eleven; he'd gotten four hours' sleep. He stared at the ceiling as the weeping and lamenting continued. They'd been moved to a new suite, on the thirty-fifth floor, directly below the old one. He knew that a few feet above him Bebe had been mortally wounded trying to save him.

He felt empty. It was like the morning after Serena had told him she wanted a divorce. Only this time there was guilt to contend with, as well.

It seemed impossible that Bebe was dead. She was much too vibrant for death, too beautiful to wither. Through his pain he realized more than a fantasy had died. Bebe wasn't just a conquest. She was a friend. That part had escaped him while she lived. But in her death, he realized that her spirit was what he'd lost. Bebe was joy—not only to him, but to everyone. She had been a gift, and it broke his heart to think he was the cause of her demise. If only she'd listened to her fortune-teller. If only he could trade his life for hers.

Christina was still crying in the next room. Mike knew he wouldn't sleep. He put on clean pants, recalling that the bloodstained pair he'd worn earlier were still in the bath. He'd ask the hotel maid to throw them away.

When he opened his bedroom door, he found Christina on a sofa, her face buried in a pillow. Serena was at the window, her arms folded over her chest. She turned at the sound of his door and walked quickly over to him, the consternation on her face turning to compassion.

"Oh, Michael," she murmured, taking him into her motherly embrace. "I'm so sorry," she said. "Bebe, of all people."

Her eyes were shimmering. Serena didn't act when it came to things like this. She might have been jealous of Bebe right down to her toenails, but she'd never have wished ill on her. Bebe's death had to have hurt her as much as it did him. That was one thing about Serena he knew with certainty: she couldn't take pleasure in human tragedy, no matter how much it might benefit her.

"You know what the worst part is? Bebe saved my life, but it wasn't for love."

"That's not true. She adored you, Michael."

"And I adored her. But that was no reason for her to die. How could I explain to her kid that her mama died because *I* wanted some fun, that I was being too damned selfish to think of her welfare?"

"Michael, you can't blame yourself. I forbid it. And Bebe would, too."

"Thanks for trying, but you can't change how I feel."

Serena pressed her cheek to his, lending her strength. "I'll see that her family's taken care of," she said solemnly. "I'm just as responsible as you for what happened. Maybe more so. I hired her, I encouraged her. I practically told her to go to bed with you."

"Nice try, Serena, but it won't work."

"Well, I can't bring Bebe back, but I'm going to do what I can to make amends. The family's my first priority. I've asked Roberto to look into it, to assess their needs."

"Thank you."

Serena was being generous—not only to Bebe's family, but to him. And so they would share this burden, too, just as they'd shared so many others. He rubbed her hands between his and looked into her eyes until he noticed Christina. She was sitting up now, listening.

"Michael, who are you talking about?" the girl asked, her tears forgotten.

"A beautiful girl who's been working with your stepfather to solve Drake's murder," Serena replied.

"What happened to her?"

"One of the men Joachim hired to harass us tried to shoot Michael. He missed and killed Bebe."

Christina shook her head. "No, Joachim would never do anything like that."

"I'm sure he didn't want anyone murdered," Mike said. "But one of his boys took it upon himself to kill."

"That's not Joachim's fault," Christina insisted. "No more than it's his fault if his chauffeur runs over somebody."

"You're probably right, pumpkin," he said. "But there's no point arguing about it. We've all got our burdens right now."

Christina got up and came over to them, wiping her eyes. "Michael, tell me honestly. Do you think Joachim's done anything wrong, whether Mercedes killed Drake or not?"

"It's too soon to be certain."

Serena rolled her eyes and walked off. At least she didn't throw more fuel on the fire. He was glad of that.

"If he's innocent we'll soon know," Mike told the girl. "And the same if he's guilty."

Christina glanced toward her mother. "At least you're willing to give him the benefit of the doubt. That's more than some people."

"Fine, Christina," Serena said from across the room, "you're right. I jumped to conclusions. If I'm wrong, I'll eat humble pie. More than that, I'll buy you and Joachim a house in L.A. for when you bring the grandkids to see Michael."

Christina scoffed. "Amazing what a man can do to open her eyes. She was a model of reasonableness around Cabral, too. You should have seen her, Michael."

"I have. But don't give your mother a hard time. She's carrying a bigger load than either of us."

"Thank you," Serena said. "But that doesn't excuse my mistakes. I owe apologies to you both."

"I think we'd all be well advised to try to get along for the next couple of days," he said. "It's going to be tense until this thing shakes out."

"It already is tense," Christina said under her breath.

He pinched the girl's cheek and went over to an easy chair, feeling a hundred years old. He dropped down heavily.

Serena came to a chair nearby. Sitting on the edge, she said, "I have news, Michael. Another development in the case arose while you were asleep."

"What?"

"Hector von Vehrling has left the country."

"Hmm. The rats are abandoning the sinking ship."

She nodded, glancing at Christina. "Yes, I think that's exactly right."

Later that afternoon, Mike sat on the balcony staring out to sea. Inside, Serena talked to her Beverly Hills office about the Happy Hosts contract, informing them she'd signed the papers and was returning them by courier. Earlier she'd spoken with her staff in London, Tokyo and New York, making a tour of the world by phone. It was make-work, he could tell. Serena used business to escape. It was healthier than drugs and booze, probably, but had its pitfalls.

After a while she came onto the balcony. Standing behind him, she put her hand on his shoulder. Serena was always good at touching in a healing way.

"What's Christina up to?" he asked.

"She's in her room trying to decide whether to pout or act mature about this."

"A chip off the old block."

Serena circled her hands around his neck and playfully gave it a squeeze. "God, what a week. Ten years' worth of misery."

When he didn't say anything, she went around and sat in the chair next to him. For a while they gazed out at the Atlantic.

"Sometimes I think I should sell everything, every last goddamn hotel, and buy an island in the South Pacific," she said. "What do you think?"

"You'd go nuts in two weeks."

She placed her hand on his. "What makes you so sure?"

"I know you, Serena."

"Maybe not as well as you think. You're not the only one who's grown up the last few years."

"Tell me, what would this new grown-up Serena do on an island in the Pacific? Start a coconut-export business?"

"You hate that I'm a businesswoman, don't you?"

"If I was being snide, I'm sorry. It's my rotten mood."

She contemplated the situation, the wheels turning. He could almost feel the heat she was generating just by thinking.

"Michael, how'd you feel about me if I gave away everything I had and took a vow of poverty?"

He chuckled.

"Seriously."

"I'd think you were crazy."

"You'd probably be right. But it's not a completely frivolous question."

"I can't picture it. You *are* your empire. Somehow you wouldn't look right in a nun's habit."

"No, Michael, you're wrong. Well...maybe not a nun's habit, but I truly don't need to own the world. If you want to know the truth, I'm coming to see there's more to life than what I do at the office."

"Somehow I don't think so."

"I understand your cynicism. I might have agreed with you a few years ago, maybe even a few months ago, but not anymore."

"Oh? What's changed?"

She hesitated. "I'm not sure I can explain it. But I *am* thinking about that island. I wasn't joking."

"Have you checked to see if Roberto has a hankering for the South Pacific? He could sing 'Some Enchanted Evening' while you crack the coconuts."

"Roberto and I are quits—in the romantic sense, at least."

He looked at her, surprised. "You're kidding."

"No."

"What happened? Was he all bass and no treble? Couldn't hit the high notes?"

Serena slapped his arm with mock disgust.

"Seriously," he said, "didn't you get laid last night?"

"No."

"I'm surprised."

"I told you, you don't know me anymore."

He looked at her. She looked at him. A question grew on her face.

"You and Bebe—did you...?"

He shook his head. "It happened just as we were about to..."

"Oh, dear God..."

"One of the greater ironies of my life."

"When we found her clothes, I thought that, well..." She sighed. "The maids asked me what to do with Bebe's things. I told them to put them in a sack. I didn't know if her family would want them or not."

Mike shook his head, the lump in his throat the size of a coconut. "I don't know, either."

This struck him as a very strange conversation. They were struggling with Bebe's death—both of them in their own way, but also together. What would they be saying to each other if Bebe hadn't been shot, if she and Michael had had their romp? Maybe Serena would have asked him how it had been and he'd have lied a little, playing it down or up, depending. Or maybe they wouldn't have discussed it at all, letting that be the message.

A week or a month or a year from now Serena might have said, "So how was it with that little Brazilian cinnamon cookie, Michael? You never told me. Was she fabulous? Do you think about her much?"

It was odd how questions about impossible things had very real answers. "She was an adventure. More than I could handle, to be honest. And yes, I do think about her sometimes. Wistfully. And with gratitude. The way I do about Yvette."

How much greater was Bebe in death? he wondered. As a person, probably much greater. But as an obstacle between him and Serena—which was all that mattered now—it was hard to say. Something about Bebe, something in his wanting her, had seemed terribly necessary, almost like a rite of passage. He sensed Serena understood that. Very well.

"Koto said the funeral will be tomorrow," Serena said, again touching his arm. "He thought you might like to know. If you want, he'll send a car."

He nodded.

"Michael, I know you're in pain. I feel so badly for you. I'm terribly, terribly sorry."

He stared off into the distance, his eyes filling. "Want to hear something funny? I don't even know her last name."

There was a long silence, then Serena said, "I liked her, you know. Maybe as much as you did."

"Maybe so."

"I'll go with you to the funeral, if you want," she said. He was glad. "I'd like that."

Serena rubbed his knuckles earnestly, sharing his pain. It was odd, but it was the closest he'd felt to her in years.

THURSDAY
September 21st

Rochina

Serena wanted Bebe's funeral to be the finest the Rochina favela had ever seen. To fill the church with flowers, they emptied every florist shop from Copacabana to Barra da Tijuca. The casket was white and gold—"Fit for an angel," Bebe's aunt said when she saw it.

Serena, Michael and Koto sat in the pew behind Bebe's relatives. Koto was the only person there Serena knew, though Michael had met the family. He'd spoken with them before the mass, hugging the little girl and the sister, who was almost a clone of Bebe.

The mortuary was the most exclusive in Ipanema. It was obvious Rochina had rarely seen the likes of the huge Cadillac hearse, or the fleet of Mercedes sedans lined up to take mourners to the internment, most of whom, it was plain to see, had only one good dress or long-sleeve shirt to their names.

Serena was determined that Bebe would go out in style. It was a small token, but an important one—not only for the sake of Bebe's memory, but for Michael, as well.

The church was so tiny that the crowd spilled into the street. The community had taken note of the event—word had gotten around that some Americans were putting on a big funeral for a girl from the favela.

For Bebe to be honored like this in death seemed a cruel irony. It made Serena wonder how she'd be mourned when her own time came. She'd discovered that commanding respect for one's influence and for one's goodness weren't the same.

There had been no rain to speak of since their arrival in Rio, but God did the predictable, blessing them with a thundershower as the mass was ending. If Michael noticed the irony, he didn't comment. Not much, it seemed, could darken his mood.

They filed out of the church as large, warm drops of tropical rain fell. Bebe's aunt stared at the gray sky, repeating a phrase over and over again. Koto translated. "The angels are crying. The angels are crying."

The cemetery was high on the mountains at a location that must have at one time been on the far edge of town, though now it was surrounded by shanties. The funeral procession wound up through the narrow, semipaved streets, stopping a hundred yards from the walls of the hallowed ground. It was drizzling as the mourners disembarked from the cars. A few umbrellas popped up, but mostly people ignored the rain.

Serena, Michael and Koto fell in with the flow, crowding through the narrow gate. The casket bobbed and weaved above the sea of heads in front of them, the rhythms of the throng more samba than dirge.

Koto moved to the front, but Michael hung back, staring off past the sea of *cariocas,* the rain spattering the shoulders of his jacket and turning his sandy hair a somber brown. Serena intertwined her fingers in his. He pressed her hand in response.

When it was over, most of the mourners took their free rides back down the mountain. Serena, Michael and Koto got in the back of their car and sat shoulder-to-shoulder, smelling damp from the rain. She pushed wet wisps of hair off her forehead and wondered what she could do for Michael.

He was obviously struggling to come to terms with his culpability. It was the remorse of a man who'd run over a child chasing a ball into the street. The ball was none of his doing, but that didn't prevent the questions. Had he been going too fast? Was he guilty of inattention? Whatever the answer, the child was dead. That was the grim bottom line.

The traffic inched down the mountain. Serena wanted to say something to Michael, but she knew this wasn't the time. Suddenly he leaned toward the window, and she looked to see what had gotten his attention. Under the overhang of a cantina was a large, middle-aged black man in a red shirt. He was watching the procession with a gap-toothed smile. But when he saw them, the smile faded.

"Koto," Michael said, "isn't that Arthur Kingsley?"

Koto leaned forward for a better view. "Yeah, that's him."

Michael reached for the door handle. At the same moment the man started down the hill. Michael got out.

"Where are you going?" Serena called.

Michael shoved the door closed and started after him. He didn't get far before stopping. The car moved ahead, coming to a halt next to him. Michael hesitated, then climbed back in.

"He disappeared in the crowd," he said.

"The bastard's up to no good," Koto said. "He's a snake."

"I've been thinking about him," Michael said. "Funny he should pop up like that. Do you know where he hangs out?"

"Yes. He's got a studio in Flamengo."

"Can you get me the address? I'd like to pay him a visit."

"Who is he?" Serena asked, realizing she hadn't the vaguest idea what was going on.

"The Jamaican Bebe and I ran into at the beach that day," Michael told her.

"Oh, that guy."

"She had a score to settle with him and it was left undone," Michael went on. "I think it may be a job that needs finishing. What do you think, Koto?"

"You know, Bebe might appreciate that more than anything else we could do."

"That's what I thought."

"I take it I'm not supposed to ask about this," Serena said.

"It's extracurricular," Michael told her.

She let it go, knowing she didn't have a lot of choice. But she did sense a difference in Michael after that. Life seemed to have returned to him.

Copacabana

"I hate my life," Christina said. "I just hate it."

She was seated across the table from Mike in the hotel coffee shop, every bit the pert nineteen-year-old she was, self-possessed, oblivious, running on instinct. Christina was a young woman, but she was also a girl, the days of being a difficult teenager not far behind her.

"I assure you, pumpkin, your mother did not bribe the police to keep you from seeing Joachim," he said.

"Then why wouldn't they let me near him, Michael?"

"People can't just walk in off the street and visit a prisoner," he explained as patiently as he could.

He hadn't chastised her for going to the jail to see Joachim while they were at the funeral. It was foolish to run around Rio in a taxi, because bad things tended to happen to innocent young girls under those circumstances—especially foreigners. But he kept his relief for her safe return to himself.

"Am I just *anybody?*" she asked rhetorically. "Joachim and I are engaged. Doesn't that count for something?"

Mike had to resist the temptation to explain, to justify, to admonish her. "I know what you're going through," he said. "And I know it's not easy to be patient. But you've got to try."

Christina gave him one of those adult-woman looks that said, "You're patronizing me, Michael. Don't."

He'd always had trouble with that aspect of the female psyche. Women loved posing problems, but rarely wanted to hear solutions. Sometimes they even resented hearing them.

"It's been a rough day for everyone," he said.

Christina maintained a thoughtful silence, something that would have been unheard of a year ago. As they looked at each other, the resentment in her eyes slowly turned to concern.

"Did you love that girl who was killed?" she asked.

"In a way, I suppose. I didn't know her very well or very long."

"I can feel your pain, though, Michael."

He took odd pleasure in the remark. "Really?"

"Yes, but do you want to know something?"

"What?"

"I promised myself I wouldn't say this, because I've tried to keep my nose out of Mother's business, hoping she'd keep hers out of mine."

Mike had a wary feeling. "But...?"

"I think you still love her, Michael," she continued. "I mean, love her the way people who truly know each other love."

He couldn't help smiling. "Think so, huh?"

"Yes. And you want to hear something even more shocking? I think Mom loves you, too. She's fighting it, but she's beginning to see it's a losing battle."

He saw that Christina was serious. "What makes you think so?"

"Mom's different. I've been watching the way she acts, the way she looks at you. She's always loved you, but admitting it to herself has gotten to be... I don't know... inevitable."

Again he smiled. "Inevitable?"

"You can only fight something like that so long."

"Listen, pumpkin, your mother and I worked out things a long time ago. A little nostalgia about lost love, and a buck, still only gets you a cup of coffee."

Christina shook her head. "No, Michael, she's changed. She even told me she's been thinking about having another baby."

"What?"

"Can you believe it? *My* mother, a woman old enough to have grandchildren."

"Don't let Serena hear you say that," he said under his breath.

"I asked if she had a father in mind or if she was going to have this one potluck."

Mike and Christina both laughed. He fiddled with his cup. "What did she say to that?"

"Just that it's the big rage now for women in their forties to have babies. I think she's a little fruity over Uncle Jeffrey, if you want to know the truth."

"Your mom's been under a lot of stress."

Just then Mike saw Serena enter the coffee shop, Roberto in tow. They were in a hurry.

"If your dear old mom has changed, she hasn't lost her knack for making grown men follow her around like puppy dogs."

Christina looked over her shoulder as Serena spotted them and turned in their direction. She was almost breathless.

"Michael," she said without introduction, "there's been a break."

"What kind of break?"

"In the case. Mercedes Monteiro da Silva."

"What about her?"

She turned to Roberto. "You tell him."

"I received a telephone call from the *senhora* this morning," he explained. "She wishes to meet with you, Serena and me. She has asked that we come to the estate of Senhora Sutcliffe d'Orléans to negotiate."

"Negotiate?" Mike said.

"Yes, Michael," the lawyer replied. "I think maybe our plan has worked."

Serra dos Três Rios

The house that Mike and Bebe had been unable to see from the road when they followed Hector to the Sutcliffe d'Orléans estate was even more magnificent than Mike had expected. It was for all intents and purposes a French château set in the midst of formal gardens. The feathery palms lining the drive prevented the mood from being authentic Loire Valley, but once inside, surrounded by French antiques, they could well have been in Orléans, France, a century or two earlier.

The butler was dressed formally. He was British, and spoke with deference. They were shown to a sitting room dominated by an enormous gilt mirror and an exquisite chandelier. Mike found the chairs uncomfortable, but was too taken up with the theater to complain.

They weren't there long before Mercedes Monteiro da Silva—known to her intimates as Mimi—made her appearance. Wearing an austere black dress, she looked grim, even defeated, as she stepped into the room, closing the door behind her. It was obvious she was deeply embarrassed, but still clung to her dignity.

Roberto made the introductions. Mercedes' resemblance to Serena was obvious, though Mike found the similarity less dramatic than expected. Mercedes was more petite and, having labored under the strain of her iniquity, appeared haggard and weary. She had dark circles under her eyes and lines at the corners of her mouth, making her look her age.

She sat alone on a loveseat. Mike and Serena took the matching Louis XV armchairs. Roberto brought a straight chair from across the room.

"I thank you for coming, *senhores*," Mercedes said with a musical accent much like Joachim's. "With your permission I will come directly to the point. I wish a bargain. If you will agree to ask the authorities to drop all charges against my son, and if you will refuse to cooperate in a prosecution against him, I will tell you the true story of Drake Manville's murder."

Mike and Serena simultaneously slumped with relief.

"Our objective is to secure the release of Mrs. Bouchard's brother," Mike said. "Nothing more."

"You have our word," Serena said.

Mercedes nodded toward Roberto. "I will trust Senhor Cabral to ensure this."

"Gladly," he said.

"All right," Mercedes said. She was sitting erect, but she drew herself up even more, the lines around her mouth seeming to deepen. "Let me say, Senhora Bouchard, that I am most regretful for the effect of this on my son and your daughter. Joachim is a loving boy and I hope you will not think badly of him because of me. I cannot blame you if you reject him, but his love for Christina is sincere."

"I do not judge your son, Mrs. Monteiro da Silva. It is for my daughter to decide about Joachim, not me."

Serena glanced at Mike, and he gave her a nod of approval. He'd been thinking about his conversation with Christina and the things she'd said about her mother. Of course, even before that he'd sensed a change in Serena, but Christina's observations had opened his eyes to the possibilities.

"For this I am most grateful," Mercedes said. Looking down at her hands, which were folded primly on her lap, she began. "Some months ago I made the mistake of going with my friend Antonia von Vehrling to a literary group. I enjoy literature, but the purpose was for me to give my opinion about Antonia's new love, Drake Manville. She wanted me to say what I think of him.

"I was most curious to see this man—a film star who would love such a fragile creature as Antonia. I have been her friend since we were children, and she wanted me to help her decide about her future with Drake. Going was a mistake, because I immediately fell in love with him and he fell in love with me," Mercedes went on. "We had no control.

I didn't want to hurt Antonia and neither did he. After the meeting, he secretly asked me to have lunch with him. We met two days in a row and began our affair."

"Then you didn't know about Jeffrey," Mike said.

Mercedes clutched her folded hands to her breast, closing her eyes. "No. If I had, *senhor,* it would have ended at that moment." She trembled. "When we became lovers, my concern was for Antonia. I loved her, though sadly not so much as I loved Drake. For weeks he and I kept our affair a secret while Drake worked to end gently his relationship with Antonia. It was a difficult time."

"You'd met Christina by then," Mike said. "Didn't her uncle come up in conversation?"

"I was aware that Senhor Bouchard was in Rio, but Joachim managed to keep us from meeting. Later I understood why."

"Then you had no idea Drake and Jeffrey had a relationship?"

Mercedes shook her head. "Not until I received a letter from Antonia telling me of...Drake's past. Of Senhor Bouchard."

Mike and Serena traded looks.

"I am not sure how Antonia found out about us," Mercedes continued. "I believe Drake must have let it slip. But this letter, which she meant to be hurtful, was devastating to me."

"You mean discovering Drake was bisexual?" Serena asked.

Mercedes closed her eyes again briefly, gathering herself. "Yes. It is a sensitive issue in my family. It is not known generally, but my own brother was...homosexual." She paused. "To my father this brought dishonor on our family. He beat my brother. It was a horrible time. My brother left the house and some months later committed suicide. His secret life became a great tragedy, not only for him, but for my whole family. I personally could not face that kind of disgrace again—not if what Antonia wrote was true. You see, I loved Drake very much. I'd given him my heart as well as my body, the first man since my husband. I was devastated and desperate to know if this betrayal was true."

Mercedes drew an uneven breath, fighting back her tears. "I gave Joachim's security advisor, Senhor Souza, money for a gun. I thought for a while of using it on myself, but then I decided that if Drake had destroyed my happiness by having a relationship with a man, he should pay with his life, not I. So I went to the villa, where I'd never been before, to confront Drake with the letter of Antonia. Using some books I'd borrowed as my excuse, I arrived without warning. He admitted me. I asked him where the maid was and he said at the market. I was glad for this.

"When I gave the books to Drake, he took them into the library. I followed, taking Antonia's letter from my purse, the gun ready if I needed it. He was behind his desk. I was shaking badly. I handed the letter to Drake and demanded that he read it. When he was finished, I asked if it was true. He calmly said it was."

Mercedes' voice cracked and she put her face in her hands. The others waited, looking at each other. Sniffling, Mercedes recovered. She lifted her chin.

"It is hard to describe what happened next. A white rage came over me. Though I had hoped I would find that Antonia's story was a lie, Drake admitted he had been with a man." Mercedes rubbed her arms as though she was cold.

"What happened next?" Mike asked.

"I took the gun from my purse," she said in a small voice. "Drake saw it. For a moment he was shocked. Then he laughed—I don't know why. Perhaps he thought it would disarm me. Anyway, he started to put the books I'd brought back in the bookcase. I was enraged. He seemed to make light of my suffering. I felt a deep hatred. More even than my love."

Mercedes fell silent. Again they waited.

"What did you do then?" Mike asked when she seemed in no hurry to continue.

"I shot him. Drake fell to the floor. For a moment I stood there, unbelieving of what I had done. Then I dropped the gun and ran, knowing my life was over. I went home to await the police."

"But the police never came."

Mercedes shook her head. "Joachim came to my room and asked me what was wrong. I told him I'd shot Drake. Naturally, he was very upset. He wanted to spirit me from the country. But I felt so empty and hopeless. I thought again of killing myself. Then there was a call from Hector. He asked urgently to see me. I did not wish to see him. I was upset by what I'd done, and for me Hector was a problem. We have a past, you see."

"What kind of past?"

"He wanted to marry me before I was betrothed to Geraldo. After my husband's death, Hector again asked for my hand. I refused him."

"Did you speak to Hector when he called?" Mike asked.

"No, only Joachim. Hector was very insistent, saying he knew what had happened and wanted to help."

"Hector knew you'd shot Drake?" Serena asked.

"Yes, *senhora*. He came to the house late that night. He told us he had found Drake's body. He'd thought that Antonia had killed him, until later at Antonia's apartment, when he read the letter he'd found on Drake's desk. It was then he realized I was the one who had shot Drake."

"So Hector's story was true," Mike said, "up to the point of destroying the letter without reading it."

"This I do not know, *senhor*. All I can say is he told us Senhor Bouchard was arrested. Only then did we realize I was not a suspect. The next day, when we learned that Senhor Bouchard's fingerprints were on the gun, we understood that I might never be arrested."

"You were content to see my brother hang for your crime," Serena said bitingly.

"I know it is terrible, but I had no sympathy for Senhor Bouchard. He was the one who destroyed my happiness."

"More like the other way around, *senhora*," Serena rejoined.

"There was also the matter of our children. Joachim was concerned for the happiness of your daughter."

Mike saw Serena flush and knew he had to intervene. "None of that matters now, ladies," he said. "The truth is coming out. That's what's important."

Serena held her tongue, but only barely, Mike could see.

"Believe me, *senhores,* it has not been easy for me to keep quiet," Mercedes went on. "I have been here since a few days after the murder. Many times I wanted to go forward with the truth. In time I realized I did not want Senhor Bouchard to suffer for what I did. I said this to Joachim. But he begged me for the sake of Christina's and his happiness to stay silent. My greatest suffering these last days was for what I have done to my family, the humiliation I have brought. My pain is so great I can hardly bear it."

"Were you aware that your son hired hoodlums to intimidate us?" Serena asked. "Did you know his men beat up Michael and threatened me with harm if we wouldn't leave Rio? Did you know these men missed killing me by inches and murdered an innocent girl who was working with Michael on the case?"

"Not until the last few days," Mercedes said, bowing her head. "I assure you, *senhora,* Joachim approved of none of this."

"What stake did Hector have in this?" Mike asked. "I understand Joachim's motive, but what was Hector's?"

"He still wanted to marry me, *senhor.* I did not love him, but Joachim urged me to cooperate until the matter was resolved."

"Until they'd hanged Jeffrey, you mean," Serena retorted.

Mike gave her a warning look.

"Well, it's the truth," she replied. "These people were only thinking of themselves."

"Yes," Mercedes said, "you are right. But I did not want this. I could see that choosing Hector because he knows this terrible secret, and having to live with my guilt, was as bad as jail. It seemed to me my life was over. Were it not for my son, the need to save him, I might not go on living. I must know that he will be all right. Now that I have told you everything, you must see that he is released from the prison."

"Provided you tell this story to the police," Mike said.

"There is one other thing, Mercedes," Serena interjected. "I'd like either you or Joachim to tell Christina this story. I want her to hear it from you, not us."

A dark look came over Mercedes' face. "You are against their love, *senhora*, even knowing Joachim's only sin was to protect his mother?"

"I'm not making decisions for Christina," Serena said, "but I want her going into this with her eyes open. She can judge Joachim's actions for herself."

"You worry for your family as I worry for mine," Mercedes said. "I cannot blame you."

"I worry for everyone in my family," Serena said, "including my brother, whose only sin was to love another."

Mercedes bowed her head once more. "I am sorry for the pain I have caused, *senhora*. Tell your brother I am sorry. Maybe he can forgive me."

"Forgiveness is needed on several sides," Serena said with a glance at Mike. "There has been much wrong done in the last few weeks. Much needless suffering."

"I thank you for your generosity, *senhora*."

"I'll pray for you, Mercedes," Serena said.

The women stared at each other. Then Serena glanced at Mike and Roberto in turn.

"Come on, gentlemen, I think we need to make arrangements to get Jeffrey out of jail."

"I'm proud of the way you handled that," Mike said as their limo rolled along the drive. "It had to be difficult."

"I'm relieved, Michael. Glad I can take my brother and my daughter home." She gazed out the window.

They were alone, having left Roberto with Mercedes. She'd asked the lawyer to accompany her to turn herself in. Afterward, he was to call the hotel with word on Jeffrey's disposition.

"You think Christina will turn her back on Joachim?" Mike asked as they came to the gate.

"She won't be as horrified as we are, but this'll put a crack in Joachim's veneer. She'll reluctantly come home with me to give herself time to think, and that'll be the end of it."

"You seem pretty sure."

"Christina and I have our disagreements, Lord knows. But I understand her. We're a lot alike, in case you hadn't noticed. Still, understanding people and getting along with them are two different things."

"You really think Christina knows you?"

"Yes. I piss her off, but yes, she knows me."

He thought again about his conversation with Christina in the coffee shop. Serena's hand was on the seat. He ran his index finger over the back of it. She looked at him and he at her.

"We've covered a lot of ground the last several days, haven't we?" she said.

"People get to know one another when facing adversity."

Serena considered that. She had that *South Pacific* look in her eye.

"What are you thinking?" he asked.

"Oh, nothing," she said, turning away.

He wondered if she was thinking about her feelings for him, about that baby she'd said she wanted.

"What is it about you that flusters me?" she asked after a while.

"*I* fluster you?"

She sighed. "Women are not supposed to make those kinds of admissions. I must be getting soft in my old age."

"You're not so old."

She turned to him, her eyes suddenly glossy. "That was a very nice thing to say."

"I'm getting soft, too."

She looked down at his crotch. "Oh?"

He laughed and so did she. Serena took his hand and kissed the back of it.

"Oh, Michael, Michael, Michael," she said, putting her head on his shoulder. "What are we going to do?"

"About what?"

"About us."

"What about us?" he asked.

She hesitated. "It's not very nice of me to talk this way, is it? Not considering we buried Bebe this morning."

"Bebe was my fantasy, Serena, not the love of my life."

"I know. I don't blame you. She was my fantasy for you."

"Is that true?"

"Yes, it really is."

"Why?"

She thought. "I don't know. Guilt. Jealousy. Self-defense. Inadequacy. False bravado. Fear. Love. You pick."

"Love is the most intriguing."

Serena scoffed. "You're a man, all right. The perfect fantasy. The wife that gives you another woman out of love."

"Ex-wife."

"Yes, ex-wife. How did I forget?"

They rode through the Tijuca Forest in silence, the tropics seeming incongruous with his mental state. He felt oddly out of sorts. Yet he felt strangely close to Serena, like the previous night, closer than he had in years and years—even before their divorce. It was a warm feeling, but also a sad one.

"Michael . . ." she said after a while.

"Yeah?"

"That comment about an island in the South Pacific . . ."

"Yeah?"

"I wasn't completely joking."

"Oh?"

"Maybe we should give it some thought."

"Maybe."

More silence.

"Michael . . ."

"Yeah?"

"If we were still married, and I said I wanted to have a baby with you after all, what would you think?"

"I'd think you were nuts."

She looked hurt.

"Sorry to be so blunt," he said, "but ten years ago the circumstances were completely different. Now we're . . ."

"We're what?"

"I don't know. Older."

"So? I could still get pregnant. And having a second baby at my age is not so big a deal."

"For whom?"

"You're being difficult," she groused. "And inconsiderate."

"Hey, I thought it was a hypothetical question."

She sighed. "What is it with us?" she said, stroking his thigh. "We can't even talk about something nice like having a baby without bickering."

"We weren't bickering. We were talking."

"Oh?"

"I mean, nobody slapped anybody."

Serena smiled, looking up into his eyes. He tweaked her chin. What was it about this woman that she had such a hold on him? Loving her seemed as automatic as breathing.

"Michael," she said, "I've got another question. This one is very serious."

"Yeah, what?"

"Could we put our agreement about celibacy on hold again?"

Why was he not surprised? He wasn't going to make light of the question, though. He owed her a thoughtful response. "You really think that's a good idea?"

"Don't you?" There was a tiny hint of alarm in her voice.

"Maybe we should give it some thought. Not that I'm rejecting the idea. It's just that there's a lot at stake."

"I'm not being frivolous, Michael," she said.

"Oh? Are you sure?"

"I said it out of love."

Mike looked at her. Then he looked at her hand on the leather seat. "Love's a big word."

"I know."

He wanted very much to take her into his arms, but he wouldn't let himself. They'd had sex frivolously once on this trip, to scratch an itch. He didn't want that again.

"You don't have to decide now," she said. "I really want you to feel good about it. It's completely up to you." She kissed him on the cheek.

Mike contemplated this woman who'd been his wife and lover. Maybe Christina was right. Maybe Serena had changed. If there was anything she was not, it was frivolous. Impulsive maybe, will-of-the-wisp even, but not frivolous.

"Awesome responsibility you've given me," he muttered.

"I have total faith in you doing the right thing, Michael. You always have."

Copacabana

Mike drained the last of his second martini as he listened to the mulatto girl sing. She was dancing, too. That was harder to take—the visual part. The girl evoked an image of Bebe, though she wasn't as pretty, nor did she have the same long lines, even in four-inch heels.

He'd thought about Bebe during the day, but a lot more about Serena, knowing this tragedy they'd lived through had brought them to a turning point. She'd admitted her fear. He understood that, better now than he would have before.

Fear wasn't his problem. It was more like uncertainty. That was why he hadn't rushed off to bed her. Getting into these things was a whole lot easier than getting out. He'd learned that the hard way.

The girl ended her number. Mike glanced toward the back of the club, where Serena and Christina had gone to powder their noses. That expression always amused him. It was one of Serena's stock phrases. "Michael, it's not genteel to say I've got to pee, so I say what my mother used to say," she'd told him the first time he'd asked her about it.

He shook his head with amusement, thinking about her— though it hadn't usually been with amusement these past years. Serena Bouchard was both easy and hard to love.

They hadn't been able to focus on each other after returning from the meeting with Mercedes. Christina had taken the news of Mercedes' guilt better than Michael had expected. Joachim's culpability in the affair was a bigger problem, and as Serena predicted, Christina refused to abandon him. The cracks were beginning to show, however. The girl was shaken, though she was loath to let on. Serena had been right about that, too.

Around five that evening, the critical event occurred. Joachim called from the jail, apparently as a result of Serena's request that Christina hear from the Monteiro da Silvas. Christina talked to him in private, but when she emerged from her room, Mike could see the relationship had suffered a heavy blow. Christina cried in her mother's arms.

After a room-service dinner, Serena had told them the family needed cheering up. "There's a nightclub in this place. The Copa Samba Room. Let's go."

"Mother, please," Christina had said. "Dancing's the last thing on earth I feel like doing."

"All the more reason to go, honey. Besides, you and Michael always dance so well together."

It was bullshit, but the kind of bullshit Serena could get away with. She prevailed in the end, and they went downstairs to kick up their collective heels. Michael wasn't in much of a mood for dancing, either, but Christina did a rumba with him and actually laughed. Serena rubbed against him during a slow dance and blew in his ear, asking if he'd decided about her proposition.

"You play to win, don't you, babe?"

"Can I help it if you're irresistible?"

After the girls had gone off to powder their noses, he was left to contemplate the singer. He watched her, though his mind kept going back to Serena and where things were headed with her. Would giving in to temptation be an act of love or lunacy?

The band took a break. As they left the stage Mike glanced up to see Koto making his way toward him. "Sorry, old buddy," Mike said, as Koto approached, "my dance card's already filled."

Koto smiled faintly. "Can we talk for a minute?"

"Sure." Mike gestured toward one of the empty chairs.

"I wanted to bring you up-to-date on Kingsley," Koto said soberly.

"What are you doing working this time of night? We've cracked the case. You should be kicking back, padding your expense account, stuff like that."

Koto nodded. "Yes, but Kingsley's been on my mind. I went by his studio and found he'd moved. Carlos Mendonca helped me track the bastard down." He produced a slip of paper. "He's still in Flamengo. Half-a-dozen blocks from his old location."

Mike looked at the address. "Thanks."

"There's more," Koto said. "It turns out he's persona non grata in half the Caribbean and is still wanted in Jamaica for racketeering. The Rio police have worked a porno investigation on him, but he's managed to avoid charges."

"That's nice to know."

"Out of curiosity, what are you planning to do?" Koto asked.

Mike stroked his chin. "I'm going to pay Kingsley a visit."

"To get the negatives?"

"That was my plan."

"Want me to come with you?"

Mike shook his head. "No, I want to do this myself."

Koto nodded. "By the way, Mendonca said Senhora Monteiro da Silva has confessed to Drake's murder. It was pretty rough, apparently. She collapsed. They had to sedate her. Mendonca also said there would be a hearing on Jeffrey tomorrow. He could be out by noon if the paperwork is handled quickly enough."

Mike glanced toward the washrooms. "Serena will see to that. And she'll be thrilled to her toenails."

"How about you?"

"I'm always happy to see an innocent man freed."

"We did our job, I guess," Koto said, nodding.

Mike stared at the table, ruminating. "You know, in my joy at hearing Mercedes' confession, I didn't think to ask her a few questions."

"What kind of questions?"

"Like how many times she'd fired the gun. Whether she'd test-fired it earlier."

"If she shot him, she shot him, Mike. What difference does it make?"

"I don't know. Maybe I'm anal, don't like lose ends."

"The police will undoubtedly ask about the second shot."

"Yeah, I suppose." Mike scratched his head. "Another thing's been bothering me. Mercedes' story matched Jeffrey's perfectly. It also fits with what Hector told us."

"That's good."

"Yes, but it doesn't fit with what Penelope Ingram said."

"What do you mean?"

"She was insistent the shot occurred moments before she saw Jeffrey run out. If Mercedes shot Drake *before* Jeffrey arrived, the lapse in time from the shot to Jeffrey's departure would be more like five or ten minutes."

"The neighbor is an old woman. Perhaps she was confused."

"I don't think so. She struck me as pretty clearheaded."

"Then what are you saying?"

Mike shook his head. "I don't know, my friend."

Serena and Christina reappeared, making their way toward them. Koto saw them and got to his feet.

"I think I'll go home and get some sleep," he said. "Let me know what happens with Kingsley."

"You've got it."

Serena arrived. "Koto, what a nice surprise. Are you joining us?"

"No, Mrs. Bouchard. I just brought Mike some information."

"You have time for a drink, don't you?"

"No. Thank you very much. My wife has become unhappy with my late hours. I think I'll go home and get a back massage."

Serena smiled tightly. "I'm sure that will make her evening."

Koto caught her implication. "Different cultures, Mrs. Bouchard."

"Well, have a nice back rub."

Koto left. Serena sat down, looking a bit more ebullient than when she'd left. Christina's moroseness was unchanged.

"Who wants another drink?" Mike asked.

"I want to go upstairs to bed," Christina replied.

"They say you shouldn't drag children to church against their will," Mike said to Serena. "Only makes them resentful. Suppose that applies to nightclubs?"

"Ha, ha, ha," Christina intoned. "Very funny."

"I'll have another martini," Serena announced. "A double."

"Sounds good," Mike said.

Christina shook her head. "Why don't you two just go upstairs and go to bed? Together."

"Haven't you ever heard of foreplay?" Serena asked under her breath.

"My God, you've had five years," Christina said. "How much time do you need?"

Mike and Serena both laughed.

"Where did I fail?" Serena said.

"Ha, ha," Christina said again.

Mike ordered another round of drinks, including a Shirley Temple for Christina, to goad her. For his trouble he got a not-entirely-gentle kick in the shins. But he was managing to get her to lighten up, if only a smidgen.

Soon after the band returned a young man appeared at their table. He was in tropical garb—khaki trousers and short-sleeved shirt with epaulets. He had black hair and blue eyes, a cross between Alec Baldwin and Keanu Reeves.

"Excuse me, miss," he said to Christina in unaccented, American English, "but I can't resist asking you to dance. Would you care to?"

Christina glanced up at him, apparently without seeing him. She shook her head. "Thank you, but no. I'm not in the mood."

The young man was only momentarily knocked off-balance. "I don't step on toes and there's a money-back guarantee if you aren't completely satisfied."

Serena, who'd been listening with interest, laughed. Christina, lost in her funk, did not.

The young man smiled at Serena and Mike sheepishly. "Sorry to have interrupted."

"You're American," Serena said.

"Yes, ma'am."

"Where from?"

"Southern California. Newport Beach."

"Oh, really? We're from Beverly Hills."

He grinned. "Oh, yeah? Small world."

"I'm Serena Bouchard. This is my daughter, Christina, and her stepfather, Michael Hamlin."

"Todd Henderson," the young man said, shaking Mike's hand.

"Won't you join us?" Serena said, eliciting a roll of the eyes from Christina.

The young man pulled up a chair. Christina gave him a cursory look. Mike could see Serena's game. Diversion.

"Are you on vacation?" Serena asked the boy.

"No, Mrs. Bouchard. I'm finishing up a stint in the Peace Corps. We arrived in Rio yesterday. Tonight is sort of a last hurrah in South America before heading home. My flight's tomorrow afternoon."

"Are you alone?"

"I was with a buddy, but he went back to the hotel. I love to dance, so I stayed. But there aren't many single ladies here."

Serena glanced at Christina. "We're a dancing family, Todd, but I'm the outgoing one. You wouldn't care to dance with me, would you?"

"I'd be delighted, ma'am."

They went off. Christina shared her disgust with Mike. "I wish she wouldn't do that."

"What?"

"Play stage mom. She knows I love Joachim."

"Maybe your mother just wants to dance with fresh meat."

Christina watched Serena and Todd doing a tango. "Who does the tango these days and calls women 'ma'am,' anyway?" she asked sarcastically.

"Apparently the Peace Corps has high standards."

"Give me a break."

"He could be a nice boy."

Christina glanced at the dancers again. "I bet he loved *The Brady Bunch Movie.*"

"A kid who gave a couple of years of his life to helping others can't be all bad," Mike said. "Who knows, maybe he's been playing polo when he wasn't too busy giving shots to sick children."

"That's not funny, Michael."

"All I'm trying to say is don't hold decency and clean living against a boy."

"For all you know he's a serial rapist."

"True. We both know you can't judge a book by its cover. But that's never a reason not to take a peek inside."

Christina gave him a long, hard look. "You want me to dance with him until dawn, don't you?"

He shrugged.

"Just answer me one thing. Is it so you can take Mom upstairs and get wild and naked undisturbed, or is it so I'll forget Joachim?"

"God, I didn't know I was that transparent," he said.

"Which?"

"Fifty-fifty."

Christina tried to look annoyed, but she chuckled instead. "You bastard."

"You wouldn't believe how often I've been called that recently."

"Yes, I would."

He gave her a playful tap on the jaw.

The tango ended, and Serena and her young swain returned to the table. She was breathless.

"Lord, it's a relief to know I'm not too old to tango. This young man can dance, Christina, believe me."

"We noticed," Mike said appreciatively. He got up before Serena could sit down, taking her hand. "How about a last dance before we repair to our room so I can soak my arthritic feet?"

Serena's brows rose. She regarded Christina, then Todd Henderson.

"I don't tango," Christina said to Todd, "but I'd love to hear about the Peace Corps. Would you mind telling me about your experiences? At least until the next fox-trot?"

"Sure, glad to," Todd said, oblivious. He sat down.

"Come, my love," Mike said to Serena as he wrapped an arm around her waist. "Let's dance."

They went to the dance floor. Slipping into Mike's arms, Serena looked over her shoulder at Christina and Todd. "How'd you manage that?"

Mike drew her close, inhaling her scent. "Simple. I told her the truth."

"What truth?"

"That I wanted to go upstairs and get laid, and needed some privacy."

Serena pulled back to see his face. "You didn't."

He nodded. "Yeah, but not in so many words."

"And Christina agreed?"

"I said I only needed ten minutes."

Serena gave him a firm pinch. "Ten minutes?"

"Actually, she agreed to dance till dawn."

Serena pressed her face into his neck, running the tip of her tongue over his skin. "That's more like it," she murmured.

Mike savored the familiar feel of her body. "I haven't decided," he said. "Are we entering a familiar port or sailing into uncharted waters?"

"I'm not sure," she replied.

"That all right with you?"

"Hell, Michael, that's half the fun. Or have you forgotten?"

The light was on in their suite, as they had left it. Serena did a spin, stopping in the middle of the sitting room, feeling happy. They'd passed an important milestone of some kind, she could tell.

After Michael closed the door, they gazed at each other for several moments. She felt unexpectedly shy. They both sensed this dalliance would be more momentous than the others since their divorce.

"Give me a minute," Michael said.

He proceeded to make a tour of the suite, checking all the closets before returning. "Sorry, but I don't want any surprises."

"Nothing kills like performance anxiety," she teased, signaling her sympathy for his concern.

"How true, how true."

Her eyes roamed his face. "Michael, I don't want you to feel an obligation. I pressured you to do this, I know."

"If it were a problem, I could have developed a headache," he deadpanned.

"I'm serious," she said, peering into his eyes.

"So am I, sweetheart."

She gave him a big, sincere hug. "It's enough if you'll just hold me. I won't insist on more."

"You've said that before," he said. "I don't think we ever managed to leave it at a few hugs and kisses."

She ran her hand down the front of his shirt, feeling his chest through the fabric. "The fires have always burned pretty intensely, haven't they?"

Michael tapped her lower lip with his fingertip. "They have. And they still do."

They kissed tenderly.

"Michael . . ."

"Yes?"

"I don't want to be a consolation prize. If you go to bed with me wishing I were Bebe, it'd be bad for both of us. I'd understand, but I wouldn't be happy."

He studied her face. "I don't mean to be disrespectful to Bebe by saying this, but had I never met her, my life in the long run wouldn't be any different. I can't say the same of you. I loved you once. And I'm not the same man I was before I met you. For better or worse, that's the way it is. It took me awhile to face up to it, but I have."

His words lifted her heart. "It's the same with me, Michael."

They kissed again and she took his hand, leading him to her room. In the faint light they undressed. She felt herself growing tingly.

"Remember Tahoe?" she said, unzipping her dress.

"Sure." Michael was on the other side of the bed, unbuttoning his shirt.

"That was one of the best orgasms I've ever had," she said. "Maybe *the* best."

"I recall enjoying it quite a bit myself," he said, removing his shirt.

She stared at his chest. "God, I really wanted you. Cornelio and I had screwed that morning, before he broke his leg skiing, but that night in your room I felt like I hadn't had a man in a hundred years."

He watched her remove her bra. His eyes made her nipples go hard.

"You had a pretty good appetite, too, as I recall," she said as the fine hair on her arms stood on end.

Michael unbuckled his belt. She pulled down her panty hose and sat on the edge of the bed to remove them. When she stood, Michael had taken off his pants. The bulge in his shorts was impossible to ignore.

"That was the last good sex I had," she told him. "Everything since then has been downhill—with the exception of that first night here. I didn't want to tell you, but that was the beginning of the end of my resistance."

"If so, you've certainly put up a good fight. And along the way you seemed to have had fun distracting yourself with Roberto."

"Purely a defense mechanism. I never really wanted to sleep with Roberto...his voice maybe, but not him."

She took the covers at one corner, while Michael took the other. They pulled them back, exposing the sheet.

Serena slid her panties off. Michael removed his shorts. His sex was thick and firm. She eyed it cautiously, feeling her juices start to flow. She put one knee on the bed.

"I know you can't say the same about Bebe," she said. "The truth is, I wish you had been able to have sex with her, because then you'd have known what it was like and you wouldn't have to wonder."

Michael put his knee on the bed. "I won't wonder, Serena."

She moved onto the bed. "You aren't just saying that?"

He shook his head. "Nope."

Michael lay on the mattress and looked up at her. She crawled the last few feet to his side and eased down beside him. She stroked his penis, her insides churning like water rising to boil. Then she kissed him long and hard, biting his lips, her desire making her more aggressive.

There was no need for foreplay—the entire day had been foreplay. Even the funeral. She had wanted him every minute since awakening that morning.

"Michael," she murmured, sucking and biting his lips, "I love you."

He crushed her to him, squeezing so hard it almost hurt. But she didn't care. Her body ached with excitement.

He rolled over on her, wedging her legs open. She dug her fingers into his flesh, and he entered her firmly, making her gasp. She rose against him, taking him in as deeply as she could. They were there instantly—at the pivotal point where desire, hostility, lust, anger and love were indistinguishable. Orgasm was only a few thrusts away. When he began to undulate, each penetration harder and deeper than the last, she wrapped her legs around him.

She came within moments, crying out. Afterward she lay soaked in perspiration. She held him in her arms, adoring him, as though he were her child. His heart continued to pound against her breast, but he found the strength to kiss her neck. She closed her eyes, the vestiges of her orgasm still echoing in her body.

"Oh, Michael," she moaned.

Nobody could do it like Michael.

F R I D A Y
September 22nd

Flamengo

Arturo's was located in a marginal commercial district not far from the sleazy clubs where the transvestites hung out. When Mike got there at nine, the shop was closed. He peered in the window at the dusty portraits—of a bride, a baby, a family. Kingsley, Mike decided, had a keen sense of irony.

There was no reason to believe the sonovabitch wouldn't show up, so Mike went to the entry of a vacant store across the street and waited. By nine-thirty his feet hurt, but he decided to hold on for another half hour, despite a growing fear that Arthur might be off shooting a wedding or a porn flick.

At least Michael had pleasant memories of Serena to keep his mind occupied. The luster of the night before was still with him. That morning they'd showered together, nearly making love again right then. But Serena stopped him just before she came, saying she wanted to be in bed. They were both eager enough that they didn't bother drying off.

Their lovemaking wasn't wanton. He felt tender toward her, and Serena seemed to feel the same. The sex had been gentle and caring.

They had breakfast with Christina, who seemed to have more to be embarrassed about than they. She hadn't danced till dawn, but she admitted she hadn't come up to the suite until after two. Yes, Todd Henderson was nice, and yes, he was a hell of a dancer. She refused to concede she'd had a change of heart regarding Joachim, though she admitted she'd told Todd he could call her once they got back to L.A.

For all the newfound love, Serena had not forgotten what she'd come to Rio to accomplish. Before Michael left, she'd made reservations on three different flights. Which one they caught would depend on when Jeffrey was released. Roberto had called during breakfast to arrange to take her to the hearing.

"Mom, I want to go, too," Christina had said. "Maybe they'll let me see Joachim."

Serena must have seen it was for a last goodbye, so she'd relented.

Christina was trying to hang in there like a loyal fiancée, but Mike had noticed a flicker of joy when the first reservations Serena got were for the flight Todd Henderson was on. There'd be tears for Joachim, but love wasn't always so blind it couldn't see the handwriting on the wall.

Before Michael left the hotel, Serena had tried to make him promise he'd be back by noon in case Jeffrey was released. "I want us to leave together, Michael." He told her he'd do his best, but that he had business with Arthur Kingsley.

"I can always get a later flight," he said. "There's no point waiting for me. Jeffrey will be anxious to leave."

She'd kissed him goodbye with extra passion. "If you don't make it back in time, plan on a party for the two of us when you get to L.A." Hugging him, she felt the automatic under his coat. "Why are you taking your gun?"

"Some people you take flowers, others you don't."

"Michael, you're going to get yourself hurt, I just know it. Being a divorcée is one thing, but a widowed divorcée is something else entirely. I don't want you to go."

He pinched her cheek. "This is boy stuff, sweetheart. No point trying to explain why I have to do it."

She hadn't fought him, but she made it clear she was unhappy with his romantic notions of duty and honor. "Bebe would agree with me," she said, but to no avail.

Standing in a back street of a sleazy part of Rio, Mike was keenly aware of the incongruity between this world and his. But he'd decided to see this thing through because of the obligation he felt to Bebe and his own need for redemption. Yet he realized more keenly than ever that where he belonged was with Serena.

That hadn't always been the case. Even when they were married he'd often felt like a visitor in her life. But now something had changed. Partly it was Serena. But he'd changed, as well. He was still the boy from Bakersfield and she was still queen of Beverly Hills, but that didn't mean what it had in the past. What had she said the other day? Something about having grown up. Maybe it was as simple as that.

The remark about having a party when they got back to L.A. was something she could easily have said in the old days, yet it had a different feel now. And the comments about wanting a baby and wanting him to go with her to the South Pacific weren't as flip as they had seemed, either. Sure, it was titillating, but it was also a concession of sorts. At least that was the way he wanted to interpret it. Only time would tell if he was right.

A couple of transvestites walked by, giving him a strange look. Mike was uncomfortable—not only because of his aching feet. Maybe this was a waste of time. Then he saw Arthur Kingsley come strolling up the street.

The sight of the bastard got his adrenaline flowing. As the Jamaican unlocked the door to his shop, Mike crossed the street. Kingsley turned at the sound of footsteps. Mike stepped into the small, recessed entry.

"Morning, Arthur," he said flatly. "Have a few minutes?"

"What? Huh?" It took a moment for Kingsley to recognize him. "Oh, the American. I remember. What do you want, man?"

Mike reached under his coat and pulled out the 9 mm Bebe had given him a week earlier. Kingsley started to raise his arms.

"Put your hands down," Mike commanded. "Now open the door and go inside."

Kingsley did as he was ordered. Mike followed him in, kicking the door closed with his heel.

"Lock the door," Mike said, stepping aside.

Arthur turned the bolt, moving slowly, apparently calculating the possible reasons for Mike's visit and the options available. "I keep no money here, man."

"I don't want money. I came to do business."

Kingsley's eyes slid to the automatic. "What's that for?"

"More efficient than a lawyer." Mike backed off a step to look around. On the walls were portraits, though not so innocent as the stuff in the window. There were girls—black and white and beige, even an Asian. There was a display case with odds and ends inside it, a stool and a wall telephone. Next to the phone was a curtained doorway.

"What's in back?"

"My studio and my office, man."

"Let's go," Mike said, gesturing with the gun. "Nice and easy, Arthur. I wouldn't want to get blood on the carpet."

They entered a small photographer's studio, which was cluttered with lights, cables running across the floor and an assortment of props. Behind it was a private office. It was nicer. There was a mahogany desk, a couple of chairs, plush carpeting and, behind the desk, a wall-mounted glass display case filled with framed photos.

"Arthur, I get the feeling this room is the real you."

"Man, what you want?"

"Bebe sent me."

Arthur's full lip sagged, exposing pink gums. "She's dead, man. Bebe is dead."

"Yes, but her legacy lives on. Sit in your desk chair," Mike said, gesturing with the automatic, "but keep your hands above your belt. They get out of my sight and I shoot first and ask you why you forgot later. Understand?"

Kingsley slowly sat down, resting his hands on the arms of his high-backed chair.

"Now," Mike said, "you've got some negatives I'd like."

"You want Bebe's pictures."

"Very astute, Arthur."

"Sorry, man, but they're gone. I sold them already."

"I don't believe you."

"It's true, man. They gone yesterday."

"Hmm," Mike said, knowing a liar when he saw one. "I'm either walking out of here with Bebe's negatives, and all the prints, or you're dead. Either way, the score is settled. The choice is yours."

Kingsley gave that a moment's thought. "Honest, man, I got no pictures of Bebe. Sold, like I said."

"Arthur, I'm going to count to ten. By the time I get there, your future, or lack thereof, will be determined."

Kingsley considered the words, his eyes moving slowly back and forth between Mike's eyes and the gun.

"One...two...three..."

"I'm not shittin' you, man. I don't got them."

"Four...five...six..."

"How can I give them if I don't got them?"

"Seven...eight..." Mike lifted the 9 mm, pointing it directly at Kingsley's head. "Nine...ten...goodbye, Arthur."

Deflecting the muzzle of the barrel a bit, Mike pulled the trigger. The glass in the case behind Kingsley's head exploded. The Jamaican flinched, closing his eyes as shards of glass came crashing down behind him.

"Shit," Mike said calmly. "Never was a good shot. Let's try again. Only let's make it five this time. One... two...three...four..."

"No, man!" Kingsley shouted, wrapping his arms around his head. "Don't shoot. You can have the fucking pictures, man. Don't shoot!"

Mike smiled thinly. "I thought you'd see it my way."

"They're in the filing cabinet," Kingsley said, pointing to the one against the side wall.

"Which drawer?"

"Top. I show you, man."

He started to get up, but Mike gestured with the gun for him to sit back down. "Thanks for the offer, but I'll do it myself."

Mike went to the file and opened the drawer. It was crammed with manila envelopes. And there was a .38 wedged in front.

"Crissakes, Arthur," Mike said, removing it. "You weren't planning on using this by any chance, were you?"

"Oh, no, man. Forgot it was there."

Mike chuckled. "God love you, Arthur, you must have been born a liar." He stuck the revolver in his belt. "Now come over here and get Bebe's negatives. Every last one. If her picture ever shows up in a skin mag, I'll come back and personally tear your heart out. Understand?"

Kingsley nodded. As Mike stepped away, Kingsley came to the file cabinet. He removed a large envelope, handing it to Mike.

"Go back and sit in your chair."

Kingsley complied. Mike put his 9 mm automatic in his belt next to the .38 and opened the envelope. He found perhaps fifty negatives and a few proofs. They were faded, but rifling through them he determined that none of the pictures showed her with a man. Koto had said that Bebe had been photographed drugged and being raped. Mike looked at Kingsley.

"This isn't all. Where are the ones of Bebe with the man?"

"These Bebe already bought, man. I swear it."

"You lying sonovabitch! They'd be the last ones you'd give up!" Mike pulled the automatic from his belt and pointed it at Kingsley's head. "This time I'm not even going to count."

"No!" the Jamaican screamed. "I will get them! I forgot."

"My ass."

Kingsley went to the files. He got a second envelope and returned to his chair. Mike pulled out the glossy photos. The first few turned his stomach. He didn't look any further.

"You disgusting piece of shit," he said. It was all he could do to keep from shooting the bastard. "This is your last chance. Any more negatives or photos of Bebe?"

The Jamaican pointed over his shoulder at the shattered glass cabinet on the wall behind him. "Top shelf."

Mike saw a framed photo of Bebe in the buff. She was on her stomach, in profile. Her chin was resting on her palm and her face was turned to the camera. She was smiling like an angel and looked exquisite. The photo was artistic— something that could have been in a perfume ad in *Vogue*. He stared at it, the memory of Bebe's exotic allure making the hair stand up on the back of his neck.

"Lord, Arthur," he said, stuffing the negatives and proofs back in the manila envelope, "for a scumbag you've got talent. Too damn bad it was misused."

"There were some fine pictures I already gave her, man."

"You obviously saved the trash so as not to embarrass her."

"Bebe and me had a deal, man."

"Your deal's just been renegotiated. Hand me the picture."

Kingsley reached up and took down the photograph. As he stepped aside, Mike saw it—the bullet hole in the plaster at the rear of the cabinet. He stared at it, goose bumps rising on his arms, a shiver going down his spine.

"Jesus Christ," he muttered.

He must have looked as though he'd seen a ghost. Arthur turned to see what he was staring at. "What the matter with you, man?"

Mike was staring at the bullet hole, but what he was seeing was the glass bookcase in the library at Hector von Vehrling's villa.

"What, man?"

Mike thought about the two shots that had been fired from the gun that had killed Drake. "Arthur," he said, "you may have done me a favor by being so damn stubborn. I was planning on shooting you for what you did to Bebe, but maybe you've earned a reprieve."

"You crazy, man?"

"Tell me, Arthur, is this your entire portfolio?" he said, pointing to the file cabinet.

"That's ten years of work, man."

Mike went over to the cabinet and took out an envelope at random. Inside he found more pornographic, degrading shots of women. Some were scarcely more than girls.

"Normally I'm not into censorship, Arthur, but for you I may make an exception. Got a match?"

Kingsley's mouth dropped open. "What you saying, man?"

"Give me a goddamn match!" Mike shouted.

The Jamaican took a box of matches from the clutter on his desk and tossed it to Mike. When he saw Mike take out a match and strike it, he began to whine. "Oh, no, man. That's my life. Don't burn it!"

Mike touched the match to the corner of an envelope. The flame caught. Kingsley started wailing.

"Shut up, Arthur. Your bad karma's caught up with you. Think of this as a chance to change your life."

Flames began to shoot up, billowing black smoke. Mike took the photos of Bebe and backed off to the door. Kingsley just stared at the burning file cabinet, continuing to whine.

"It's been a pleasure doing business with you," Mike said. "I want you to stay and enjoy the fire. If the smoke gets too bad, you can come out." Then he turned and left, walking through the studio. He let himself out as curses and angry shouts came from the back of the shop.

Walking briskly up the street, Mike pictured the bullet hole in Kingsley's wall. He wondered if fate had bestowed a brilliant insight, or if it was a case of too much adrenaline in his blood. His mind spun as he thought once more of Penelope Ingram insisting she'd heard a shot before Jeffrey left the villa.

At the corner he flagged down a taxi and gave the driver the address of Koto's office. There were a few things to do before seeing Serena and Jeffrey.

Rio de Janeiro

As he rode, Mike held the photos in his lap. Knowing what he had sickened him—it made Bebe's suffering more real. For the first time he truly understood her anguish.

Bebe would want them destroyed. He should have tossed them in the burning file cabinet with the rest of Kingsley's smut, but his soul cried out for a more dignified ending.

They were near Koto's office now and, looking out, Mike saw they were passing the street barbecue in the small park Bebe had pointed out the day they'd gone to lunch at the Colombo. He told the driver to pull over.

Mike got out and walked back to the park. The portly sidewalk chef, a jovial black man, was starting a fire in his grill, getting ready for the midday rush. He beamed as Mike approached, greeting him in Portuguese.

Mike looked into the flames in the oil drum. "Need some fuel?" he asked.

"O que deseja?"

Mike held up the manila envelopes and pointed at the flames. The man shrugged. Mike tossed the photos in the fire. He clutched the framed photo against his chest and watched as first the paper caught, then the celluloid, transforming instantly into a huge cloud of smoke. The man laughed and looked up at the black cloud rising to the sky. He lifted his hands to the heavens. Mike thought of Exu, the *umbanda* god. Maybe it was an omen. Bebe probably would have thought so.

Mike stood there, following the smoke with his eyes until it had disappeared in the cloudless sky. He had a feeling of certainty that Bebe was somewhere good, enjoying this right along with him. "You've got your pictures back, Bebe," he mumbled. "Now you're free."

* * *

Santa Teresa

They pulled up in front of von Vehrling's villa in Koto's Toyota. Mike got out. Koto came around the car, and they went through the gate and up the stairs. Mike rang the bell as Koto stood, puffing.

"What does it prove if you find another bullet hole?" the investigator asked.

"That there were two shots fired in this house."

"And?"

"It would be interesting to know who fired them, and when."

Mike rang the bell again. No one answered. After a minute he sighed.

"What's the penalty for breaking and entering here?"

"If you take nothing, no one will care."

They went around back and broke a kitchen window. Mike crawled through and let Koto in. They went immediately to the library. Mike moved behind the desk and stood where Drake would have been when he was shot. Then he opened the bookcase and began removing volumes. Behind the fourth handful of books they found a bullet hole in the wall.

"There it is," Mike said, "the missing bullet."

"So how did it get there?" Koto asked.

"Mercedes said she returned some books to Drake as a pretext for her visit. He must have opened the bookcase. Obviously one of the shots was fired sometime before the bookcase door was closed."

"You're saying she fired twice, missing with one of the shots?"

Mike stroked his chin. "That's the logical explanation. Except that..."

"Except what?"

"It still doesn't explain why Penelope Ingram heard a shot moments before Jeffrey ran out the villa."

"She seems to mess up every plausible theory about what happened," Koto said. "Maybe *she's* mistaken, Mike."

"Possibly." He studied the hole in the wall, contemplating the problem.

"What are you thinking?"

"I'm wondering if it's possible Jeffrey fired one of the shots."

"Jeffrey?"

"We know he had the gun in his hand."

"But why would he shoot a bullet into the wall when Senhor Manville was already dead?" Koto asked. "It makes no sense."

Mike stared at the bloodstained carpet. "True. But then, a lot of things about this case don't make much sense. There's also no explanation as to who put the books away and closed the glass door before the police arrived."

"Perhaps Senhor von Vehrling or the maids did it."

"If so, they'd have seen the bullet hole. No mention was made of that. And they had nothing to hide in that regard. Of course, Hector has conveniently disappeared."

"Do you want to ask the maids about it?"

"Koto, I think Mercedes is the one we need to talk to. Maybe she can give us a plausible explanation for the second shot. I never did get a detailed, blow-by-blow account from her. What she did and saw is bound to explain it." He checked his watch and saw it wouldn't be long before the first flight left for L.A. "We've got to hurry, though. There's not much time."

Rio de Janeiro

They found Carlos Mendonca at his desk, munching on antacid tablets as he did his paperwork. He glanced up and, seeing them, put down his pen.

"*Senhores,* come in." He motioned for them to sit. "Senhor Hamlin, it is a surprise you are still in Rio. The *senhora* and her brother left for the airport some hours ago. Why aren't you with them?"

"I don't like to leave a place without tidying up after myself, Carlos. There are some nagging questions in my mind."

"Truly?"

"Yeah. What are the chances of talking to Mercedes Monteiro da Silva for a few minutes?"

A somber expression came over the detective's face. "Not very good, I'm afraid. The *senhora* has taken it upon herself to close the murder case very quickly. Early this morning she slashed her wrists with a piece of glass and bled to death in her cell. She was not discovered until it was too late."

Mike's mouth sagged open. "Mercedes is dead?"

"Yes, *senhor.* Suicide. By the words of the matron, she was very...uh...Koto, *desanimada?*"

"Despondent."

"*Sim,* despondent. *Obrigado.*"

Mike and Koto exchanged looks.

"The priest came to her cell last evening. The prison matron said the *senhora* was crying all night, babbling incoherently about her son. Then when she stopped, the matron thought it was for sleep. But the *senhora* cut her wrists and died. It is a tragedy for the family, but it saves the government much trouble. Better if all the prisoners did it, perhaps."

"Well, I guess that takes care of my tidying up," Mike said.

"What is it you wished to ask?" Mendonca said, popping another antacid in his mouth.

"Koto and I found a second bullet hole at the villa, Carlos. It was behind the books and glass doors, which explains why it was not found."

Mendonca glanced at Koto, who nodded. The detective stroked his chin. "How did you know to look, *senhor?*"

"Serendipity. Dumb luck. A hunch, I guess you could say."

"Interesting."

"I don't suppose Mercedes said anything to you that might explain that, did she, Carlos?"

Mendonca reflected. "No. We asked her how many times she fired the weapon. I'm sure she said only once."

"Something's not adding up," Mike said.

"She might have been mistaken," Koto said. "Two shots could have gone off in rapid succession. In her excitement, and because she thought she pulled the trigger only once, she might have been unaware of the second shot."

"She missed with one shot and hit Drake with the other?"

Koto shrugged. "What other explanation is there?"

Mike sighed with frustration. "I don't know. That's just it."

"You do not question her guilt, *senhor,*" Mendonca said, "*certamente.* She killed herself because of shame and humiliation. This is not the act of an innocent person. Several times she told us she shot Senhor Manville. There was no doubt in her mind—how could there be in yours?"

"Maybe I put too much faith in the words of little old ladies."

"*Senhor?*"

"I guess I'm just too anal for my own good, Carlos."

SATURDAY
September 23rd

Rio de Janeiro

Mike, with Koto at his side, walked in silence toward the ticket counter. It had been only ten days since he and Serena had arrived in Rio. That first morning the airport had seemed like the gateway to a vibrant, exotic, sensuous, colorful world. Rio had been all that, and dangerous, too. It was like no place he'd ever known. His life had been changed by what had happened here, and yet he was leaving with mixed feelings.

He certainly wasn't feeling the joy and relief Serena must have felt boarding the plane the day before. And as for Jeffrey, he could only imagine. It must have been like an escape from hell.

Mike was troubled. He'd spent the night anguishing over the inconsistencies in the case. He hated getting obsessed over details that probably didn't matter in the grand scheme of things, and yet he couldn't get those two shots out of his mind.

The line at the ticket counter was fairly long. Koto had hardly spoken, but Mike knew there were a few things that remained to be said between them.

"I wish all this hadn't ended on such a down note," he told the investigator. "After what happened to Bebe, the case should have been wrapped up nice and clean. I can't even leave feeling good about what we accomplished.''

"You can't let go, can you?"

Mike smiled. "You noticed?"

"Me, I'm not going to second-guess Senhora Monteiro da Silva."

"I guess slashing her wrists was a pretty strong statement, wasn't it?"

"Let go, Mike. Just let go."

"Good advice, I'm sure."

The line advanced and Mike kicked his bag ahead.

"It's none of my business, I know," Koto said, "but I'm wondering, will you and the *senhora* be getting back together?"

Mike smiled broadly. "What makes you think we would?"

"Forgive me for saying this, but from the first day I saw you and Mrs. Bouchard, it seemed you should be husband and wife. I was surprised to learn you were divorced."

"Koto, you may be an even better detective than I thought."

"Then there may be a happy ending?"

Mike laughed, clasping Koto by the shoulder. "Dreams of tropical islands can be ephemeral, my friend."

Koto furrowed his brow questioningly.

"Let's just say the proof will be in the pudding," Mike said, knowing his words weren't much clearer. The thing was, he didn't know the answer himself.

The line was advancing slowly. Mike checked his watch. "There's no reason you have to stay here, Koto. You're on your own time now."

"I want to see you off," Koto said. "I got an extra bonus, and there was all that money to Bebe's family. I am very grateful. Mrs. Bouchard is a good woman."

"Serena has her virtues."

"I hope you will be happy together." Koto bowed his head, then said, "If Bebe had lived, she would say the same."

Mike nodded. "I know." He reflected for a moment, then, on impulse, bent to open his suitcase. Digging through the bag, he pulled out the framed photo of Bebe and showed it to Koto.

"I salvaged this from Kingsley's studio," he said. "I was going to keep it, but it occurs to me it belongs here in Rio, not on a mantel or in a closet back in the States. You decide what to do with it. Keep it, give it to Bebe's family, whatever you think is right."

Koto studied the photograph, his eyes turning liquid.

"She was beautiful," Mike said.

Koto nodded. "Maybe one day Branca would like to see the beautiful woman her mother was."

"Yes, I bet she would."

Mike was next in line to be checked in. He closed his suitcase and, when his turn came, lifted the bag onto the scales.

The agent was a pretty Brazilian girl. "Going home to Los Angeles, Mr. Hamlin?"

"I'm not quite sure."

The girl smiled as though it were a joke. "I hope you had a pleasant stay in Rio."

"I loved Sugarloaf."

She nodded. "Everybody does."

Minutes later they were headed for customs. Koto walked beside him, the photo of Bebe tucked under his arm. Mike sensed that something was troubling his friend, and he didn't want to leave without giving Koto a chance to get it off his chest.

"Is there something you want to say?"

"You're a better detective than I thought, too," Koto said, returning the favor. He smiled sheepishly. "I guess I can't let you go without telling you. My conscience would bother me, even though I know keeping my mouth shut is in your best interests."

"What?"

"Yesterday, after I dropped you off at the hotel, I got to thinking about the two shots. I knew it was eating at you, so

I decided to talk to the maids and see if they could tell me anything that might help put your mind at ease. I drove to their village in the country and found them last evening at a relative's. I asked about the bookcase, figuring they'd say the door was open and that either they or Hector von Vehrling put the books back in and closed it before the police arrived."

"And?"

"They said just the opposite. The room when Ana first entered it was just as we saw it, except with Drake's body and the gun."

Mike reflected. "Which means the door to the bookcase had to have been closed by either Drake, Mercedes or Jeffrey."

Koto nodded.

"If it was Drake, that means the first shot was the one in the wall, behind the books, and that he was killed by a second shot."

"Certainly not one that was fired immediately after the first, as I suggested when we were talking to Mendonca," Koto said.

Mike rubbed his chin, thinking. "But it could have been Mercedes or Jeffrey who closed the door...which would be bizarre, to say the least."

"Exactly," Koto said. "For what reason? Even if they were neat freaks, it wasn't consistent with their probable states of mind."

"Yeah, with a dead man at their feet."

"If they wanted to hide anything," Koto said, "you'd expect it to be the gun, or even the body."

"Which takes us back to Drake."

Koto nodded again. They came to the entrance of customs and stopped.

"You did want to make my flight home interesting, didn't you, you son-of-a-gun?" Mike chided.

Pericles Kotomata shrugged. "What can I say, Mike?" The men looked into each other's eyes.

"Maybe the case is closed as far as Mendonca is concerned," Mike said, "but I'll have to keep it open a crack... at least until I have a chance to talk to Jeffrey."

"Sorry to do this to you."

Mike put his arm around Koto's shoulders. "Hey, what are friends for?"

A silence fell over them. Mike looked down at his feet. "My only regret is not being able to say goodbye to Bebe," he said.

"That's my main regret, too."

They embraced. Even if it felt a bit awkward, it seemed like the right thing to do.

"Have a *choppe* sometime and think of me," Mike said. "I'll do the same when I get home."

"Godspeed, and give my regards to Mrs. Bouchard."

Mike saluted him and went off to catch his plane.

Los Angeles

It was late when Mike's plane arrived at LAX. He hadn't told Serena which flight he'd be on, but he'd left a message with Agnes. He assumed that Serena would be waiting and was surprised to find Eddie Brown hanging around outside customs instead. The chauffeur had a big grin on his face.

"Welcome home, Mr. H.!" Eddie said, beaming. "Sure is good to see you!"

"Hi, Eddie." Mike glanced around, realizing there was no Serena. He noticed Eddie was holding a large envelope, which the chauffeur immediately handed him.

"Mrs. B. told me to give you this," he said, taking Mike's suitcase.

For the briefest of moments Mike wondered if Serena could be heartless enough to deliver a Dear John letter this way, but he realized he was being paranoid. More than once during the long flight he had considered the possibility that things might look different to her once she got back to the real world. Nor was he sure how he'd feel. The love they'd rediscovered could have been left behind in the tropical air and samba nights.

He examined the envelope, recognizing the "Michael" scrawled across the front as being written by Serena. "Am I supposed to look inside now or later?"

"That's up to you. But Mrs. B., she done told me to tell you she's sorry she's not here. She had to go to New York."

"New York?" Mike said, feeling his first real stab of disappointment.

"Yes, but she's arrivin' back in a couple of hours. As soon as I take you to her hotel in Beverly Hills, I got to come back here for her."

"We're going to the Beverly Bouchard?"

"That's my instructions. Mrs. B. thought you'd need to rest after your flight."

The envelope seemed less ominous. Mike tore it open. Inside was a travel photo of a pretty girl on a beach. She was wearing a flower lei and little else. The note said, "What do you think?" and was signed, "S." There was a P.S. at the bottom. "If you're not too tired, wait up for me."

Mike showed Eddie the photo. "How's this for an invitation?"

"To what?"

"With Serena, you can't be a hundred percent sure, Eddie."

They went to the limo, which was being guarded by a cop with an extra twenty in his pocket. Eddie had a liberal expense account.

The air smelled like L.A.—Disneyland/Mediterranean spiced with smog. Mike got in front with Eddie.

"I'd like to make a side trip to West Hollywood first. Do you know where Jeffrey lives?"

"Miz Bouchard's brother? Drove him home yesterday."

"Good. That's where we're headed, Eddie."

The drive to West Hollywood was long enough for Eddie to catch Mike up on the sports news. The Dodgers still had a shot at the playoffs, even though the Giants had taken two out of three in the series just completed at Chavez.

"I guess you're too tired to care about the Dodgers," the chauffeur said, realizing he'd been doing all the talking.

"I've got a lot on my mind, Eddie."

"Don't sound like you got in much beach time down in Rio."

"A little."

"Was the ladies as hot as they say?"

"Yeah. That and more."

"You goin' back?"

Mike shook his head. "I don't know what I'm going to do."

"Oh, it was one of those trips. The way Mrs. B. was all-smiles, I was wonderin' if you'd come back the same way."

"I guess I haven't, have I?"

"You got lady problems, Mr. H.?"

"Yes."

"Oo-ee. I know how that is."

West Hollywood

Jeffrey lived in an art-deco bungalow off Sunset Boulevard in a neighborhood that managed to be tired, pretentious and false, all at the same time. Somehow it fit him.

Jeffrey answered the door in a Planet Hollywood T-shirt and shorts, holding a glass of Scotch. His Persian cat, Poopsie, was under his arm.

"Michael!" He looked past him, probably expecting Serena.

"I'm alone."

"It's so good to see you!" Jeffrey said, the slur in his voice indicating he was well into his cups. "Come in, come in. Did you just get in? God, you look beat."

Once Mike was inside and the door closed, Jeffrey put Poopsie down. The cat bounded off.

"Jesus, Michael, I owe you. God, do I owe you." His eyes flooded.

Mike could hear soft piano music. The house smelled of booze and incense.

"I was having a drink and thinking of Drake," Jeffrey said, making it sound almost like a confession. "Can I pour you one?"

"No, thanks."

Jeffrey gnawed on his lip. "Actually, I've spent the last twenty-four hours drinking and thinking of Drake."

Mike nodded.

"You can't believe how hard it's been," Jeffrey said, his voice shaking. Tears overflowed his lids. His thin body began to tremble. Then he stepped forward and hugged Mike, careful not to spill his drink.

Mike patted Jeffrey's back self-consciously. Jeffrey sniffled, then eased away as smoothly as he'd eased in. "Sorry to be such a sop."

"Jeffrey, we need to talk."

The emotion on Jeffrey's face shifted to calculation. "Oh?"

"I came directly from the airport."

"Talk to me before fucking Serena?"

"Yeah."

"Well, maybe we should sit." He led the way to the front room. His walk had faint echoes of his sister's. "Excuse the dust. I haven't had time to get a cleaning service in. Ralph brought Poopsie over this morning. She's the only normalcy I've found since I got home."

They sat in opposite overstuffed armchairs. Poopsie leapt onto Jeffrey's lap, curling into a ball. He stroked her and drew on his drink. Mike could see a wariness underneath the controlled veneer. The Jeffrey who'd wept under the painting of the tortured saint in Rio was not very far from the surface.

Mike figured the moment was right to spring his little trap. "I found the bullet Mercedes fired into the bookcase," he said casually. "The one you heard fired when you were coming up the street."

Jeffrey blinked.

"The police were about half an hour too late in figuring out that it was your shot, the second one, that killed Drake."

Jeffrey hesitated, then drew on his Scotch, trembling ever so slightly. Mike realized immediately that he'd guessed right. The sonovabitch had killed Drake Manville, after all!

They looked at each other for a long time. Poopsie purred. The ice cubes tinkled in Jeffrey's glass as he took another sip of his drink.

Mike felt the revulsion in him building.

The tears in Jeffrey's eyes overflowed and rolled down his cheeks. He wiped them away with the backs of his hands, his manner reminiscent of Serena's.

"They can't make me go back to Brazil, can they?" Jeffrey finally managed to murmur. His voice was small, hollow.

"Probably not."

"What are you going to do about it, Michael?"

"That depends."

"Are you going to tell Serena?"

"I haven't decided."

"Oh, God, you're going to blackmail me."

"Let's say we're going to negotiate. For starters, I'd like to hear the whole story, exactly like it happened, blow by blow."

Jeffrey drained his glass. "Shit," he said under his breath. "Don't you think I've suffered enough already?"

"This is nothing compared to what could have been," Mike said, barely controlling his anger. "Because of me you're here instead of in that jail cell. I'd say the truth is a pretty small penance to pay. You owe me, Jeffrey."

"All right, for heaven's sake. But don't condemn me, Michael. It *was* an accident."

"Look, I don't want to be jerked around. I want to know what happened at the villa that day. So start talking."

"Okay, okay." He took a deep breath. "I did see a woman running out of the house, like I told you. I guess because of my jealousy I assumed it was Antonia."

"And?"

"I went inside. Drake was dusting himself off. I asked what the hell had happened and he told me he'd just about had his fucking head blown off. He pointed to the hole in the back of the bookcase. Then he starts putting books away, talking about how crazy women could be. He went on and on, acting like he didn't give a shit how *I* felt."

"Mercedes missed, but didn't know she had, is that it?"

"Hell, I didn't even know it was Mercedes he was talking about till Serena told me just before the hearing. I assumed it was Antonia. Drake had made some remark about being lucky she couldn't hit the broad side of a barn. In my mind 'she' was Antonia."

"So what did he do once she fired and missed? Play dead?"

"Yes, he was afraid she was going to come around the desk and administer the coup de grace. Fortunately, she didn't." Jeffrey gulped. "God, what am I saying? Better she'd shot him than me." A deep frown furrowed his brow. "But then they still think she did it, don't they? I mean, Mercedes is in jail for the crime I committed."

"You don't have to trouble yourself over that, Jeffrey. Mercedes killed herself in her cell yesterday."

"Oh, my God."

"It's unfortunate, considering she was innocent, but then she was no Mother Teresa. She tried to murder Drake, but failed. The gods are probably having an interesting time with that one."

Jeffrey put his head in his hands. "I don't know whether to feel relieved or sad or what. All I know is I'm sick to my stomach."

"Leave your guilt for later," Mike said. "Right now what I'm interested in is your story. You enter the library and find Drake getting up off the floor, complaining he'd nearly been killed by a woman. What happened next?"

"Well, I was pissed off. I'd been dying, missing him. I went there hoping he'd say he still wanted me. Instead he

complains about nearly getting his head blown off by some
bitch.''

"So what did you do?"

"I told him he got just what he deserved. Well, he didn't
like that. He said I was jealous. That it had been a mistake
to get involved with me, that I was the biggest mistake he'd
ever made. It could cost him his happiness."

"That obviously didn't please you."

"Michael, I was wounded. Mortally wounded. And mad
as hell. There's not a lot of difference between hate and love,
you know."

"Go on."

"Well, the gun was just lying there. I picked it up and
pointed it at him. He told me to put it down. Said I was a
poor imitation of a woman. I asked if he thought it would
hurt any less to get shot by a queer." Jeffrey closed his eyes,
shuddering. "He smirked. My father used to look at me that
way. I—I . . . just lost it. I didn't mean to kill him. I didn't
even want to hit him. I only. . .wanted to make him sorry for
what he'd said, what he'd done."

Jeffrey began crying. "I loved him, Michael. And I can't
begin to tell you how miserable I am now. I'm suffering,
really suffering. My soul's as dead as if they'd kept me in
that jail."

Mike waited as Jeffrey wept into his hands. He cried for
a good minute. Finally he looked up, red-eyed, miserable.
"So, what happens now? You aren't going to tell Serena, are
you? You might just as well shoot me as tell my sister."

Mike didn't say anything.

"You don't expect me to go back voluntarily, do you?"
There was an edge of hysteria in his voice. "It'll be bad
enough worrying that the government's going to change the
extradition treaty. God, what if they want to trade me for a
Nazi or something?"

"Jeffrey, nobody knows you shot Drake Manville except
you and me."

"What?"

"On the flight back I worked out a theory, but I wasn't sure about my hypothesis until you confirmed it."

"You mean you tricked me?" Jeffrey said indignantly.

"I just got you to tell me the truth."

"You bastard!"

"You were the one to pull the trigger, partner."

Jeffrey fell mute, chastened. He stroked his cat, calculating as Mike waited.

"I know you're just dying to drop the other shoe, Michael, so do it. Say what you intend to say."

"I've been thinking maybe there's a better way to pay your debt to society than jail."

"How?"

"A young woman died trying to save your ass, Jeffrey. You didn't pull the trigger in that shooting, but because of what you did her little girl's an orphan."

"Serena told me. She said she gave the family a hundred thousand."

"Yeah, and that was thinking her brother was innocent."

"You want me to pay more?"

"That little girl's taken care of, but there are thousands of orphans in that country, Jeffrey, thousands who could profit from your unused millions."

"You want me to give my inheritance away?"

"How about half?"

Jeffrey gulped. "Half?"

"You can survive on half and still write a fat check each year to United Way—in the memory of Drake Manville."

"You have a nice sense of irony, Michael."

"You'll be a happier man."

"Serena controls the trust. I can't do it without her consent."

"Ask for it. She'll respect you for your generosity."

"You're a bastard, Michael. You know that, don't you? A real bastard."

"Yes."

Jeffrey sighed, shaking his head. "Much as I hate to say it, you're probably right. I may be able to live with myself if I do something for others."

"You live up to your end of the bargain and Serena will never hear what really happened. She may as well love the new charitable you instead of the one who shot Drake Manville. Besides, you may not realize it now, but in the long run you'll feel better about yourself."

Jeffrey wiped his eyes with the backs of his hands. "You're probably right," he said again.

"And I'd just as soon spare Serena the burden. She's still got lots to worry about with Christina and Joachim."

"Not anymore. Christina kissed off the polo player before we left Rio. I think my sweet little niece is already on to bigger and better things."

"The kid in the Peace Corps?"

"They sat behind me on the flight back. She told him the whole story. He was smart enough to be sympathetic. Naturally, she immediately fell for him." He shook his head. "Women are so gullible."

"Aren't they, though."

Mike mused at how well things had worked out for Serena. She'd gotten her brother out of jail, her daughter away from a spoiled, rich lothario with questionable values, and she had her ex-husband halfway on the hook again.

Jeffrey looked at his empty glass. "So what's with you and Serena?" he asked, seeming to have read Mike's thoughts. "To me, she sounded like she's planning a honeymoon."

"Oh?"

"Maybe I'm spoiling the surprise," Jeffrey said with a chuckle.

"You forget, we've already had a shot at it."

"Yeah, but a guy could do worse, Michael. I'll say that about Serena, even if she is my sister."

"Love is a complicated business."

"Tell me about it." He sniffled again, wiping his nose.

Mike got up. "So much for the lonely hearts club. I think you and I understand each other, don't we?"

"I guess I still owe you, don't I?" Jeffrey said.

"Maybe it's crazy Rio you owe. As far as I'm concerned the case is closed and in the hands of the gods. I'm out of here, Jeffrey. I'm beat."

They went to the door.

"So, let me be clear, Michael—are we *really* square?" Jeffrey asked.

"As soon as the orphans of Brazil start sending you crayon drawings as tokens of appreciation, we're square."

"Love's not cheap," Jeffrey said sadly.

Mike thought of Bebe's white coffin bobbing above the heads of the crowd as they'd filed into the cemetery. "No, Jeffrey, it's not."

Beverly Hills

It was damned near midnight. Serena peered out the window of the limo as Eddie Brown drove briskly along Santa Monica Boulevard. He'd reported that he'd dropped Michael safely off at the hotel. Presumably everything was ready.

She'd left instructions that there be two bottles of Dom Perignon on ice. Joyce over at Rodeo Realty had promised to have pictures of every known island for sale in the world waiting in the suite for Michael to peruse. Serena had done everything she could think of, but she didn't feel confident. Michael knew she loved him, but somehow that didn't seem enough.

Just then a car next to them honked. Serena turned to see a carful of kids, two bare asses pointed directly at her. The car swerved onto a side street. Serena and Eddie exchanged looks in the rearview mirror.

"Sorry about that, Mrs. B."

"Hope it isn't an omen."

"It's the wheels, not you, ma'am. Happens all the time. Specially in West L.A."

"Bad manners and money seem to go together," Serena said with a laugh. "I probably did that once myself."

"Somehow I don't think so, Mrs. B."

"No, more likely I wanted to. There aren't a lot of things I haven't been at least tempted to do."

"Yes, ma'am."

They were nearing the hotel.

"Eddie, did Michael say anything when he opened the envelope?"

"Not that I recall, Mrs. B. I think he liked it."

"What man doesn't like firm flesh?" she said under her breath.

"Ma'am?"

"Nothing. Did Michael seem pleased to be going to the hotel?"

"I guess. He didn't say much."

"Men of action tend to be that way."

"Yes, ma'am."

A few minutes later they pulled up in front of the Beverly Bouchard. Serena was out before Eddie or the doorman could get to the door. She handed Eddie a *C* note, much to his delight.

"Wish me luck."

"Like the man said, Mrs. B., when you're good you don't need luck. Thank you, though, for making this *my* lucky night."

Serena touched her fingers to her lips, then pressed them to Eddie's cheek. "I need all the help I can get. Believe it or not, I'm as nervous as a virgin on her wedding night."

"*You*, Mrs. B.?"

"I was a virgin once, Eddie." Laughing, she headed for the door. "That bag in the trunk goes to the presidential suite."

"Yes, ma'am."

An assistant manager met her in the lobby with a key. "Good evening, Mrs. Bouchard," the young woman said. "Mr. Hamlin arrived and everything was ready, just as you instructed."

"Thanks, Cynthia," Serena said, after glancing at her name tag. The girl accompanied her to the elevator and Serena added, "The young man at the door needs a cup of coffee or a Coke or something. He's a touch slow to the curb. Will you see to it?"

"Yes, Mrs. Bouchard."

A bellhop came running with her suitcase in time to accompany her in the elevator. Serena smiled at the assistant manager as the doors closed. "Thank you."

The last expression on the young woman's face was relief.

"Been busy tonight?" Serena asked the nervous-looking young man holding her bag.

"About average, Mrs. Bouchard."

"We boost that average, you get more tips."

"Yes, ma'am."

When they arrived at the top floor, Serena headed directly for the presidential suite. Stopping at the door, she put her finger to her lips. "When I open the door, just slip the case inside. No noise."

The young man did as she asked, and Serena handed him a twenty. A single lamp was on in the sumptuous sitting room that hadn't yet housed a president of the United States, though it was regularly occupied by moguls connected in one way or another to Hollywood. Serena rarely used it.

She made her way to the master suite. A candle was burning, affording the only light. Michael was in bed and, judging by the sound of his breathing, he was asleep. Serena came up beside him.

He looked peaceful. A sheet covered all but his upper chest and he appeared to be naked. On the bedstand were the real-estate photos and brochures and a half-empty glass of champagne. She checked the bottle and found it practically full. She poured herself a glass, drinking half of it before repairing to the chair in the corner, where she undressed.

After a trip to the bathroom, she returned to find Michael still sleeping. Even though they hadn't spoken, she decided he wasn't a man intent on rejection. Still, she couldn't be certain what he'd been thinking.

Lifting the sheet, she slid over to him, snuggling against his warm body. Michael moaned. She put her hand on his stomach, then slid it down through the tangled hair to his groin. As she took his penis in her hand, he stirred.

A few strokes and she felt him coming to life. He groaned again, lifting his head and squinting at her. "Serena . . ."

She put her finger to his lips. "First we make love, then we talk."

"Jesus, what a way to wake up," he mumbled.

She didn't have to wait long. He was groggy, but he came to life, his penis hardening in her hand. She was glad. She'd been thinking about this—about him—for hours.

She climbed astride him as he clasped her buttocks. He was as deep inside her as a man could get. She could have come like this in moments, if she let herself, but she sensed Michael didn't want to yet.

She lay on his chest. "What do you want?" she whispered in his ear.

Michael gently rolled her onto her back, staying in her. He kissed her lips tenderly, loving her.

She adored this man. Being with him was better than breathing. How had she ever thought she could live without him?

Michael sensed the depth of her feeling. He was taking his time, savoring the moment, savoring her. Serena surrendered to his love, his affection making her more aroused by the moment. Usually he came when she did, but this time she would follow his lead, waiting until he simply couldn't wait any longer.

She immersed herself in his pleasure, finding in that a greater pleasure for herself. When his undulations quickened, she knew he was close. A new and different sort of excitement went through her. She found power in his power.

She couldn't help herself—she began to moan, the throb
of her orgasm starting to build. Then he surged inside her
and they came together, each crying out.

They lay in each other's arms. There was an intimacy in
what had happened that she had never known before. He
stroked her head.

"I love you, Michael," she whispered. "Do you love
me?"

"Yes."

She snuggled closer. For several moments she was silent.
"I think you should know that the last two times I haven't
used any birth control."

The comment brought him out of his lethargic state.
"None? Isn't that kind of irresponsible?"

"Why? Because we're not married?"

"For starters."

"What are we going to do about it?" she asked.

"You sound like you have a proposal."

"I asked you to marry me the first time. If it's going to
happen again, you'll have to ask me. You might have better
luck than I did."

He chuckled. "Serena, Serena," he said, but nothing
more.

They lay for a time holding each other. After a while, she
started feeling anxious.

"I have an agreement in principle to sell the entire Bouchard holdings to the Four Seasons chain," she said.
"That's why I went to New York. The details still have to be
worked out."

"You're getting out of the hotel business?"

"I'm ready for a new challenge."

"Like what?"

"I don't know. Exporting coconuts, raising our kid—one
or the other."

"Aren't we getting ahead of ourselves a little?"

"Maybe. So shall we go to Tahiti and talk about it?" she
said. "While we're at it, we can see if the climate agrees with
us before I lay down the money for an island."

"Hmm."

"Am I pushing too hard, too fast?"

"I'll go to Tahiti with you, but there's something I want to do first."

"What?"

He kissed her. "I want you to come camping with me."

"What?"

"You heard me."

"Michael, I don't camp. I watched Meryl Streep in *The River Wild* and got all the nature I need for a lifetime."

"I want you to come with me to the mountains."

She propped her head in her hand so she could see his expression. "You're serious, aren't you?"

"Yep."

"Why? Is it some kind of test?"

"Maybe."

"But why? What's it going to prove?"

"I want to see you wash your dirty face in a mountain stream and climb rocks and watch birds soar and chipmunks play. I want to make love with you in a sleeping bag and kiss your chapped lips."

"Jesus, you're a masochist."

"After, say, two nights in the woods, we can go to my place in Vegas and have a shower."

"Then what?"

"If we're still talking to each other we can get married."

Serena laughed, then kissed his chest. "A test of fire."

"Yeah."

"Two days, huh?"

"Yeah. My knees can't take more than that."

She pressed her face to his skin, inhaling his scent. "I can think of a thousand things ten times more romantic than going camping."

"Maybe that's the point."

"You mean doing it your way?"

"Yeah."

"God, with all that nature, I probably *will* get pregnant."

"Maybe."

"And what do you expect to get out of all this, Mr. Hamlin?"

"Something I've wanted for years."

"What?"

"Seeing you naked in a mountain stream."

"Seriously?"

"Seriously."

RISING
Tides

EMILIE RICHARDS

The reading of a woman's will threatens to destroy her family

As a hurricane gathers strength, the reading of Aurore Gerritsen's will threatens to expose dark secrets and destroy her family. Emilie Richards continues the saga of a troubled family with *Rising Tides*, the explosive sequel to the critically acclaimed *Iron Lace*.

AVAILABLE IN PAPERBACK
FROM OCTOBER 1997

Elizabeth Lowell

Tell me no Lies

An international crisis is about to explode unless a desperate trap to catch a thief succeeds. Lindsay Danner is the perfect pawn in a deadly game. Now it's up to ex-CIA agent Jacob MacArthur Catlin to make sure Lindsay succeeds—and survives.

"For smouldering sensuality and exceptional storytelling, Elizabeth Lowell is incomparable."
—Romantic Times

AVAILABLE IN PAPERBACK FROM OCTOBER 1997

EMMA DARCY

*at her most daring with an
unforgettable tale of ruthless sacrifice
and single-minded seduction*

THE SECRETS WITHIN

When Tamara Vandlier learns that her mother is
dying she is elated—and returns to the family
estate to destroy her mother's few remaining
months, in return for her own ruined childhood.
Loyalty turns to open rivalry in this novel that
explores the dark, hidden secrets of two branches
of a powerful Australian family.

**AVAILABLE IN PAPERBACK
FROM AUGUST 1997**

DEBBIE MACOMBER

THIS MATTER OF MARRIAGE

Hallie McCarthy gives herself a year to find
Mr Right. Meanwhile, her handsome
neighbour is busy trying to win his ex-wife
back. As the two compare notes on their
disastrous campaigns, each finds the perfect
partner lives right next door!

*"In the vein of When Harry Met Sally,
Ms Macomber will delight."*
— **Romantic Times**

**AVAILABLE IN PAPERBACK
FROM SEPTEMBER 1997**

JAYNE ANN KRENTZ

Joy

When a couple win a mysterious emerald
bracelet in a poker game, their peaceful
Caribbean holiday becomes a rollercoaster of
adventure, desire...and deadly peril.

*"Jayne Ann Krentz is one of the hottest writers in
romance today."*—USA Today

MIRA

**AVAILABLE IN PAPERBACK
FROM SEPTEMBER 1997**

Take 3 of
"The Best of the Best™"
Novels FREE
Plus get a FREE surprise gift!

Return this coupon and we'll send you 3 of "The Best of the Best" novels from MIRA® books and a surprise gift absolutely FREE! We'll even pay the postage and packing for you. We're making this special offer to introduce you to some of the world's very best romance novels written by the world's very best romance authors. Accepting these free books and the gift places you under no obligation to buy any further books. You may cancel your subscription anytime, even after receiving just your free shipment.

REPLY TODAY - NO STAMP NEEDED!

THE BEST OF THE BEST, FREEPOST, CROYDON, SURREY CR9 3WZ
Readers in EIRE send coupon to PO Box 4546, Dublin 24

YES, please send me 3 FREE Best of the Best novels and a free surprise gift. I understand that unless you hear from me, each month I will receive 3 of the best books by the world's hottest romance authors for only £3.75 each*. That's the complete price and a **saving of 25%** off the combined cover prices. Postage and packing is completely free. I am under no obligation to purchase any books and I may cancel or suspend my subscription at any time, but the free books and gift will be mine to keep in any case. (I am over 18 years of age)

B7YE

Ms/Mrs/Miss/Mr _____
BLOCK CAPITALS PLEASE
Address _____

_____

_____ Postcode _____

THE BRIGHTEST STARS IN WOMEN'S FICTION

CAROLE MORTIMER

Gypsy

She'd always been his one temptation...

Shay Flannagan was the raven-haired
beauty the Falconer brothers called Gypsy.
They each found her irresistible, but it was
Lyon Falconer who claimed her—when he
didn't have the right—and sealed her fate.

**AVAILABLE IN PAPERBACK
FROM SEPTEMBER 1997**